Patrick Robinson is a former sports columnist for the London Daily Express. He has written close to 30 books, some sports, some military. Translated into 27 languages, more than 22 best sellers, #1 spots, with two different books, on both the New York Times List, and the London Times List. One of his horse racing books was the official gift of the United States presented to the Queen by President Reagan. He wrote Lone Survivor for Navy SEAL Marcus Luttrell. Sold over 4 million, top of the bestseller list for eight months. Major movie.

Patrick Robinson

MAIDENS IN THE VALE

AUSTIN MACAULEY PUBLISHERS™

LONDON · CAMBRIDGE · NEW YORK · SHARJAH

A CIP catalogue record for this title is available from the British Library.

ISBN 9781528974592 (Paperback)
ISBN 9781528978422 (ePub e-book)

www.austinmacauley.com

First Published 2023
Austin Macauley Publishers Ltd®
1 Canada Square
Canary Wharf
London
E14 5AA

Dick Neve whose highly active brain created the original idea for *Maidens In The Vale*. He handed over the writing to me, but remained on board until the book was completed. He is without doubt the best literary researcher I ever worked with. Because Dick was not just a gatherer of facts, but as a writer himself, he's an instinctive judge of what was important and relevant, even when it showed up unexpectedly. And that's a rare gift, as any experienced writer will tell you.

Prologue

The elegant house in Maida Vale was quiet in the late afternoon. And Sasha came down the stairs silently, hoping, even praying, that her older sister would not hear her. She wore her school blazer over a white shirt and blue jeans.

At 15, she might have looked older, if dressed differently. But her golden hair was uncombed, she wore not a semblance of makeup, and on closer examination her tear-stained face suggested she had been crying for a month.

Not quite, Maybe three weeks. At school she had long been regarded as a beauty, but this no longer applied. Sasha no longer cared what she looked like. And she fought valiantly to try to get the big brass handle of the front door to turn without squeaking.

Once outside, she ducked below the garden hedge to avoid detection from her step-father's study. And then she crept furtively down the path to the wrought-iron front gate. Essentially the tall, crouching Sasha looked like a burglar on a half-term break.

Beyond the gate, and on the pavement, she ran, across the street and through a mews walkway before emerging onto a busy shopping arcade a couple of blocks north of Bayswater Road, where the urban sprawl of west London meets Hyde Park.

Only then did she slow down and readjust the one-foot square painting of the third-century Roman Catholic Virgin Martyr, Saint Agatha, which she carried under her left arm. And she was still crying as she begged her God to forgive her for mortal sins beyond imagination.

Sasha prayed silently as she walked ... *I never meant it ... please, please God don't send me to hell—but I'd rather be there than stay here ... I never meant to offend ... I never wanted any of this ... but I'm too afraid ... please God ...I'm begging you to keep my dearest sister safe ... but please help me ...*

Passers-by stared as the heartbroken, sobbing schoolgirl made her way into the area which surrounds one of the top colleges in the capital. She made no attempt to dry her eyes, and when she reached the high residential tower block she waited out beyond the fence, until a group of people headed for the entrance.

Swiftly, she joined them and followed them into the lift, waiting until the last one made an exit at the 14th floor. And then she pressed the button up to the Penthouse, where the hallway was deserted. Sasha went directly to the door marked 'Roof-garden.'

This meant a short flight of steps and then an emergency exit door with a wide push-bar. But Sasha had been here before, just checking. And once again she stepped out onto the roof. But this time she stared at her painting, her thoughts locked upon the appalling suffering of Saint Agatha of Sicily, the eternal Bride of Christ. And now she placed the framed picture against the low rampart wall, before stepping back and clasping her hands together.

She drew a string of rosary beads from her pocket, and climbed onto the wall, 200 feet above the street, and 18-inches wide beneath Sasha's shoes. And then, quite clearly, she said, "Reverend Mother Anna, please pray for me." She followed this with Saint Agatha's famously brave prayer of departure …*Lord, you have given me patience to suffer … receive now my soul.*

Five seconds later, inconsolable and terrified, she jumped.

Chapter One
A Sinister Overture

A light southerly breeze drifted in from the coast and the new Spring leaves quivered, as well they might. Two daggers would strike fatally on this night. And both would involve a very beautiful woman.

There are only two occasions in the entire English social calendar when the very act of al fresco dining is shipped out, as it were, into the long grass. One is the Royal Meeting at Ascot when the silk-hatted gentry of the English shires gather in various car parks for champagne and poached wild salmon. The other is on an often too-chilly evening in the grounds of Glyndebourne on opening night.

This late Spring festival is always in May, and on this particular evening the dinner-jacketed opera lovers of southern England were together among the rhododendrons and sloping lawns of this secluded country estate. With one half-hour to go before the beginning of the opera, this was strictly cocktail hour. Uniquely, among the world's opera houses, the Glyndebourne interval spans 90-minutes, which is when the serious al-fresco picnic/dining takes place.

As always, some of the most beautiful women in London had joined their country cousins in cocktail dresses, exquisite jewellery, and high heels in the damp grass. Tickets were both expensive and rare, black-tie compulsory, picnic tables necessary, butler optional. Hardly anyone shows up at Glyndebourne without an outdoor banquet, and vintage champagne for half-time.

With a half-hour before the start of one of the greatest operas ever written, the lawn had become a scene of perfectly-mannered English reserve. Latecomers barely received a second glance. Anyone who should be here was here.

One particular latecomer, however, turned a few heads regardless. Wearing a dark-blue calf-length dress and a tailored jacket which was probably hand-stitched in a Paris atelier, she was a tall, striking, beauty in her early 20's. But there was something else about her as she strode out of the winding path through the trees and onto the lawn.

For one so young, there was an air of subtle haughtiness about her. And it had nothing to do with the fact that she was Russian by birth, wealthy in her own right, and carried a lethal weapon sheathed in a Hermes evening bag. No one knew anything of that. But the *soignee* Miss Sophia Morosova, without one second's effort, was making a noteworthy entrance to one of England's grandest evenings.

A diverse collection of young bucks, trying to sip champagne and look sideways at the same time, could hardly wait to see into which little gathering she would settle. Old school? Faded aristocracy? Parents (please, God)? New money striving to look old? Some slightly flash young Master of the Universe with an eight-litre Bugatti Divo at peace in the parking lot?

None of the above actually. Miss Sophia headed directly to a most unlikely little clique of three people, all of them plainly foreign, and one of them, in his mid-60's was an especially tough-looking character. Old Reggie Willoughby-Sanders, a member of the Glyndebourne Board of Directors actually mentioned, "Christ! Who the hell's he? Looks like an escapee from the Lubyanka!"

But it was to this unsmiling patron of the opera that Miss Sophia headed. And she embraced him warmly, planting the traditional Russian three-kisses on his swarthy left and right cheeks. This brought her sufficiently close to a little giveaway ribbon pinned on the left lapel of her uncle's dinner jacket. It was discreet, dark red and solitary … the coveted insignia of Hero of the Russian Federation, the highest honorary title bestowed by the Russian Government upon either military or civilians, whose immense heroism merited exalted public recognition.

Although no one had ever escaped from the Lubyanka, old Reggie was darned nearly right. But not quite. Rudolf Masow was a 5ft 10ins, bushy-eye-browed hard man, with a scar on his right cheek, and a nose which may have been broken more than once. But he was not unattractive. As a youth he'd obviously been handsome, and that still showed, And he was currently employed as a 'Cultural Attache' in the Russian Embassy in London. Which of course virtually guaranteed he was a spy.

And since Rudolf had been a high-ranking spy for practically all of his working life, he was certainly a very good one; sufficiently well regarded to walk off with the Embassy's treasured allocation of four free tickets for Glyndebourne "in the interests of cultural co-operation with the home country." The Trustees annually collected four in return for the Bolshoi in Moscow (air fares and hotels included).

Rudolf's basic experience of cultural matters was largely restricted to the dank, rainy streets of Eastern Europe, and the Soviet Union. He had been nearly murdered on the docks of The Hague, beaten up in the backstreets of Berlin, and severely worked over in the Red Light district of Hamburg. Recent Russian records do not reveal the fate of his opponents, many of whom were never found.

But, like so many Russians, Rudolf loved the opera, and he reached for a bottle of vintage 2000 Krug and poured a glass for his niece, enquiring as he did so about the health of her MaMa, a sad and tragic figure currently residing in a mental health institute on the outskirts of Moscow. Unlike many of her fellow citizens, Mrs Morosova was incarcerated entirely of her own free will, having suffered a shocking mental collapse owing to the appalling antics of her husband.

"A toast to Veroniya," said Rudy, raising his glass to the memory of his sister. "And let's make that enough sadness for tonight." Sophia too raised her glass. "To MaMa," she whispered, solemnly and, privately, "I miss you."

Rudolf leaned over and kissed her on the cheek, saying quietly, "I'm so glad you came. Revenge is a sweet thing for Russians. And tonight will be especially important." But swiftly he lightened the mood, gazing at her impeccably trimmed, short brunette hair also cut by one of those Parisian stylists who can make a girl look as if she belonged at the wheel of a Bugatti Divo.

"Very stylish," chuckled Uncle Rudy. "Perfect."

Sophia grinned, sipped her champagne, and was already staring at a party of a dozen people gathered companionably under a Glyndebourne oak. Their mood was apparently joyful, which was understandable since three of them were Glyndebourne Trustees, headed by the Chairman himself, Lord Fontridge, a Law Lord and Life Baron, owner of the nearby 2,000-acre Laughton Towers estate.

His Lordship—Freddie to his pals—was a Lord Justice of Appeals, one of the highest ranking judicial figures in England. He had taken his place in the House of Lords, and had been invited into Her Majesty's Privy Council, where his wise and learned opinion was frequently called into discussions. He, and fellow Council members Prince Phillip and Prince Charles had interests in common, all three men being former high-goal polo players. Lord Fontridge was also Chairman of the exclusive South Downs Polo Club at Alfriston.

But his Lordship harboured one hidden idiosyncrasy, which could never be spoken. Freddie Fontridge was involved in one of the highest-priced and secretive call-girl rings in London, specialising in young girls, schoolgirls actually, 15-18. Lord Fontridge, at the age of 67, had no children of his own. He preferred, occasionally, to rent them at extremely high cost.

The risk of public disclosure was small, but obviously horrendous. Nonetheless the compulsions of such men are fierce, a near fixation on the newly-developed bodies of teenagers, their innocence, if nothing else, still intact. Very beautiful, mature women never held temptation for his Lordship. Instead he had the key to a private West London sex-agency, which was exclusively in this field, and was, understandably, clandestine in the extreme. And he saw no wrong, and recognised no breach of morality, in his obsession. Indeed, he believed, somewhat lyrically, it kept him forever young.

Sophia never took her eyes off him. And only those who knew her well could detect a sense of unease in her manner. Even Rudolf was wondering whether her lovely brown eyes were usually narrowed to this extent, even in the sinking sun of a May evening.

And he said quietly, again in Russian, "Is that him? The one waving the opera program? Silver-haired, a lot of teeth."

"Yes," she replied. "I would recognise him anywhere … as long as I live, probably."

Rudolf nodded gravely.

There was an excellent plate of Russian blinis on the picnic table, and an enviably large pot of caviar, direct from a Caspian Sea sturgeon. "Have a couple of those, my dear," said her uncle. Sophia tried two, liberally spread with the divine and gleaming little black eggs. After which she tried two more, uncertain as she was about her next hot meal. She'd be gone by the time Picnic Extravaganza began, first interval.

It was almost time for the bell, the traditional summons for the diners to enter the opera house. "No hurry," muttered Rudolf, "Keep watching."

Glyndebourne has a reputation for efficient seating of its 1,000-odd patrons, especially on a busy opening night. Some of them headed straight for the auditorium striding up the lawn like hunting dogs off the leash. Everyone was on the move, though the Trustees were strolling in a more leisurely manner, the Russians bringing up the rear.

Inevitably, the lobby was still crowded but once inside, Sophia bypassed the seating stewards and headed directly to her aisle seat where she sat unobtrusively, Rudolph's empty place beside her.

Back in the lobby the Russian attaché sought out the lady in charge of programs, and holding a single cream-coloured envelope, said: "I wonder if you could have this delivered to Lord Fontridge before the curtain. He does expect it."

The lady smiled, called an assistant, and handed her the envelope, ordering crisply, "Thank you, Diane. Lord Fontridge, second row, the Trustees area. He's waiting."

She turned to mention that she sincerely hoped Mr Masow enjoyed the performance—but the ex-Soviet spy had vanished, an art form in which he was world-class. But the program lady had seen his barely forgettable face, and in another setting, she might not have been still breathing.

But Rudolph was strictly off duty tonight, in attendance only to enjoy the opera. Well, that, and to pray fervently, that his dearest Sophia would not lose her nerve.

He waited on the aisle, as the ghostly opening fanfare echoed through the hall. Indeed, Sophia and Rudolf had barely made their seats before the massed violins of the Glyndebourne orchestra filled the great domed auditorium with the achingly sinister overture to Verdi's *Rigoletto.*

Almost 120 years after his death, Verdi, the bearded Italian socialite, composer of 25 operas, was, right here in deepest Sussex, once more gripping an audience with sounds from the very heavens, in which he undoubtedly dwelt.

Outside, high in the ancient Spring trees of Glyndebourne, a light summer breeze drifted in from the nearby south coast of England. And the new leaves trembled. As well they might. Two daggers would strike fatally on this night. And both of them would involve a very beautiful woman.

Rarely, even from the Milanese maestro, does any overture sigh so beautifully with such promise of evil, perhaps even murder. Especially when immaculately-played by the London Philharmonic Orchestra, in residence tonight. And a thousand tiny electric tremors zipped along the spines of even the most resolute opera-lovers, as they were engulfed once more by the orchestral swell of *Rigoletto,* created by perhaps the finest composer the world has ever seen.

This was the work of one of opera's gods, whose dark statue still stands timelessly glowering in the foyer of La Scala. Glowering was in fact the natural facial expression of Guiseppe Verdi, and almost every sculpture of him seems to highlight the furrowed brow, the stern uncompromising look of the Maestro.

Such an expression was, however, less often seen on the complacent face of Baron Fontridge, Lord Justice of England, Chairman of the Glyndebourne Trustees. But right now his expression was tortured. He actually looked as if he had seen an apparition. And the words on the now opened letter, written to him with the purest malice, shook before his eyes:

My Lord,

I do hope you remember me. Such intimate moments, with my little sister looking on, before you thrashed her bare skin with that leather belt. I always wondered why you wanted to hurt her every time you had me. She was only 15, and I was 17. I still relive the agony and the shame every night of my life. Your brutality seemed so unfair to us both.

Meet me by the stone bridge by the lake immediately after the first act. I'm afraid there will be a price.
Yours,
Sophia.

PS Should you not keep this rendezvous, I will be in the offices of The Sun newspaper by 11am tomorrow morning.

Lord Fontridge never heard one note of the overture. His mind was transmitting a brand new dimension to the word 'fear'. He tried to fold the letter away and slipped the envelope into his inside pocket. He tried to bring a sense of self-righteous anger—"some shoddy little blackmailer trying it on." But that didn't work. The ghastly spectre of The Sun hitting the street with an end-of-the-world typeface proclaiming "ROYAL ADVISER ACCUSED OF SCHOOLGIRL RAPE," stood before him.

"Mother of God!" breathed Lord Fontridge. And where the hell was his accuser? Was she in this this very opera house? What was he supposed to do? There was literally no one to whom he could turn for help. Right now his only course was to attend the bridge, face this Sophia, whoever the hell she was. And find out if the price was worth paying.

Right now he was in the deepest throes of self-denial, repeatedly saying to himself alone, 'What is this woman talking about? Little sister? Brutality? What price to pay? Why me? I've never heard of anything so outrageous. Does she have any idea who I am?' Worse yet he was trapped in his second-row seat. No escape. He was also trapped by his very own personal demons.

But, even more profoundly, there came the whispered words of another voice, from deep within—I am afraid she knows exactly who you are. And Lord Fontridge understood he must either silence Miss Sophia. Or face total ruin, humility, socially, legally, and perhaps even financially. Such overpowering national disgrace is suffered by very few.

Rigoletto proceeded, essentially without the head of the Board of Trustees. The rich and melodious baritone of the hunchback himself thrilled the audience, as did the Italian tenor playing the sly and seedy Duke of Mantua. But perhaps it was the purest notes of the truly enchanting soprano playing Gilda who stole the opening hour, as she drifted towards an inevitable fate, born of her impassioned love for the Duke.

In barely disguised torment, Baron Fontridge tolerated the First Act. And as the long interval approached, he knew he must leave, right in front of his fellow Board members. Several rows back, there was already an empty seat. Miss Sophia Morosova was out of the auditorium, and pulling on a pair of soft black leather driving gloves, as she made her way down the lawn, on her way to the bridge.

On stage, *Rigoletto* himself was a study in anguish. He stood terrified of the curse, which runs thematically throughout the opera: *La Maledizionne*. His voice betrayed his terror, and his agony. Lord Fontridge, perhaps above all other opera-goers, understood precisely how the hunchback felt about the oncoming disaster.

Excusing himself for the slight disruption, Fontridge stepped past his fellow Trustees, and made his way out of the theatre. He walked along the footpath to the great lawn, and then set off down towards the lake, and the stone bridge. It was a five-minute walk, but it took him longer, as his footsteps slowed, in anticipation of the ordeal, which undoubtedly awaited him. He still had not the slightest idea either of what to say, or indeed to do. Both his mood, and the night air were growing darker.

And now, up ahead, he could see a shadowy figure just beyond the bridge. And as he walked on towards the shore of the lake he had to admit it was a rather relaxed looking, shadowy figure, a tall girl, standing beneath a willow tree, looking down at the evening ripples lapping from the lake. When he reached the stone crossing, he hesitated, then strode forward, summoning all the pompous authority his many offices afforded him.

He was tall, a handsome man, with a dashing smile when required, and now he said briskly, "Good evening, madam. I believe you mistakenly wished to see me?"

"No mistake, my lord," replied Sophia. "Perhaps you would like to step a little closer, in the interests of identification. I, of course, will never forget you, but I think it would be better for both of us if you could recognise me."

"Well, I don't think there's any need for that," he replied, "None at all. But you might inform me what you actually want."

"I want you to look at me, perhaps for old time's sake …"

"I've told you," he replied, now standing about six feet from her. "No need. I've never seen you in my life." His gaze was instantly captured by the driving gloves she wore, slightly incongruously. They were in no way a lady's evening gloves. Indeed they were more suited to the hands of a Formula One Grand Prix competitor.

Fontridge looked momentarily puzzled, but Sophia smiled, and took a step forward, holding out her hand in a rather affectionate gesture. "Come along, Freddie," she chuckled, remembering for the one millionth time the name her own step-father had used when addressing this very brilliant lawyer seven years ago. And Lord Fontridge, his dinner jacket unbuttoned, took her by her gloved left hand.

Sophia, however, moved quickly. And she came forward smoothly, guessing where the gap between the aristocratic fourth and fifth ribs were located, on the right side, facing him. And as their bodies lightly touched, she rammed the eight-inch blade of her bone-handled Italian stiletto into his white dress shirt, and directly into the nearside ventricle of Lord Fontridge's heart, which went into immediate spasm.

The eminent Law Lord gasped, the very last gasp he would ever make. The pain was overwhelming, his eyes looked as if they might explode from his head, but Sophia was still smiling as she whispered in his ear.

And these were the final words he would ever hear, before she grabbed her letter from his jacket pocket, and crammed it into her trusty Hermes bag. Then she twisted his body around and shoved Freddie Fontridge backwards into the shallow waters of the Glyndebourne lake.

Still jutting grotesquely from his central rib-cage was the stiletto, upon which there would not be one smudge of a finger-print. With the body face-down half-submerged, Sophia had one more task to complete. She leaned down and picked a small flint rock out of the water, about four inches wide at the base, and shoved it into her pocket.

Lord Fontridge was already dead, and knew nothing of this ritual. And, since he knew not one word of Russian, neither would he ever understand the departing statement of one of his former victims … "*Dosvidaniya, ty ublyudok.*"

Goodbye, you bastard.

Chapter Two
No Cathedrals for Sasha

But it was the tower, that stark and sightless high peak of evil,
which hardly ever faded from her mind. Sophia Morosova
prayed at the grave-side for her sister—trembling at the true
reason for her suicide.

Sophia left her dagger behind. She had delivered the fatal thrust with the kind of expertise only available from men like the former KGB assassin who had coached her. Rudy would, she guessed, be very proud of her. She had obeyed his instructions to the letter, right down to the last order: leave the dagger in, it stops the bleeding.

And now she walked on a casual stride towards the car park—no running. She realised it was much darker now, and the body could not possibly be discovered until the ground staff arrived tomorrow morning—unless they decided to dredge the lake tonight. And how unlikely was it, that the body could be found, floating just below the surface, in the pitch black after *Rigoletto* had concluded?

No chance of that, thought Sophia as she slipped through the lines of cars, and climbed into her own, ironically named, black Ford Escape SUV. She headed west along the coast towards the old A23, which runs north to Gatwick Airport, site of some of the most anonymous commercial hotels in England. This was a place where anyone could get completely lost, especially a Paris-based Russian nobody, travelling on at least a half-dozen impeccably forged foreign passports, and driving licenses.

Sophia looked more French than English, especially her clothes and her hairstyle. After Cambridge she had gone to France and taken a course in fashion and design at the *Paris L'institut Marangoni,* on the *Rue de Miromesnil* in the grandest of the Paris *arrondissements*—the 8th, the hub of the city, with the *Champs Elysee* running through its heart. There was nothing suburban about Sophia, but the self-possessed world of people who essentially make frocks for a living was too whimsy for her.

Sophia sought something more serious, and more exciting. She had no idea what that would be. But, two terms at *L'institut* had done it for her, and, on reflection, here on the A23 speeding innocently away from the scene of a crime, she was probably on a better track. She loved Paris, and wherever this new adventure finally led her, so far it definitely beat the hell out of shifting hemlines, and shoulder pads.

The journey away from Glyndebourne took her just under one hour. She parked in a space close to the London Gatwick Hilton, and checked in using her Canadian passport—one large double room, king-sized bed, double lock on the door ... plastic card key—Please Do Not Disturb.

At around 10.20pm she checked her watch. And again coincidentally, it was approximately the same time Sparafucile was plunging a much larger dagger into the heart of *Rigoletto's* daughter, Gilda, giving way to the classical, tortured final scene, with wondrous music from the very gods. Not to mention the heart-wrenching, unforgettable plea of the hunchback ...Non morir ... non morire o ch'io teco morro—Don't die ... don't die, or I shall die beside you ...

Not even Rudolph knew where his niece was, as he fought back utterly foreign Russian tears. Quite separate now from this overwhelming operatic performance, Sophia slept for a fitful eight hours, awakening over and over again, fighting back the grotesque dying image of Lord Freddie. This was a lot worse than Gilda's tragic end, until finally Sophia awakened at first light, on Sunday morning, wondering if his Lordship was properly dead.

She ordered a light breakfast in her room, and then checked out, retrieving her credit card (in a false name, of course) from the receptionist and then paying in cash. Rudy never missed a trick in the noble art of vanishing without trace in the immediate hours after a contract murder, approved by the State.

Sophia once more turned her SUV towards the north, driving up the short stretch of dual carriageway which led to the M25 highway, the one which completely encircles London. She drove clockwise up through Surrey and out towards the West of England, that's sharp left at the junction with the M4.

Probably the fastest, and definitely the busiest freeway in England, the M4 orders travellers off the highway and down a local road for those heading into the picturesque Thames-side town of Henley, home of the most famous Regatta in the world. Sophia went for the familiar, ancient stone bridge which has straddled the river since the 12th century. It's famously arched and narrow, right at the top of the dead-straight 2000-metre racing stretch over which the fastest rowing crews on earth have raced every summer for almost 180 years.

Princess Grace Kelly's brother Jack won the coveted Diamond Sculls here back in 1947. Which was sweet revenge indeed, since his father, the three times Olympic sculling gold medallist and construction tycoon, Jack Senior, had his entry rejected by the Henley Stewards in the 1920's since he had once worked as a bricklayer!

That particular entry was in such flagrant defiance of the rigid social rules of the Regatta at the time, it almost gave the Stewards a couple of haemorrhages apiece. Today, of course, they would probably have been in the slammer for an infringement of Big Jack's human rights.

Sophia Morosova drove across the bridge in light traffic. She knew it well. Too well. And she parked at the Red Lion Hotel, before walking down to the water, where she stood staring down the racing straight all the way to Temple Island. A hopeless romantic, Sophia used to come to Henley with her mother for long walks downstream along the rural Berkshire riverbank.

And once more she was pondering the exploits of her grand-father Pietr, who had rowed in the great Soviet Navy eight which won the Grand Challenge Cup, rowing's Holy Grail, twice in the 1960's. She and her mother had so often stood and gazed at these historic waters.

"Right out there," MaMa always said. "My father raced out there. His crew was unbeatable in all the world." And then, to her daughter, "You have so much to be proud of. Always remember moy angelochek, we are Russian and sometimes we are better than anyone."

For all her early life, this place, along this river, was sacred to Veroniya Morosova. Her famous father had died too young, but, for her, his memory would never settle in Moscow, and never along the Volga, nor even on the shores of the northern oceans, where he served for many years as a Chief Ship Starshina (Chief Petty Officer) in the Soviet Navy's Baltic Fleet.

No. For Mrs Veroniya Morosova, Pietr's memory would always be here, close to the scene of his greatest triumph, the one that saw him presented with the rarefied Russian Award of Honour, alongside his crewmates and coaches at an unforgettable ceremony in the sprawling dockyards of Murmansk. It was a medal which set Pietr, the steel-armed stroke-man, apart. It was the Medal awarded only to those who attained the very pinnacle of Russian sport.

20

But somehow his spirit never belonged there, up by the Arctic Circle. It belonged here, right along the Remenham shore, where once thousands had roared the Russians to victory. In Veroniya's opinion, the modern population of Russia may not be aware. But surely God would. And the soft green fields of the Upper Thames would always be in her soul.

But now her older daughter Sophia stood alone. And she began the one-mile walk, across the bridge and down past the fabled Leander Club towards the little church. It was a walk that unfailingly assaulted her senses, somehow bringing her closer with each step to the memory of her mother, and the strong, defiant spirit of her grand-father.

Russians in England. Good Russians. People of culture and stern responsibilities. Sophia walked in the footprints of her mother, and was now watching the blades of a lone sculler skittering across the water before the stroke. For people of a racing crew heritage, this was paradise on a summer's day. And the walk was one of the most beautiful in southern England. It was also a walk she dreaded. Every step of the way. And tears streamed down her face with every yard she travelled.

The towpath was deserted as she made her way along the riverbank, but suddenly it widened and to her right was one of those old fashioned English stiles, an easy little climb-over. These things were built originally to prevent livestock escaping and falling into the river, while allowing pedestrians to traverse the fence simply. They must have worked fine, since they are still in place, all over the country, and have been for about seven thousand years.

Sophia climbed over, and headed up a rough little road for 150-yards, at which point she came face to face with the one-thousand-year-old Church of St Nicholas, a village place of Roman Catholic worship when it was built, but left in the lurch, surrounded now only by woodland, after the ravages of the bubonic plague (Black Death) which swept England in the late 1500's, killing 80,000 people in one year alone.

The destruction of the village has rendered St Nicholas Church a very beautiful oasis at the foot of the lush hills above the river. It stands mostly in shadow surrounded by a rather elegant brick wall, headstones in the little churchyard standing resolutely on its well-clipped, always dark green grass. Its stone tower wreaks of history, stretching back through the entire millennium, right into the pages of the Domesday book.

Which meant, of course, it was Catholic for at least 600 years, before the English King Henry VIII decided to fire the Pope to facilitate his divorce. This was important to Sophia, a devout Roman Catholic—just knowing that the holy ground upon which she stood, was somehow connected to the ancient church of Rome.

Sophia Morosova unclipped the gate and walked to one of the newer graves, which bore a small grey marble stone, bearing the chiselled words:

Sasha
Born Moscow 1996-died London 2011
A Tragic Child of God
Eternal light will shine upon her

Above the chiselled lettering was a carved symbol of the most highly venerated of the seven Virgin Martyrs of the Roman Catholic Church, Agatha, the Patron Saint of Sicily. This beautiful high-born noble woman suffered savage torture, humiliation, prison, burning on hot coals, and ultimately death at the hands of a junior Roman Governor, who desired her for himself.

But Saint Agatha had refused to turn against her vows to Christ for a life of celibacy, prayer and service. She defied the courts of Rome over and over, and was saved from her agony by Saint Peter, who visited her in a vision, healed her terrible wounds, and took away her pain. She died within days, with a brave smile and a famous final prayer, "Lord, you have given me patience to suffer—receive now my soul."

These were also the final words repeated by Sasha Morosova before she plunged to her death. And there, beside the grave, just as she always did in this place, Sophia knelt before the headstone and wept without restraint for her younger sister. There would be no enormous Cathedrals and churches built in her name all over Europe, as there were for Saint Agatha. But here in this shaded churchyard there was, at last, a distant sense of consolation. And the sun came out, lancing bright beams through the trees.

And they cast aside the image of the satanic 20-storey skyscraper, which had haunted Miss Morosova's waking hours and all of her dreams for seven endless years. That tower had haunted her worse than the sight of Sasha's smashed body at the City morgue. More even than the sight of her younger sister's bedroom, with the name Alexandra painted on the door.

That single word had represented a terrible reminder for Sophia that Sasha was gone, after that 200-foot plunge from the skyscraper. God alone knew how she made it up to the roof-garden. But she did, and the only certainty the young girl left behind was her sure knowledge that there was no place on this earth for her.

But it was the tower, that stark and sightless high peak of evil, which hardly ever faded from Sophia's mind. The sunbeams along the Thames had done their best, but only temporarily. Sophia Morosova prayed at the grave-side, as she always did for her sister's safe deliverance into the Kingdom of God, and she did so trembling all over again at the true reason for Sasha's suicide.

It was the belt, that thin, hard leather strap whipped down three times onto Sasha's backside, by a naked Lord Fontridge, who preferred to conclude his afternoon adventures by a display of self-proclaimed power. He was not a brute, the three strokes were fairly light. It was simply a compulsion for a man used to handing out justice, and right here after the disgraceful rape of a 15-year-old girl, his Lordship consolidated his status. At least in his own mind he did. He was also proving that in the 21st century, no one can trust any figure of authority, who ghosts along behind the masterful mask of legal, or even lordly power and prerogative.

Anyway, the light beatings virtually destroyed the 15-year-old Sasha. Such screams from a young girl Sophia hoped never to hear again.

The truth was the fates had ganged up on Sasha. His Lordship occasionally raped her. But preferred Sophia who was 17 and still in the sixth form at St Margaret's School, Pangbourne. There was a quasi-legality about that. But the lash of the belt was just too much for the younger sister. She had long dreaded the sound of a black London cab pulling up outside the house, for it sometimes contained Fontridge. But somehow, after he had whipped her, it was too awful to bear.

After the second time, Sasha was virtually unreachable. Her slender, boyish figure betrayed the age of this classic child/woman. And now it was wracked with sobs. She took no food, was unable to speak, and was curled up on her bed, facing the wall, clutching her Sunday school dress.

It went on for three days and three nights. All of Sophia's entreaties fell on newly-deaf ears, and she wondered whether the outrages against her sister had taken the cruellest toll of all, perhaps rendering her unreachable for the rest of her life. No one understood the horror like Sophia. No one else had seen the shuddering convulsions of her sister, who was certain in her own teenage mind that she had somehow offended God.

And on the fourth day, Sasha was dead. She had escaped from the house where the 17-year-old Sophia was supposed to be in charge, and then run through the west London streets to the residential tower block which they could both see from their bedroom window. High on that roof, it was now known, Sasha had carried her treasured framed art print of Saint Agatha, and, clutching it closely, she prayed one final time to the still-revered third-century Bride of Christ.

She then placed the picture against the wall, and jumped 200-feet to her death.

At the time, Sophia actually thought Sasha was in their step-father's study reading. And no one else was home when the police called with the shocking news. They sent a squad car around, collected Sophia and drove her to the morgue. Her father was not expected home and the Russian-born sixth-former coped somehow with the suicide of her beloved sister.

Mostly her eyes were dry. Because, in a sense, she understood that Sasha's end was inevitable. It was a rare cut-and-dried case, no doubts, no explanation required. Sasha was too afraid to stay on this earth. And she made very sure she left it. A kindly London policeman had handed Sophia the only item in Sasha's school blazer pocket—a crumpled piece of paper from her Latin exercise-book. It contained the scribbled final words of Saint Agatha … *receive now my soul* …

And now her big sister completed her self-imposed obligation. She took the flint rock from her coat pocket and smeared it on one side with half the contents of a tube of thick stone-mason's cement. With immense care she placed it directly beneath the words on the headstone.

And then she stood up and smiled, and she looked again at the little rock. It was a gigantic symbol sealed onto a modest grave—in Sophia's mind it was a memorial as high as that cursed tower block back in west London

"If this churchyard lives for another thousand years," she muttered softly, "No one will ever know why it was placed there. Except you and me, my darling. A keepsake from the spot where that bastard died."

She stood up and made the sign of the cross, in the Catholic/Russian manner. "Goodbye, my dear, I'll come back soon."

And as she did so, the ancient chimes of St Nicholas struck 11 times, evoking in Sophia's mind the popular, bearded and happy vision of the fourth-century Catholic Saint. It also reminded her that he was also the Patron Saint of her homeland, Russia, and one of the rare saints whose feast day is still observed by the Russian Orthodox Church. Sasha, quite certainly, rested in the correct place.

*****

At 11am, 85-miles to the south, head groundsman Harry Ainsworth and two young Sussex policeman were hauling the lifeless body of Lord Fontridge out of the Glyndebourne Lake.

They dragged him out of shallow water facedown and rested the waterlogged ex-Chairman on the grass. Then the two policemen rolled him over onto his back, and all three of them could see the bone-handled blade of the stiletto still rammed into his heart.

"Fuck me," said Harry.

The two policemen merely gaped. Now mud-splashed, standing in their waders, out of breath, and sweating like a couple of Japanese wrestlers, they had both been up half the night. They'd been up ever since the 38-year-old Lady Fontridge had called the local police station shortly after 3am, by which time her husband had not returned home.

She had explained carefully how the opera had ended at around 10.45pm and how her husband quite often stayed for a drink with the other Trustees, the cast, and volunteer staff. On opening night they all met in the ornate committee room, for a kind or self-congratulatory celebration that yet another fabulous opera season had begun in this most spectacular setting. To hear old Charlie Willoughby-Sanders banging on you'd have thought he'd sung the lead tenor for the Duke.

Privately the late-duty station sergeant, Bob Hammond, thought the great man was probably drunk, or he had "taken off into the bushes with one of those randy young dancers." But this only proved that Bob did not know the difference between opera and ballet. It did not make him any less of a policeman. And he cottoned on to this severe situation, involving a Lord Justice of Appeal, extremely quickly.

This missing man was a pillar of society, next in line for High Sheriff of Sussex. He chaired many committees, and was reputed to be a professional associate of the Royal family, as well as a belted Baron of the realm. There were several people in this part of the county who, in the scheme of things, mattered. But this multi-millionaire grandee really mattered.

And if Jane Fontridge was sufficiently concerned to be calling the police at this hour … well, Sergeant Bob Hammond was on the case. Not because he was in any way certain that something was wrong, but because there would be all hell to pay if there truly was something amiss with his Lordship, and the Sussex constabulary had made no move.

Bob summoned into action every one of his available officers, on or off duty, within a 25-mile radius of the opera house. By 4am there were three squad cars, blue lights flashing in the grounds of Glyndebourne. It was raining lightly, but four officers in hi-visibility rain-macs, carrying powerful police flashlights were searching the main lawns and pathways.

Two more searched the car park where there was just one vehicle still in residence—a black Mercedes Benz in the reserved section for staff and committee executives. It took them no more than five minutes on the satellite communication system to headquarters to establish the owner was indeed Lord Fontridge of Laughton Towers.

By now the Chief Constable of Sussex, Sir George Kenny, had been alerted. One of the most important Appeal Court Judges in England was missing. And it looked very much as if he were still in the grounds at Glyndebourne, at least his car was still there, and he had not been seen since moments before the interval of *Rigoletto*.

Chief Constable Kenny was a County man through and through, having served long years as both a Chief Inspector and a Chief Superintendent, after which he was knighted for outstanding service. Also he played the trumpet in the local Sussex County Orchestra. And now he was standing in his pyjamas speaking to his Deputy Chief on the phone in the country town of Lewes, in which he was born, and from where he now ruled over nearly 3,000 officers. His reaction to the case of the departed Baron was kind of universal.

"Fuck me." said Sir George.

And he dressed swiftly and then instructed his driver to head straight for Malling, where the County HQ was situated, right across town from the old Victorian ramparts of Lewes Jail, whose former inmates included Eamon de Valera, the Irish rebel leader in Dublin's Easter Rising, 1916, and the notorious London gangster Reggie Kray.

Indeed the Sussex Constabulary was as steeped in matters of crime as any force in the land. But even as Sir George headed to HQ, his organisation had somehow missed a trick. A big one at that. Aces and Kings. On the very outskirts

26

of their operational territory was Gatwick Airport and all of its hotels. Sir George's missing murderer was asleep, nearly, right there, in the Hilton, fourth floor, room 428. At 3.52am they were seven hours from finding a body.

By now there were squad cars racing towards Glyndebourne from every which way. The opera House was less than two miles from Malling, where the principal ops room was already fully staffed. A bank of computers was recording every inch of the search, the phone lines were alive with call-backs from young policemen reporting for early duty, and statements were being processed from patrons who had attended *Rigoletto*

Beyond all that was an unmistakable sense of urgency. Lord Fontridge had been a lifelong prosecuting lawyer, and for many years a circuit court judge, presiding at Lewes Assizes in the majestic Crown Court on the High Street. There were criminals all over the place, both incarcerated and on the loose, with reason to hate him.

Not many of them would have dared to seek revenge against a Judge. But every senior policeman understood they were never thinking about the many. They were thinking about just the one; the deranged villain, now out of jail, and bent on harming the man who sent him there. Never mind the vicious crime, nor the victim. Just the man who had passed sentence.

It does not happen often. But it has happened. Despite the common knowledge that if any villain tries that, the police are going to lock him up and throw away the key, occasionally some idiot tries it on, apparently not caring about a future incarceration for the rest of his life. Judges live with that slight danger, and the police are always aware of it.

If Lord Fontridge had been the victim of foul play, there would be no effort spared, because such a crime threatened the heart of British justice. By 6am, the Special Search Division was screening through the records of every criminal Lord Fontridge had ever sent down, dead or alive.

And Sir George Kenny's storm-troopers were on the case. The Glyndebourne search would be ramped up at first light, and six more squad cars were already swerving into the grounds of the opera house. Harry Ainsworth was on duty with several more of his staff, in company with police officers.

If Lord Fontridge was lying unconscious in the grounds, they would find him. The search would begin around the central building where there were many hedges and clumps of bushes. As the morning wore on, they would fan out, combing the hidden corners of this vast estate.

By 9am the police knew the Law Lord had left his seat in the second row, and was then seen leaving the theatre itself, around four minutes before the interval. The program lady confirmed that. They also knew about the letter. The program lady revealed that. And two of the Trustees suggested that Freddie Fontridge had seemed unwell throughout the First Act: he was pale, sweating and on edge.

The search switched to the shores of the lake around 10.30am. Harry Ainsworth's assistant found his Lordship face down in the water some six feet offshore, just below the surface. It took them 10 minutes to pull on waders and drag the body in. When they turned it over and revealed the stiletto, the game changed significantly. The search for a missing person had turned into a murder hunt. Viable suspects: None. Motive: Unknown.

Chapter Three
Prepared to Kill

*The Japanese rapist rolled off the bed. He was still conscious,
but unaware with what he was dealing—no ordinary tigress this
... Veroniya was, after all, born on the western border of Siberia,
home to the largest, most ferocious big cat in the world.*

At this particular time it was almost impossible for Sophia Morosova to look forward to anything. A visit to her sister's grave was in itself depressing, but the emotional jolt of having murdered one of the senior Law Lords in England brought its own brand of somnolence to her mind. Yes, he deserved it. Yes, she'd agreed to do it. And no, she was certainly not sorry. But nonetheless, the image of poor old Freddie hitting the Glyndebourne Lake with an Italian dagger sticking out of his chest was a bit depressing.

It took the joyful ambiance of a unique England country pub to dispel her mood, and she entered the old wooden-floored bar of the Angel on the Bridge, with the merest suggestion of a smile. This is one of the few pubs right on the river in the entire 100-mile stretch of the upper Thames, and the only one in Henley. It was historically old, in Sophia's opinion probably as old as the bridge itself. It was probably as old as St Nicholas Church, though how its supreme, gold-battered haddock and chips had dodged the Black Death only God understood.

Sophia walked to the bar and ordered her lunch. The same dish she and Veroniya had also ordered on the many times they had stopped here in the middle of the day—the sublime fresh haddock and chips, gold-battered as the chalk board menu confirmed. Sometimes they had lunched on the downstairs terrace, close up to the water, before the piercing eyes of the cruising swans, and in the western shadow of the venerable arched bridge itself.

Other times, in the winter they chose a table near the log fire in the small dining room. Wherever, the Angel on the Bridge was like home to Sophia, although the landlord did not recognise her. It had been so long since both her sister and her mother had been taken away. And she had not been here since.

Today she ordered a glass of spring water, and went downstairs to wait on the terrace for her lunch to arrive, and her mood was lifting, even before the first racing eight, in training for the Regatta, shot the bridge and powered on, upriver towards the village of Sonning. Eight blades struck resolutely 32 strokes per minute, the oarsmen were all wearing the pink livery of the Leander Club, the sport's fortress on the river, founded 1818, the oldest rowing club in the world.

Sophia stared at the strokeman, the one facing the coxswain, the one setting the pace for the others to follow, often the most skilled and savvy member of the crew. And in her mind she saw the faded image of her grand-father, Russian strokeman in another age, and then Chief Petty Officer in a Soviet warship ploughing through the frozen wastes of the Baltic Sea.

She always felt a part of this river, and she sat day-dreaming a while, going over the precise events which had brought her here on this sunlit late morning in England. It was no doubt, the demise of her mother, which had caused such a terrible family catastrophe.

The visits of those awful older men, with their clothes off, grabbing at the girls, while darling Sasha just whimpered in the corner sobbing and crying. It was always the same, many different men, some of whom hit her, and the ghastly one from Sussex who beat Sasha with the belt.

It always happened when their mother was away visiting her family in Russia. It happened only around the long English school holidays when Mrs Morosova returned to Moscow for one month at a time. Post-Christmas, Easter and in the seven-week break in the summer. The times when only their step-father was in London.

He was always there to greet the men when they arrived. But there was that appalling night when her mother returned unexpectedly three days early.

Both Sophia and her sister were locked in their bedroom with some horrible man from Japan or somewhere, who was striving to make love to the petrified, screaming Sasha, aged just 15 now.

Veroniya had suddenly entered the kitchen, where her second husband Boris was drinking coffee and checking bank statements. His wife suddenly heard Sasha's screams and demanded to know where her daughters were, and what in God's name was going on upstairs.

Boris had moved to block the doorway, "Nothing is wrong," he said. "The girls are just playing with a good friend of mine."

Veroniya was not buying that, and she yelled, "Let me

pass!" But Boris stood his ground and told her to sit down and shut up, "The girls will be down very soon," he shouted.

At which point his enraged and frightened wife, picked up a steel frying pan and, holding it with both hands, slammed it into the right-hand side of his head. Boris went down like a sack of potatoes. And Veroniya charged up the stairs to the second-floor of the house.

And then came the worst part of all. She unlocked the front bedroom door and rushed in, to find a middle-aged Japanese businessman, raping her sobbing 15-year-old daughter, with Sophia bleeding from her lower lip, cowering on the floor.

Veroniya almost went into shock. But, with the instincts of a tigress defending her young, without a word, she raised the frying pan again, and smashed it into the man's head, swinging it back and clubbing him with it for a second time, The Japanese rapist somehow rolled off the bed. He was still just conscious but unaware with what he was dealing—no ordinary tigress this. Veroniya was born on the very western border of Siberia, home country of the largest, strongest big cat in the world.

And right now there was not one single member of the Siberian tiger tribe, who would not have been proud of the defensive battle being fought by one of their own. The Japanese man tried to rise, and scrambled towards her, fists clenched, but Veroniya came at him again, a predator prepared to kill, and she smashed the steel edge of the pan into his ear, a colossal blow which flattened him as thoroughly as she had already flattened her own husband. Right then, Veroniya fainted.

With the two girls clinging onto her, begging their mother to wake up, a critical sequence of events began. First of all the Japanese man almost died. Boris came up the stairs pouring blood from a head wound, and saw the scene of undiluted horror in the girl's bedroom. Sasha's blood was on her legs, Sophia's lip was swollen and bleeding, dripping on her unconscious mother.

Veroniya herself was not moving, but she was sprawled on the floor in urgent need of medical attention. The Japanese rapist was obviously very badly hurt, spread out on the carpet, white-faced and streaming blood from his right ear, and from a bad open gash above his right eye, which would need several stitches. If, Boris thought, the man survived.

Step one was plainly to get rid of the man from Japan. Boris called an ambulance and told them a house guest had fallen down the stairs and was

31

seriously injured. He asked Sophia to clean up Sasha, to get towels for his own head wound and to prevent Veroniya's victim from making any more mess than he was already doing.

Then he called a personal friend, a Russian doctor, who also lived in Maida Vale, and asked for him to come to the house as quickly as possible. By the time he arrived, one hour later, Veroniya was conscious but seemed unable to make any sense of anything. Doctor Anton gave her an injection, to make her sleep, and quietly asked Boris if his wife had recently suffered some kind of a major trauma.

Boris denied this but mentioned that she had suffered from fainting spells for some time, and he would like to get her into some kind of a rest home, back in Russia near her family, for a few months in order for a full recovery to be possible. He asked for his help, and for Dr Anton to accompany him to Russia to ensure Mrs Morosova would receive the best possible care in a top institution for the emotionally disturbed. In any language that's a mental home for the seriously deranged. Difficult to get into, a lot more difficult to get out.

Dr Anton was swiftly persuaded however, with a £10,000 cheque, and he agreed to keep Mrs Morosova in a Harley Street clinic, mildly sedated, until they were ready to travel. Neither Sasha nor Sophia ever saw her again.

For two years now, they had been subjected to systematic rape, sexual and physical abuse, so badly and for so long they actually thought this was what happened to everyone; that this was what women were for. Boris had threatened torture, or even death, if they ever told anyone, especially their mother.

On one chilling evening, after they had both been raped, just before Sophia's 17th birthday, he had heated the fire poker until it was red-hot, and then held it up in front of them. "If either of you," he said, "Ever think of telling anyone about our games, I will take this poker and wipe it straight across your face." Both terrified out of their wits, 24 hours a day, they kept quiet.

Privately, Sophia thought that Sasha might be going mad, that the whole procedure with these hideously disgusting men might have caused her to lose her reason. She just acquiesced when they undressed her, just lay there when they raped her, and obeyed other unusual commands.

For Roman Catholic teenagers this young, it was like something out of the dark ages, but for these two there was nothing else. They could not remember knowing anything else. And so it continued, two or three times, every week in the school holidays, men arriving at the house at all hours, prepared for sex with two wonderful looking schoolgirls, one of them, in law, a juvenile.

It seemed that it would never end. And then one day it did: when little Sasha jumped off the roof of a skyscraper. Suddenly everything was too dangerous for their step-father. He sent Sophia back to her boarding school at Pangbourne, where she would cope with the sudden absence of her fifth-form sister. He put the house on the market, and shipped himself back to Russia 'on business'. No one in England ever saw him again. And the house, expensively located in a mews off Prince Regent Drive, close to the Regent's Canal, sold for well over

£3 million, all of which was put in Trust for Sophia.

Boris was rotten through and through. But he did one other favour for his step-daughter before he left. Boris asked his brother-in-law Rudolf Masow to act as guardian and Trustee for his surviving daughter, Sophia, while he was away, which, he assured, would not be for long. Boris, of course, had no intention of returning to the scene of his crimes. Ever.

And so the torment of the mews house near the Regent's canal in Maida Vale ended. With Sasha, so shockingly gone, Sophia settled back into school, and did everything she could to cast the memories aside. She told no one what had happened, neither on the fateful night of her mother's sudden return, nor indeed of the events that led directly to Sasha's death. Of the men who had ravaged her and her sister nothing more was heard, anywhere.

Sophia, of course, knew their names as mentioned by her step-father, and occasionally saw the name of Fontridge in the newspaper. The man from Japan was called Yunto, but when they were clearing out the house she found a note in her step-father's desk which contained the words 'Yunto Takahashi,' then the words Hong Kong.

There was only one who was unmistakable—a real weirdo named Sir Josh Hartley, who had blond hair down to his shoulders, very tight trousers which were mostly around his ankles, child-like tee shirts with nursery rhyme characters, and dodgy teeth.

Since he always wanted to kiss both girls, his visits were a living nightmare. He was a whip-thin beanpole of a man, and he always insisted on having them both, and saying the crudest description of the act of love, out loud, over and over. Sophia thought he was almost certainly insane. Of them all, she absolutely detested him.

The long-haired 68-year-old was very rich, but he always arrived at the house behind the canal on his bright yellow racing bike. As ostentation went, Sir Josh was a master. He was always in the news and in magazines, usually being lionised for his charitable work with young children, especially in care homes.

However, he was best known as a disc jockey for the BBC—radio and television. In later life, even Sophia would wonder how such a man could ever have been hired by Great Britain's national broadcasting corporation. Sir Josh Hartley was one very weird, and very dangerous little predator, and he worked behind the cover of being England's most caring celebrity.

Sasha began to tremble almost uncontrollably when she heard the jaunty ring on his bicycle bell when he pulled up outside the house. He used it instead of the doorbell, and her step-father was always waiting. Sophia never forgot that.

The biggest man who visited the house was a 6ft 3inch American in his mid-40's. Their step-father called him Buck, and he was, in a Hollywood kind of way, good-looking, dark haired and very fit. Over many months of eavesdropping and listening, Sophia worked out his full name of Buck Madden. She also ascertained he was a very high-class tennis player, and once overheard him suggest her father visit him in Virginia, wherever that might be.

But this particular sportsman was the cruellest of them all, a true sadist, far worse than Fontridge. He never wanted the girls to undress, but preferred to strip their clothes off, always smacking Sasha hard. Once he smacked her too hard, and Sophia went, for him, whacking him with a shoe in the place she guessed it might hurt most.

Buck lashed out at her with a terrific backhand blow across her jaw and watched her skid across the carpet, smacking into a radiator and cutting her forehead just below the hairline. Then he laughed and raped her right on the floor, with blood still streaming down her face. Buck might have had a decent backhand on or off the tennis court, and the crowds loved him at Wimbledon. But he was a brute. An unmitigated, sexually deviant brute.

Sophia Morosova hated him worse than she would ever hate anyone in her life, even more than she hated Fontridge.

There was another American on the list too. He was a rather gentle guy aged around mid-50's, grey-haired and well-dressed; talked kind of funny to Sophia's ear, referring to the sisters as y'all, and pronouncing the word 'chair' as chayer.

His requirement was simple. He wanted to lie on the bed, stark naked, kissing two naked schoolgirls. No variations. And he acted like they must love it as he did, not being present when both girls threw up for a half-hour as soon as he'd gone. Sophia loathed the sight of the self-satisfied American from the Deep South.

Her step-father never used a name, and she'd never heard a conversation between them. She only once heard anything. One evening just before her father opened the bedroom door, she heard the American snap, "Goddamit, I've had real trouble with that Katrina. Thank God that bitch has gone now." Secretly, Sophia and Sasha thought he might have murdered someone, and from that moment they were more scared of him than anyone.

The only other visitor that Sophia could remember was a Spanish type, medium height, athletic build and very strong. Her step-father called him Eduardo, and he only came to the house in the summer. He was very rough with them, and only wanted Sasha, at 15. He made the older girl watch.

He never spoke to either of them, never smiled, just took whatever he wanted, dressed and left. But Sophia could hear him speaking to their step-father sometimes for 15 minutes. She never knew more than his first name, but gathered from her eavesdropping that he was some kind of a horseman.

Once she saw a photograph in her father's desk which showed the man mounted, wearing long boots and holding some kind of a long-handled wooden mallet. The sight of him upset her so much she tore the photograph into pieces and threw it in the fire.

All these secrets she kept from the world. Never told one living soul; all through her school years, and all through her three years at Clare College, Cambridge (founded 1326), where she read English and History.

And now, as she sat watching the Thames run softly past her, she had two things on her mind—1) the gold-battered haddock which was on its way, and 2) Uncle Rudolf whose presence in her life had always been important, but never more than it was right now.

The Russian secret intelligence officer had been there right from her earliest age. Both girls and their mother visited each summer while they lived in Russia. It was three weeks on the wonderful beaches of the southern Crimean coast, near Yalta, where Rudolf owned a dacha right on the water.

The house was a living testimony to his astounding skills as an undercover Russian agent. It was a summer house so extraordinary it needed not one improvement as Rudolf moved up rapidly to become one of the paramount assassins in Vladimir Putin's KGB.

Sophia never had the slightest idea what her uncle did for a living, but those vacations in that sunlit Crimean paradise stayed with her down all the years. This rugged southern coastline was probably the prime real estate in all of the Soviet Union. Discovered by the Czars, it contained spectacular oceanfront Palaces, and magnificent summer residences all backed by the towering Crimean Mountains.

Czar Alexander III built the Massandra Palace there in 1889. Shortly afterwards, Czar Nicholas II built the Livadia Palace which, in the manner of the Romanovs, was not that much bigger than Windsor Castle. Leo Tolstoy spent summers there, while writing *War and Peace*. The fabled White Dacha was owned by Anton Chekhov. Generally speaking Veroniya and her two daughters, felt as comfortably at home in south Crimea as did Chekhov's *Three Sisters*.

Even Joseph Stalin, always a world-ranked social climber, never lashed out on a home of his own, but took over the Massandra Palace whenever he felt like it. Never mind. Uncle Joe found plenty of other ways to lash out.

Perhaps Sophia and Sasha had something profoundly in common with the Russian aristocracy, and the immortal writers—every last one of them treasured their memories of the rugged Crimean coastline for all of their days.

Sophia remembered particularly that Uncle Rudolf had all the time he needed to take them all out in his sailboat, all the time necessary for long walks along the beach and over the rocks.

He loved them all, but she knew he liked little Sasha more than anyone. Nothing was too much when it involved Sasha's happiness. And Sophia remembered too his utter dismay when he learned of her suicide. And he was never happy about the plight of his sister, Veroniya.

All through her slightly-lonely school and university years, her Russian guardian remained attentive. He took care of her Trust, ensured it was invested wisely, and provided a home for her during vacations—usually a rented house somewhere in the Henley area, with a permanent staff of two ladies, usually from the Russian Embassy in London.

He made sure Sophia came to London often, and she frequently stayed as his guest in the Embassy, dined with her uncle and befriended several other members of staff and their families. But of course there were the unanswered questions, touched upon but never examined.

And for years, Sophia Morosova revealed nothing to the man upon whom she depended for everything. At least until her 21st birthday that was the case, but after that point in her life she would inherit money from another Trust. This would not make her truly wealthy, but she was never going to worry about anything financial. Independence would be hers for the first time.

Unless of course she ended up with a highly dodgy husband, and that was never going to happen given her experiences with men. At 22 she had never been on a date, never kissed a boyfriend, never allowed any man to touch her. The house in Maida Vale, and all it represented, had destroyed every last one of her natural feelings of affection. Except for Uncle Rudolf, although that was entirely different.

The longed-for gold-battered haddock arrived, and as a gesture of friendship to the river, she tossed a couple of equally golden chips to a passing swan who snapped them skilfully. And then she settled down to savour the perfectly cooked fresh fish. And of course the apparition of the gaping Lord Fontridge was never far away, and with that came the permanence of Uncle Rudolf, and how much she now needed him and his sage, but often brutal counsel.

And her mind reeled back to that 21st birthday dinner she'd had three years ago at the Embassy with just her uncle, and how after all this time, he kept implying that he wanted to know what had really happened to Sasha. That birthday had been a life-changing celebration in more ways than one. But the conversation on that evening led directly to her present plight. If it had never happened, she would not be sitting here today, essentially preparing to escape England, while on the run from the forthcoming police manhunt she knew was inevitable.

But the dinner had been lovely. Uncle Rudolf had presented her with a gorgeous emerald necklace and earrings, which had belonged to her own family, and she had proceeded to drink too many glasses of a 1995 Chateau Latour. Still, if you can't do that on your 21st what's left? At least that was Uncle Rudy's take.

And still he had persisted … What really happened to Sasha? And finally, after four long years of silence, Sophia had cracked, caved in on her birthday, and told him that which she had vowed to tell no one. She broke down and told him every last detail—the rapes inflicted on her and her sister, the beatings, the ghastly sexual humiliations. The sheer terror of living in such a totally threatening environment.

She told him about her step-father and her suspicions that he must have actually been selling the bodies of his own wife's daughters. She even recalled the many weeks when a working crew rebuilt walls, ceiling and floor of their large front bedroom. "Soundproofing—that little bastard," Rudy had growled.

And long before she finished her story, he had three times mentioned, "I don't know where Boris is, but I will find him. Ever since he married my sister I've never trusted him one yard. The man is a monster. He murdered little Sasha. And now I must kill him."

Sophia's eyebrows had shot skywards. "Kill him!" she exclaimed. "Isn't that a bit extravagant?"

"For a pig like that?' replied Rudolf. "Certainly not. He should not continue to take up room on this planet."

"Well, good luck with that," said Sophia. "We don't even know which country my step-father's in. Could be America. Could even be Russia. And God knows what name he's using. If anyone's going to get killed I'd rather it was one of those hideous creeps who raped Sasha and me."

"Why not the man who arranged it?" said Rudolf. "Why not the Procurer-in-Chief? Come along, Sophia. Always take out the head man if you can. Don't bother to break the arrow, kill the archer. That's an old Russian proverb."

"Russian!" smiled his niece. "Sounds a lot more like an old Lubyanka proverb!"

"Aha," said Rudolf. "Sometimes the two must be inter-changeable. In the interests of … well … justice."

Russian agent Rudolf Masow often surprised her. But on this day he had astounded her. First of all she had never seen him this angry. He was under tight control, as would be expected from a spymaster. But there was a slight shake on his hand when he refilled her glass, and his lips seemed somehow white-rimmed.

"This man arranged, for criminals to violate the two most beautiful members of my family. Two beautiful children." These were the precise words of Rudolf Masow. "If you think for one split second," he added, "That I am ever going to let that pass, then, Sophia, you do not know me very well."

Right now she was inclined to go along with that. Here was her beloved uncle proposing to murder her step-father. But, to her, it had a hollow ring, like a Shakespeare tragedy. Rudolf was seething and he could see nothing beyond his rage. But to her, the death of her step-father would mean little. He'd gone, and was already a distant memory. His death would be irrelevant.

But the memories of those terrible onslaughts on her young body remained stark and real, and her subconscious never let her forget. She remembered every night of her life. She could have fired a bullet through the head of any one of those men and never thought about it again.

And that's what she had told Rudolf, who told her, "That's the Russian in you. That cold longing for revenge. Remember modern Russia was created by the passion of the Bolsheviks, a cry from the heart to rid themselves of 300-years of slavery under the Romanov Czars.

"And when they eventually struck, they struck hard and fast. And they did not kill just one of this ruthlessly selfish ruling family—not just Czar Nicholas. They executed them all; his wife, his son and heir, and his four daughters, each one a Grand Duchess of Russia. Even his dog. The concept of Revenge is built into our souls. But it must be complete. Otherwise it is not revenge at all. Just a token attack which will soon be forgotten."

"You mean, Uncle Rudy, that it is our Russian moral duty to ensure that each one of the men who raped us must die?"

"I do," he said sternly, as if addressing a senior officer in the KGB. "For you and I, and for your mother who fought back so bravely. But mostly for my darling Sasha." And the iron-souled ex-Soviet assassin made no attempt to hide the tears which were streaming down his cheeks.

It would have been a simple matter to dismiss the whole conversation as the sudden ranting of a very angry man. And the dark-red insignia of Russian Heroes, often pinned to his lapel, confirmed that red was indeed the colour of angry men.

Rudolf was not even one percent joking. He meant every word. And such sentiments were more than possible for such a man. And Sophia knew it. However, her objection would be personal, not moral. She did not give a damn whether Rudy killed any of them or not. But the violation had been to her, not to him. And the only real satisfaction, even peace, which she could ever experience, would be if she delivered the mortal blow herself. It was the Russian in her.

And this she had told her uncle, right there at her own birthday dinner, and he had reacted slowly with much thought. "Very well," he said. "You have my blessing in all that you do. But in this case there will be a condition: that you allow me to help you plan, and to coach you and teach you, and above all to act as your guardian angel throughout the operation."

Despite a distinct atmosphere of disbelief, and indeed unreality, Sophia allowed herself to be led into an unknown place, one of murder and revenge. And she was uncertain, unable to accept what she was most definitely doing. But the everlasting apparition of those cruel and disgusting men loomed into her mind over and over, until she ultimately believed there was no freedom for her, until it was done.

And what would the consequences be? Nothing, not compared to what she and her sister had tolerated. Nothing, Zero. Sophia could never be tortured more she had been already. And that was the moment. She knew it. Uncle Rudolf knew it. And the sands of time were running swiftly through an hour-glass down in Sussex.

Which was more or less why Freddie Fontridge had been sloshing about in the Glyndebourne Lake, after one expert and savage thrust from a dagger. And indeed why she was sitting here overlooking her Russian grand-father's river, eating this wonderful fresh fried haddock. And why she knew she would be scared to turn on the BBC television news tonight. Even in the Russian Embassy.

Chapter Four
"Someone Bumped Him Off"

*The police do not normally stage manhunts and refuse to
rule out foul play, when some doddering elderly Baron,
who's been drinking champagne, falls into a large pond
in the middle of the night, and accidentally drowns.*

Sophia walked across the street to the Red Lion Hotel and backed out of the forecourt. A couple of motorists, one on either side of the road slowed to a halt to allow her to get in position. Then she gunned the black SUV with the diplomatic plates straight over the old bridge, and made a beeline for the M4 Motorway and London.

The 36-mile drive took her almost 75-minutes, driving into the city with heavy traffic from Heathrow airport. It was a typical busy Sunday afternoon, weekenders returning from the country, international visitors preparing for their nightly assault on London's theatre-land. Sophia swung off the freeway at Hammersmith, and drove along Kensington High Street, before scooting left up Church Street, and then swerving right, into Kensington Palace Gardens, home of the Russian Embassy.

There were several huge houses associated with the Russians and Sophia passed through Security and headed for the biggest one, on the left opposite Kensington Palace. She was immediately waived through, and a guard met her at the main door and then drove the Embassy car to the parking lot. Uncle Rudolf was there to meet her and the two of them walked through the red-carpeted hall into a pleasant reception room overlooking the gardens.

They had done this so many times before, but Sophia was always glad to escape the rather gloomy entrance hall. In fact the whole place was pretty gloomy, grand but glum, with heavy brocaded curtains, dark colours and large-scale carved wood all over the place, especially around the staircases.

But still, what could a girl expect for lodgings which cost her native country only a one pound coin per year in rent? Not much, she supposed. But then the Brits paid the Kremlin only one rouble a year for their massive and much brighter

Embassy in a panoramic setting on a curve of the Moscow River. There was less than 80 staff in Kensington, as opposed to 250 Brits in their Moscow Embassy. It never did seem quite fair to Sophia, but at present she had many bigger things on her mind.

Rudolf ordered tea for two. And when it came he told the Russian staff waitress to pour and add milk. Both Sophia and her uncle had acquired the British way of doings things. This did not, however, include stabbing judges, which had a distinct Italian mafiosi edge to it.

This afternoon Rudolf was all good humour and encouragement, telling his niece that she had done marvellously well, not a trace of evidence left behind, only a highly bewildered Sussex police force. "My enquiries have required a rather light touch," he said, wryly. "But I do assure you they do not have the first idea what really happened to Lord Fontridge. I'm guessing you delivered the blade precisely as I taught you?"

Sophia nodded. "And do you have any regrets?" he asked.

"Absolutely none."

"Excellent. And it is worth remembering that most murders are solved because several people knew who did it. Perhaps even more when people understood exactly why it was committed. In this case neither one applies. The Sussex police have no clues, and they are most unlikely to get any. I have, by the way, booked you on the 10am out of St Pancras to Paris tomorrow morning. Two hours and 20 minutes and you'll be home in your apartment.

"Travel on your Spanish passport. I'll join you there on Friday late afternoon."

They both retired to their rooms at around 5.30pm and regrouped just before 6 o'clock for the evening news. Rudolf sat smiling. Sophia nearly went into cardiac arrest at the sheer scale of what she had done.

Lead item on the newscast:

The body of one of England's most senior Law Lords was recovered from the Lake at Glyndebourne opera house this morning just before noon. The 66-year-old Lord Justice Fontridge was pronounced dead on arrival at Sussex County General Hospital though police were not revealing the exact time he had died. Neither would they reveal the cause of death, even though a suspicion of foul play was not denied.

Lord Fontridge had been attending the opera *Rigoletto*. He was a senior Trustee at Glyndebourne, and a member of Her Majesty's Privy Council. Lord Fontridge had expected to take up his duties as High Sheriff of Sussex later this year. The local police commander at Lewes HQ also confirmed they were in the process of a county-wide manhunt for those who might throw light on the circumstances leading to the death of the eminent Judge.

There followed pictures of his Lordship both at home and in the High Court, there were photographs of the grounds at Glyndebourne, including several shots of officers still patrolling the woods. There were also shots of the nearby Laughton Towers estate where Jane, Lady Fontridge was under sedation and said to be suffering from shock.

This seemed rather mild and factual, but when the program switched back to the studio, an entirely different atmosphere prevailed. They wheeled in the chief crime reporter for the network, Henry Marsden, who said flatly, "Lord Fontridge was plainly murdered—since the police do not stage manhunts and refuse to rule out foul play, when some doddering elderly Baron, who's been drinking champagne, falls into a large pond in the middle of the night, and accidentally drowns."

Henry knew full well, of course, there was nothing doddering about Freddie Fontridge; an excellent polo player, and former Master of the South Downs and Eridge Foxhunt with whom he still rode, whenever his demanding legal schedule permitted. But his Lordship was gone now, and you cannot libel the dead, so Henry had waded in with a spot of extra colour. Doddering it was, despite the fact that the fit and lean Lord Fontridge was in incalculably better shape than the red-faced, overweight, quasi-drunk, divorced crime reporter

"I'd say there were close to 50 journalists and cameramen here, between the opera house and the Towers," Henry added, "And every last one of them believes someone, for whatever reason, killed his Lordship. It could have been some criminal he sent down during his many years as a judge, it could have been anyone. But it was someone, and the police know it. You can trust me on that."

He added for good measure, "These journalists are mostly down from London. They are experienced and professional. And I have not spoken to one of them who even considers that this was accidental death. Right now we are all just waiting here for the police to admit it was murder."

At this point Sophia turned off the television. She and Rudy had a relaxed dinner, and the assassin of Lord Fontridge passed another restless night. Rudolf drove her to St Pancras Station early on Monday morning, and she picked up three newspapers and took her seat on Eurostar a full half-hour before the train was due to leave.

The headline in the London *Daily Mail* almost sent her into shock :

Slain Peer Dumped In The Lake
Manhunt begins for Law Lord's killer

As tabloid screamers go, that one was right out there on a limb. An unnamed police source had told the *Mail* reporter, "Between you and me, old son, someone definitely bumped him off." It may of course have been a flagrant lie, but it may not. And Sophia Morosova's heartbeat was pounding at roughly the same speed as the 100mph train as it thundered through the green fields of Kent.

The conservative broadsheet, the *Daily Telegraph* was a great deal more careful and admitted no one was making the murder official. They used the old newspaper trick of the 'mystery,' which traditionally means the police did not want to answer reporters' questions. Which is, of course a lot less sexy than:

DEATH OF SENIOR LAW LORD
SURROUNDED IN MYSTERY
Police reluctant to announce
suspicious evidence

The London *Times* was a bit more daring, in the natural idiom of its swashbuckling Australian proprietor:

DID HE JUMP OR WAS HE PUSHED?
Law Lord's Death at Glyndebourne
baffles Police
Scotland Yard called in

All of them ran major front-page pictures of Lord Fontridge himself, the *Daily Mail* combining a large study of the Judge in his scarlet courtroom robes and 18th-century wig, with an elegant shot of the Glyndebourne Lake, which suggested His Lordship was somehow conducting a trial in the bulrushes.

There were full-page picture spreads in all three papers of Fontridge, taken throughout his life, the courtroom, the country estate, his opening appearance at the Privy Council and, of course, his very senior position on the Board of one of the most famous opera houses in the world. He was a very eminent man.

Sophia, faced with the reality of her action, nonetheless was unrepentant. The flashes of memory were entirely involuntary—Freddie Fontridge whacking that belt down on Sasha, and then making her watch while he raped her elder sister … God knows, if anyone deserved that stiletto, it was the sneering, sadistic Law Lord from Laughton Towers.

Sophia sat reliving her nightmares as the train plunged into the darkness of the Channel Tunnel, and without the bucolic distractions of the Garden of England, she found herself quietly confirming her hatred of Fontridge. *Regrets? You must be joking. I'd do it again. Any time.*

Once in daylight, the Eurostar sped up to 186mph, flashing across the flatlands of Northern France, too fast even to notice the haunted white stone walls surrounding the ghosts of the Great War—too fast even to search for the giant memorials which still salute silently the tens of thousands who perished on the Somme a hundred years ago.

Before she realised it, Sophia was pulling into the Gare du Nord in Paris. With just her light travelling bag, she moved swiftly outside to the taxi rank and jumped aboard a small Peugeot and requested: *"Rue des Beaux-Arts, Saint Germain."* The journey took a half-hour in traffic until finally they stopped right across the street from *L'Hotel,* Oscar Wilde's old hangout. Generally speaking, she had always loved his work and his incomparable wit, but sincerely hoped to have a lot more luck evading the British law than he did.

Home for Sophia these days was a lovely two-bedroomed rented apartment which cost too much, but was so beautifully situated, high above this arty, bookshop and restaurant area, that she considered it worth every penny. Just around the corner from *Boulevard Saint Germain.*

It was also a short walk from *Deux Magots,* the near legendary sidewalk French café, which was once the daily rendezvous for Hemingway and his pals. Today it was still the best place in the entire City of Light to watch the more interesting Parisians stroll by. Sophia Morosova had her coffee and croissant there every morning, regardless of the weather.

She slipped through the front door of her building and called, *"Bonjour, Gaston,"* as she passed the doorman, and then she took the elevator to the sixth floor and let herself into her apartment. She'd been gone exactly one week, and whichever way you looked at it, Sophia was a very different young woman now than she was on the day she left.

She was a bit more cool, a bit more cunning and a lot more wary. She was better equipped, by any standards, to face the only future there could ever be for someone who had suffered as she had, as a teenager. Also she wielded an Italian stiletto with the same determination and skill she'd once reserved for her hockey stick at St Margaret's.

This evening she would stay at home. The restaurant across the street would bring her dinner, and she had a bottle of very classy white burgundy from Meursault in the fridge. She would spend the time reading magazines she'd brought from London. One was rather important, it contained a six-page feature about a BBC disc jockey, whose photo graced the front jacket.

Sophia could spot that despicable little creep at a thousand paces. She'd read the magazine article already, all about the gloriously generous life of the sainted benefactor Sir Josh, hero of British culture. She was rather looking forward to reading the story again, more slowly. In greater detail.

*****

Almost 180-miles northwest of Paris, the scene in the Sussex Police HQ was one of controlled despair. The officers had searched the grounds for every possible clue, found nothing significant, and were already in the process of trying to interview members of the Glyndebourne staff.

They were also in the process of interviewing patrons, most of whose names they knew. There were only 12 anonymous seats in the auditorium, and these were occupied by the embassies: four each for the Americans, the Italians and the Russians. The Americans would respond upon request, the Italians would be all smiles and gracious assistance, and the Russians would not even return the phone call. Could you please provide us with the names of the people who used the Russian complimentary allocation? You have to be joking. You'd never get past the switchboard. Such a request would be treated by the men from the Kremlin as "typical western spy mania."

46

Meanwhile, the body of the late Lord Fontridge lay in the Lewes morgue while everyone waited for the coroner's report to be made public. And for the police to announce, finally, that he had been murdered. Sir George Kenny, the Chief Constable of Sussex, was, in truth, no nearer solving this crime than he had been at three o'clock on Sunday morning.

No one had the slightest idea who had stabbed the peer. No one could accurately know when it had happened. And no one had the remotest thought about a motive. They certainly didn't know who, they didn't know when, and they didn't know why. Which was highly irritating for Sir George. They had only just received permission, from her doctor, to speak to the sedated Jane Fontridge.

In all the great sprawling mass of this crime, there was but one semblance of a clue. And it led resolutely into a clunking dead end. Edith Carstairs-Rogers remembered that a man had asked her to have a letter delivered to Lord Fontridge moments before the curtain.

She had handed it on to young Diane Mason who had carried it down to his Lordship on a tray, and actually remembered him starting to tear it open before she left. That was helpful, but the key was, could Edith, a local worthy, remember who had given her the letter? Would she recognise him again?

Her answer was a resounding no. "There were several people wanting programs at the time," she said. "I hardly looked up. I saw the letter he had put in front of me, he was very polite and I just took it, and called Diane over. I hardly gave the man a glance. And I most certainly would not recognise him again. I'm pretty sure I'd never seen him before."

So far as Sir George was concerned that more or less wrapped it up. They had nothing. He believed the letter mattered. His Lordship had opened it, and, possibly, a little over an hour later, he was murdered. There must have been a connection.

But this was not a local Sussex matter. This was a major national incident. And his men were tired by this Monday evening. Everyone was tired. Sir George himself was knackered. He did not relish the idea of becoming the major lynchpin in a nationwide investigation. Because it was an extreme certainty that when the press grew bored of the story, they would turn on the police, worse yet they would turn on Sir George. He'd seen it before, and he could see it now:

Why Oh Why Has This Sussex
Bugler Failed To Find Killer?
Is Sir George still the right man for the job?

"Jesus Christ!" he muttered. Of course he knew he did not possess quite the talent of Louis Armstrong, but at the slightest provocation, the slightest suggestion of trouble, the press disparagingly called him 'the Bugler.' He'd even considered retiring from his back-row seat in the orchestra, but the conductor had told him not to be so bloody daft. The newspapers would use the insult, whether or not he was actively still playing.

However, on this Monday afternoon, he had no time for self-recrimination. The fact was, he needed help. And he needed it quickly. He quietly closed the door to his office. And three minutes later another phone buzzed, on the desk of Detective Chief Superintendent Charles Barton, New Scotland Yard. He and Sir George had been friends for several years, dating back to 2008 when the young Detective Constable Charles Barton had miraculously solved a really unpleasant murder in the cosmopolitan North Lanes district of Brighton.

Charles himself dismissed it as 'a fluke.' Sir George called it "bloody brilliant," nothing less. And whenever the Sussex Chief was in London they always had lunch or dinner together, talked "shop" and swapped stories. They usually inflicted serious damage on a couple of bottles of Bordeaux, sometimes at the Mayfair home of Charles himself. His mother Lady Penelope Barton always addressed the Sussex Knight as "Darling Georgie," a level of flippancy, which might be expected from the daughter of a Scottish Duke, which Lady Penelope indeed was.

Tonight DCS Barton was delighted to receive the call. "Hello, George," he said, "Funny, I've been expecting you."

"I'll bet you have," he replied. "I'm calling you from a bloody madhouse."

"That also does not surprise me," said Barton, quietly. "But it's more or less what to expect when someone dumps a Law Lord in the bloody Lake a couple of miles from your own office. I hear he was stabbed. Anyone called you a bugler yet!"

"Jesus, Charlie! This is serious. I need help. And I need it fast."

"I know that," said Charles. "That's why I was expecting you."

"You mean you will give me a hand?"

"'Course I will. I'm rather looking forward to it. You want me to come down?"

"Do I ever? Can you come tomorrow morning?"

"I can. Eight o'clock. Your office."

"Perfect."

"Oh, and George. One thing. I hear that four Russian Embassy comps are still unnamed. Can you let me know the four people sitting directly behind the Russians?"

"Sure. But what do you want them for?"

"Eight a.m. sharp. See you then."

Charles Barton was not an average detective. And while his old school, Eton College, had produced 19 British Prime Ministers, its roll-call of on-the-beat coppers was strictly limited. In fact no one ever traced an Old Etonian actually swinging his truncheon, patrolling the dark streets of East London where Charles Barton's career had begun.

He had gone to the expensive University of Aylesbury, and taken a degree in Criminology, but his school record had counted against him. And, no matter the influence of his family, Charles faced the prospect of walking in the grim footsteps of Jack the Ripper in the East End of the capital, as a beat policeman, no better. Or else joining a bank in the City, where his father was an undisputed Titan of Finance.

Too bad, he'd died early, leaving every penny to his adored wife Lady Penelope. Regardless, Charles chose the dangerous night-time streets of London. And, if ever accused of reaching the heights of Scotland Yard through family connections, his reply, never varied … "Fuck off, old boy. I came up through the ranks."

Charles lived in one of the most pricey stretches of Mayfair, South Audley Street. He occupied a large private apartment on the third floor of the family house. But today, the taunts he'd tolerated for years from fellow beat coppers had died away, owing to his meteoric career, which effectively made him their boss.

He was a tall, good-looking, dark-haired member of England's ruling class. He had a quiet demeanour, which only marginally disguised a brain which could calculate facts at an incredible pace. His mother thought it was absurd that a young woman of his own background had not yet snapped him up. But she understood that was slightly awkward since he was already married … to New Scotland Yard, to which he was ever devoted and faithful.

A long-standing Saturday date with a titled former debutante at an exclusive Ball at Claridge's, had once clashed with the somewhat grisly murder of an MI6 man in a back alley in Kilburn. "Of course he won't let you down, darling," said a frowning Lady Penelope on the phone to Lady Carol. Wrong, Charles was in the back alley.

"He's hopeless," added Lady Penelope, this time to the girl's parents. "If that damned workhouse on the river summoned him on his wedding day, he'd leave someone standing at the altar. Trouble is, he thinks he's Sherlock Holmes, a man I always thought faintly ridiculous. Can you imagine? He lived in Baker Street, like some Jewish tailor!"

Charles may have floundered around at Eton with only four O-level passes, but he was, like Sherlock, a detective of the blood. His endless devotion to Sir Arthur Conan Doyle's master sleuth, and the hundreds of hours he'd spent studying those crime-ridden novels, had in the end paid off. At the age of 24 he'd single-handedly nailed the elusive killer of a French children's nanny: the tattooed kid from next door. And once, trapped with four criminals on the roof of a furniture store in Camden Town, he'd flattened one of them, with a four by two, when the thug had pulled a gun on him. The others surrendered.

"I sometimes wonder how a young man of your background could possibly be so rough," the presiding Magistrate had stated when passing sentence.

"That's easy, sir," Charles had replied. "I went to Eton. And that was harder than Colditz Castle."

And even as he climbed the ladder to the very height of the Metropolitan Police detection divisions, he stuck always to the creed of Sherlock himself : *When you have eliminated the impossible, only the truth remains.* At 37, he was the youngest Detective Chief Superintendent in the modern history of Scotland Yard. He was also President-elect of the much-revered Sherlock Holmes Society.

The fact that he attended the most famous school in the world gave him a rather relaxed attitude to command. He never shouted at people, never belittled them publicly, since he was safe inside an inbuilt view that he was somehow superior to most people. Etonians never lose that, at least the successful ones don't, and neither do most of the less successful. Even the catastrophes are usually pretty darned sure of themselves. It's the English way. And Charles Barton was extremely popular. He was a proper commanding officer.

And the relationship between New Scotland Yard, HQ of the Metropolitan Police, and the other British county police organisations, suited him perfectly. The Met is nothing like the FBI. It's not a national crime-fighting unit, and it's not regarded as superior to the others.

However, it has a lot more money than anyone else, it's far better equipped with laboratories and high-tech divisions. It has more officers, and an unspoken advantage that very brilliant young men seem to end up at the Met. Regular county Police Chiefs do not appeal for help from the Met, as inferiors to the Masters. They call on New Scotland Yard as friends, often suggesting they share the responsibilities of the most important cases.

This is not compulsory, but foolish is the County Boss who does not call in the experts at the Met, when a case threatens to swamp him and his staff. Such was the position of Sir George Kenny with the matter of the stabbed Lord Fontridge. And he would be mightily relieved tomorrow morning when he saw Barton step out of his Metropolitan staff car and into the Sussex rain.

Chapter Five
The Butterflies of Death

*"The Russians don't actually send people to England at vast
expense to study poetry. They send them for things like espionage,
political intrigue, kidnapping, or assassination. They call them
Cultural Attaches. Which is like calling the Kremlin an Arts College"*

Back in London, the Detective Chief Superintendent was making his way home to South Audley Street, carrying a package of newspaper cuttings and internet print-outs, which had been compiled for him over the past couple of days. He asked his driver to grab an evening paper on the way, and was amused to see the editor had decided to 'splash' on the murdered lord. The editor was lucky. Sussex Police announced the coroner's findings shortly after 3pm and that gave the afternoon publications a scoop.

Yes, It Was Murder
Law Lord Fatally Stabbed
Scotland Yard officers headed for East Sussex

In reality this particular Scotland Yard officer was taking the quick route to Mayfair, along The Mall, around the statue of the Duke of Wellington into Hyde Park, with a swift right turn into Upper Brook Street, before a zig-zag final 500-yards. It was 7pm. Lady Penelope was awaiting him. They were dining alone tonight, which was a rarity.

"Oh, hello, Charles," she said. "Excellent. You have the paper, let me have a quick look, will you? Just the theatre guide."

Charles kissed his mother lightly on the cheek and handed it over.

"Oh goodness me!" she exclaimed, "That dreadful business in Sussex is all over the place again. I can't imagine what Freddie Fontridge was doing in the stupid lake in the first place. Never mind dropping dead in it. Poor darling George. I expect the press will find a reason to be absolutely beastly to him."

"Actually, Mum," replied Charles. "It's more like poor darling Freddie. Someone stabbed him to death before he hit the water."

"Stabbed him! What d'you mean stabbed him?"

"The usual procedure," said Charles, offhandedly. "Long-bladed knife shoved straight into his heart. Normally does the trick."

"Into Freddie's heart! My goodness, how terribly disagreeable!"

"Well, yes. Pretty bloody unattractive really. Old George is up to his neck in the investigation. I'm going down to Sussex early tomorrow. Try to give him a hand."

"Who was it? I mean, who killed him?"

"Actually, Mum, if they knew that, I probably wouldn't be going."

"No, I suppose not. Well, anyway, let's have a drink, I told Hudson to feed us at eight."

"Good idea. I've been reading up on this murder all day, Forgot about lunch. What'll I get you? G and T? I'm going for a sizeable Johnny Walker Black."

"Fine. But tell me a bit more about the late Freddie. He was a bit of an odd-ball. I knew his first wife, but a lot of people think he might have been queer. This new wife was a bit out of character, you know, youngish, sexy, ex-dancer. But we all thought Freddie was never much interested in women."

"Perhaps he wasn't. Perhaps he was kind of neuter like that grumpy old prime minister, the one who never married, and played church music."

"I suppose that's possible," said Lady Penelope, "Perhaps he was killed by a very disappointed lady."

"Don't know about that, Mum. But someone was very disappointed about something."

"Will the murder be solved?"

"Don't know really. A lot of them aren't. And this one's very difficult. They have no suspects, hardly any clues, and no motive."

"And you're going down there to sharpen them all up, I suppose. Is that the idea?"

"Not really. I'm going down there very quietly to help George have a careful look around, and see if I can come up with anything. I've been told that Glyndebourne can name just about every person attending any opera.

"My very private contact at Malling tells me, on the quiet, the only unidentified seats in the entire theatre were the four comps given to the Russian

Embassy, who will, as ever, reveal nothing. But mysterious murders with Russian spies close at hand … well … you'd want to have another look."

"How do you know they were spies?"

"Mum, the Russians don't actually send people to England at vast expense to study poetry and go to the theatre. They send them for things like espionage, political intrigue, and the occasional kidnapping, or assassination. They always call these people Cultural Attaches. Which is a bit like calling the Kremlin an Arts College."

They passed a companionable evening, and Charles retired at around 10pm to be packed and ready when his Scotland Yard Sergeant, Tom Reilly, who'd come up through the ranks like most Scotland Yard coppers, showed up at 6am in a staff car in company with another officer, who would appear insignificant, but who would be, in reality, a Detective Inspector with a specialty in 'motives for murder.' Roger Wells by name.

The drive took two hours even though they ducked and dived through Putney and finally picked up the orbital M25 and sped down the M23 for almost the rest of the way. George had coffee and toast ready for all three of them, and by 8.30 they were on their way to Glyndebourne, where four Sussex officers met them by the Lake.

Charles wandered about by himself for a bit, having established the precise spot where Fontridge had been hauled out of the water. Eventually he told them at least now they could pinpoint the time of death.

And he walked through the wet lawn from bridge to water, before saying, "There's the mark where you pulled him out. He's a big guy, and he's made heavy indentations, plus the heels of his shoes made grooves on the grass. There are no such matching marks anywhere else. Assume his Lordship was stabbed right there and fell into the water. He was definitely not killed and then brought here for burial at sea, as it were."

Sir George nodded, but asked how Charles could nail time of death from just that.

"Well, if he was murdered here, if could not have happened after about 5.30 when dozens of people began to arrive. It could have happened after 6.30 when everyone was in the theatre, except we know Fontridge was in there as well. It may have happened immediately after he left the theatre just before the interval—around 7.26. But not one moment after that because there were several hundred people all over the garden. And, what's more, they stayed here for 90-minutes."

DCS Barton paused to make a couple of quick notes. And then said, "Now we know he did not return to his seat. So perhaps he was still out in the garden after 9pm when it was getting dark. But I somehow doubt it. There were stewards and staff cleaning up after the picnics. And they were probably there for an hour. No one commits murder when there are obviously people around."

"And after the performance?" asked Sergeant Bob Hammond.

"Even less likely," said the DCS. "People tend to exit slower than they entered, and at Glyndebourne, in my experience, they stroll back into the gardens for a nightcap, finish the sandwiches and open flasks of coffee and brandy. It would have been very nearly midnight before the grounds were empty, and we can assume no one was murdered in the hour or so before then."

He then told his little audience that something could have happened between 1am and 3.30, but again unlikely. "And not after that, because the place was swiftly swarming with police with flashlights, because his Lordship had not come home."

He said they could all assume that Lord Fontridge had not been hanging around in the grounds for eight hours since he left his seat, waiting to be murdered. "No," said Charles, "I think it is very nearly definite that Lord Fontridge walked out of that theatre at 7.26 and was killed within six or seven minutes before the crowd flooded out onto the lawn. No one would have seen his body because it was just below the surface of the water."

The search party went slowly back to the theatre, and Charles Barton talked for a while with the management staff. And once more it was confirmed that the Russian comps were the only unknown seats. And the police could offer nothing by way of identification.

Finally Charles Barton asked if he could have the names of the four people sitting in the row immediately behind the tiny Russian bloc. They checked the register, and gave him the names on the tickets on the aisle. The two which were situated farther into the row were a little more difficult, since they were not regulars.

The two on the aisle were—season tickets in the name of Johnny Fairchild and friend. "Quite a well-known Brighton jeweller," said Sergeant Bob Hammond. "Just along South Lane, near the seafront."

"I'd like to talk to him," said the DCS.

"You want to call him first?"

"No, I'd prefer just to arrive and speak in person."

Two minutes later, Tom Reilly was at the wheel, driving the men from Scotland Yard straight out to the A27, direct to the south coast city of Brighton. The shop was quite grand, beautifully furnished with some expensive items behind glass cases.

Johnny himself was there, an obvious confirmed bachelor, as they say, highly intelligent, beautifully dressed and plainly successful. He was happy to speak to the detectives from London, and invited them into an opulent office, with a staff member, who, it should be said, was not terribly … well … manly. But they were pleased to offer assistance, and Johnny Fairchild knew exactly who had occupied the seats in front of him, not their names, but he knew they were from the Embassy."

"Russians," he said, "And the head man sat one seat in from the aisle. He handled the tickets, and seemed to know quite a bit about opera."

"Were his companions men?"

"I'd only seen him once before, and they were then. The seats were not always occupied by the same people."

"How about last Saturday?"

"He was accompanied by a young lady. I noticed her dress, expensive, dark blue, and she had the most beautiful matching earrings, small sapphire butterflies in a brushed gold setting. They were exquisite."

"Very observant," said Barton.

"Professional," said Johnny. "I doubt you and your people ever miss a dead body. I never miss a sapphire butterfly!"

Both policemen laughed. And when asked if there was anything else he might remember about the Russian group, Johnny Fairchild had something to say. "Do you know," he added, "When the lady came back after the interval, she had changed her earrings, and was wearing some ordinary little pearl studs. I thought that was very strange."

"Hmmmm," said Barton. "You're sure it was the same lady?

"Well, I suppose so. She was sitting right on the aisle, and of course she had her back to us. But I didn't notice anything. She had the same short hair, but, honestly, I only noticed the new earrings."

"Quite so," said Barton. "But I would like to ask you a favour. For the new opera next week, would you take me as your guest, right behind the Russians?"

"Oh my god, Superintendent … so bold … think how people would talk!"

Again everyone laughed. DCS Barton was beginning to like the proprietor of the upmarket jewellers, and they swiftly came to an arrangement. Scotland yard would pay for the two Fairchild season tickets, in return for identification of the Russian head man, and a seat right behind him for the next performance. Johnny did not care one way or another about the other four cops who would be on guard in the lobby and outside the theatre door.

It was a very successful visit. And DCS Barton could not stop thinking about the mystery of the earrings, and the unspoken question: had the Russian switched women, not jewellery? If that were so, and a second person had not returned after the interval, they had a real suspect. But no one could deal with that until they got a handle on the Russian's name, and that of his companion. And that was not going to happen for another few days, until the opening night of *La Traviata,* another Verdi extravaganza.

The policemen had several laughs on the way back to London. Tom Reilly mentioned that he wasn't too sure about the DCS's 'date' with Johnny Fairchild. But Charles reminded him that the alternative was even more sensitive—"How about three days and evenings together in a car in Kensington Palace Gardens trying to spot the Russian?"

"Christ, sir!" said the driver. "Now that would have caused a bit of chatter!"

Detective Inspector Roger Wells added, "Definitely better to attend *Traviata* with Johnny. Just so long as there's no bloody hand-holding!"

The staff car containing the Scotland Yard wits finally made it back to the high-rise Yard headquarters on the Victoria Embankment, overlooking the river. It was 8pm by the time Barton and Wells checked into Charles's office for a general de-brief on the day.

"You don't really think this Russian guy took out Fontridge, do you, sir?" asked the DI.

"Not really. We've nothing to suggest that," said Charles. "Except most of the patrons were relatively well-known to the Glyndebourne management, and Vladimir, or whatever his name is, represents one of the few strangers in the theatre."

"I realise that, sir. But those Soviet undercover diplomats are usually looking for people involved in serious matters, espionage and stuff. Old Fontridge, outside the court, has nothing on his record to suggest anything like that. I spent six hours reading up on him yesterday. He's a lawyer who's never done anything much more sensational than dropping his fucking polo stick."

"Aha, Roger, that may be," replied Charles, smiling. "The part that interests me is those bloody earrings. I can't get my mind off them."

"Little sapphire butterflies. Jesus Christ!" said Roger Wells.

*****

Sophia Morosova elected to remain by herself for the two or three days before Uncle Rudolf showed in Paris. She browsed a couple bookshops along *Rue Boneparte*… she mostly ate at home, aside from her morning walk to *Deux Magots*. And she often walked along *Les Bouquinistes* on the left-bank of the Seine, to see the hundreds of paintings which were always on display, from artists hoping to hit it big in this riverside treasure-trove of second-hand art books and prints.

She avoided any form of ostentation, no glitzy art galleries, no high-end restaurants; nowhere she could see anyone who might recognise her. It was a relief to receive a message from the Embassy that the Russian Bear had landed. Which meant dinner in private this Friday night, with Rudy, in the diplomats' dining room, which was usually half-empty, owing to the known chasm of skill between Russian cooks and Parisian chefs.

Still, the wine cellar at the Embassy was always top of the line. It had been since Czar Alexander had refilled the cellar of the Massandra Palace with literally thousands of French bottles in the 19th century. Somehow the tradition had persisted through Russia's consulates around the world. Say one thing for the Bolsheviks; they may have despised the very marble floors upon which the Czars had walked, but they were swift to pick up a few hints on Romanov high-living.

The grand white stone Russian Embassy in Paris is one of those buildings which stands, in a sense, in the heart of the city, but is situated nowhere in particular, idling around in the 16th *arrondissement*. Its address is on the *Boulevard Lannes*, only a mile from both the Arc de Triomphe and the Eiffel Tower. And yet, it is just up the road from the prime French steeplechasing racecourse of Auteuil, and just across the Bois de Bologne from the world-famous French classic venue of Paris Longchamp.

58

Is it city or rural? Or just a Russian stronghold in a no man's land of its own making? Judging by the high, black iron railings around its exterior, stronghold is the right word. Also it's long on guards, and armed officers. Russia does not really do 'cosy' even among friends, and when Sophia arrived in an Embassy car, she still had to go through a fairly rigorous security check, including the standard one for visitors (or, in her case, at least, one of them).

Happily, Rudolf saw her arrival and sent someone to rescue her. And he could scarcely have been more delighted to welcome his niece into the stronghold. He told a security man to take her light travelling bag up to her room, and then took her into a private lounge and ordered a couple of stiff but elegant Russian vodkas, which came in a decanter with two crystal glasses.

"Aha, perfect," said Rudolf. "My favourite, and also the favourite of the late 'Mad Monk' Grigori Rasputin."

"How could you possibly know that?" laughed Sophia.

Rudolf looked positively pained. "This is the vodka first distilled through silver charcoal for Nicholai Alexandrovitch Romanov," he said. "That's Czar Nicholas II to you."

Sophia took a gallant swig. "Tastes a lot like Stolychnaya to me," she said, chuckling.

"Probably is." replied Rudolf. "But it's Embassy policy to make our guests feel they are drinking with Russian royalty."

"The ones your Bolshevik employers murdered!" she said. "That's irony for you. And anyway, I'm not a guest. I'm a local."

"You are also a *Czarina*. At least you are to me. And so was your little sister. Don't forget the big picture. You and I are dealing with high crime on a very personal level. I also have one piece of news for you … Glyndebourne called the London Embassy, and asked for the names of the staff who used the complimentary tickets for *Rigoletto*."

"You didn't tell them?"

"No, but the police then called, and assured us it was purely routine, since they were investigating the death of Lord Fontridge, and those four tickets were the only anonymous ones in the entire theatre."

"You still didn't tell them?"

"Of course not. Never even returned the call."

"And will you?"

"Certainly not. They have no right to question diplomats without a thundering good reason. But the Brits are very good. I expect them to find certainly me. At which point I shall be the soul of helpfulness. I will speak to them freely, and I shall give them your home address if they ask."

"You'll do what!"

"I shall tell them where my niece lives, and how I took you to the opera. I shall not, of course, tell them that you left at the interval and I replaced you with Ludmilla from the typing pool, in an identical dark blue dress and a wig to match your beautiful hair. And of course neither will you. You had a lovely time at Glyndebourne, would love to go again, and drove back to London with me. There is no closed circuit television in any of the car parks. I checked."

"But why will you tell them about me?"

"Because there's nothing so off-putting to any detective than scrupulous honesty, and helpfulness, an open-door policy. And that's mine. Remember they have nothing."

"Those Brits unnerve me. They always act in such a superior way."

"Let them. They still have nothing. No suspects. And especially—no motive. And don't worry about their airs and graces. There was a mighty Russian Empire while the Brits were still eating tree roots. And even their damned army, which they are so proud of, was not a patch on the Cossacks. And what about the Charge of their half-witted Light Brigade in Crimea? Disaster. Into the Valley of Death Rode the 600 Morons."

And, warming to his task, he added, "And what about that vulgar little nutcase from Austria, the former housepainter, who damned near flattened London with his bombs—who stopped him, eh? We did, that's who. We threw his invading army out of Moscow. We drove them out of Leningrad after one of the cruellest sieges in military history. And we finally destroyed the Hun's retreating army, in the frozen wastelands of southern Russia and Eastern Europe—before we blasted our way into Berlin, caused the housepainter to blow his brains out, and forced the remnants of the Nazi army to surrender."

Sophia was silent. And then Rudolf said, "We are Russians. And we have more to be proud of than most other nations. We don't need to bother about the glories of the British Empire—we lost more than half of all the dead in WWII. But we never quit. Unlike the French. We kept going. With our traditional Cossack bravery in war. Until our enemies either died, or wished they'd died.

"The Brits and the Americans did not save Europe. We did. In blood and courage. And let no one forget it. And in case anyone does, remember too, we also smashed the armies of Napoleon after he'd tried to take Moscow. Half a million Frenchmen died on the retreat."

It always surprised Sophia how passionate Rudolf could become on the subject of being Russian. "But it's not just war and history that cause the British to act so superior to us," she said. "It's everything: cultural, musical, writing, even, I suppose, the opera or the ballet."

"That's just because they think we're all like our former peasant leader Nikita Khrushchev," he said. "Fat little farm labourers from the potato fields. But Russian culture stands up against anyone. The Brits, for instance, think they own some of the world's great music—written by whom?—Edward Elgar who composed some catchy little military tunes? George Handel who was German, and wrote something called the Messiah? Which was ironic for a nation of Teutonic Barbarians who, for no reason, tried to destroy my country, starved and killed millions. After those two, Handel and Elgar, there was nothing much in Britain until The Beatles!"

Sophia burst into laughter, and Rudy added, "Anyone care to stack that up against Pyoter Tchaikovsky, Igor Stravinsky, Nickolai Rimsky Korsakov, Dmitri Shostakovich? Or even the immortal cellist Mstislav Rostropovich? As for writers, that's not a contest—they've got Shakespeare who died about 7,000 years ago; and I suppose Dickens who was a part-time child welfare officer, with silly little characters like Mr Pickwick.

"And in Russia, we have the greatest literature ever written, by Leo Tolstoy, Dostoyevsky, Alexander Pushkin, Vladimir Nabokov, Boris Pasternak, and our beloved Aleksandr Solzhenitsyn, whose three-volume Nobel Prize winner, *The Gulag Archipelago* quite literally changed history. And has any work been more riveting for the modern world than *A Hero For Our Times* by Mikhail Lermontov? Sophia, we bow to no one."

His niece just leaned back and applauded the list of men who between them had written *Swan Lake, The Nutcracker, The Snow Maiden*, dozens of operas and ballets, the *"Leningrad Seventh Symphony,"* which inspired superhuman courage among the people of St Petersburg—to stand up and repel the invading Nazi army, men, women and children, if necessary, until there was no one left alive.

Right there on Rudolf's list were the authors of *War and Peace, The Brothers Karamazov, Lolita, Anna Karenina, Doctor Zhivago, Crime and Punishment, A Day in the Life of Ivan Denisovich*: very probably the greatest fiction ever written.

"I understand, Uncle," she said, "But I am more troubled by the moral issue of our plan—the decisions to kill. My God! No one would ever believe it."

"Precisely," replied Rudolf Masow, and, perhaps justifying his own particular trade, he added, "Down all the years we Russians have always dispensed with those who were too evil, too dissipated, too dangerous, too different, or too self-obsessed: people who work to a different set of rules, who think they can do as they wish, regardless of the shocking damage they may do to others.

"To us, they must be removed from society, before they inflict more harm on the innocent. Such men, the ones on your tiny list, check almost every one of those boxes. You trust me, Sophia. The moral issue favours us, not them. And they must not be allowed to live among normal people.

"Sophia, I know you are a religious person, as was my sister. What would God have thought of the men who ravaged the two young girls in Maida Vale? I'll tell you, He'd have hit them with a fucking thunderbolt before they'd put their pants back on.

"Look how He reacted to Sodom and Gomorrah. He would have wrought enormous revenge. We Russians feel the same as God about these kinds of people. The moral issue is with us. Not them."

Despite herself, and despite Rudolf's colourful way of making his point, Sophia felt rather better after that. She understood he was probably confirming the righteousness of his own profession. Russia did after all always try to eliminate those who intended them harm. In the last hundred years that included the entire upper echelon of the Romanovs, they plainly murdered the "Mad Monk" Rasputin (a dangerous influence), all the way through to the near-miss Novichok nerve-agent, involving the Russian double-agent Sergei Skripal in Salisbury, 2018.

She was not sure exactly what Rudolf did, but he operated in the highest possible regard for the Kremlin, and she did think he may have been a State assassin. But she'd never asked him, and now he'd laid it out before her. His strategy was now her strategy. And he would always be in her corner, which was a private place of high morals. And she drew strength from the absolute certainty of Rudy's position … *some people are just too evil to be allowed to live.* In his view, the men who ravaged her and Sasha, must die. And he would personally mastermind the operation.

They dined together at the Embassy, as planned, and Rudolf took the magazine article about Sir Josh Hartley to bed with him. That kept him awake for an hour, but he liked what he read, and when he finally drifted off to sleep, turbo-charged Grand Prix engines shrieked through his dreams.

Chapter Six
The Verdun Experiment

Since their historic wartime deaths total ran into millions ...
the Russians were no strangers to carnage on the battlefield.
To the men from the Kremlin, one more death, if justifiable,
was usually a small price to pay for justice. Or, Revenge.

Nonetheless, Rudy was awake very early on this Friday morning, having slept soundly in anticipation of the second section of his master strategy. Sophia, who had slept hardly at all, was bleary-eyed, not ready, and only just packed when Uncle Rudy came zipping up to the front door of the Embassy with her ride to the Gare de Lyon, for the high-speed train to Marseille, the TGV6103. At 7.37.

It was a 40-minute journey, straight down the Champs Elysee, with two crossings over the bridges of the winding River Seine. By the time they arrived at the station, they had hardly spoken, mostly because Sophia kept falling asleep. He accompanied her to the door of the carriage, with instructions not to call him unless the situation was dire. His driver would be at Charles de Gaulle on Monday morning.

He kissed her goodbye five minutes before the big silver-and-blue TGV hauled out under the electric power wires which would literally hurl it 250-miles to Lyon in two-and-a-half-hours. And as Sophia faced a full three days without Rudy she was seized quite suddenly by the chill black cloak of self-doubt. And she blurted out, "But what if I get caught? What if I'm arrested, and locked up for the rest of my life, or executed? What if one of my future projects ends in disaster, thousands of miles from home ...?"

Rudolf Masow smiled at her kindly, and said, "If I am your guardian angel, you will not be caught. My trade is unorthodox but honourable. Soviet, and then Russian State Security. We *never* get caught. Never have been. There's not even an official state document naming the murderers of the Romanovs ... and they *never* discovered the actual killer of the Mad Monk Rasputin ... even though he was poisoned, shot three times, and hurled into the freezing River Neva."

"But Rudy ... that was long ago. What about *now?*"

"Always the same, my darling. More recently, 1978, the Bulgarian dissident, Georgi Markov, stabbed with a poisoned umbrella on Waterloo Bridge. The Afghan President, Amin Hafizullah, the Kyrgyzstan President Soltan Ibraimov, all murdered. Alexander Litvinenko, a defaulted Russian spy, killed by radio-active poison in a London café. And none of the murderers were ever identified.

"That's not to mention about a dozen Presidents and emirs of Chechnya and the Caucasus, all taken out successfully. No charges. And no one ever found out who poisoned the pro-Western Ukrainian Leader Victor Yushchenko, or the dangerous Russian businessman, Alexander Penepillchny who dropped dead 100-feet from his own front gate in London, poisoned for his own treachery.

"From Dutov to Trotsky, from the Afghan President Imre Nagy in 1958, right down to the traitor Sergei Skripal and his daughter, in Salisbury, 2018. Not one of the perpetrators was ever caught and charged with anything. For the final time, Sophia … we *never get caught.*"

She kissed him goodbye, and whispered, "Let's pray my luck holds."

But Rudy wagged his forefinger at her. "Never use that word," he admonished. "This has nothing to do with luck. It's professionalism, the elimination of mistakes. Never forget that. And never forget the critical path of the assassin—meticulous planning, zero traces left behind, and a totally unexpected escape route."

She blew him another kiss, and stepped slowly into the train, making her leisurely way to her reserved seat. And that was just about the last half-speed moment of the journey, because this French rocketship rarely dropped its speed to less than 100mph. The blue-and-silver monster shot across the bridge over the River Marne, and then sped right along the Forest which for eight centuries shielded French Kings residing in the great Chateau de Fontainebleau.

Sophia slumbered, finally awakening as they raced across Burgundy, past the escarpments of the Cote d'Or, past the birthplace of some her very favourite white wines, the world renowned vineyards set on the magical east-facing Jurassic limestone—*Gevrey-Chambertin, Meursault,* and *Montrachet.*

She changed trains at the city of Lyon, after the first 340-miles of her journey, abandoning the mighty TGV express with some reluctance. But the next leg of the journey was just as luxurious, the 226-mile high-speed run south to Marseille, mostly across Provence, all along the left-bank of the Rhone River, until it reached Arles. This is now a thriving modern city, which, however, will be ever remembered for its shining summer light which was an inspiration for Vincent

Van Gogh, the legendary French artist who lived there for a year and painted 300 pictures, including all of the Irises and Sunflowers.

There are two major junctions here, where the Rhone splits in two and flows through the town. And the main railroad between Italy and Spain also divides. Sophia Morosova peered out of the window expecting the place to be covered in sunflowers and irises, but was deeply disappointed to see busy streets and apartment blocks.

"If you ask me," she mumbled, "Vincent wouldn't have given five francs for this place. He'd have been challenged to *find* a sunflower, never mind paint it!" Amused, as she often was, by her own acerbic wit, Sophia smiled the rest of the way to the ancient Mediterranean seaport, where she again changed trains.

They pulled into *Gare Marseille-Saint-Charles* with its monumental stone staircase leading up to its 14 hilltop tracks. Saint-Charles is the final terminal on the Paris southern network. It is one of the biggest railway stations in France.

Sophia had more than an hour to look around, before she boarded the TER express which runs along the 140-mile length of the Cot d'Azur, all the way into Italy. The weather down here was very warm and sunny, and it reminded her of the task which lay ahead. As such she once more opened the magazine with the long article about a man she loathed almost more than anyone on earth. Almost. Not quite.

The truth was that magazine had shone light into the joyful life of Sir Josh Hartley, which was of course a pretty ritzy name for a former English lout. But it definitely sounded a lot better than Bert Wilson, the name awarded to him by his mother and father, who worked as a ditch-digger in Essex.

The magazine was a mere passenger in the long list of publications simply longing for a glimpse at the high-life enjoyed by England's great human benefactor who played records on the BBC for a living, earning him more money in a month than his father made in his lifetime. And the Queen had knighted him for it.

But the girl who wrote the story had obviously been very expert and Sir Josh had let his hair down. At least that was Sophia's opinion, although she added bitterly, "She was probably about 15-years-old. She's a good writer for that age!"

The article pointed out that Sir Josh had so many friends in very high places, his life was conducted almost exclusively out of public reach. He had a private plane—don't they all?—and smoothed around in a silver Rolls-Royce with darkened windows. His charitable works saw him invited to nearly every major occasion on the London social circuit.

He even attended the Royal Meeting at Ascot, although his wispy, shoulder-length, dyed blond hair looked ridiculous flopping out from under his silk top hat. He knew nothing about racehorses, but nonetheless, here was Sir Josh, wandering about the paddock chatting to owners and aristocracy. Rumour had it, he'd actually had tea with the Royal family.

"Jesus!" said Sophia, wryly.

But it was one of those owners who pointed the arrow in the critical direction. His name was Sir Brian Willcox who had a half-dozen thoroughbreds in training with a couple of unfashionable yards in Newmarket. Sir Brian had, as it were, rather blotted his copybook.

A City banker, he had twice been involved in extremely serious 'insider trading' scandals, one of which very nearly brought down a prominent merchant bank. Sir Brian, his own fortune intact, locked safely away in Switzerland, Liechtenstein, and the Cayman Islands, hurriedly vanished from the City for a couple of years.

Then he suddenly showed up in a very sleek apartment in a high-rise building, overlooking the harbour in Monte Carlo, which was just one more confirmation of Somerset Maugham's classic description : *A sunny place, for shady people.* Among his new friends was Sir Josh Hartley who'd often invited him to stay at his country house in Oxfordshire, and in return he'd invited Sir Josh for a few days at the apartment in Monte Carlo, "any time you like, old chap. Whether I'm there or not."

And for the last three years, Sir Josh had come down for the Grand Prix weekend, which Sir Brian hated, but Sir Josh loved. The packed little town was swarming with strangers, prices for everything were through the roof, restaurants were full, even the casino was operating 'by Invitation only." On this weekend, you would not catch Sir Brian within a hundred miles of the place. On the other hand, Sir Josh just loved being applauded every time he entered a restaurant.

Young Samantha Brodhurst recorded all this faithfully for the magazine. Rudolf Masow and Sophia Morosova had taken careful note. And now, the Russian-born traveller read it over again as the train sped along the Cote d'Azur, sometimes down close to the water, sometimes higher in the mountains, a summer trip through the jewel of the Mediterranean.

It took over three hours, sliding along the ocean's turquoise rim, through Cannes, through Nice, and eventually through the most densely populated sovereign state on planet earth, Monaco. Sophia never looked up as they made that brief stop, and then pressed on towards the Italian border, finally pulling into the station at Menton, the last stop in France before the frontier of Italy. The next stop, the oceanfront city of Ventimiglia, was the end of the line.

Sophia disembarked at Menton, slinging her overnight bag over her shoulder, and setting off on her well-researched 15-minute walk, which led to the charming little two-star hostelry, in which neither the jet-setting Sir Brian nor Sir Josh would have been caught dead.

It was Claridge's Hotel on the unobtrusive Avenue de Verdun, a street named slightly innocuously in memory of the greatest and longest military battle in world history: the Battle of Verdun, fought between French and German troops on February 21st to December 19th, 1916, during which time there were more than 700,000 casualties (dead, wounded and missing).

It was a grotesque encounter representing all the horrors and pointless massacres of yet another fight over a tiny piece of land out near the German border. The best book about it was entitled *Death of a Generation*. And here stood Sophia Morosova, a citizen of a country whose historic wartime death totals ran into millions. No strangers, the Russians, to outright carnage on the battlefield. And always, to the men from the Kremlin and the Lubyanka, one more death, if justifiable, was usually a very small price to pay for justice. Or, sometimes, revenge.

Sophia checked in, passing the time of day with the receptionist. At 3.45 in the afternoon, she was still carefully concealed in her long brunette wig, sunglasses and stylish, wide-brimmed straw sunhat, but she'd been travelling since just after 7am, and she'd been tired before she started. At this particular moment she felt absolutely exhausted, and crashed out on her bed for a two-hour recovery.

Her phone had been left behind for obvious security reasons, and was currently hidden in Uncle Rudolph's care. So she was awakened by her miniature alarm clock, which was only about three inches high, with a wake-up shout like Big Ben. Sophia sat up with a rush, quickly conscious, and ready for the next step of her quest.

She scribbled in her omnipotent notebook. And her plan was complete—right here in the Avenue de Verdun. The plan was, so far as she could tell, immaculate. Experimental certainly, but immaculate.

She dressed and headed straight back to the drab little railway station at Menton, and 10 minutes later boarded the local train, six-miles back to the Monaco terminus which, this weekend, was probably the most crowded place in Europe.

She jostled her way out and headed southeast for the harbour, straight down Boulevard de Swiss, and cut through the narrow Passage de la Porte Rouge, into the winding Avenue de la Costa. Sophia negotiated a sharp hairpin bend and swerved left. She was navigating this turmoil of a city, in a country about the size of Hyde Park, like a pure-bred Monegasque. And she'd never been here in her life. Ah, the miracle of electronic cartography.

Three more minutes and she was on the Avenue d'Ostende, and she walked to the harbour side of the street, strolling quietly, while staring up at Number Nine, a tall duel-purpose block of bankers' offices and apartments on the opposite side of the street. She stared particularly at the eighth floor, so faithfully recorded by the probably 15-year-old Samantha in the magazine.

As Sophia had feared, this was a high prestige tower, known locally as *Le Beau Rivage*, the beautiful shore, which was a pretty important compliment to a miniature State with more than 30 percent of its population made up of registered millionaires. She could see there were magnificent views over Monte Carlo Harbour, and also down to the Formula One racecourse, in particular the Turn-Two Beau Rivage, the 130mph uphill sprint from the start, a place of screaming turbos and hard-driving.

Right here, beneath her Jimmy Choo shoes, was a racetrack of legends, where the great ones had fought out monstrous battles for supremacy—Juan Fangio, Graham Hill, and Jackie Stewart; Alberto Ascari, Jack Brabham, and Bruce McLaren; Ayrton Senna, and Michael Schumaker. The supreme racer Ayrton Senna once crashed near here at the notorious Portier's Corner, right before the tunnel, after leading for 67 laps.

The *Beau Rivage* building was a Monaco Grand Prix landmark, and it would possibly be difficult to breach, with closed circuit cameras, doorman, and security on the upper residential floors. She needed prior knowledge about the impediments, if they existed. And she crossed the avenue and pushed open the front door to the building. There was a doorman, and she walked straight up to him and said, *"Bonsoir, monsieur."* She then explained she was going up to see Sir Brian Willcox on the eighth floor tomorrow, she'd mislaid the precise number—*s'il vous plait?*

The doorman told her he would be on duty tomorrow, but he might be watching the race outside … if so, she should proceed in the elevator to the eighth, and go straight ahead. The lovely Sophia just did not look anything like a burglar or a terrorist. In fact she looked like precisely the type of lady Sir Brian would befriend. On her way out she scanned the lobby for cameras, but did not see one. She did however see a sign for the fire exit.

She made her way swiftly up the hill to the enormous train station and picked up the local, back to little Menton. Half-an-hour later, at 9.30pm, she was sitting comfortably at a café table just down the road, awaiting her *pot au feu,* the classic French beef stew, a dish from the heart of France, and guaranteed to satisfy the ravenous hunger of a Russian exile who'd had nothing to eat all day.

The stew was served with a warm, crusty French loaf and a half-bottle of deep claret from the left bank of the Gironde, up near Chateau Mouton Rothschild; not quite that good, but a real treat all the same. Sophia loved France.

And that night she unaccountably slept either the deep sleep of the innocent, or the very tired. She was uncertain which, but Sophia almost jumped out of her skin when her dwarf Big Ben alarm went off at 8am. Scorning the very concept of *le petit dejeuner*, she set herself up for a day without even the prospect of food on account of Uncle Rudolf 101—*you will linger nowhere in Monaco, all day, until you are out of France.*

As such she returned to the café of the beef stew, and ordered an *omelette au jambon et au fromage* accompanied by a warm baguette, apricot jam, and *café au lait*. At 10am, she once more slung her travelling bag over her shoulder, and walked to the Menton train station. The fast local, now crowded, and late, once more sped her 12-minutes along the line to Monaco, which was even more thronged with visitors for today's Grand Prix.

Since the race did not begin, like all European Grand Prix, until 2pm, she would not actually report for duty until around 3.30pm—which she knew was cutting it fine, but right now she was a professional, which meant, in the words of Uncle Rudy, "the total elimination of mistakes. It has nothing to do with money."

He may or may not have been completely correct, but so far as she knew, he was still breathing, which undoubtedly made him worth listening to, given his lifetime vocation on behalf of the Soviet, and later, Russian State.

It took her almost 20 minutes to extricate herself from the Monaco station, and twice as long as yesterday to find her way down to the harbour-side area, dealing as she went with barricades, one-way systems and many, many policemen, every one of them trying, hugely unsuccessfully, to make life easier for the race spectators.

Sophia was pleased she came early, but despite Monaco's absolute insistence on being the safest place in Europe, with the lowest level of crime, lowest level of public inconvenience, it was still a genuine hassle on this day of the year. Never mind, she thought, all the hassle in the world was a lot better than getting run down by one of those turbo-charged racing cars driven by some maniac at 400mph through the main streets.

She finally arrived on Avenue d'Ostende, but made no attempt to make it across the street, since on this day that might mean instant arrest. And anyway her business was on the town side not the seaside. All the sidewalks were crowded, but Sophia was checking out an escape route. She could not possibly afford to walk towards one of the hills, leading up to the station area, only to find it blocked.

Between now and 3pm, an hour into the race, she would traverse the route from the *Beau Rivage* to the railway three times, thus logging every way out, every side-street, which may mean escape or failure … no mistakes. By the time this marathon of reconnaissance was completed, the race was underway. And Sophia completed her final task before entry into the building.

She slipped into a local *Magasin de Vin et Spiritueux*, which she'd already passed several times, and scanned the shelves selling champagne. She found one she recognised, a non-vintage bottle of *Veuve Clicquot*, which she purchased at an exorbitant price, and had it gift-wrapped. She also bought herself a small plastic bottle of iced spring water which she glugged as elegantly as possible, while sitting on a bench behind the *Beau Rivage*, right in front of the round fountain in the Square Beau Marchais.

The clock ticked on, and out on the track a desperate duel was unfolding between the British world champion Lewis Hamilton, and the 31-year-old German pretender, Sebastian Vettel—Hamilton in the 950hp silver Mercedes AMG, Vettel in the world-famous scarlet livery of Ferrari, the Italian master engineers whose howling V-6 turbo-charged engine was right now pushing to its limits of 15,000rpm's.

Hamilton held the lead as he had done for an hour, Vettel locked on his near quarter, pushing, harassing, striving to hit the gas at the first sign of weakness from his younger rival. They charged for the tunnel with the harbour on their left, and 200,000 people were on their feet roaring with excitement, as Hamilton held fast, and rocketed into the brightly lit underground stretch, in the lead by less than a dozen feet. At this moment, Sophia Morosova entered the *Beau Rivage* tower, having already spotted the doorman outside with friends watching this epic struggle, just a few feet away on the track.

The lobby was deserted. And Sophia walked directly to the elevator. The doors swung back immediately and she stepped inside, and hit the button for the eighth floor. The small hallway in which she found herself had once been occupied by a security guard. She could see his empty desk and chair. At this moment, however, he was in the kitchen, leaning out the window, trying to spot Hamilton and Vettel through a pair of opera glasses.

She walked directly along the corridor to 8G and tapped on the door, holding in her left-hand the gift-wrapped bottle of *Veuve*. Moments later, the unmistakable figure of Sir Josh Hartley answered the door, and raised his eyebrows at the sight of this very beautiful young woman, asking for Brian Willcox.

"Sorry luv," he said in an impenetrable British accent far closer to one of the family ditch-diggers than a Knight of the Realm. "He won't be back 'til Tuesday—can I give 'im a message."

"Well, he's an old friend, he and my father worked together. And he told me at my birthday party I could watch the finish of the race from his apartment. I should have called but I didn't have time."

Hartley chuckled, and said, "'Course you can, luv. I've already opened a nice bottle of champers, get a glass and come out to the balcony. Hamilton's led all the way …"

Sophia flashed him her most alluring smile, left her bottle on a small side table inside the front door, and glided over to the bar, pouring a drink from an icy bottle wrapped in a large white napkin. She was thinking nothing beyond her hatred of the man. She remembered the way he had raped her little sister, and used the most disgusting slang she had ever heard. He kept saying it, over and over, as if there was no other word in the English language except the one that started with an "f" and was an expulsion offence at St Margaret's.

At the age of 18 she'd nearly been given her own marching orders after once uttering it loudly, when she was cracked on the knee by the opposing goalkeeper, in a rain-swept hockey match against their hated Berkshire rivals from Downe House.

She put down her drink and noted that Hartley was even more of a beanpole than when she had last seen him. He was older now, weaker, more fragile. "Thank God," she murmured. At last, she was alone with him, with no Sasha to worry about. This time she held every ace. She was, finally, the predator.

And she began a power-run which would have been celebrated for many years on the hockey right-wing at St Margaret's. Sophia kicked off her shoes and came out of the blocks like an Olympic sprinter. It was all of 50-feet to the balcony, and she was travelling flat-out when she raised both hands in front of her, and slammed them into the back of Sir Josh Hartley, one flat palm for each shoulder blade.

He dropped his drink over the balcony, and then catapulted forward, bent from the waist, over the rails, perhaps more startled than he had ever been in his life. As for Sophia, she stuck by Uncle Rudy 102—and her hands flashed down to his ankles, grabbed them both, around the front, and heaved, shouting out with the effort, like one of those ridiculous female tennis players. Almost in slow motion, the flat soles of the Hartley Guccis rose to the area in front of her eyes, and she shoved them forward, unnecessarily.

Because this appalling man was past the point of no return, toppling forward head first, towards the track, where Hamilton and Vettel had just screamed past at 150mph. Sir Josh Hartley executed a perfect double-summersault dive … bent at the waist … with the merest suggestion of pike.

The body had powered forward with all the pent-up energy supplied by a young fit woman with seven years of undiluted hatred in her soul. She'd hit him in the back with such enraged force he actually cleared the track fence, smashed into the asphalt, obliterated his skull, severed his spine, and rolled towards the centre line, right into the path of an oncoming yellow and black Renault RE18.

It was just accelerating up to 160mph, racing into third place in the hands of the young Gilles Romanet, heir apparent to Alain Prost, national hero of the 1990's, whose daredevil driving has never really been replaced in France.

The Renault slammed into the body of Sir Josh at 150mph as it tore along this incline with not a semblance of breaking. Romanet never had time to react and he gripped the wheel, as his carbon-fibre racer disintegrated, firing hunks of plastic all over the track and into the spectators.

The impact was horrific. But young Gilles was protected by the hard Renault chassis, which bent but did not shatter. The wheels too, held fast which certainly saved his life. But a huge groan split the sunlit air, as the nearby section of the crowd erupted with disappointment. Not for the suicide of the disc jockey. No one knew who had flown over the balcony.

They groaned for the lost chance of Gilles Romanet and the mighty French engine of Renault. But, in a few more moments, the entire 200,000 were disappointed, as track-marshals flagged down the drivers, switched on the danger lights, and abandoned the race.

Romanet had just stopped spinning. The incline had helped to slow him, but not enough. And the battered hulk of his car crashed hard into a reinforced barrier, at last coming to a halt. Gilles, a mere five seconds after he'd hit the disc jockey's body, stepped out, miraculously unharmed, ultimately saved by the highly-treated carbon-fibre of the rigid cockpit.

The catastrophe had taken precisely 10 seconds. Doormen, *concierges*, security men, had seen nothing, not a single unauthorised entry or exit from the exclusive *Beau Regarde* apartments. The high-speed battle between Mercedes, Ferrari and Renault had captivated every Monegasque, to the exclusion of all else. This was the accident from nowhere. Within hours the Monaco police would be hunting a phantom.

Chapter Seven
No Evidence, No Clues

"Get a hold of the BBC Director General for a quote ...
I don't care what he says, but if he won't talk, try to
persuade first ... then threaten a piece that asks:
Did the BBC drive Hartley to suicide?"

There was a frenzy of sheer chaos on the track below the *Beau Rivage*. Police swarmed in, to surround the devastated body of Sir Josh Hartley. It was impossible to identify him, and no one was concerned whether he'd actually jumped or been thrown over the railings. That would come later, just as soon as someone worked out that England's most celebrated disc-jockey had just been hit by a 150mph Formula One Renault in the middle of the Monaco Grand Prix.

High above the racecourse, Sophia Morosova did not waste one split second looking down at the uproar she had caused. The prospect of tomorrow's headlines, and the raptured intensity of the television news tonight, never crossed her mind. The death of this disgusting sexual predator was history. She had only one thought. She had to get out of here fast, everything was planned to facilitate her freedom, and to avoid at all cost the prospect of a lifetime in *Le Bastille*—"Or," she wondered, "Wherever the hell the French incarcerate their female assassins."

She moved nearly as fast away from the balcony as she had when she'd hit the weirdo rapist. She grabbed her shoes, expertly wiped the glass she'd touched, and then grabbed the gift-wrapped champagne from the table. She used the wet napkin to move the door-handle, dropped it and walked resolutely along to the elevator. Thankfully the security men throughout the entire building were riveted to the track below, peering out of the windows.

The hallway was deserted, and the elevator took her swiftly down to the street lobby. There was still no one there, but she had no intention of exiting through the front door, mere yards from where Hartley had landed. And she headed straight for the sign to the Fire Exit. As planned, it led through a dingy passage at the end of which was an illuminated sign which said *Sortie d'Urgence*. Below it was a heavyweight one-way industrial door, with a wide opening bar. Sophia hit that with both hands, a move to which she was becoming accustomed.

She found herself back by the round fountain, in the *Square de Marchais*, wishing to hell she had another bottle of the ice-cold spring water. But there was no time to find a drink, no time to linger. Sophia headed for the hills, the steep ones up to the railway station, and she already wished the full bottle of champagne in her shoulder bag weighed a bit less. It was getting heavier by the minute.

But she pressed on, walking along the narrow, but correct streets, straight through the route her tireless reconnaissance had confirmed. And again she silently offered thanks for Uncle Rudy 103 … *leave nothing, repeat nothing behind.* She also recalled with gratitude Uncle Rudy 104 (Russian Military) … *Time spent in reconnaissance is seldom wasted.*

Before her was a 10-minute wait. Her pre-bought first-class ticket was in her purse. And she vanished into Monaco's immaculate station lady's room, where she dispensed with her blond wig, removed her sunglasses and sunhat, and fished her Spanish passport and driver's license out of her shoulder bag. She resolved to dump her disguises out of the train window every couple of miles after they crossed the Italian border, 10 minutes from here. Hopefully into a river.

When she boarded the *Ventimiglia* express, right on time, she looked very different, having also changed out of her sassy skirt into trousers, with a dark red shirt instead of her white one. She glanced in the carriage mirror and decided she was unrecognisable. She especially liked the dark red shirt—same colour as Uncle Rudy's decorative ribbon—Hero of Russia. "That ought to be me," she murmured.

And she sensed a feeling of great relief as the local train pulled out of the station, carrying her for the last time, transporting her away from the French Riviera, where she had already caused pandemonium. Back at the scene of the crime, someone had already identified the dead man. Sports writers, who had come for the Grand Prix, were now in pursuit of a bigger story than any of them had ever dreamed. And some of them were already being yelled at by news editors in the principal capitals of Europe, especially from London, home of the lately departed Sir Josh.

Residents of the *Beau Rivage* were clamoring to help. An eager lady on the eighth floor claimed to have seen Sir Josh as he came off the balcony 'like a bullet.' "I'd swear to God, that man leaped to his own death," she said.

"Merci, madame," said the police, but they were plainly not as sure as she was. A few minutes later they were in the apartment, searching through the Hartley luggage, wondering, to a man, the age-old cliché of crime novels ... *Did he jump ... or was he pushed?* Same kind of thing as Lord Fontridge, really. Only a lot higher, 100-feet to be precise.

They were, of course, groping around in the dark. The owner was not there, had not been there for two weeks. The house guest had left the area, albeit in a somewhat unorthodox manner. And the place was otherwise deserted. The security men were useless, AWOL. And even the veteran doorman, who admitted being absent from his post, watching the race, mentioned only that he had seen the disc-jockey come in to land, right before his eyes.

The truth was, there was not one shred of evidence to suggest Josh had been heaved off Sir Brian's balcony. Unless something earth-shaking came along in the next few days, the Monaco coroner was going to come up with a verdict of "Death by misadventure."

And that's how it would stay. Particularly, as an unrecognisable Sophia Morosova was currently clattering along the ocean-hugging railroad towards the border with Italy, beyond which neither the *Liguria* nor the *Piedmonte Carabinieri* would want anything to do with the whole procedure.

She was going to the end of the line at *Ventimiglia*, for a quick train switch, and then onto the mountain train for a 12-mile ride up through the craggy eastern peaks of the Alps Maritime, once a favourite haunt of Leonardo da Vinci, and an unending inspiration for his sculptures.

The lonely northern Italian railway, crosses the *Alpine Tamaro* River, and then climbs all the way to the city of Turin, which, as the nation's first capital, is often known as the 'Cradle of Italian Liberty.' Which Sophia, incidentally found strangely comforting.

She slept much of the way, and tired as she was, allowed the almost four-hour journey to pass her by. At 9.30pm, the Mountain Train was pulling into the huge *Torino Porta Nuova* high-speed railway terminus, before she was even properly awake. She stepped into a city which was absolutely strange to her. The only time she'd even seen pictures of the place was in a 60-year-old movie based on Tolstoy's *War and Peace*, with Audrey Hepburn as Natasha Rostova.

But Uncle Rudy's supreme command of his laptop had made her less of a stranger, indeed an expert on this intercity train station, long before she arrived, and she walked hurriedly, directly towards the nearest taxi rank.

The journey through the city took almost an hour in surprisingly busy streets, but luckily Miss Morosova checked in, first-class, and the beautifully-mannered Air France executive escorted her personally to the airline's lounge where she would rest for the next few hours before her 6am Monday morning take-off for Paris.

She'd switched to her French passport for this leg of the journey, which was a 350-mile flight, straight over the Swiss Alps to Paris, in a British Aerospace Avro jetliner. International travel had come a long way since the Carthaginian General Hannibal came trundling past Turin with his 37 African battle elephants, on a month-long trek over the Alps. Sophia would land at Charles de Gaulle in a mere one-hour and 40-minutes, hopefully with a Russian Embassy car to meet her.

*****

London. Sunday night. As big media events go, this one was right up there. By the 5 o'clock news bulletins, the whole of Europe understood that Britain's big-hearted charity Czar, Sir Josh Hartley, had been unimaginably killed in the middle of the Monaco Grand Prix racetrack—slammed into by a 150mph Renault RE18, after a 100-foot plunge from the balcony of a trackside apartment block.

Monaco police were mystified. There were about 200,000 potential witnesses, but only one, a next-door neighbour, would admit to seeing anything. Cause of death was obvious, Sir Josh was killed instantly when he hit the asphalt. The racing car driven by France's Gilles Romanet hit only a dead body, despite the terrific speed of his car, which was in third place at the time.

Such was the pandemonium upon the arrival of Monday morning's first editions, late Sunday night, ranking Scotland Yard officers were called in for a midnight conference: to decide whether to inform Monaco authorities they wished to be a part of the investigation into the violent death of this British subject. Or indeed whether to stay out of it until Monaco requested assistance.

None of the newspapers were yet suggesting it was an accident. But neither were the police ruling out foul play. In short. Sir Josh may have been shoved. But there was no evidence, and no one was claiming to have seen a suspicious person.

Though later a women's publication would demand to know in a tear-jerking "Why, oh Why?" editorial:

Who Would Do Such A Thing
To This British Saint
To Whom So Many Owe So Much?

But for now New Scotland Yard was simply glaring at the London papers in a meeting chaired by Detective Chief Superintendent Charles Barton, everyone pondering the question of whether someone had murdered Hartley. But even the national editors were not committing themselves on that one.

The London *Daily Mail:*

150mph Grand Prix car kills Britain's Charity Legend
SIR JOSH HARTLEY PLUNGES
TO HIS DEATH IN MONACO

The Sun:

Monaco Grand Prix Halted when …
FRENCH F1 CAR HITS AND KILLS
SIR JOSH HARTLEY

The London *Daily Telegraph :*

Fatal 100-foot plunge at Monaco Grand Prix
MYSTERY OF HARTLEY'S
DEATH ON THE TRACK

Charles Barton was too much of a suspicious senior policeman to accept, at face value, that no one pushed Sir Josh, simply because no one had seen it. At least no one admitted they'd seen it. Charles was firmly of the opinion that the very rich, earning £400,000 a week, never kill themselves. Not those with large country houses, Rolls Royces, private planes, and lifestyles like an Indian Rajah.

Except for chancers like the Czechoslovakian-born Captain Robert Maxwell, who was not anything like as rich as he seemed, and ended his financial woes by jumping off the stern of his yacht in the middle of the Atlantic in 1991. Not for nothing was he known in some circles as The Bouncing Czech.

Charles Barton sighed the sigh of the deeply irritated. "I don't think we want to get involved in a murder hunt in Monaco, while the local police are not even certain whether it was suicide or not. My own views remain open, but unless the media forces our masters to insist we do something, we'll just follow it closely.

"I'll have a chat to the Monaco authorities, and we'll see how it's proceeding two or three days from now. We've enough trouble trying to solve real crimes, right here in our own backyard. That's all, gentlemen. For now."

Charles moved swiftly away, to South Audley Street, and everyone else essentially scattered towards home. Meanwhile, in what used to be known as Fleet Street, the big newspapers were already working all night on this one. The huge-circulation *Daily Globe* had moved senior men from their Paris and Rome offices directly to Monaco. A plane had been chartered for the four biggest London publications and the *Globe* had three men on board.

One of them was a renowned feature writer whose task was to write a graphic 'shock, horror' piece about the atmosphere in Monaco, a country now humiliated before the world ... *Get ahold of Prince Albert if you can ... if not go for one of the other royals down there ... Tuesday night for Wednesday ... and don't fuck it up, old boy... this is BIG!*

Other writers were being detailed to interview the major yacht owners, whose boats were all over Monte Carlo harbour. The hard news men were talking to the police, interviewing anyone who lived in the *Beau Rivage ... and get ahold of that old broad from the eighth floor who thought she saw something ... offer money if you have to ... also interview the doorman, that French bastard who abandoned his post ... and that fucking layabout who was supposed to be a security guard on the eighth. We're looking for a headline saying* **THE DISASTER WHICH SHOULD NEVER HAVE HAPPENED!**

Newspaper cameramen were being briefed all over London, before they left for the Riviera ... *Get me pictures of the smashed French car ... shoot the building from the outside ... and get it back fast ... we want artists to work on a diagram of the fall, and the track ... get pictures of the police investigators ... photograph the inside of the building ... get up to the eighth floor ... pay if you have to for shots of the apartment interior ... also pay the doorman for a photograph ...*

On the home front the tension and rush of activity were just as bad ... *Get new photographs of Josh's home in Oxfordshire ... doorstep his mother in Bolton, and don't leave 'til you've spoken to her ... forget the police ... they know less than we do ... doorstep the BBC ... interview everyone who's ever worked with Josh ... and get ahold of the Director General ... I don't care what he says, but try to persuade... then threaten a piece that asks: Did the BBC drive him to suicide!*

Journalists, cameramen, feature writers—the same barbed message for them ... don't come back without it. The same mentality. After 66 years, it still reflected the *Daily Express* legend which emanated during the tragic Lynmouth floods in North Devon, 1952—still the worst river disaster in British history, 34 dead in one terrifying evening.

An earnest young reporter filed an opening paragraph to his story which read "God sat on a hill and witnessed a scene of absolute devastation wrought by nature in this tiny Devon village."

Back came a cable from the standard tyrannical *Express* news editor: "Thanks, Tom. Interview God and get pictures."

That old Fleet Street mindset would never die when a world-class news story broke. And heaven knows this was world-class. With modern instant emails flashing back and forth, the snazzy payoff lines of the golden age of newspapers in the 1960's and 70's. But the last line never needed writing. It was unseen, but still there—always would be:

Failure unacceptable.

Chapter Eight
The March of the Paper Tigers

There is an unbreakable doctrine at the KGB,
which is also the creed of the Bolsheviks ...
Some people are simply too evil, or too different
to be allowed to live among the normal population.

Television newsrooms, with their overpaid presenters, and overstaffed reporting corps, would always be paper tigers in the minds of men who had actually worked for the hard-driving masters of the great Fleet Street publications with circulations once riding up towards five million daily, and beyond.

Nonetheless, the television channels had to join in this stampede for 'exclusives'—which was currently ruffling the hair of their highly groomed front men. Hiring planes, loading enough equipment to film a remake of *Star Wars,* the outside broadcast teams made their plutocratic way down to the south of France with about seven assistants and secretaries, each trying to book them into five-star Riviera rooms and suites to reflect their staggering importance to the world.

For this particular assignment they would, between them, set world records for re-runs, replays and stock footage, since the actual event had taken approximately 10-seconds, and the last thing Prince Albert wanted was newscast after newscast informing the world that his Monaco Police Force had no results, and no one knew when the Grand Prix would be re-raced, if ever.

There was also the sinister, unwritten warning that no one should venture above the second floor of any building in the Principality, for obvious reasons— A) You might go over one of the too-low balconies, B) Some lurking homicidal nutcase might heave you over, and then vanish forever.

The television men, in the total absence of anything worth filming would be edged ever further along the easy-to-understand formula of ... *did he jump or was he pushed?* Which of course thrilled the newspapers, who were also proceeding along that same path with infinitely more caution. They still needed to be right more than the crowd whose reports were inevitably, ephemeral flickering pictures. But they liked the broadcast backup to their general guesswork.

The near-universal melee to cast light upon the demise of Sir Josh continued unabated for three days, and there was a feeling of disquiet—that no one was doing quite sufficient to avenge this beloved British institution. Readers' letters to the press contained a mild air of indignation ... *What about the police? Why has Scotland Yard not gone down there? Has anyone come forward? Was he or was he not murdered?* Most correspondence ended with the written, or even unwritten assertion: *I think we should be told.*

And every day there was an official in a high place trying to make a name for himself. A drastically unsophisticated Labour Member of Parliament put it to the House that Sir Josh Hartley was a man of undisputed national stature *(Righto, boys and girls, what about an old faithful from the Beatles, YES?).* And from beyond the airwaves, a nation thundered its approval.

"In light of that, Honourable Members, I was thinking in terms of a State Funeral, and either a burial or memorial in Poet's Corner, Westminster Abbey. He deserved it. Such dignity in the face of death."

"You mean a funeral on the level of those of Sir Winston, Field Marshall Viscount Montgomery of Alamein, Admiral Nelson and Lady Thatcher?" Thus spoke the Prime Minister.

And he was swiftly followed by the Oxford-educated Foreign Secretary, a Classics Scholar, who added, "And a memorial among the literary eminences of our nation? I mean, Dickens, Samuel Johnson, Keats, Kipling, Milton, Tennyson and Wordsworth. Not to mention Lord Olivier ..."

And no one heard a seasoned old Tory MP from the shires mutter, "Christ! He was a fucking disc-jockey for our national Communist broadcast network."

"For the people," added the undaunted Labour member for Little Soddington.

*****

At 7.40 on Monday morning the Air France flight from Turin International touched down at Charles de Gaulle. Sophia Morosova was out very quickly and headed for the waiting area outside the terminal. The procedure never varied— Just stand there, say nothing to anyone, and when the Embassy car pulls up, open the door and get in.

The wait was just three minutes, and she was instantly on her way, a 24-minute run direct to *Boulevard Lannes*. She and Rudolf had breakfast together in a private Embassy room, and began a debrief on the recently completed mission.

"I noticed he had died," he said.

"Yes," she replied, "Several hundred million other people noticed the same thing. I think the Americans might call it the shove heard round the world."

"In my trade we consider the bigger the uproar, the safer the perpetrator."

"Please God," she smiled. "But I am certain I made no mistakes. I remembered my disguises. I escaped in the opposite way they would think. And I was in the train and out of there before they even knew who'd died."

"Good girl."

"Better yet, my train had me over the border and into another country within 10 minutes of leaving Monaco station."

"And, Sophia, it's still only Monday morning. The papers are still saying the police are not ready to announce foul play. Which is a certainty they have not one suggestion of a suspect. I think, my dear, you've done it."

"You mean we've done it. Because it's all thanks to you."

"Thanks to the unbreakable doctrines of the KGB, and the creed of the Bolsheviks. Some people are too evil to be allowed to live." And then his words trailed off, as if he could no longer bear to say anything else. But he did, just … *little Sasha … darling little Sasha.*

And then Uncle Rudolf brightened up. "I have to say, Sophia, if you hadn't finished him … he still would not have had long to live. And now …?"

"And a very difficult problem lies ahead," she said. "I know his name and I know what the world thinks of him. And I know his importance. But I'm not sure where he lives. Whether it's China or Japan. All I know is, I must find him. God, will I ever forget the last time I saw him…?"

"Not many people can cast aside a trauma like that," said her Uncle. "But it's best not to dwell on it …"

Rudolf was just trying to help, but he was too late. For a rare time in this long-planned mission, Sophia broke down and wept shamelessly. It was her little sister's screams. It was always the memory of those screams that so upset her in the daytime, and turned her night-time dreams blood black.

On that terrible last night the Japanese man had punched her viciously in the mouth when she flew at him, as he tried to rape the 15-year-old Sasha. The blood was nearly as bad as the screaming, pouring both from her split and swollen lips, and down Sasha's legs. Sophia remembered lying on the floor, dazed, trying to spot a weapon, any weapon, trying to get up, trying, if she could. to kill this hideous man.

And would she ever forget her mother bursting into the room with the steel pan? The man had tried to fight back, but Sophia knew that Veroniya, at that moment, was ready to lay down her life for her and Sasha. She remembered it every day; her mother smashing that pan into the man's head. She could still hear the sound as her mother had shouted a kind of Russian battle cry, *Die, you bastard, die!* And that last thump of the pan on his head.

After that there had just been silence. Neither she nor Sasha had known why their mother was just lying on the floor. It was as if she was dead. And well she might have been. She had never spoken again. And Sophia had never seen her again. The staggering trauma, both in what she had seen, and what she had done, had rendered Veroniya unreachable. That was the verdict of both the English and Russian doctors.

Eight weeks after that, Sasha died too. Like her mother, she had lost her reason, after the savagery of that evening. Everything came down to that; the sense of loss, the sense of outrage, the sense of invasion, the sense of hurt and overwhelming injustice. Which was why nothing could stop Sophia's tears. And she looked up at Uncle Rudy, and just said, with difficulty, through her heartbreak, "I will get him, Rudy. I will get him."

Uncle Rudolph took her in his arms. "Yes," he said, "You will get him. With my help, you will most definitely get him."

But there would be no immediate progress. Sophia was home in Paris, and Rudolf had to return to the Embassy, where, from Kensington Palace Gardens, he would have a very good view of the unfolding drama over the deceased disc-jockey in Great Britain's capital city.

Chapter Nine
A Legal Time-Bomb in the Letters Page

She also claimed there had been other minor incidents,
involving young girls, but since Sir Josh had recently
paid for a brand new roof for the church, even the vicar
was not mad about pursuing these lines of enquiry.

In the opinion of the British Prime Minister, any time the nation is basically in tears, it is unwise to stay silent. In 1997, even the Queen was compelled to return from Scotland to London to share the national grief after the divorced former Princess of Wales was killed in a car crash.

She occupied a place in the hearts of the public because of her beauty, and her tireless work for charity. Sir Josh was also a tireless worker for charity, and, although he came up light in the beauty department, was almost as beloved as the People's Princess.

Thus the PM was acutely conscious of the necessity to do something. Aside from the somewhat silly request for a State funeral, he was genuinely concerned that it would not be terribly clever to ignore the outpouring of sadness in the country, despite the fact that Sir Josh's death might yet be proven to be either murder or suicide. In fact later that afternoon, the PM called from Downing Street to New Scotland Yard to speak to the Commissioner.

And he reminded the most senior policeman in the capital that both the Government and the Law should be seen at least to be paying attention. The Scotland Yard Chief went along with that, but in turn reminded the PM about the murder/suicide conundrum.

They spoke for 10 minutes and decided that Scotland Yard should put out a news bulletin pointing out the problems of working with a foreign government, which had very different priorities. But it would assure everyone they were on the case, ready to move at a moment's notice, at the first sign of suspected foul play. Scotland Yard had Sir Josh Hartley's interests very much at heart.

In turn Downing Street would put out a press release, confirming the Prime Minister's concern, and stating that he would be in regular touch with the

Commissioner of Scotland Yard, with whom he shared a determination to keep the public informed should there be any suggestion that the life of Sir Josh Hartley had been wrongfully terminated.

Despite the flagrant lack of any evidence, the massed scribes of the newspapers and broadcast industry had been so insistent that they believed something was afoot, the British public had more or less decided that someone had shoved him over the balcony. For three reasons 1) You can never trust Johnny Foreigner, 2) There's never smoke without fire, and 3) That many national journalists can't all be wrong, right?

Not many people considered the fact the newspapers and broadcasters are in it for the money, their business is to sell papers, sell advertising space, and keep their high salaries and expenses coming. The way to do that is to ramp up circulation and viewership. It's 10 times the story to imply Sir Josh was probably murdered, than it ever would be to say he died accidentally.

And since the furore seemed unlikely to die down, the PM's closest advisers were suggesting that Prince Charles, heir to the Throne of England, should also put out a statement pointing out what a loss this man was to so many good and necessary causes. The Prince, who had received many a big cheque thanks to Sir Josh, for his principal charities, agreed.

All of which guaranteed a lot of ink and a lot of air-time for anyone who could shed light on either Sir Josh's character or his work ethic. The possibility of a first Sainthood, for a disc jockey, in 2,000 years of Christian history stood before the Vatican, which is of course the only State on earth smaller than Monaco.

Only the heavyweight brains of the PM and the Yard Commissioner understood clearly that the entire concept of instant Sainthood is unwise in the extreme. Stuff can come out of the woodwork. If he had been murdered, then by whom? And, more importantly, why? They both knew this sudden Sainthood business was a dangerous road upon which to embark. Even the Commissioner felt he should remind the PM that Saint Teresa of Calcutta was canonised nineteen years after her death in 1997. And there was a left-wing element in England going for instant Sainthood for a DJ.

Nonetheless, the press releases and bulletins went out and were given heavy coverage. One of the BBC classic channels was playing Mozart's 1791 Requiem in D-Minor almost non-stop all day. Chopin's Death March, from Sonata No.2 in B-flat Minor, filled in the gaps. These were very gloomy days on the airwaves, and even one of the country music channels joined in the melancholy mood of London, playing constantly the American Brad Paisley's winsome funeral ballad, *When I get Where I'm going.*

Whatever else, Josh Hartley's death had touched a note. And the very slight mystery surrounding his death did not alleviate for one split second the esteem in which he was held by the public. And even grumpy old Tory MP's were obliged to admit there had never been a word of scandal about Sir Josh Hartley in all the years of his remarkable career.

But on Thursday, there appeared the tiniest chink in his armour. Buried down-column in the letter page of *The Times* was an item from a lady in Rochester, Kent, which constituted a legal time-bomb. It may or may not have been true, and a lot of people felt it should not have been published. It read:

Dear Sirs,

I have read almost non-stop of the wonderful deeds and generosity of the late Sir Josh Hartley. But there is one person who may not subscribe to this admiration. And that's my daughter, now aged 18, and likely to be embarrassed by this letter. Three years ago Josh Hartley took a group of Sunday school girls from our church to see a Disney movie. And halfway through it he offered my daughter, sitting next to him, some popcorn from his own container.

To her horror the popcorn was not the only thing in that big cardboard box. My daughter actually screamed in the cinema not knowing what was jutting up through the kernels. She was so upset, I went down that night and reported it to the police, but the station Sergeant could not stop laughing. Nothing was ever done. Not even a call-back. It's high time the statements of women were taken seriously.

Just so you know,

Still angry...

Rochester, Kent. (name and address supplied).

Letters pages in the London nationals are often skimmed rather than read. Many, many people miss little gems, or even bombshells, which lurk in those columns. But every big newspaper has a person whose job is to check them thoroughly, every night. So does Scotland Yard.

And on this Thursday morning there were two sets of eyes taking a very hard look at the communication in *The Times*, direct from Rochester, Kent. One was

Detective Chief Superintendent Charles Barton. The other was Harry Cook, a sub-editor at the *Daily Mail*.

The professional antennae of both men were vibrating, Barton's because he felt the deep background of a victim often led to a murder being solved. Harry Cook because this might be where the *Daily Mail* blew a gaping hole in the reputation of 'Sir Josh-fucking-Perfect.' It was hard to fathom which of them was more eager. But, for the moment, Mozart's Requiem played on.

Charles Barton was quickest into his stride, because he could demand the lady's name and address from *The Times*, and get it, fast. There was a Detective Constable cleaning this up within minutes. But Harry was struggling a bit, since *The Times* was never going to hand over their advantage on a story this big.

Two young Scotland Yard detectives were speeding across Waterloo Bridge in a squad car before Harry had decided whether to beg, borrow, buy or steal the name and address from *The Times*. The letter-writer was at home, and only too pleased to elaborate precisely what had happened to her fifteen-year-old daughter in the cinema.

She also claimed there had been other minor incidents, involving young girls, but since Sir Josh had recently paid for a brand new roof for the church, even the vicar was not mad about pursuing these lines of enquiry. But the Lady from Rochester was insistent. Her daughter's description of the incident was far too graphic to have been invented. And she was very certain there was something very odd, weirdly sexual, about the great benefactor—"Knighthood and Sainthood be damned," was her actual phrase.

The two policemen thanked her, assured her of the Yard's sense of discretion and returned to have a chat with Charles Barton, who listened with rapt attention. He had been certain the solution to Lord Fontridge's murder rested with the Peer himself, somewhere in the deep background. Same with Sir Josh. It was merely a matter of unearthing the facts, however unlikely they may seem. He immediately put two men to work gathering a list of the charities the DJ had supported, especially those involving children, children's homes, special schools, and hospitals.

His final instructions were to listen to anything, the smallest detail, the smallest complaint, the merest suspicion. And follow up with every possible method. "These kids are older now, but a lot of them will be local to the hospitals," said the DCS. "Get after them, find them, talk to them, and if you need any further assistance … you've got it."

*****

Sophia Morosova was now 211 miles from London which had been turned, courtesy of the media, into the pivotal centre of the quasi-unproven scandal of the departed Sir Josh. She could still catch up here in Paris, but quite frankly she didn't care. That sadistic bastard had gone for ever, and she hoped he'd died of fright, like her sister, little Sasha, who was too scared to go on living.

So far as Sophia was concerned, it was well and truly over, and if anyone thought they could find out anything about his death, good luck with that. She had never felt more relaxed, sitting here at 8am, in the morning sun, on her high balcony, sipping *un chocolat chaud,* which she poured from a special chocolate pot she'd bought in a Paris market.

Never mind relaxed, she also had never felt more popular. That morning Uncle Rudy had called from London to ask her if she wanted to go to the opera again on Saturday—such a wit, old Rudy. And she had replied, predictably, "Are you actually out of your mind!" Which brought forth a great bellow of laughter from the Russian Intelligence officer.

Then, one hour later, she had a call from her oldest and best school friend, Kate Mildmay, who wanted her to come to England today, and then come to the races with her parents on Friday.

"I don't know much about horse racing, really," said Sophia. "What's going on? You never asked me before."

"That's because I never go myself," replied Kate. "But Dad's got a runner in the Woodcote Stakes. He probably won't win. But it'll be fun. It's the Derby meeting at Epsom Downs. They run that on Saturday, but the Friday's quite big, it's the Oaks and Coronation Cup. They call it Ladies Day, but don't ask me what that's all about. Anyway, we'll have a laugh, and we'll have lunch in the owners' room. Dad just shouted to tell you to come to dinner tonight at home."

"Sounds a bit too good to miss. I can try for the mid-day flight Air France. But I might not get on."

"You're already on," laughed Kate, "I just reserved you a seat and Dad paid. Don't be late. I'll pick you up at Heathrow, Terminal 4, about 2pm. See you then … apparently we have to look halfway glamorous on this day, but men don't wear morning coats, and I'll never worry about you in your Paris fashion outfits … see you later, 'bye…"

"Christ," muttered Sophia to herself. "There's no peace. I'll say that. But I can't wait to see Kate. It's been over six months."

The Mildmays had always been very good friends to Sophia, always ready to invite her down to their sprawling tree-lined house in Winkfield Row, near Ascot, Windsor and Sunningdale, a mecca for City big-hitters like Kate's dad, the banker Richard Mildmay. He'd had a near miss in 2008, but had fought back boldly to even greater riches.

Their home had been a sanctuary for Sophia, whose own family was erratic at best, her step-father commuting between London and Moscow, trading oil futures, or whatever he did, once he'd left the Russian capital. That was after Vladimir Putin had frightened the life out of the oil oligarchs by putting one of them in the slammer for seven years on charges which mystified everyone.

The upshot of this was Boris headed west for London with every last rouble he could lay hands on. It was a lot, but he also left a lot behind, and he had to make periodic trips back to Russia to free up whatever he could of his once-vast fortune. He'd been a very rich, but slightly mysterious man, when he married the lovely Moscow widow Veroniya, when Sophia was but two-years-old. Sasha was actually born after their real father had died.

But life was very complicated for the oligarchs, and Boris's frequent trips back to Russia were not always successful. By his own absurdly high standards, he felt as if he were on the breadline. The truth, however, ran deeper. Much deeper.

Step-father Boris was not in fact an oligarch, and the oligarchs were not his peers, they were his clients. Boris Morosova, in deadly secret, ran the most exclusive high-end prostitution racket in Moscow. His tireless impersonation of a big oil exec could have seen him on the Red Carpet, nominated for one of Hollywood's little golden statuettes, the ones with no genitals. Though, upon reflection, in his case, this might have been judged inappropriate.

Boris was in fact a poster boy for big-spending Moscow. He had two areas of operation, an astronomically-expensive nightclub, plus an executive booking office for his fleet of city prostitutes. Both of them were located in Moscow's Golden Mile in the affluent district of Khamovniki, less than a mile southwest of the Kremlin.

The nightclub was discreetly situated in a small side road, and represented a symphony in dark red velvet curtains, deep-pile carpets, same colour, with gleaming white table-cloths and armchairs also upholstered in dark red velvet.

French Champagne ran at $5,000 a bottle, a large scotch on the rocks $500, the prices especially designed to keep out persons of low rank, including newspaper journalists. Especially newspaper journalists. The Club was named *Ode to Joy*, in Russian, *Ony-Panolth*, which no one really understood, but the oligarchs got the drift—behind these doors was a version of love and sexual gratification on an empirical scale.

The girls, imported from all over Europe, were without exception spectacular looking, and cost Boris's patrons $25,000 for a night, after a few bottles of champagne of course. The plush executive and booking offices two blocks away were strictly financial, equipped with two banks of desk-top computers with global links. The place was manned night and day, arranging *Les rendezvous* with beautiful women for billionaires all over the city. They say there was a time when the sun never set on the British Empire. There was also a time when the cash registers of Boris Morosova's sex Empire never stopped printing money, night and day, summer and winter.

But it all came to an end when Vladimir slammed his own version of brakes on the oligarchs—jail terms, threats and massive fines. Where once these mighty men had strutted around Moscow with their heads held high, now they stayed in the shadows, living opulent but discreet lives, offering no signs of riches beyond most people's dreams. And they stayed the hell away from high-profile operations like *Ode to Joy*.

Many of them set up headquarters out of Russia—Paris and London. With an obvious government crackdown on immoral living, Boris was one of the first men to ship out of the city. And he found it hard to live without his enormous income.

He purchased a house just to the west of central London and set about creating a new business. For many months, earning money, in London, possessed him, and since, like most very rich men, he had an utterly ruthless sense of self-preservation, he followed the sacred creed of America's Wild West—*A man's gotta do what a man's gotta do.*

And if that meant selling the sacred bodies of his very young step-daughters, well … that was the way to go. It was, of course, the deepest irony that the Trust Fund established for Sophia and Sasha's futures, was established from Veroniya's side of the family, from her devoted husband Mikhail Obolensky before he was killed in a car crash on the Moscow freeway.

When Boris married Veroniya, he made three moves which seemed, on the face of it, the very soul of goodwill and generosity. He never adopted the girls, but he gave them his name, and signed away all rights to their Trust Fund, and indeed all rights to the former Mrs Obolensky's estate. He put the Maida Vale house in Veroniya's name, became the girls' guardian, and the last word in all matters appertaining to their welfare.

Actually, changing their name was questionable, since the fabled Obolensky dynasty still remained a part of Russian folklore. Indeed Sophia's distant relative was Prince Alexander Obolensky who scored two tries for England when they beat the New Zealand All-Blacks for the first time in 1936. It's still called 'Obolensky's match.'

For a man such as Boris to have power over girls descended from such a bloodline, was one of fate's cruellest blows. The saving grace was that he was rarely home, and he was definitely not registering the essentials of school holidays, half-terms, parents' days, concerts, and sports days which make up the curriculum of a major English girls' boarding school.

Perhaps the enormous effort of creating a full-blown *Joshi Kosai* operation in the middle of Maida Vale had sapped his strength. But the three years of profitable JK had made him a very large bundle of cash at £10,000 a time through the long school holidays, and had enabled him to be sufficiently generous to Sophia, that she, hopefully would bother him no more.

So the Mildmays scooped her up, and received a couple of tubs of wild caviar from the Caspian Sea, in jars the size of beer-barrels every Christmas. Richard Mildmay and his wife, who were both very fond of Sophia, thought, secretly, they had easily the best of that bargain. They'd known her since she was 12, which represented a bonanza in the world's most expensive food, the near precious black eggs of the Beluga sturgeon, hand delivered from the elite Russian importers in Kensington.

All courtesy of the now distant, but quietly-detested step-father.

Sophia made it to London Heathrow right on time. So did Kate, and the two former gazelles of the St Margaret's field hockey team sped down the M4 and through the lanes to Winkfield Row in just over 20 minutes. It was a good reunion for the family, which had welcomed the young Russian exile for many years, and still did. Sophia slotted right in with the Mildmays as always, and they had an amusing and very classy dinner of roast pheasant accompanied by a couple of bottles of Chateau Lynch Bages—Richard's favourite.

The conversation often threatened to become bogged down along memory lane, as the two girls fell about laughing with astounding tales of their antics at England's most expensive girls' school. Mrs Mildmay at times looked mildly shocked. But her husband skilfully dragged the chatter back to tomorrow's Woodcote Stakes at Epsom, when his two-year-old colt Winkfield Lad would take his chance against some of the fastest young sprinters in the country.

His long-time trainer, the Newmarket baronet, Sir Mark Prescott, was characteristically pragmatic about the race. His words to Richard Mildmay were: "He's fit, he's in great form, and we've got a chance. If he comes down that bloody hill okay, we're in with a shout."

It was a six-furlong dash nearly all downhill, which placed juvenile sprint records in danger every time it was run on fast ground. And tomorrow would be very quick since Epsom had been without rain for nine days, a warm late Spring wind having made the decline from Tattenham Corner swift as a Grand Prix race track. Most racehorses, by the way, hate running downhill, which rules out half the field in any race down Epsom's steep gradient.

But Winkfield Lad was light-framed with a low action, and may just feel right at home on this unorthodox turf runway. Such hopefulness keeps all owners as optimistic as Lazarus, and most of them could talk for an entire evening about such a conundrum. Richard Mildmay was no exception, despite the bookmakers' confident offering of 10-1 odds against his colt.

Being interrupted every few moments by hilarious tales from the Upper Sixth at St Margaret's only amused him, but by 11pm he had convinced everyone at the table that a tenner each way on Winkfield Lad might be the best investment they ever made. So everyone retired to bed with heightened ambitions to skin the bookmakers alive once Richard's colt got himself into gear on the morrow.

Sophia, who, was, of course, no stranger to a bit of excitement these days, was up first, dressed to kill in a very stylish little Chanel number, made the coffee, buzzing around the kitchen as she had done for much of her life. Then she settled down to read the morning papers, which were delivered to the Mildmay back door every day sometime after 6am. The Mildmays took the *Mail, The Times,* and on Fridays and Saturdays, the *Financial Times* and the *Racing Post*—just in case something major was happening on the turf.

With very little on her mind except the prospects of Winkfield Lad, she picked up the Post and turned inside to find the race cards for the Epsom summer meeting. The Woodcote Stakes was right there, jockey silks presented in colour, with form, number, owner, trainer, rider and draw for each horse. Readers were encouraged to check the previous form of each horse by turning to another page, which contained about 10,000 numbers, and tiny incomprehensible phrases, which to Sophia might just as well have been written in Hindustani.

"Yes ... well ..." she muttered, and skipped swiftly back to the main cards. The numbers behind Winkfield Lad were 04110—which she guessed meant he'd won a couple of races and was now allowed to run in this exalted company. While she was about it, she also checked the runners in the Coronation Cup, first run in 1902, to celebrate the ascent to the Throne of King Edward VII, Queen Victoria's sex-loving son whose athleticism in the sack was legendary even before the days of rampant, tawdry television series.

Sophia digested these historic landmarks, the Coronation Cup, not, of course, the athleticism. And she skimmed down the runners just to see if France had an entrant. However she had noted only the favourite on the front page of the Post. Its name was Double Domo, and, having finished a close-up fourth in last year's Arc de Triomphe, the five-year-old from Sha Tin, Hong Kong, was expected to leave this field standing over the switchback 12-furlong race worth over a half-million pounds sterling.

He'd be ridden by a top French jockey, but the owner's name on the race card stopped Sophia Morosova dead. She almost shot coffee down her nose, coughed and spluttered. Then she looked again. And there it was, a name she kept hidden in two places for eight years—in the deepest recesses of her mind, and on an old piece of paper in the false bottom of her jewellery case ... *Yunto Takahashi*.

Sophia had stored her memories of this man in secret places most people don't even know they have. The savagery of that last night which sent her mother mad, and her sister to her grave, swirled before her. She actually thought she might faint, and rushed upstairs to her bathroom where she was violently ill.

She somehow preserved her pristine Epsom Ladies Day dress, wrapped in a huge Mildmay bath towel, but it still took her 20 minutes for her heart to slow down, and for her tears to stop. There was nothing she could do about them. They just flowed, whenever she was reminded of that night ... just the sight of his name ... that's how bad it was.

When she returned to the kitchen, Kate was already sipping coffee and checking out the form of Winkfield Lad. She looked up and asked if Sophia had made the coffee since there was no one else around. And then said, suddenly, "Christ, Sophia! Are you okay? You're as white as a ghost."

Her friend smiled weakly, and assured her, "I'm fine. Just felt a bit shaky when I first got up. Probably a hangover."

"Don't mention that to Dad for God's sake. He thinks his cellared wine is so good a hangover is impossible!"

"I know that—and it's always the best wine I taste all year. And anyway I'm feeling much better now. All ready to start planning our tilt against the bookmakers. I'm going for £25 each way on Winkfield."

"If we see 10-1 let's take it. I know some of Dad's city friends will be there and by the time they've finished we'll probably start at 5-1 or worse."

"That's a bit above my pay grade. But we'll be there early for lunch so we can place the bets before the crowd arrives."

Winkfield Row was probably invented as an adjunct to London high-life. It's no more than 35 minutes from the most fashionable racecourses in the south of England: Newbury, Royal Windsor, Ascot, Sandown Park and Epsom. It's just up the road from some of the prime private golf clubs, Royal Berkshire, Wentworth and Sunningdale. It's also up the road from The Guards' Polo Club at world-renowned Smith's Lawn, and five minutes from the Royal Windsor Horse Show. In Winkfield Row, anyone who was not a member of at least two of them was regarded as someone akin to the Vietnam Boat People.

Aside from the unforeseen trauma of Sophia's morning, the rest of the operation was very relaxed for everyone. Richard Mildmay's chauffeur picked them up at 11.30, and completed the 20-mile journey to Epsom with no traffic problems. But the hillside parking lots to the historic English racecourse were already busy when they arrived. Which did not affect them, since the chauffeur dropped them off at the front gate, and then went off to park the dark blue Bentley. No one could remember when Richard Mildmay did not own a Bentley.

Sophia kept her secret Intelligence strictly to herself. She knew the Coronation Cup went off at 3.30. She knew Yunto's hateful colours were basically red with white markings. His horse was Number Six. His trainer was the Newmarket veteran Alec Shiplake. They would be in the parade Ring shortly after 3pm.

The Post's preview of the race contained much about Mr Yunto Takahashi, who had flown in from Hong Kong just for the race. The plan was for him to collect his winnings, and the Cup, and make an evening flight back to Hong

Kong where he had runners this weekend. Mr Takahashi was a big hitter in the Far East—he was a member of the exclusive Hong Kong Jockey Club, and a major investor in the China Horse Club, the new force in world racing, part owners of an American Triple Crown winner.

Mr Takahashi was one of the richest men in the world with a fortune estimated at more than 120 billion dollars. He was Chairman and CEO of the secretive Okinawa Conglomerate Trust, which had the closest possible ties with six major US Banks. Huge investments in oil, shipping, high tech, and sales of military hardware swept silently through the offices of OCT, just as silently dropping gigantic commissions into the pockets of the aforementioned Yunto Takahashi.

Sophia slipped into the ladies room to make her notes on a blank page of the race card. She had already grabbed the 10-1 about Winkfield Lad, and a half-hour later watched the Woodcote Stakes, jumping up and down with excitement over the last furlong, as the Mildmay colt came storming up the hill to the finish, gaining with every stride, but going down a neck and a half-length to the favourite.

She and Kate had made a small amount of money on the each way bet, but her father had made more with a £1,000 each-way bet of his own. The win bet cost him £1,000 but he got 2-1 a place and walked off with a £1,000 profit. "Next time," said Sir Mark. "Next time, Richard, you'll have a real bet. This is a damn fast two-year-old—we'll get him on a flat track. I don't think he loved running downhill."

Almost an hour later, Sophia and Kate were at the Parade Ring behind the stand awaiting the horses for the Coronation Cup. At least, Kate was. Sophia was waiting for the man whose very name had almost made her pass out with anger and hurt that very morning.

Owners and trainers were beginning to walk in, and Double Domo had already marched past, saddled up ready for his jockey. Sophia saw a well-dressed trainer walk in with three Asian men, Chinese, Japanese, Koreans? She did not know which. But she knew one of them must be Yunto. The Post had made it clear he was here to win this big prize, as if he didn't have enough cash already.

The trouble was, she did not know which of the three was him. They all wore dark suits, and they all wore Panama hats. She needed help here but there was no one to ask. But at that moment assistance came from a very unexpected quarter—the Queen of England to be precise. The Royal party of six had just entered the parade ring, and was walking slowly while the Queen cast a very expert eye over the runners.

As she passed Alec Shiplake and his Japanese owners, they all made a short bow—probably a *domo* in the etiquette of Japan—and just raised their hats in deference. And that was when Sophia saw it. A long pink scar against the light brown skin of the man to the left of the three, across his temple, and right across his ear. She actually gasped, and her hand flew to her mouth, as she recognised the surgical stitches made to the huge gash left by Veroniya's steel frying pan— the desperate, murderous swing which had probably saved her own life on that night seven years ago.

"You won't be so damn lucky next time," she murmured, surreptitiously raising her cell-phone and taking a very sharp photograph of the owner of Double Domo. She'd never need it. That face was embedded in her mind, for all the days of her life. And they would meet again.

Slowly the close connections of the Coronation Cup runners were dispersing out to their select vantage points to watch the one-and-a-half-mile Group I race, 15 runners, Double Domo now even-money favourite. And the contest went rather tiresomely to plan. They swung around Tattenham Corner travelling downhill, left turn at nearly 40mph, with the Japanese runner in second position right on the fence.

At the two-furlong pole he struck the front, going quickly two lengths clear. They reached the bottom of the hill and faced the stiff uphill climb, and at that moment the Newmarket maestro, Frankie Dettori, brought John Gosden's experienced four-year-old Whiplash, from right off the pace, having cruised easily down the hill.

And now he asked him. Dettori really asked him, setting him alight with one crack of the whip. And he drove him up that hill, hands and heels, but still asking him. And Whiplash responded, lowering his head, jamming his ears back and fighting for victory.

The huge crowd stood up and roared as Dettori again went to the whip, and once more the gallant Whiplash answered his call. Fifty yards out Double Domo still had it. But on the line the big straining white face of the bright chestnut Whiplash hit the front, a neck to the good.

Sophia who'd been screaming "GO WHIPLASH! … GO FRANKIE! … PLEASE. PLEASE FRANKIE!" at the top of her lungs for the past 15 seconds, nearly died of happiness.

"Did you back him?" asked Richard Mildmay.

"Didn't need to, darling," replied Sophia, tears of joy still rolling down her cheeks. "I was just hoping."

Richard just looked highly bemused, as he often did at the off-beat remarks of both his daughter and her closest friend. Not so the winning trainer. John Gosden looked slightly knowing, as if suspecting the triumph of Whiplash was something he'd thought might happen all along … just a hint of a wry smile, so familiar to racegoers. It betrayed nothing like the overwhelming delight on the faces of both Sophia Morosova and Frankie Dettori.

Chapter Ten
Barton in Paris

"It would be remiss to leave out anyone, just because it was inconvenient. We have interviewed everyone. And you were among the last, since you attended the opera on anonymous Russian Embassy tickets. You and Rudolf Masow."

In many ways, the opening races of Epsom's summer meeting had been a day of triumph for Sophia, with a £25 profit, and as much information as she could possibly have hoped for. She knew Yunto's corporation, she knew his status and address in Hong Kong, she knew he was a member of the HK Jockey Club, and above all, she knew precisely where he'd be on Saturday next week in the hours before his three-year-old colt Fighter's Dream ran in the HK$5 million Kowloon Gold Cup at Sha Tin.

All she needed was a chance to enter the Jockey Club rooms at the 40-year-old racecourse, with its majestic capacity of 85,000, and world-class races, one of which carries a prize of HK$10 million. This was a task for Uncle Rudy, whose global network of Russian ambassadors and diplomats would compare favourably with those of the late Czar Nicholas himself.

And all the way home, through the Surrey Hills and ritzy Berkshire, Sophia sat back and smiled. Revenge really was the warmest feeling, and, she knew, without one semblance of doubt, there was a lot more to come. Ahead of her was a peaceful weekend. Tonight they were dining at a very swanky restaurant on the River Thames—Richard's favourite. And tomorrow they would all watch the Derby on television, with Kate's two younger brothers who were coming home from Charterhouse School for the day.

Sophia would leave for Paris on the 6pm Air France flight from Heathrow on Sunday. It was only an-hour-and-20-minutes, very swift for most shoppers bound for the French capital. It was pretty swift, too, for Sophia. But for her, it was just the first step on a much longer journey, halfway around the world. And before that there was much to be arranged with one of Russia's top international secret agents.

*****

While Sophia and her closest friends were completing dinner along the Thames on that summer Friday evening, a thoroughly disgruntled Yunto Takahashi was scowling bleakly in the first-class cabin of Virgin Atlantic fight 206, bound for his staggeringly overcrowded homeland of Hong Kong. To be honest, he felt a bit of an idiot, having made a 12,000-mile round trip, halfway around the globe for certain victory in a major Group I contest over one of the most famous racecourses in the world.

Indeed, in the minutes immediately after the race-finish, he understood perfectly well how the WWII Japanese Admiral Masafumi Arima had felt as he led his Emperor's 'Kamikaze' pilots screaming towards the decks of the US aircraft carriers. To be fair, Yunto never would have yelled the Imperial war-cry of "BANZAI!" Not in the owners' and trainers' section at Epsom.

Indeed he was, these days, more in tune with his adopted nation's sense of "face," or, "the loss of face"—the Chinese dread of humiliation. And in truth, he still felt it, cruising over the English Channel at 33,000-feet. But his post-race musings kept straying to Admiral Arima, the national hero who crashed and died on his first mission, but missed his target. Like Double Domo, really.

Like so many men of uncountable wealth, he was at heart a very poor sport, being accustomed principally to a personal business creed of "victory at all costs." Defeat was essentially out of the question, and when it came, on Satan's wings, it really was the most bloody awful experience.

And of course, being so financially powerful, he was unused to being interrupted, far less argued with. In these rare moments of sorrow, old Yunto just kept on rehashing events from his own point of view ... *Jockey's an idiot, Alec Shiplake had totally let him down, ground was too fast, Double Domo wasn't ready etc., etc.*

Accompanying him on the journey was his personal assistant and bodyguard, the slimmed-down ex-Sumo wrestler Jim Ho, who retained his job mostly by never disagreeing with Yunto for even a split second. He treated 'boss like god' ... *boss never wrong ... boss genius ... obey boss at all times.* Which was more or less how Yunto expected the whole world to behave.

Dettori and Gosden break ancient law—Never argue with God. That's Buddha, by the way. Which made Yunto very disconsolate. And he sat in his wide seat, sipping water, working out how to explain things to his friends in the

Hong Kong Jockey Club. Pondering how his own jockey had been caught by surprise, and how this must never, ever happen again. *If Alec wants to stay employed, he'd better understand that.*

"Boss not pleased with Shiplake-san," said Jim Ho. *"Boss being very brave, like Kamikaze warrior. Shiplake-san need new jockey. Very dumb rider make boss too sad."*

The Japanese tycoon was so distracted by his shocking misfortune, never mind the hundred thousand pounds he'd picked up for finishing second, he had actually come out in a slight rash brought about by his humiliation. He seemed to itch everywhere, and his left hand kept straying to the eight-inch scar across the side of his head. It always irritated him at rare times like this. But nothing like so much as the vicious, criminal woman who had inflicted it, and her two disgusting whore children, who he'd paid good money for and had been cheated.

The Boeing 787 Dreamliner did its level best to ease his pain as they flew quietly and smoothly east across Asia, but his mood was no better 11 hours later when they finally touched down and taxied to Terminal 1 at Chek Lap Kok international airport. It was 4.55pm Hong Kong local time.

"Saturday now, boss," said Jim Ho. *"New day. New luck. One week from now, we make big revenge in Kowloon Gold Cup. Very big revenge. Boss save face, like always."* Yunto smiled for the first time for over 6,000-miles. *Hong Kong... we win here in hometown.*

*****

Detective Chief Superintendent Charles Barton kept his date with Johnny Fairchild on the Saturday night while Sophia was still at the Mildmays. The two men met on the Glyndebourne lawn where the Brighton jeweller had set up a beautiful little table for drinks, with two other friends. They were all there early, ready for a chat with 'Johnny's policeman'—*so bold—a first date, after only one previous meeting!*

But it all went according to plan. During the interval DCS Barton buttonholed Rudolf Masow in the lobby, and asked him, with immense politeness, if he'd mind having a brief chat as part of a strictly routine enquiry into the death of Lord Fontridge a couple of weeks ago.

The Russian diplomat was the soul of cooperation, and volunteered to have the chat right now, outside, on one of the Glyndebourne garden benches. The following day, Sunday morning, Charles Barton telephoned Sir George Kenny and reported the results.

"He could hardly have been more helpful," he told the Sussex Police Chief, "Admitted right away he'd been to *Rigoletto*, with his niece actually, and had of course heard about the murder. He recalled Sophia leaving just before the interval, but noticed nothing unusual afterwards. They'd had a picnic supper on the lawn and then watched the second part of the opera before driving back to London together."

"Did you get their full names?" asked Sir George.

"Of course. He's Rudolf Masow, cultural attaché at the Russian Embassy in Kensington. He's given me a phone number if we need any more help. His niece is Sophia Morosova, she's 24, lives in Paris now. He willingly gave me her name and number. Quite frankly, George, I'd be amazed it either one of them had the slightest knowledge of the murder. I don't think Masow had even heard of his Lordship before he read about it in the papers."

"Well, Charlie. It was always going to be a needle in a haystack search; just combing through the patrons of Glyndebourne. But there's no other way really. Somebody killed him. But I just cannot imagine why an outsider, even one who hated him, would have dreamed of turning up in the middle of a bloody opera hoping to stab him at half time. That's just fucking bizarre."

"I agree, but stab him they did. And the person who did it was almost certainly in the audience. So whether we like it or not, we're both back standing by the bloody haystack."

Sir George chuckled. And then he said, "Charles, I've known you a long time. And I can tell by your voice, you think there's something afoot. It might not be much, but you're holding out on me, you bugger …"

"Steady, George … and I wish you'd pick your words more carefully, given my recent record dating those of a less masculine persuasion!"

Charles Barton's old friend laughed loudly as he usually did at the Scotland Yard man's droll turn of phrase. But he still persisted, "Come on, spill the beans, I know you're up to something."

"Well," replied Charles, slowly, "There is just one thing. Johnny Fairchild, in case you don't know, is a highly intelligent, very successful man …"

"Christ! You're not thinking of marrying him, are you?"

"Shut up, George! I'm trying to tell you something. Now listen. The reason I went back to the opera was Fairchild told me one thing that stuck in my mind.

He noticed when Rudolf's niece returned to her seat after the interval, the dark-blue sapphire earrings she had been wearing had gone. She was wearing little pearl studs instead."

"And you have it deep in your imagination that it is possible they switched ladies not earrings. The second-half woman was a substitute, and that Rudolf's niece had actually hopped outside, stabbed his Lordship to death, then vanished."

"Well, something like that. Although it's probably about a 10,000 to 1 chance. The fact is, George, I can't quite let it go, Fairchild's observation was too cool. And I'm going to fly over to Paris tomorrow morning and chat to Miss Sophia, face to face. I have to say that if my somewhat outlandish theory is in any way correct, Rudolf had a damn funny way of trying to protect his niece."

"He had no reason to tell me anything—she's a foreign national, living in a foreign country, an occasional visitor to England. Also he has diplomatic protection against any police enquiry, and here I am trying to treat her like a Mafia Don wielding a stiletto. And that uncle cheerfully gave me her address and phone number. Told me to call him if I needed anything else. I'm probably on the verge of absolutely nothing. But I'm still going to Paris."

"Keep me posted, Charlie ... you never know."

****

Charles Barton had a busy Monday morning at the Yard. He managed to get out by 11am, and his driver had him sharply down to Heathrow, albeit with no ticket, no reservation, and no lunch. He managed to get a seat in business class on the Air France 1pm flight to Paris, but only after producing his Scotland Yard credentials, which had a way of scaring ticketing clerks half to death.

The flight was on time, and landed at Charles de Gaulle at 3.20pm (local time). The DCS was in the front hall of Sophia's building at 4.20. The French cab driver would probably have overtaken Lewis Hamilton.

Gaston directed him up to her apartment, and called her immediately to say *Le Gendarme* was on his way. Sophia was getting used to this. Her Uncle had called that very morning with the same message. Longer time-frame; information identical: Scotland Yard on its way.

Charles rang the doorbell. And in truth was instantly taken by surprise by the striking looking young woman who faced him. She was quite tall and looked at him with clear eyes, before saying quietly, *"Bonjour, Inspecteur,"* which made Charles feel like *Clouseau.*

"I'm sorry to intrude, mademoiselle," he said. "And I'm even sorrier I had no time to telephone first."

"Oh, that's okay," she said, "I've been expecting you. My Uncle Rudolf told me you would probably visit. Although he did not mention you would actually drop into Paris from out of the blue. Anyway, please come in. How about a cup of tea?"

"That would be wonderful," he said. "I've been up since 5am, subsisting on one breathtakingly stale croissant baked by Air France. A cup of tea might revive me. By the way, my name is Charles Barton. Are you English now? Or still Russian?"

They stepped inside, and Sophia gave him a quick genetic run-down, "Born in Russia, went to England aged eight, school and university in England. British subject, French resident."

"Excellent. Just to get it all squared away, do you normally go for a Russian samovar or a tea-pot?"

Sophia then did something, which was truly rare for her, meeting a man, any man, for the first time. She burst out laughing, but instantly recovered and said, "Tea pot every time. I'm not a bloody Cossack!" She said it as if she were joshing with Kate Mildmay, which in itself was unusual, since she had known Kate for 10 years and this policeman for less than two minutes. And she still added, "Tea-pot from Marks and Spencers, fake willow pattern, on sale as I recall."

Charles Barton chuckled, and marvelled at the way a certain class of British people know each other, in a way which applies to no other nation. It's as if they were members of some kind of club, or more likely a secret society. As Lady Penelope always said: "There is no nation on earth so reviled as the Brits for our outmoded sense of class snobbery. And no nation on earth where outsiders are so cruelly punished." Spoken, of course, by the socially fireproof daughter of a 14th generation Scottish dukedom, a lady with a reckless wit, but still fireproof for all of her days.

Charles Barton and Sophia Morosova knew each other instantly. Eton and St Margaret's, Pangbourne. They spoke the same language.

Sophia made the tea. And she observed the undernourished Charles, speaking with extreme care about the opera, and the wondrous setting at

Glyndebourne. He actually had no idea what to ask her, short of, *Any chance you murdered that Lord Fontridge—just checking!*

He decided to concentrate instead on just getting to know her—an exercise he might have entered into with some enthusiasm, whether or not Freddie Fontridge had been inexplicably murdered. They finished their tea, and Sophia was aware of two things, 1) he had asked her nothing of any importance, 2) he was starving. Which led to a brainwave.

"Superintendent, I am going to lead you to a couple of top-class croissants. Right around the corner at *Deux Magots.*"

"Excellent," he said, "Heard of it. Never been. Hemingway's pub, I think."

"That's the one. How did you know that?"

"Oh, my mother. She's always banging on about Paris. If you didn't know her, you'd think she was Marie Antoinette's aunt."

Sophia was getting used to laughing with this Englishman. And they left the apartment, and strolled to the legendary sidewalk cafe. She ordered for them both, and told the DCS that in the absence of half a side of roast beef, she'd gone for a large croissant she was certain he'd like.

Charles was as certain as anyone could be that Sophia Morosova had categorically not rammed a stiletto into the ribs of the English Law Lord. In fact right now he was just noticing her earrings, small dark-blue butterflies. And for a man who was uncertain, earring-wise, of the difference between a butterfly and a fruit bat, he trod very carefully indeed.

"Pretty earrings," he ventured, knowing he was walking barefoot through broken glass. "Tell me something, do they ever hurt after wearing them for a long time. Do you ever want to change them in the middle of dinner?"

"Often," said Sophia. "As a matter of fact I always bring a spare, very light clip-ons, fake pearls."

"Anyone ever noticed?"

"Probably not. At least no one ever mentioned it."

Uncle Rudy had briefed her well. Ludmilla's performance at Glyndebourne had been flawless, except for the earrings. But the Russian spy, had been trained to sonar-level standards of observation, and he had noticed, like the jeweller sitting right behind him. And he'd warned Sophia that the oncoming Scotland Yard policeman might bring up the subject, and her reply must be forthcoming, and frank … yes, she probably had changed them.

"I still can't understand why you wanted to see me," Sophia remarked.

And at this point, as a part of his murder enquiries, neither could Charles. And he answered between bites of his buttery croissant, which had been made even more lavish by liberal spreading of *la confiture de fraises*. Which both Sophia, and certainly Charles, privately thought was a bit heavy, for strawberry jam.

"Miss Morosova," he said seriously. "We are in the middle of a major murder enquiry. It is our slightly educated opinion that the victim was stabbed by someone who was in that audience. We have about 40 officers combing through the lists and interviewing every last person we can find who watched *Rigoletto* that night.

"It would be highly remiss of us to leave out anyone just because it was inconvenient to speak to them. We have to interview everyone. And you were among the last to be found, since you attended the opera on anonymous Russian Embassy tickets. You and Rudolf Masow. And I have to say it seems that neither of you had ever even heard of Lord Fontridge before. I also have to say you are among my least likely murderers."

"Well, that's a relief," she smiled. "I'd find it quite depressing if you arrested me."

"I'd say you were safe—for the moment," said Charles. "Zero motive. Almost Zero opportunity. Zero criminal record. Too young ... and ... well, a bit too pretty. And a lot too nice. Thank you Miss Morosova."

With that he theatrically clapped the pages of his notebook shut. And Sophia, she just clapped, laughing again at this amusing Yard Superintendent. And she thought, probably for the first time in her life, "What a truly attractive, clever man."

They made their way back to the apartment at around 6.30pm, and when they stopped outside her door she said, "Gaston will get you a cab. What time's your flight?"

"'Bout eight."

"Will there be anything else, Superintendent?" she asked with a grin.

"I'm afraid not," he said. "Except just one thing ... I wonder if I might invite you out to dinner tonight? It's a bit forward, I know. But I haven't got anything much happening this evening!"

"What about the flight?"

"There's dozens of them to London."

"Then I would love to accept your invitation. And by the way, does this mean I can break all known protocol and call you Charles."

'Well, that would be stretching things a bit …" he laughed. "But since we're both on foreign soil, I suppose it would be okay … just so long as you're alright with Sophia."

"Come in, Charles," she said with a flourish of her front door. "Why don't you sit there and get us a reservation somewhere. If you don't know anywhere, I'll do it when I come out of the bathroom."

"Leave it to me, Sophia. I'm not nearly as helpless as I look."

And as she left the room, she whispered, "Christ! Dinner with one of the Big Bosses of Scotland Yard, in Paris. Wow! Things are looking up." It never remotely occurred to her how close to the wind she was sailing. Charles Barton was simply not that type of character.

But she did know a little about the structure of Scotland Yard, probably thanks to many years of Uncle Rudy skirting skilfully close to the law. She knew that the Yard had hundreds of ambitious young policemen scheming their way upward. At the top, on the roof, as it were, was the small group of senior detectives—and Detective Chief Inspectors. Above them were the very few Detective Superintendents. And highest of these was Detective Chief Superintendent—the title Charles Barton had skipped right over as he introduced himself.

As far as Sophia knew there were only two beings higher than that, the Commissioner himself, and above that, only God, who like Prime Ministers never wore a uniform. And on this evening, she, Sophia Morosova, was out to dinner with a BIG Boss, a man who answered only to the Gods of the Yard. Except, she was certain, he *was* one of the Gods of the Yard.

"Christ!" said Sophia for the second time in as many minutes.

Charles booked them a table at well-known restaurant a few blocks away off *Rue des Beaux Arts.* It was unimaginatively named, *"Le Bistro,"* along with about four thousand other *"Le Bistros"* in Paris. Except this one had been here for about 150 years, probably the height of trendiness in 1870 when it first opened in the time of French Emperor Napoleon III.

It had also been run by one family, and contained a superb wine cellar, a large part of which had been cemented up behind a false wall during those unhappy WWII years when Hitler's thugs had decided to help themselves to anything they liked. The DeFarges family of Normandy kept *Le Bistro* going, down all the years, and still it was hard to reserve a table. It was not overly expensive, it was the ambiance. The restaurant was one of those City hotspots, a hangout for actors, artists and writers. Exactly as *Elaine's* was on New York's Upper East Side for decades until her death in 2011.

They both had a rarefied list of regulars, Jacqueline Onassis, Woody Allen, Norman Mailer and George Steinbrenner at *Elaine's*, an equally select group at Le Bistro that no one ever names on pain of banishment! Sophia had never been there, and was truly amazed when they walked up to its front door, with its famous hand-painted columns, and went straight in.

Her lower jaw actually dropped, when the *Maître d'* came straight up to them, bowed, and said, "Welcome back, Charles, it's been too long. How's Mama? And introduce me to this beautiful lady!"

He dealt with the preliminaries, assured the famous restaurateur that Mama was still as scathingly amusing as ever, and Monsieur DeFarges vividly recalled the famous occasion in this very room when she had described the imperious General de Gaulle as looking like a "lovesick bloodhound"—right in front of a couple of ministers from the Elysee Palace.

Still laughing, he led Charles and Sophia to a small round table in a hidden alcove in this slightly darkened but still beautiful room. The pressed table-cloths were immaculate. And the large 19th century portraits, softly lit, had been there since the place opened, and were now almost certainly worth more than the property itself, especially as one of them was painted by Edgar Degas.

Sophia was slightly overwhelmed by all this, but in truth was absolutely fascinated by the this apparently high-society sleuth who came here thinking she might have murdered someone … perish the thought!

Charles dealt with the wine, and suggested the summer truffle salad to start, then attack whatever she felt like. If you'd like fish, the *sole meuniere* is always great, the veal chop would feed a battle-trained division of the French Foreign Legion, and the *lapin en peluche*—baked rabbit with *foie gras* is wonderful, my mum's favourite.

"I'd love the *sole meuniere,"* said Sophia. "What about you?"

"Veal chop for me, I might be on stale croissants for the rest of the week!"

The food was delicious, the wine exemplary, and the conversation as interesting as Sophia could remember. She started off asking Charles where he lived, and he told her, with stupendous understatement. he had a little place in West London. Her mind raced to a basement flat in Fulham, or the wrong end of

King's Road, where most of her pals lived. It took her 20 minutes to prise out of him that he lived in the family's small mansion in South Audley Street, a couple of hundred yards from the US Embassy, same distance from two Royal Parks, and 300-yards from the garden wall of Buck House itself.

"And who exactly is this grand lady who cleverly gave birth to you … how many years ago?"

"Thirty eight, plus three months and a couple of weeks. And the lady is the daughter of a tribe of claymore-swishing Scottish madmen, who these days in the absence of the English, shoot mainly grouse. A couple of them think they should be Kings of England. Charles Stuart and all that."

"You mean Bonnie Prince Charlie?"

"Yes, I do really. I think they named me after him, but I dropped the 'Bonnie Prince' after I became a detective. It might have encouraged the criminal classes."

She simply could not help laughing at him. Except that it was with him. He possessed a nearly unique blend of wry sophistication, worldly know-how, and just enough youthful carelessness to be probably the most attractive man she'd ever been out with. Of course this was from very small field of runners. Zero, actually.

Charles Barton represented the first date she'd ever been on. She was terrified of men, all men, as skittish as a high-strung thoroughbred filly out on the gallops for the first time. She was not however in any way afraid of Charles. Which might yet rank as one of her most diabolical mistakes.

She weighed up the evening. He'd told her so much, stories from deep inside famous murder trials, some of which he'd prosecuted. He told her about the night he crashed a four-by-two wooden strut into the skull of a gangster he'd thought might shoot him. And how the judge thought Old Etonians simply did not behave like that. "I wanted to tell him it's a bit different when you're staring down the barrel of a gun, specially one held by a little bastard like this."

"Did he recover?"

"The Judge?"

"No! The gangster."

"Hope not. Otherwise I might have to hit him again."

This was the most fun she'd ever had. And, of course, in return she'd told him about herself. Nothing about Sasha; nothing about her step-father; a bit about her mother's nervous breakdown, but not the cause of it. A lot about St

Margaret's, and Cambridge University; nothing about her three-year sexual ordeals; and as little as possible about lovely Uncle Rudy. The word, assassin, was kept strictly under wraps.

As they stepped out into the Paris night, she automatically slipped her arm through his, and they strolled back to her apartment still chatting companionably. On the top-floor, when they reached her front door, she had no time to thank him, because he said, "Sophia, that was as nice an evening as I've had for many years. And I thank you."

At which point he kissed her lightly on the cheek, and said, "I have to go— there's a midnight flight to London, Air Krakatoa, I think. It's their only plane!"

She wanted to laugh, but suddenly he was gone, down the stairs, never even asked for her phone number. She felt disappointed by that, but then, he already had it, courtesy of Uncle Rudy.

She shut the door behind her, and leaned back on it, wondering why her heartbeat was so obvious. She'd never felt quite like this before. And she could not stop thinking about Charles Barton. Perhaps she never would. At least that's what it felt like, at 11pm on this Paris night. And she took herself slightly sadly to bed—afraid that in this cruellest of worlds, she might never see him again.

Chapter Eleven
A Door Opens in the House of Lords

Only one thought was in his mind. Why was the cupboard
locked? Not for these old law books, surely? If they were
that valuable, why were they in this unlocked deserted office? Carefully he
lifted them out, placed them on the writing table.

Sophia was unable to sleep. Three hours after she'd arrived home from *Le Bistro*, she was just lying there, in the dark. She heard the bells of Notre Dame's North Tower chime three times, and she turned restlessly in her bed. She was just wondering where her Detective Chief Superintendent was at this moment. Did Air Krakatoa make it to London?

And then, at five minutes past three, the telephone rang. Who the hell's that? But she answered it politely enough, certain it was a wrong number. But it wasn't. A familiar voice said cheerfully, "Good-night, Sophia. Just to let you know I'm safe!"

Since her heart-rate more or less trebled in the shock of that moment, speech became hit-or-miss, and she just blurted out, "Charles, are you in Krakatoa!" Then she corrected, "Sorry, I meant London, you know England and everything …"

The DCS laughed quietly, and told her, "Yes, I'm home. Little place in West London where a weary policeman can rest his head. But, listen, I'm sure you're tired, and I'm sorry for waking you … it's just that … well, let's face it, I must have been thinking of you—not as a suspect—something a bit different from that."

At this point, Sophia was regaining her confidence, and she said, "I do hope so. I was a bit fed up you left in such a hurry …"

"If I hadn't gone then, I'd still be there. And I have to be in my office at 6am. You actually witnessed a supreme effort of self-denial …"

"Is that what it was? I nearly put it down to lack of interest!"

They both laughed at each other, and then Charles called the conversation to a halt. "Listen," he said, "I have to go. I need to be up in a couple of hours, and we'll have another chat later in the day …"

"Okay, good night, Superintendent."

And she could hear him chuckling as he put down the phone.

She had no idea why, but after she'd put the telephone back on her bedside table, sleep came easily, a long untroubled seven hours, befitting a girl who'd just been on her first date. A bit late in life, but still a first. But when Sophia awakened once more to the sound of Notre Dame, this time striking 10, it somehow heralded a new and stark reality in her life.

Today was Tuesday. Tomorrow would be very busy, mostly on the phone to Rudy. Last minute briefing. And on Thursday she must take a flight to the Far East. Because her own life seemed to have taken on new meaning since yesterday afternoon, she now gave deep consideration to calling the whole operation off. Just to let it go, let the past rest. But, in her heart she knew this was impossible.

Her mission was carved in pure marble, and without its accomplishment, her life, she knew, would be meaningless. Sasha was counting on her. And her little sister had tolerated quite sufficient disappointments—and she, Sophia, had vowed to put them right.

How could she possibly live with the knowledge that she had deliberately walked away from all that she knew had been ordained for her? Her promise. Her word. Her blood bond with her sister. And one thing she knew beyond all doubt, and she whispered softly, "I would rather lose my own life trying, than let down my mother and Sasha. Rudy would do it all for me. But I cannot let that happen. Some things you have to do yourself."

*****

Sophia Morosova climbed out of a cab at Charles de Gaulle airport and presented her Canadian passport to the desk official at Cathay Pacific's business class check-in section.

"Thank you, Miss Cerdan," said the uniformed girl. "Our Hong Kong flight is on time. We'll announce it in the lounge, and you'll be escorted to the aircraft."

Sophia headed towards Cathay Pacific's complimentary *café au lait* which had made the airline such a favourite with business travellers. She took a delicious looking French pastry while she was about it, and sat down in a soft, comfortable chair with a couple of very specific magazines she had brought from home.

One was strictly fashion, and one was more attuned to high society in the Far East, a kind of glossy version of *Crazy-Rich Asians.* Both contained an important detailed article on the life of one of the richest men in Hong Kong. Big racehorse owner. Probably genius.

"Probably rapist," muttered Sophia.

*****

She slept much of the way on the 12-hour journey across the world, and she awakened to the bright light of Hong Kong as the aircraft stretched out its landing wheels for Chek lap Kok airport on this Friday afternoon. She hoped Uncle Rudy had not let her down. If he had it would be another first.

Slipping through the light immigration checks on her Canadian passport, and then Hong Kong customs, 'Miss Cerdan' walked out onto the main concourse carrying just her shoulder bag. She reached the sidewalk, and looked around for the black SUV Rudy had sworn would be there. Half-a-minute later it pulled up right next to her, with the passenger side window down. Inside was a smiling chauffeur. "Very on time arrival," he said. "Hop in quick. Russian Big Boss waiting. He's not good at that."

Sophia climbed aboard, and in the back seat was a small, stiff carrier bag from an upmarket London store. "For you," shouted the chauffeur. "Don't open 'til we reach offices of Consulate General."

And with that, he stamped on the gas, and so far as Sophia could tell, would never slow down 'til he reached one of the greatest tower blocks in this City of wall-to-wall skyscrapers. Sophia's guide book told her there were 8,500 of them, 1,400 of them over 330-feet high, 350 of them over 500-feet. One of them 108 stories, 1,600-feet straight up, the flashing light on its roof presumably to warn any passing space shuttle.

Sophia's driver sped past Disneyland, scooted under a major freeway, found Route 1, and floored it, all the way down to Hong Kong Island. It took him 42 minutes—Hamilton and Vettel might have made it in an hour. They pulled into the gigantic *Sun Hung Kai Centre*, on Harbour Road, and the chauffeur helped her out, next to the main entrance.

"You get in there, please," he told her sternly. "Go to 21st floor—Protocol Division, find Big Boss. Hurry up, Boss real bad at waiting."

She promised to do her best and proceeded into the elevator to keep her appointment with the Russian Consul General. She was on safe ground here. Uncle Rudy had once saved his life in the backstreets of Bucharest.

*****

Back in London, Detective Chief Superintendent Charles Barton was in his office, high up in the New Scotland Yard Building. He was thinking of Sophia, but did not know where she was. He knew she was away for a few days, but given the enormous pluses and minuses of the world's time zones, he didn't really know if it was breakfast time or midnight, wherever she might be.

He'd spent the last few days investigating, quizzing the task force of police officers in Sussex, pondering, checking and examining every shred of evidence involved with the murder of Lord Fontridge. That last part took very little time, since there wasn't any evidence. Save for that bone-handled dagger jutting out of his heart. And the still-mysterious riddle of whether Sophia and her pearl earrings had actually shown up for the second-half of *Rigoletto*. And it was her word against … well … who knows? No one had ever said she didn't.

And the fact that Charles thought she was wonderful did not really lessen the chances of her lying to him. He couldn't believe she would. But she might. He was still enough of a cop to accept that.

No, nothing could be taken for granted. And he still believed that the solution to this murder rested with Lord Fontridge himself. Somewhere there was a secret, somewhere there was something going on, something that no one knew about. There always was. The family was saying nothing. No member of the public had one thing to say. It was all too tightly held.

Tonight, however, that might change. Charles Barton was going to take a look around the House of Lords. His high Scotland Yard credentials would probably keep him safe, but he did not much want to be questioned by their Lordships' night security officers. He'd better tread very lightly.

Ten o'clock was his start-time, late enough on Friday night for the place to be largely cleared out for the weekend. Late enough for the offices to be deserted. He knew where Lord Fontridge worked when he was there. Scotland Yard had interior diagrams of every important building in London, including Buckingham

Palace, the Foreign Office and the US Embassy in Grosvenor Square. Charles had already discovered precisely where the Sussex Law Lord had his own office, as a member of the Privy Council. Most Peers had to share.

Charles would require no driver tonight. He wanted nothing which might be remembered by anyone, he wanted no sign of activity, particularly suspicion of a slightly dodgy entry into the inner sanctum reserved for Great Britain's Lords and Masters.

He left his office, walked down the short corridor and took the elevator to the ground floor. The place was busier than most office blocks at this time of night, but demonstrably quieter than usual. Friday nights at Scotland Yard, like most places, exuded a special calm after the air of permanent urgency which is present all day in a top Police HQ.

His car was waiting outside the door, a black unmarked SUV, and he drove away slowly, out through the heavily-guarded official Yard entrance, through the barrier, and onto the embankment. He turned right at Big Ben and slipped along Parliament Square, until he reached the entrance to Old Palace Yard, the Peers' entrance, on the southern section of the west façade.

He hoped to high heaven his hand-drawn map was an accurate guide to the vast 170-year-old Gothic Palace with its 1,100 rooms and 100 staircases, which led up, down and sideways. "Wouldn't be the biggest test in the world to get absolutely lost in here," he muttered.

Along to the south he could see the beautifully-lit Victoria Tower where the old Queen had her special entrance, befitting a monarch of perhaps the world's greatest-ever Empire. The Royal way-in was set with suitable grandeur at the base of what was then the tallest and largest stone square tower in the world, 325ft high.

It's still the tallest Tower in the Palace of Westminster, and would be an outstanding edifice in any capital city in the world, except perhaps downtown Hong Kong, where it would probably be used as a rabbit hutch. Anyway, Charles hung a left before he reached the Tower, and pulled up at the Palace Yard entrance at the signal of the police officer on guard duty at the gate.

"Oh, good evening, sir," he said. "Staying long?"

"Hello, David," replied the DCS, who prided himself on knowing the names of as many officers as possible. "No, not long, Anywhere I can park?"

"Yessir, stick it over there," he replied, pointing to an empty space. "I'll keep a watch on it. I'm here 'til midnight."

"I won't be that long," he replied, and drove over to the Peers' Carriage Porch, and slipped into the spot PC David had indicated.

Charles walked through the door and was immediately stopped by another policeman, and recognised equally quickly. "Oh, hello, sir," he said. "Need any help, this place is like a bloody maze."

"No thanks," he said. "Just going to my usual. Won't be long."

"Yessir," he said. "Anything you need, just shout. We're just about emptied out."

"Thanks, constable," said Charles, evenly, and he headed for the most brightly-lit corridor leading off the main hall, resolving to climb swiftly up the first staircase he saw. The office of the late Lord Fontridge was on the third floor. And he knew the number thanks to the Yard's often-improved diagrams. God alone knew how long he would be walking around up there.

The third-floor corridor was lined in oak panelling, and bookshelves full of ancient leather-bound volumes behind glass. The light was gloomy, there was no one around, and the atmosphere among these musty, high-vaulted ceilings was spooky. The place could have been purpose built for a Gothic horror story. Charles would not have been unduly shocked if Bram Stoker had glided around the corner looking for Dracula's coffin.

He organised his bearings, lined up the door numbers and set off. It actually took him only five minutes, and he was outside the Law Lord's office, without encountering Bram even once. Actually he didn't encounter anyone. No staff. No Security. No Peers, who plainly thought their week's work was over.

Still, at three-hundred quid a day, the work of a Peer of the Realm has to end sometime, especially on a Friday. That was the final thought of the DCS as he approached the Fontridge workplace. In his hand he held a small set of master-keys which everyone knew would open anything, very smoothly. Charles was quite disappointed when he discovered the door was not locked, and he could walk straight in.

He pulled on his tight-fitting, thin, leather gloves, and shut the door behind him. He locked it with his master key, and fished out his tiny flashlight to check the lie of the land. He did not think he should switch on the main lights, which might trigger an alarm. Instead he saw a desk-light on His Lordship's writing table, and elected to light the whole room from that; dimly, but not too bad.

He searched like the expert he was. Desk drawers were not locked, and there were no files of any importance in them. He guessed the Law Lord kept his critical documents somewhere in the Inner Temple or wherever he made his HQ. This was a thoroughly simple, but fruitless examination of the office of a busy Appeal Court Judge. However, around the room were several oak-panelled cupboard doors, and although he had little hope of striking hidden treasure, Charles was still, at heart, a cop.

And he tackled them methodically going from door to door, checking each cupboard, most of which were empty. The first three contained nothing. Number four was locked, and five to eight contained a few files of old law court trials; none of it interesting. Charles decided to check the locked-door cupboard, and apologised to himself for wasting time and effort.

He used the smallest of his master keys to tackle it, and needed his flashlight to see into the interiors. More disappointment. There were just three antique volumes, probably valuable. One of them was entitled, *A Century of Successful Appeals 1800-1900*. Another was called, *English Law Challenged. 1821-1910.* The last one was a treatise on the history of a life-sentence.

But, there was only one thought in his mind. Why was the cupboard locked? Not for these old law books, surely? If they were that valuable, what were they doing in this unlocked, deserted office? Carefully, he lifted them out and placed them on the writing table.

Then he returned to the formerly locked cupboard and began a diligent search of the empty space. He checked the three interior walls, pressed them, tapped them, applied pressure. Nothing; rock-solid construction, same with the ceiling to the cupboard. Then he tried the floor, placed his flat palm downwards and alternated the pressure. There was an unmistakable looseness to the wood.

Not only did it give to the touch at the front, it actually rattled, very softly, but very definitely. And there was an unusual seam on both sides. He pressed against the front of the 'floor' where the door shut, and lifted. It rose like a lid, and he felt inside, but there was nothing; just a flat surface to a false-bottom compartment. But then he noticed something. That false bottom was sleek and cold, not like any of the wood.

He flashed his tiny light beam. This was not the floor of the secret compartment. It was the unmistakable lid of a slim metallic laptop computer; hidden from the world. Hidden from everyone, except the late Freddie Fontridge. Charles lifted it out and placed it on the writing table. Then he carefully put the cupboard back in order, closed it, and locked it with the master key.

There was a computer charger wire on the table, running from an electric outlet in the wall. Charles could see no other computer in the room. And his search had been sufficiently thorough to eliminate the possibility of one. The charger was for this hidden link to cyber space. Charles scooped it up, slipped it into the tailored large inside pocket of his Burberry raincoat and left, making certain not to lock the door.

It actually took him longer to get out than to get in. A couple of wrong turns had put him into the maze, as specified by the constable. Charles's thoughts were, as so often, irreverent … if I don't get this right in a minute I'll have to take a nap on the bloody woolsack! Not many people have referred to the sanctified Seat of the Lord Speaker that casually. Still, grandson of a Scottish Duke … what d'you expect?

The DCS hit the next down-staircase and found himself right around the corner from the main door. He wished the duty policeman good-night, reached his car and headed back to the Yard, It was almost 12.30am, the smallest hours of Saturday morning.

On the other side of the world Sophia Morosova was preparing to go to Sha Tin Races, as the escort to Uncle Rudi's old secret police buddy, the Russian Consul General. He planned to stay to watch the Kowloon Gold Cup, and then leave her to do her best inside the main lounge of the Hong Kong Jockey Club. Quite frankly, he didn't like her chances much. But she seemed confident enough.

*****

The Russian bureau chief was much like Rudy himself, but bigger, a great bear of a man with twinkly eyes and a physique like King Kong. He had the same combination of good humour and hidden steel that made Rudolf Masow such an interesting, and probably successful, 'diplomat.' Which was a bit like calling James Bond a bureaucrat.

His name was Ivan Andropov, like Rudy, well into his sixties, and resident of a tower block near the Hong Kong waterfront which was otherwise occupied by Russian executives, bankers and corporations. He and his wife Martina occupied a huge apartment, attended by a maid and a butler, who doubled as a chauffeur. When he'd told Sophia, 'boss not good at waiting,' he knew of what he spoke.

The Russian Consul-General's Hong Kong office was an enormous profit centre, not only for the daily hundreds of visa applications and payments, but for all manner of transactions which went through this quasi-Embassy situated in the most highly commercial couple of square miles on planet earth.

Ivan Andropov knew more about money than almost any member of the Russian Government. His influence in the Russian business community was without equal, which made him something close to Emperor status in Hong Kong. He was a social giant, as well as a regular giant. His big, highly polished shoes could walk through any doorway in the brittle A-List society of this former outpost of Great Britain's Empire. He was King Kong in Hong Kong.

Ivan was a good and loyal member of the Communist Party, a son and grandson of devoted followers of the Bolshevik creed. His grand-father, another giant former potato farmer, had fought hand-to-hand in the streets of Saint Petersburg in the Revolution of 1917, on behalf of the people. The Andropovs were a beloved family in the Kremlin. Ivan could stay in the money-churning lap of luxury, which was Hong Kong, for all the days of his life, should he so wish.

Sophia was staying with Mr and Mrs Andropov that Friday night, and the plan was for the Consul General to take her to Sha Tin the following afternoon, and have her ensconced in probably the holiest room in the Far East—that's the Hong Kong Jockey Club, founded 1884, and granted Royal Charter 60 years ago by Her Majesty Queen Elizabeth II.

Alas, the beloved Royal Hong Kong Jockey Club is no more. The Chinese removed that reminder of Empirical glories past in 1996, by striking the word out of the title in their avowed proletarian way, and reducing it to HK Jockey Club, which sounded to Lady Penelope's ear, 'like a betting shop in South London.'

Nonetheless, the locals struggled gamely to preserve overtures of Royal Ascot, rather than the Great Hall of the People, making membership by nomination and election only. The Club itself was fairly expert at that, having banned any Chinese members until well into the 20th century. It was to this prickly gathering that the social colossus of Hong Kong escorted his buddy Rudolf's very beautiful niece on the day of the Kowloon Gold Cup. 'Til the day he died Ivan would never reveal the true name, and certainly not the mission, of the lady who accompanied him.

In fact, he was rather more careful than she was. And before they even left home, he remembered her passport; the Canadian one which was about to become lethal, because it bore her name, the name she had used entering Hong Kong; the name by which Takahashi would know her. "Better give me that passport," he had said. And she handed it over, meekly.

"Will I need it again?" she asked.

"Never," replied Ivan. "I'll have it destroyed. Which is of course another of the enormous talents of the Russian foreign network. Getting rid of evidence. We're actually world ranked at it, probably number one." And he laughed loudly at the supreme drollness of his remark.

When they arrived at Sha Tin, he introduced her as Miss Louise Cerdan of Toronto, whose family had raced thoroughbreds at Woodbine Racecourse for many years. No one questioned Ivan Andropov about anything, and Sophia was greeted with kindness and civility by everyone she met. Her expensive wig looked wonderful, and her discreet black-tinted sunglasses shielded the exact contours of her face.

It was not until the race before the Kowloon Cup that she spotted Yunto Takahashi, sitting with the same two men he'd been with at Epsom, hatless now, the scar visible to anyone. Again Sophia had to look away, just to feel slightly less appalled.

They were sitting a few tables away, and the discussion everywhere was about his favourite for the race, Fighter's Dream, who would probably go off at odds of around 5-2. It seemed people were wishing Yunto well, in the wake of Double Domo's narrow defeat at Epsom. Personally, Sophia hoped the damn thing would come last, but that would not be the drift of her conversation when the correct moment presented itself.

She kept a careful eye him throughout the preliminaries, but lost sight of him during the race itself. Once more Yunto came face to face with defeat, Fighter's Dream finishing fast, passing horses in the straight but going down by a half-length and a head. Sophia nearly felt sorry for him, but not quite, even though Yunto's horse was probably best. But what's the loss of another four million to a man as rich as Mr Takahashi?

After the presentation of the trophies, Ivan Andropov left and told her the car would be awaiting her in the members' car-park. If she did come home for dinner, that would be fine, if not, he hoped to see her on her next trip. They shook hands formally and Ivan was gone.

The Takahashi team was seated back at their table where, sundry HKJC members came to offer condolences to one of the losing owners. Sophia was talking to friends of Ivan's, who knew a lot about horse racing, and she made a few mental notes while still watching Yunto.

There was, however, one mental note, she was not able to log—and that was a nearly unknown fact that, but for Yunto, none of this would have happened to her. But for the Japanese tycoon, there would have been no forcing of her and Sasha into prostitution, no schoolgirl sex-rings centred around the house in Maida Vale; and, above all, Sasha would still be alive.

One of the lesser-known of Japan's post-WWII accomplishments was the full commercialisation of sex with teenagers. Older Japanese men have often had a penchant for slim and innocent young girls still attending school. And, with the government standing indecisively in the background, the industry bloomed in Tokyo, in particular in the Akihabara district.

Schoolgirl prostitution is known there as Enjo Kosei; the business model for the sexual exploitation of teenage girls in Japan is Joshi Kosai, that's JK to aficionados like Yunto Takahashi. Even today, long after formal government disapproval, there are at least three 'Maid Cafes,' in Akihabara, offering prostitution with high-school girls.

One of the best known is named, *That's Amore*, and is generally considered the flag-bearer for this ancient, but somehow very modern example of Japanese culture. Outside the premises are usually found provocatively dressed, very slim young girls in very short skirts. When they attract men they often retreat to another Japanese cultural bedrock, the Love Hotel.

This strong demand for teenage sex has spread to southeast Asia and Mongolia. But Tokyo is its home, and the Cafes explain themselves quite delicately, stressing 'our adorable culture,' and its 'childlike charms,' its 'innocent cuteness,' the 'weak but pure inexperience of these young girls.'

And one night, sharing a drink with the proprietor at *Ode to Joy* in Moscow, Yunto Takahashi explained to Boris Morosov the joys of teenage-prostitution— not, repeat not, paedophilia involving children, but with girls aged over 15, who, when made up would pass for a 20-year-old. "There are men all over Tokyo," said Yunto, "Married of course to much older wives, who would pay anything for a night with a 15 or 16-year-old. I suppose I am one of them. There are Maid Cafes earning million yen a month!"

Now Boris was not sure how many dollars this was, but it sounded pretty good to him, and he already knew the oligarch client-base in Moscow's high-priced sex industry was shrinking. And he already understood the inevitable move to London was not so far away. And he resolved to put some kind of a teenage sex operation into action as soon as he settled into the English capital. Naturally, he never told one single soul about this. Especially his wife.

Yunto Takahashi was one of Boris's finest clients. Money and its expenditure did not figure in his calculations. He was just too rich. And by his own admission he just lived for sex with 15- and 16-year-olds—$25,000 a time. What's that between friends? Boris Morosov resolved to do whatever it took to keep the sexually-driven Japanese plutocrat high on his client list.

Which was, more or less, why he undertook the drastic step of selling the daughters of his own wife for prostitution—working on the theory that if the girls were physically developed enough, they were certainly old enough, and, anyway, they might even grow to like it … just as long as Veroniya never finds out.

And that was precisely why Boris's step-daughter Sophia found herself in the Hong Kong Jockey Club, planning the murder of Yunto Takahashi, a sensational crime which would rock the world's stock markets, and threaten Hong Kong's financial survival.

Right now there was a large crowd around Yunto Takashashi, but as the time for the next race approached it began to thin out, and Sophia stood up and approached his table.

He was certainly the type of man who would have noticed her anyway, and he stood up as she approached and offered his hand. "Good afternoon," he said, "I am afraid you find me in my second defeat of the week." You could tell he was not used to it, and Sophia gave him a smile of sympathy, and said quietly, "Yes. I noticed. I saw Double Domo lose at Epsom. Matter of fact I backed him!"

"Oh, I'm really sorry," he said. "My jockey got that race wrong, he was outwitted by Dettori. And I have to admit I'm disappointed by today."

"I noticed that Fighter's Dream likes to come from behind with his best work at the end," said Sophia, drawing on knowledge that was all of two minutes old. "Sha Tin's not easy for that type of horse."

"Quite right," said Yunto, "The straight's not much more than a quarter-mile long. Hard to get going for a late runner … won't you sit down for a few minutes?"

Sophia sat, smiled and flirted as best she could, trying to reconcile sex with hatred, which was about as easy as giving away seven lengths in a quarter-mile home straight. Like Fighter's Dream today.

She could see Takahashi assessing her slender figure, a lot more like Audrey Hepburn than Jennifer Lopez. Still, since he prefers 15-year-olds, she decided, that was unsurprising. But the race meeting was moving on and it was the Japanese-born finance tycoon who made the first move. "Will your escort be coming back for you?" he said.

"No. I'm afraid I made it clear to him that I am not available for what he wanted. No matter the price."

Yunto smiled, "You mean there is a price?"

"Not for a great bruiser like him. I prefer my lovers sleek, more manageable. He's just not attractive to me."

"Ah, but give me the key ingredient, the price or the person?"

"Oh, the person, always. The price is not really relevant. I'm not tempted by the money, but since I like to travel, there's not much time for proper love. And even a lady of my obvious standards has to earn a living!"

Yunto Takahashi was almost beside himself with excitement, and the vision of a night of pure sex with this Canadian goddess, stood before him. "What price did you reject from the big man?"

"Well, since you mention it, his final offer, before departure was in the area of five thousand America dollars."

"Oh," said Yunto, suddenly the shrewd businessman. "I'd very gladly match that."

"Aha," she replied, "But I would not have slept with him for one hundred thousand dollars. I told you, it depends almost entirely on the person. I treat the whole transaction as if I'm on a date! That has to be established before I even discuss finance."

"I see," said Yunto. "Would you like a glass of champagne?"

"How kind of you. We might even be approaching the start line!"

Yunto Takahashi was in love. Or something like it. He would in truth have paid anything for the opportunity to love this Canadian beauty for however long she allowed it. He poured her a glass, topped up his own, and asked her a few personal questions, which she duly lied through her teeth to answer.

Finally, he asked her, "Miss Cerdan, your very presence in this room means you are a person of a certain class. Would you then do me the honour of dining with me tonight at my apartment, a penthouse which has one of the highest and most beautiful views in Hong Kong? I should like to present you with a check for $100,000 American dollars as a gift, and a mark of my personal esteem."

"Why, Mr Takahashi, I should be delighted."

Chapter Twelve
A Black Op in the Hot-Tub

He bellowed in impeccable Cantonese, "We've got a fucking maniac loose on this island. I don't care if we shut the place down for a week… this murderer cannot get away—this is total lock-down. Road, rail, and sea. Now get out and catch this bastard!"

It was six miles from Ivan and Martina's apartment to Repulse Bay, one of the most expensive waterfront residential communities in Hong Kong, south of the main business district. Yunto Takahashi lived on the top floor of the most expensive tower of them all, Buckingham Heights. Sophia had just spent the last hour packing her shoulder bag in preparation.

The three gifts from Uncle Rudolf were safely put away: one small transparent package containing white powder, which Rudy said was both tasteless, and fireproof in the noble art of knocking someone unconscious inside three minutes, and then keeping them comatose for at least a half-hour.

The second item was typical Uncle Rudy, ruthless to its core, but with just a touch of romanticism—it was a Japanese dagger for an evil Japanese victim. And not just any old dagger. This was a 9-inch long Japanese *Tanto* blade, the slightly curved weapon-of-choice for the nation's feared, disciplined and skilled loyalists—the Samurai warriors who had served the clans of Japanese nobility for hundreds of years … the *Minamoto* and the *Taira* Clans, all direct descendants of the Imperial House of Japan.

The Spirit of the Samurai lives on in Japan, and Sophia fervently hoped the deadly *Tanto* blade she now carried would bring her a warrior's victory, not so long from now.

The Samurai devotion to the great Lords of Japan gave them power even over the Emperor. The Code of Honour which bound them together was based on Discipline and Morality—*Bushido*, they called it. Or, "The Way of the Warrior." When the Samurai came forward, weapons drawn, they were universally regarded as unstoppable.

Sophia believed she was personally entitled to a touch of *Bushido,* with its unwritten protection. "I wasn't born to it," she told herself. "But I am closer to a Samurai right now than any other St Margaret's Old Girl has ever been. And my target will find that out … Just holding this dagger … my God … I can feel the Samurai. This is a holy mission. And I am moral. The Spirit of the Warrior lives in me tonight."

Uncle Rudolf's third piece of equipment was Russia's latest model A26 Kalashnikov stun gun, a state-of-the-art piece the size of a small television remote, a shocker of electronic power when unleashed on an attacker. Like most modern research projects the objective was to make it small, smaller, smallest. There have been a lot of high-pressure tasers, carried mostly by police forces in lawless countries. But so far they have been as large, though not quite as heavy, as service revolvers.

This new Russian number, however, was a high-tech tiger of the art form, a high voltage stun-gun, not much bigger than a cigarette pack, and it will pump out 50 million volts in one brain-numbing burst. It won't kill—but its opening 8-milliamp charge will knock anyone flat on his back, and keep him there for several minutes. It has a reciprocating inner-trigger which can slam another bolt of electricity into any victim who looks like he might get up.

In Rudolf Masow's opinion this was only for situations which might be described as dire. He'd told Sophia it would be in the package he'd left for her, for emergency use only … slip it in your jacket pocket, and don't touch it unless your life is threatened, only then do you aim and fire.

Well, here it was, in her jacket; her fail-safe equipment. And here she was on her way to Repulse Bay, where the anxious Yunto Takahashi was awaiting her, just as the evening sun was preparing to set.

The six-mile journey passed quickly, and Ivan's chauffeur dropped her right outside the door. Before she left, he told her, "I'll be right here, parked over in the parking lot. As you come out of that door, I'll flash my headlights once. Then we're gone. We move quick, otherwise Russian boss have heart attack."

Sophia, the modern day Samurai, walked into the main lobby, presented herself at the desk and gave her name, observing the single security camera making its timely sweeps, like a miniature search-light from Stalag-17. But Sophia spotted it, and knew the tried and tested avoidance procedures. A glance to her left as she spoke to the guard, and the camera missed her.

"Okay, ma'am, you're expected, penthouse floor." She exited the elevator at the very top of the building and stepped out into a hallway where there were two security guards, one in uniform, one not.

"Good evening," said the senior guard. "I am afraid I must ask you to leave that shoulder bag right here. Visitors not allowed to take any bag which could conceal anything into the apartments."

"I cannot leave the bag here, it has my passport, money and private documents." said Sophia. "Please call Mr Takahashi and tell him I'm leaving."

"No need, madam. We have system." And he pointed to a bank of safe deposit boxes. "We store bag in there, lock it and give you the only electronic key. You aim that at door and it locks, with a brand new code every time. Only person in this world can open that door is you. We don't even know the code. No one knows. Just you."

Sophia smiled. "Okay," she said, handing over the bag. "Now you place it inside, and I lock it."

"Excellent," said the guard. "Never had any problem. Bag right there when you come back. And the only person who can get it is you! Good system, right?"

"Good system," agreed Sophia. But inside she was devastated. She was a Samurai warrior stripped of her weapon. She may as well leave and try again, some other day. This had become a waste of time. But she walked along to Yunto's front door just the same, and tapped on it lightly.

He answered it almost immediately and she was surprised to see him dressed in a deep purple velvet robe, and wearing light slippers with some kind of a gold crest woven into the dark leather. Sophia thought it might be the Society of International Rapists, but decided not to check.

He said, "Welcome, Miss Cerdan, I am delighted to see you." And then before she had a moment, even to reply, he walked over to a table and picked up an envelope. "I thought it best to get the transaction out of the way," he smiled. "This contains the cheque for $100,000 US dollars I promised. You may open it if you wish. But that's not necessary. It's drawn on an American bank with branches in Canada, Europe, wherever."

"Oh, thank you very much," said Sophia, placing it in her jacket pocket. "I won't open it. I know a gentleman when I see one."

Yunto gave her a quick bow—a Japanese *domo*—and said, "Let's go outside and I'll show you the view."

But as soon as they stepped onto the roof garden, Sophia noticed a large hot-tub, steaming in the light evening air, and instantly guessed the view he was planning to offer her, as if she hadn't seen sufficient of that for one lifetime. Words could scarcely describe the depth of sheer loathing she had reserved for this conceited little billionaire for seven years now. Since Sasha died … and Mama left.

He was right about the other view however. It was truly stunning, the harbour and the islands as far south as it was possible to see. And the momentous skyline of Hong Kong to the north. "Magnificent," she said, "No other word. Thank you for inviting me."

Yunto smiled and fired her another *domo,* before his acute sexual anxiety clashed with the remnants of his patience, and he almost blurted out, "Miss Cerdan. I have been anticipating this for very many hours. And now that we are on a proper business footing, I would like to suggest we take a very leisurely dip in the hot tub. It's a very relaxing way to start what I hope will be a lasting friendship."

And in that moment Sophia saw her chance. It would be a Black Operation, the action of a Samurai warrior. Take your pick. But this was her moment. And in her mind she heard the calm voice of Uncle Rudy … *Let's go Sophia … GO! GO! GO!* … Ten minutes ago, she'd just about abandoned all hope of completing her mission this evening, but not anymore. She glanced around, spotted a small outside bar behind two low Japanese maple trees, looked back at the tub, and made a very bold decision. "Perfect," she said, "Let's jump in the tub."

She hesitated for a single moment, and then suggested, "I really would like a drink, sir. You know, the English and colonial habit of a gin-and-tonic before dinner. We even did that in Canada. If you don't mind, I could pour one for myself over there—but I won't have one if you won't."

Yunto Takahashi beamed widely. "Of course," he said, "I can have them sent to us, or we can pour our own."

"I'll do it," she said. "You hop in the tub and I'll make the drinks."

The Japanese tycoon, slipped off his robe, and his excitement was obvious. Sophia looked away, wishing no further reminders of the worst day of her life. She walked to the bar, filled two long glasses with ice, and poured from a bottle of expensive Bombay Gin. She found the tonic water and a small dish of cut limes and mixed the drinks with a tall, glass stick. Then she fished into her pocket, found Rudy's package, ripped it open and tipped the contents into Yunto's glass, the one on the left, the one she would pick up with her left hand.

When she arrived tub-side, Takahashi was relaxed, lying back in the bubbling hot water. "Your gin and tonic, sir," she said, handing him the glass, smiling.

"Thank you, my dear," he said, and he raised his glass and clinked it against hers. "To health and happiness," he toasted, elegantly, hardly believing his luck as Sophia sipped her drink and then began taking off her clothes. He was transfixed by her beauty, watching as she stripped down to her underwear, and taking alternate sips of his drink—one for each garment. At least that's how it worked out, as Yunto, his imagination aflame, tried to stop himself rising into a too-early sexual frenzy.

Finally, Sophia Morosova stepped into the tub, facing him with her legs curled up, still sipping her drink. Yunto had gone strangely quiet, leaning back, a large smile on his face, staring at the darkening sky, instead of at her. Sophia put down her drink on the wide edge of the tub. Then she stretched out her legs, and put herself into a kneeling position.

Yunto's eyes were still open, and she moved astride him, whispering, "Yunto, you are a very beautiful man." But Yunto had gone the way of the rising sun, except his was the setting sun, and he no longer saw anything.

Sophia no longer saw the view. She only saw the tortured face of little Sasha, the horror on the face of her mother as she slammed the steel pan into the head of the man who had raped her 15-year-old daughter. She cupped Mr Takahashi's face, and then slipped her hands around his throat. She felt for the prime position of the windpipe, just as Rudy had shown her in his many lessons on how to kill people.

She tightened her grip and squeezed. She held it for 10 seconds, then lifted up his head and slammed it under the water, her thumbs pressing more and more pressure into Yunto's windpipe. Then she counted to 10 again, and lifted and slammed downwards again, cracking Yunto's skull against the tub. "That one's for Sasha, you bastard," she gritted. "And this one's for my precious mother, you unspeakable Japanese pig."

Six times she lifted and slammed downward. But the last two were irrelevant. Yunto Takahashi, his brain starved for oxygen, had died in a white powder sleep. He was stone dead, drowned, throttled, drug overdose, fractured skull. Take your pick. But Yunto had finally paid for years of sexual abuse of very young girls, all over the world. But the one that nailed him was the maiden from Maida Vale.

Sophia had followed the mantra of the KGB assassins, who normally used a garrotte for this kind of work. But if it became necessary to barehandedly throttle someone, they always took the windpipe route, not the blood vessels, both of which would kill, but the windpipe was always quicker, and more efficient.

She let the limp body slip out of her grasp, and back under the water. And now she had but one thought, "I have to get out of here. I have to get past Yunto's bodyguard and away." Even for a brand new Samurai warrior, this might not prove as easy as it sounds, and she did bear in mind that this particular warrior had somehow been disarmed by a 5ft 4inch Chinese janitor.

Without even a second glance at the deceased tycoon, she grabbed his robe and used it as a towel, then pulled on her underwear and then her dress. Her shoes were under a chair and a little difficult to slip into since her feet were still a bit wet. But she wriggled her toes into them, put on her jacket and made for the doorway, back into the apartment.

But now she was not alone, big Jim Ho, the ex-Sumo champion was sitting in a wide chair reading the racing results. He looked up as she came into the room.

"Hello, Miss," he said, "Boss ready to come inside?"

"I think he wanted to stay in the water for a little longer," said Sophia, swiftly gauging her time to the bottom of the elevator, as, probably, four minutes, depending on the speed of the deposit box, which held her shoulder bag. "He said he was feeling tired but would be ready for dinner."

"Okay, Miss," replied Jim Ho cheerfully, "I go now. Check on boss."

To Sophia this meant the huge bodyguard would know in less than one minute's time that Yunto Takahashi was dead. He would know before she even got in the elevator. Worse yet he would want to know where she was, and what she knew about a possible murder.

Sophia Morosova just said, "Oh, just one thing, Jim …" And by now she had her right-hand on the small Kalashnikov stun-gun. He turned back to face her, looking quizzically at this total stranger who had left the boss in his bathtub. Too late. Sophia coldly fired a heart-jolting 8-milliamps directly into the left side of his chest, which achieved the not inconsiderable feat of landing Big Jim flat on his back.

His 320lb bulk shuddered the entire building. At least it seemed that way to Sophia. Big Jim grunted and looked dazed, which was too much for Sophia, who let him have it again, snapping back the reciprocal trigger, and slamming another zillion volts into his body. Big Jim went down for the count. And Sophia went through the apartment door a lot quicker than Fighter's Dream had blown out of the starting gates that very afternoon.

She hurried along the corridor, and walked very casually up to the same guard and said, "May I open the box now? I'm just leaving."

"Of course, ma'am, just aim and press the button, and it will swing right open."

Which indeed it did, and she slipped the shoulder strap over her head, wished the security man good evening, and stepped into the elevator.

Downstairs, she saw the flash of headlights across the parking lot, and headed straight to the black SUV. And the chauffeur, without a word, gunned it along the coast road, heading west to Heung Yip, directly to the ancient harbour, a hectic half-medieval, half-modern fishing wharf, which, in many ways, has remained unchanged from the regime of the Hong Kong inshore pirates of the 19th century.

Sophia checked her wristwatch. She'd been out of that penthouse for a total of nine minutes. According to Uncle Rudy, Big Jim Ho could not be on his feet in less than 20 minutes, not if she zapped him twice. And the driver already had his foot to the boards. "Step on it!" she called, above the howl of the engine, as they ripped down the highway towards the restless netherworld of the old seaport of Aberdeen, where east meets even more east, and fishing deals between the sampans are shouted out, night and day.

They roared through the narrow pass of Ocean Park, hitting top speeds right along the foothills of Victoria Peak, the jutting central mountain, and the only summit on Hong Kong Island which can compete, from a level standing start, with the thousands of high-rise towers to its north, now twinkling with evening lights.

They shot over the *Ap Lei Chau* bridge to the outer reaches of the harbour, a patchwork quilt of fishing sampans scattered over the entire bay, all of them home to the mysterious *Danjia*, more commonly known as the *Tanka* Boat People, the Gypsies of the Sea. Their proud native traditions, like those of most other gypsies, are upheld rigidly, but, in truth, might not bear too much investigating.

But the *Tankas* are a lot more colourful, claiming to be the original ethnic minority of South China, driven to the sea by ruthless laws and judges. Many of them had landed, mingled and become lost in a form of civilisation. The rest pitched up in Aberdeen Harbour, perfected their history by word of mouth, and made no move to move on. They parked their red-masted sampans right in the middle of the harbour, and for hundreds of years went fishing, sold their catch to Hong Kong and the mainland.

They essentially told any Chinese authorities who enquired, "Forget it, pal. We're staying right here." And since nothing short of a couple of hundred sea-mines was going to alter this, there they stayed ... the *Tanka* Boat People.

Over time, of course, things changed. High rises were built overlooking the picturesque harbour. Office blocks were constructed. Paved roads, shops and the rest of the paraphernalia of modern life were built. They are very much still there. So are the Boat People. Right out there in the middle of the huge harbour were hundreds of sampans, and they too have changed with the times.

These days, almost everyone is fitted with a diesel boat-engine. The red sails of old China have been hauled down, but much of the original Chinese hull-shape has remained—still the old high bow, and the long curved aft deck, rubber tires hitched over the hull in preparation for mooring alongside.

Never mind half of them haven't moved for 20 years, they live on, out there in a kind of motley fleet from the Xia Dynasty which started stir-frying 1,600 years before Christ. Some of the boats are converted into excellent Chinese restaurants now, with regular western patrons. But the overall sight is one of colourful, cheerful, barely controlled chaos. And it was to this seething ocean-going bedlam, packed with totally unseaworthy Chinese watercraft, that Miss Sophia Morosova found herself rapidly heading.

They swung left after the bridge, past Cham Wan Towers, and down to the wharf. She was so thrilled at the speed her driver made, she jumped out of the car, squared up for a *double-domo*, then, in her gratitude, threw him a triple—before almost running down the gangway to which he had pointed. She was stunned by the sight of this sprawling, apparently endless, mismatch of marine engineering, some of the boats more than a century old.

But it was not the sights that most amazed her. It was the sounds of non-stop Chinese music, drifting off the boats, loud, off-key and definitely not coordinated which struck her first. It was like 10,000 brass bands playing blindfolded. A western musician simply would not have believed it.

But even more than that, it was the smells, the sizzling smells from the floating restaurants, where fresh snapper, black bream and barred soap-fish were being stir-fried, baked and grilled, blended with sauces from unwritten recipes created thousands of years ago. China, the most striving modern society on earth, remains a nation whose ancient past strides resolutely in step with the 21st century.

Right now Sophia, in a single heartbeat could have dived happily into a plate of stir-fried black bream with scallions and soy sauce, since dining with Yunto now seemed unlikely. But she was too busy running for her life, unaware that in those exact moments, big Jim Ho, was back on his feet, stumbling across the penthouse towards the roof garden door shouting for the boss, at the top of his cavernous lungs.

Sophia was running, dodging and sidestepping along the narrow walkway, and suddenly she was seized not only by her worst fears, but simultaneously by a tough-looking Sea Gypsy, in rough work clothes, and a hat like a lampshade. She tried to twist away but his grip on her wrist was like iron, and the first thing he did was to tell her to shut up.

"I'm Fred Hong," he said. "Work for Mr Ivan. I get you away. I know you are Louise Cerdan. Get in boat right now. We're out of here in 10 seconds. Ivan says very important. I don't refuse Ivan, or he cut my balls off. Ha Ha. Get in boat!"

Sophia got in. Fred jumped right after her. "Right," said Fred, "Sit there, keep still," as the red-masted rust tub eased away from the jetty. He took the wheel, and the two boys who had cast off, came and shook hands with her. "Part-time workers," said one of them. "Very big adventures now with Captain Fred Hong. Probably don't go back to University again—high pay, dangerous work!"

But, within the last 90 seconds, two things had happened. One of the boys brought Sophia a lampshade hat, and some old clothes, which would quickly make her look like Jiang Qing, Madame Mao, after a bad day on the Long March. And, less than seven miles away, big Jim Ho was staring aghast at his dead boss who was still in the hot-tub.

Captain Fred Hong opened the throttle on his diesel engine, and the old sampan lurched forward, turning to her port side, into the historic trading lanes of the South China Sea, probably 15 minutes ahead of one of Hong Kong's greatest manhunts.

Back in the penthouse, Jim Ho lifted the boss out of the water. He understood that Yunto was exceptionally dead, but there was definitely no sign of exterior wounds, no blood, which more or less ruled out stabbing or shooting. No, boss died from heart attack, poison or drowning. Big Jim had not noticed the marks of strangulation Miss Cerdan had left behind.

He rested Yunto on a sun lounge, and hurried in to telephone the Hong Kong police department where the duty officer's own heart skipped about 30 beats. "Mr Yunto Takahashi murdered!" he shouted, shuddering at the magnitude of the crime. One of the richest men in the world killed in his own apartment. Even the middle-management duty officer realised this was the most important telephone call he would ever take.

"You sure?" he yelled, unnecessarily.

"Very, very sure, sir. Boss dead in hot-tub. You come quick. Repulse Bay, Buckingham Heights. Bring ambulance. Very, very serious."

The officer took down the phone number, then sounded an alarm, which was heard throughout the Hong Kong Police Department, island-wide, nation-wide, then world-wide. Every member of Hong Kong's massive police force of 34,000 uniformed and civilian officers, was either called into immediate duty, or put on permanent standby, to report at a moment's notice.

In any country, an alarm like this would be a drastic matter. In Hong Kong, with the world's second largest disciplined modern police department per capita, it represented something approaching World War III. The Commissioner himself was dragged to the phone, and in turn he dragged his own Deputy Commissioner, the executive in charge of Crime and Security, that's high crime, murder and terrorism.

Big Jim Ho had rung a bell, which was clanging coast to coast in the former Crown colony. A murder had been committed in a top-priced apartment block, and the man who'd died was of such stature, such financial importance, of such international prominence, it could shudder the Hong Kong Stock Market on Monday morning in the long hours before Wall Street awakened.

The Stock Exchange of Hong Kong is the third largest in Asia behind Tokyo and Shanghai. It's the sixth largest in the world, with over 2,000 listed corporations, half of them from mainland China. It's the fastest growing Stock

Exchange in the world, at least it was before Sophia Morosova throttled probably the biggest name on its roster.

The Commissioner himself laid out the opening strategy—20 squad cars to Buckingham Heights, surround the place, seal off the building, block all roads leading into, and away from the south side of the island, that's Arterial Route I. Mobilise every police car we have, road blocks on all freeways, shut the tunnels, close the ferries.

He wound up his opening instructions by bellowing in impeccable Cantonese, a sentence which meant, broadly, "We've got a fucking maniac loose on the island. I don't care if we shut the place down for a week… the murderer cannot get away—that's what an island is for—this is total lock-down. Now get out and catch this bastard."

He added that he did not actually give "a monkey's fuck" what it cost, because his own life would not be worth living if his officers managed to fuck it up.

Actually the Commissioner was normally a mild-mannered man, not given to extremes of any kind, and certainly not to extremes of bad language. That's a fair barometer of how he felt about the already lamented death of Yunto Takahashi. And as a result Hong Kong went into lock-down.

Chapter Thirteen
A Sampan to Macau

*Fred Hong was now steering calmly, relieved to be carrying
an English lady murderer, rather than the usual, surly ex-Soviet
spies, carrying the deadly, nerve agent, novichok-5. He was
Russia's go-to man for dangerous people, out of Hong Kong.*

The police shut down Route 4 all the way along the north side, starting at the West Harbour Tunnel, which also shut down, along with the closure of the cross-harbour rail tunnels. The Route 2 tunnel under Kowloon Bay was slammed shut, trapping vehicles inside. Same with the Route I Cross Harbour Tunnel. All ferries out of Aberdeen and Stanley Harbour heading for the outer islands, were closed down for the indefinite short term.

Within two hours Hong Kong was isolated, with all main route transport into and out of the island at a complete standstill. Thus, 7.5 million people, in one of the world's great financial hubs, were essentially trapped, marooned. It was, by 10pm the biggest manhunt ever mounted by the Hong Kong Police. The tiny state, with the second highest Police/Citizen Ratio in the world, was on the hunt for an unknown female murder suspect.

And they were mobilising 2,500 police cars, flashing blue and red lights on the roofs of the BMW fleet, the Toyota land cruisers, the Lexus Fleet, the Audi fleet, the Mercedes Benz wagons, even the Saracen armoured police division was out there, as ever looking like spare parts from the Gulf War. The police sirens split the night air all across the island.

The new squadron of 50 American-built electric police motor bikes were out there, swarming the streets, with unfettered power to search anyone, anything, anywhere.

All seven government helicopters, called in to support the HKPD, were buzzing seaports, sweeping down towards road blocks, frightening the life out of everyone. Especially the Super Puma L2, each one packed with a couple of dozen armed officers. In the Commissioner's opinion, a show of extreme force might just force the murderer to come out with her hands high.

Wherever the hell she was, surely she could never withstand the onslaught of the Hong Kong Police army. Because let there be no doubt, that's what it was; on land and in the air, an attacking force, with a free hand to do anything required to capture, or kill, their quarry.

At sea, it was just as bad for any fugitive. Hong Kong has a Marine Coastal police service unmatched anywhere in the world for such a relatively small land mass. They have more than 100 patrol boats, including six 100-foot Australian-built Divisional Command launches. They have 14 fast, 35-knot armed patrol launches; eight nearly-as-fast Pursuit Craft; 18 heavy-duty inflatables, Searider 5.4 RHIB craft, manned by two experienced armed seamen. Plus 34 Inshore Patrol Craft and Police Launches.

Hong Kong Island had a ring of dark blue steel around it. Its maritime muscle is probably the most dangerous coastal police force in the world, battle hardened by clashes with pirates, drug runners and terrorists. Mostly they're trying to prevent people from getting in.

But tonight they were smoothly adapting to prevent an escape. And every last vestige of diesel power they possessed was scanning the waters, searching the surface with radar, floodlighting the harbours and waterways. Hardly a single cruising black bream could swim peacefully in dark waters.

And even the Commissioner was having a difficult time, already under siege by politicians and financiers, who were wondering what was going to happen when the world woke up to the dangers of Hong Kong, the dangers of investing there, never mind living there. Would the Hang Seng Index crash on Monday morning, with stock prices diving, for no real reason?

But the stock market does not need a real reason, a scare in Hong Kong is a scare everywhere. Would there be a flight of capital from the former British Colony? Would shares in the all-powerful Okinawa Conglomerate Trust crash, and take many similar investment corporations with it? Would there be a flight to safety? Nobody knew, but the omens were plainly bad.

And the words of one of America's greatest investors, hung grimly in the night air : "Remember the Stock Exchange is a psychopath—and nothing much is going to change that."

Headlines were already being set all over the Far East, every one of them on predictable lines:

Yunto Takahashi Murdered

World's Richest Man Found dead
in the hot-tub—woman sought

Which more or less caused the Commissioner to repeat himself : Find this killer ... and find her fast.

And his troops were doing their level best. By 11pm they had arrested 52 women, all over the island, eight of them residents of Buckingham Heights. All 52 had bomb-proof alibis, and the 5ft 4inch security man who worked next to the elevator, had never laid eyes on any of them.

So unless some of them had been parachuted into the penthouse ... well, plainly this needed to be filed under the heading: Too anxious (zero connection to Truth). Still, the Hong Kong Police were following the first part of the creed of Sherlock Holmes—trying to eliminate the impossible.

Meanwhile, sitting comfortably under her Madame Mao hat, the world-travelled murderer of Yunto Takahashi was enjoying a dish of exquisitely stir-fried black bream in scallions, ginger and soy. It was, she thought one of the best dinners she'd ever tasted. Mrs Hong was a wizard, no doubt of that, and she'd cooked it very fast ... "Very hot wok make tender fish," she had said.

Sophia could not argue with that. In fact it crossed her mind that if Fred and Wing Tai Hong ever decided to open a restaurant in Rue des Beaux Arts they'd put several locals out of business in the first week. *Deux Magots* could find themselves making sweet-and-sour croissants, just to stay in the game.

Fred was now steering calmly, probably relieved to be carrying mad English lady murderer, rather than his usual Russian cargo of surly ex-Soviet spies, or packets of the now world-famous, but deadly, nerve agent, novichok-5. He was Russia's go-to man to move dangerous cargo or dangerous people out of Hong Kong, asap.

Fred was highly-paid to make the 37-mile crossing of the Zhejiang estuary, and into the 'Las Vegas of the Orient'—Macau, the largest gaming empire on Earth, home to 20 of the world's biggest casinos. His sampan would be flat out at seven knots, which made it like all the other working fishing boats which trundled in and out of Aberdeen, all day and all night, seven days a week.

As boats go, the whole fleet out of Aberdeen was unobtrusive, a bit ramshackle, chugging along, usually slowly, with a couple of line fishermen casting over the side. Net fishing is banned in these polluted waters in a government attempt to bring the stock back.

The police, in their big, sleek fast-patrol craft, never gave them a moment's thought, speeding past them on missions of such importance these low-life fishermen could never possibly understand. There was scarcely a single record of any Aberdeen fishing boat being apprehended by the law. It was simply two different worlds; suave well-paid officers in their high-peaked black caps and sharp, dark-blue uniforms, and those who merely scratched some kind of a living out of ancient waters.

Thus Captain Fred chugged onward, occasionally seeing the lights of the patrol boats hurtling around the bays. Before him sat Miss Cerdan, talking to his wife. Fred guessed how important she was, but it never once occurred to him a police launch would signal him to stop. They never had, and he doubted they ever would.

In turn the police officers on the water never gave his old sampan a second glance. And of course they had no idea that the Captain of this old tub was being paid more for his night's work than any policeman earns in a month. And right now they were slipping through moonlit waters, the bom-bom-bom of the old diesel engine scarcely noticeable above the howl of distant sirens, both on land and offshore.

They were a mile off Lamma island now in the West Channel, heading up to the lonely waters which ebb and flow around two completely uninhabited islands, Chung, which they'd pass on their portside, and Hei Ling Chow to starboard. The night was warm, and the South China Sea was calm. Captain Fred raised barely a bow-wave as they plodded smoothly on towards Macau. Sophia considered this elderly fishing boat to be the most peaceful place she'd been in years.

*****

Not so big Jim Ho. He had 16 police officers in the apartment. The ambulance crew had removed the body of Yunto Takahashi, and now the law was in search of clues, anything which might appertain to his murder, anything which might throw some light on the identity of the lady who had plainly killed him.

Jim tried vainly to keep order, and in particular he was personally attempting to find the envelope which contained the banker's draft for $100,000, which he had personally collected for the boss. He looked everywhere, and sorrowfully realised that Miss Cerdan had taken not only the boss's life, but also his cash. He regarded it as one of life's ironies that most evil people still get paid. She could deposit that check anywhere and it would be honoured. It worried Jim but he understood he was now powerless, like everyone else around here.

He had done his best to help the investigation, produced details of the check, assured them the murderer was a Western woman … *spoke strong British … charge boss extra crazy high-price … then fuck boss in bathtub, then throttle him … most diabolical English blond floozie … who will get boss's money.*

Big Jim was unable to elaborate further with a precise description on the person who throttled boss … *very, very sorry,* he told the police. *But anyone from west of Macau—they all look the same to me—Russians, Africans, Europe, all the same, west of Macau, that's my frontier—not Oriental, not register with Jim.*

In fact, Jim Ho need not have troubled himself. At this actual moment, Sophia Morosova was leaning on the rails of the fishing boat, ripping the check and its envelope into little pieces and dropping them over the side. That's how much she hated Yunto Takahashi. She could not bear even to touch his money.

And now, two miles up ahead she could see the moonlit peaks of Lantau Island. And Captain Fred told her the next place after that was the island of Shek Kwu which marked the halfway point. And she sat silently for the next couple of hours, occasionally dozing off, listening to the ripples of these foreign waters.

Captain Fred told her when they reached the low-lying Soko Islands, where he said the shallow ocean was at its deepest between Hong Kong and Macau. "Probably 60-feet below the keel," he said, and that was where Sophia accomplished her next task, dropping the *Tanta* knife and the stun-gun over the side. The remnants of the white powder drug package were rolled tightly into the end of the Tanta's scabbard.

They swerved north of the island of Lung Sou Gok and headed along the eastern shores of the Pearl River estuary, into Macau just before 0230, straight into the inner harbour, which was as busy as it was at midday. She returned her hat and Madame Mao disguise, then said goodbye to Captain Fred and his wife. She thanked them for everything, and climbed into a taxi waiting on the harbour rank, for the six-mile ride through the docks and warehouses of East Macau, directly to the airport.

She removed her long, expensive blond wig and, with some regrets, dumped it in a trash can with a steel lid, in the ladies' room before she collected her ticket. Everything was clean, but Macau is forever a little outpost of the airways. It has only one main runway, though it thrives, like everything else in Macau. And that, in these days of jet airliners the size of warehouses, and airports the size of small cities, is perhaps amazing. Macau's international airport is only marginally bigger than the flight deck of a US Navy Nimitz-Class aircraft carrier. Although a lot less dangerous.

There was a surprisingly comfortable first-class lounge, and Sophia collected her ticket, organised by Ivan Andropov, and settled herself into a deep sofa, facing away from a couple of brightly-lit slot-machines. That's Macau, not even here, in the very last strides of departure, can they miss an opportunity to relieve a few world-weary travellers of a final few bucks.

Sophia on the sofa slept for most of the night, and was awakened by a call from the steward informing the few passengers that Tigerair's 0915 Boeing 737 non-stop to Taipei, Taiwan, would be boarding in 15 minutes. Her British passport, skilfully forged under the name Margaret Harvey, was accepted immediately by the ticket desk. Visas are not required Macau-Tapei.

It was a journey of almost 500-miles to the northeast, across the open, heavily disputed international waters of the South China Sea, parts of which are claimed variously by China, Japan and the Philippines. In days gone by, these were the diabolical haunts of fiendish Chinese pirates who terrorised the entire area.

They terrorised it almost permanently, until the 1850's when the Brits sent in the 12-gunned 900-ton two-masted steamer, *HMS Rattler*, to end the situation, leaving probably 1,000 pirates dead, several of their ships sunk, de-masted or burned. One of the most ferocious actions was right off Lantau, past which Sophia had just sailed, probably right over the pirate wrecks from their catastrophic Battle of Nan Quan, in which the gunboat *Rattler* ended their reign of terror.

Tigerair of course was unconcerned by this, streaking over the historic seas at around 400mph, and landing at its home port of Taipei shortly after 11am. Sophia's British passport saw her swiftly through immigration, and she took refuge in the magnificent first-class lounge of Emirates Airlines, which would be her stealthy, unnoticed hideaway for the next 12-hours, before boarding. It was not very convenient, but Sophia knew she was darned lucky to have a way out of Hong Kong which was virtually untraceable.

So far as she was concerned, she was almost home free, but somehow, after travelling for more than 14 hours she was still in China. Taiwan, officially the Republic of China, was a bit of an offshoot, but still, to a foreigner, China. The mainland country called itself the People's Republic of China. Nothing would please Miss Morosova more than the moment when the big, new Airbus-380 from the United Arab Emirates took off for Dubai, her last stop before Paris and home.

The 4,000-mile journey into the Arabian desert was overnight, chasing back the time zones. It would take her over South China, Burma, Northern India, Nepal, and Pakistan. Then across the Arabian Sea, with the south-eastern tip of Iran to starboard, before landing in Dubai at around 6am on Monday morning. She was staying with the superb Emirates Airline until they landed at Charles de Gaulle around lunchtime in Paris. After that Sophia planned to sleep, at home, for approximately one week.

The best part of the entire operation was the United Arab Emirates. They tended to her every need before and after boarding. they cosseted her in Dubai, and wished her farewell in Paris. They also asked her to be sure to fly with them next time she went to Taiwan. Sophia did not enlighten them that this would occur only when another heaven and another earth had passed her by.

After her 20,000-mile round trip in less than five days, *Rue des Beaux Arts* had never looked more enticing. She paid the cab driver, returned to her regular name, Sophia Morosova, whose regular passport would confirm she had never been out of the country in the past couple of weeks.

She gratefully wished Gaston, *Bonjour,* and, upon arrival home, made herself some Earl Grey tea, since she had made a private vow never to touch her favourite Lapsang Souchong China tea for the rest of her life. At least not until two apparitions had faded entirely from her mind … the mighty Jim Ho, zapped half to death on the floor of the Buckingham Heights penthouse; and the grotesque death mask of his boss out there underwater, in the hot-tub.

She sat in the warm air of the City of Light, out there on her own roof garden, once more hearing the bells of Notre Dame Cathedral, relaxing, loving the world, and praying for the safe delivery of little Sasha into the Kingdom of God. It was her everlasting prayer … that eternal light will shine upon her; the very words she'd had carved on the tombstone at Saint Nicholas Church along the green banks of the Upper Thames.

And damn Yunto Takahashi. Damn that disgusting pig to hell. She had to admit. She felt a lot better already.

*****

Nonetheless, despite drawing all the curtains, and crashing into her bed at 4pm, the week-long sleep lasted exactly two hours. Her cell-phone rang, from England. And on the line was Uncle Rudy, whose precision planning, and indeed his long friendship with Ivan Andropov, had probably saved her life, and certainly her freedom.

And here was Rudy on the phone. "Hi," she said, as cheerfully as possible. "How did you know I was home?"

"I knew within five minutes what time you boarded the aircraft in Dubai. I knew what time you landed in Paris." he replied. "The only thing I did not know was you'd lost your dagger! But I found that out too."

"Don't miss much, do you?" she replied.

"I try not to. But anyway, I'm really calling to check that you're home safe. The Hong Kong Police have nothing, except they know it was a western woman who killed him. But beyond that, zero."

"How d'you know that?"

"Ivan told me. How d'you think? You may have got clean out of there, which Ivan says was nothing short of a miracle, given the loss of your principal weapon. But you left a world-class commotion behind you."

"Who, me?"

"Yes, dearest Sophia, you."

"What did I do?"

"Well, you crashed the world's stock markets, just for a start."

"Who, me? I did no such thing."

"Sophia, would you like me to read you the second-lead headline, front page, today's *Wall Street Journal* …?"

"Okay …"

"Here goes … don't faint …

Hong Kong Island Shut-Down
Stock Markets crash as OCT
Chairman found murdered

"And, *Financial Times* front Page ...

World Markets in Free Fall
Asia's Richest Man found Murdered in Hong Kong
Hang Seng Index leads stock market crisis

"And, the London *Daily Telegraph* ...

Hong Kong Murder Sparks
Global Stock Market Crash
Yunto Takahashi, one of the world's richest
men found throttled in his hot-tub

"And *The Sun* :

Stark-Naked Billionaire
Found Dead in The Bath
Hong Kong Tycoon Rocks World
Markets for the Last Time

"Christ!" said Sophia.

"That's more or less what I said myself," replied Rudolf. "But just because the papers are making a bloody fuss, and shares have temporarily crashed, there's still no need to get excited. The main thing is the HKPD have not the slightest clue who committed the crime and they are searching the Island and all ocean points around it, just to prove they know nothing."

"What do I do?"

"Absolutely nothing. Live your life entirely normally and generally act as if nothing has happened."

"Can I read the newspapers?"

"Of course not. They know less than the police. Forget it ever happened. Anyway, I'm driving down to Henley tomorrow just to put some fresh flowers on the grave—and to say a little prayer. I have to go now, but remember, there are people who are just too evil to be allowed to live. Bye, now… and take care."

Sophia did not make the one-week of sleep, but she was unconscious until lunchtime on Wednesday. She strolled along to *Deux Magots* and ordered a couple of *croissants* with her café au lait. It was a restful and familiar place, the waiter chatted, a couple of people whom she knew by sight wandered by, and the most dangerous police force in the world wasn't hounding her.

And yet … and yet, she was restless. She didn't know why, though it was mostly because her mind was roving back and forth through the adventures of the astounding last month of her life. But there was something else, another kind of fear, and it took a second cup of *café au lait* before she faced up to the fact that it was the fear of losing touch completely with Detective Chief Superintendent Charles Barton.

She knew he'd called several times, but left no message. The last time on Sunday night. And now he'd given up. And she had a very hollow feeling deep inside that he might think she had killed Lord Fontridge, and that she was now on the run.

This, she decided, was a crisis that needed her attention. And every day she ignored it, would make everything worse. She couldn't just call Scotland Yard and ask to speak to him. But neither could she stay idling around in *Deux Magots*. She was fed up to her eyebrows with travelling … *if I turn up at Charles de Gaulle one more time, they'll probably give me a uniform.*

She considered trying to fly Emirates to London, remembering they already had 16,000 uniformed staff. But decided this particular situation was becoming so plainly urgent she needed the convenience of an airline that took off for Great Britain's capital city every half-hour.

Back to Air France, no ticket, no reservation. She'd handle that at the airport, and with those sharp thoughts in her mind, Sophia suddenly became the hunter, rather than the hunted, and she set off in search of the most interesting man she'd ever met.

Chapter Fourteen
She's Innocent, Rules the Coroner

The report did, of course, shed a glaring light on the totally
obvious. Which would save everyone a whole lot of trouble
Because the case was closed. Sir Josh had died by accident.
Monaco had it right. No reason to suspect anything.

Lightly-packed, Sophia made it to Charles de Gaulle by 3.30pm. She found a flight at 4.15, and arrived in the Heathrow terminal just before 6pm. She boarded a taxi but had no idea where to tell him to go. She settled for Brown's Hotel in Albemarle Street, where she and Kate's family used to meet for afternoon tea.

The drive was slow, heavy traffic, and it was almost seven before she arrived and told the doorman she would not be checking in. "Just visiting," she said, jauntily. Hoping he could not see her heart pounding through her raincoat.

She sat in the lounge, searching through a notebook, looking for a number, not an office number, not a cell-phone number, just the number of the house in South Audley Street, the one he'd given her.

What if his mother answers? What if he's not there? What if his mother wonders if I'm calling from Wormwood Scrubs or somewhere? Christ, can I go through with this?

The answer to the last question was probably, no. But she went through with it anyway, nervously entering one of the elegant wood-panelled call boxes, and dialling the number of the house in South Audley Street. To her horror, the voice that answered was that of a female.

And it did not take a leap of imagination to guess it was Lady Penelope Barton, a bastion of Burke's Peerage, who was on the other end of the line. The easy drawl of the aristocrat, the rigid confidence, the marginally disguised sense of faint irritation.

"Good evening. And what may I do for you?"

Sophia gulped. "Er, I was wondering if I could possibly speak to Charles," she managed.

"Well, you most certainly could if he were here," she said. "But I am afraid he's not back from work yet." And Lady Penelope, tuning in instantly to the proper tone of the caller, added, "I do expect him, though. May I ask who wants him?"

"Yes, my name is Sophia Morosova. We met in Paris a couple of weeks ago."

"Ah, yes. Of course, Charles told me in great detail, how much fun he had— mentioned you had dined with a very old friend of mine, Ronnie DeFarges— such a nice man."

"Gosh, yes," replied Sophia, cementing her place in the great lady's good books, with a word like 'gosh.' In England, you only learn that at very, very posh girls' boarding schools. The rest of the population usually says "Christ!" even Sophia, in off-guarded moments.

"Where are you now?" asked Lady Penelope.

"Actually. I'm at Brown's Hotel."

"Good heavens, what could you possibly be doing there? It's full of commercial travellers, absurd little men in plastic shoes!" Which was an unorthodox way of describing one of the classiest hotels in the West End, for years an accepted haven for wealthy country squires and landowners, on rare visits to London.

Sophia burst out laughing which also pleased her Ladyship, who like most of that generation prided themselves on that deadpan outrageous, delivered without a smile.

"I'll tell you what, my dear," she said, "Why don't you come over to the house, and wait for Charles here? We can have a drink and you'll be more comfortable."

"Well, thank you very much," replied Sophia. "If you're certain Charles won't mind."

"Judging by what he told me, I don't think he'll mind at all," said her Ladyship. "Not one bit. See you in a minute."

The doorman called her a cab for the short ride, through Berkeley Square, up Curzon Street and into South Audley, walking distance, but not with a weekend bag.

She rang the bell and was greeted by an immaculately dressed lady, probably approaching 70, but with the appearance of someone in her 50's.

"Sophia, my dear, come in. I feel as if we're old friends." That old English class system, guiding the socially fireproof, as always.

She put down her bag in the hall and followed Lady Penelope into a beautifully furnished study, with dark green walls, and deeply upholstered sofas. From somewhere or other, the butler was summoned and asked to bring a couple of gin-and-tonics as if there was no other drink on earth.

Sophia took one sip, and decided she'd better take serious care as she did not want to sit here and get pleasantly drunk before Charles actually showed up.

"Well, thank you very much," she said, before enquiring whether or not Charles was likely to show up in the next few hours.

"Oh, he'll show up," replied his mother. "He's dining here tonight and he always telephones in amply good time if he's not going to make it. Just a few good manners, that's about the only thing he did learn at that ridiculous school his father sent him to."

Sophia had never actually heard Eton College described quite like that. But Lady P went on to describe her family's disquiet when her husband announced he was sending Charles to the 580-year-old Thames-side school opposite Windsor Castle.

"You see, my dear, we are Scottish Stuarts, and have been Catholic since long before Eton was invented. It's important to us that children are kept well clear of King Henry VIII's barbaric ideas about religion. He actually sacked the Pope and put himself in charge of the Church. Eton was founded by his damned grand-father, or uncle, or something. It should not be a place for us."

"I can quite see that," replied Sophia. "We've had our problems with people like that in Russia."

"Oh, of course. I forgot you have Russian blood," said Lady Penelope. "And that's something we have in common. I have a few ancestors who were somewhat tight with the Romanovs. Through one of Victoria's daughters I believe. She had about three hundred of them so it's a bit difficult to sort them out all these years later."

Sophia thought Lady P was an absolute hoot. And she very confidently said, "My mother married Mikhail Obolensky, my father. But I was only about two when he died."

"Oh, my gosh!" replied her Ladyship. "I know exactly who he is—my grand-father was at Brasenose with Prince Alexander—the rugby player. I was told they always had oysters and caviar for breakfast—especially before a big match!"

At which point Sophia heard the front door open and then slam shut, followed by a very familiar voice calling, "Evening, Mum, I'm back."

"Just as well," she called back. "I have a very nice surprise for you."

And in through the study door walked Detective Chief Superintendent Charles Barton who could not believe his eyes.

"Hello, darling," said Lady Penelope. "I believe you know Sophia. She and I, by the way, are probably distant cousins, direct line through Ivan the Terrible!"

Sophia found herself in a flat-spin. Still laughing, she did know whether to get up and greet Charles, wait for him to walk over to her, or thank Lady Penelope again. Just then Hudson came in to see if the young master needed a scotch and soda. Which threw Sophia into such a dither she stood up and nearly kissed Hudson by mistake.

Charles very smoothly put an end to all of these shenanigans, walked over to her and held out his arms, prior to giving her a huge, lingering bear hug, right in front of his mother and the butler. And while he was at it, he whispered in her ear, "Where the hell have you been? I was just starting to get worried. I've called about a dozen times."

Sophia who'd been practicing the exact number of whoppers she was going to tell him, smiled and just said, "I'm so pleased to see you. You have the kindest mother, and she's been looking after me. I called the only number you gave me, and here I am."

"Very lucky for you, Charles," said her Ladyship. "What a pity to lose a lovely girl like this just because you're trapped in that silly police station, or arresting some pick-pocket in Marks and Spencers."

One of the principal heads of Scotland Yard smiled benevolently, and told Hudson he would definitely have that scotch and soda, and then he thanked his Mum graciously for taking care of Sophia. "Ivan the Terrible would be absolutely thrilled," he added.

"And another thing," interrupted Lady Penelope, "Sophia, my dear, I should tell you my butler is actually named Gordon McPherson, his family have worked for us for generations. I think he's the fourth.

"But many years ago I made the mistake of showing Charles old re-runs of a television series called *Upstairs, Downstairs*. From that moment, he's insisted on calling Mr MacPherson 'Hudson.' Very childish of course, but I'm afraid it's been going on since Charles was about eight, and poor old Gordon's been Hudson ever since. I even call him Hudson myself!"

"It's also a lot more appropriate than I get credit for," added Charles. "The actor who played Angus Hudson the butler, was Gordon Jackson a Scotsman— he and MacPherson had the same accent, the same Christian name, and were both butlers. I probably should have been a casting director."

"My God!" said her Ladyship. "That's an even worse job than you have now—you'd be shouting at all those appalling left-wing Hollywood rapists. On reflection you're probably better off at Scotland Yard."

Charles, as a kind of aristocratic double act with his Mother, really was the best company, and Sophia was thrilled to be invited for dinner, and even more delighted when Lady P announced there was no question of her returning to any hotel, and that she was more than welcome to stay here for the length of her London stay.

Hudson served an excellent dinner, wild Irish smoked salmon followed by a small rack of lamb from a cousin's Pembrokeshire sheep farm way down in West Wales near Haverfordwest. "Welsh lamb," said Charles, opening a very agreeable bottle of burgundy, "It's their best export, just ahead of their male-voice choirs and Catherine Zeta Jones."

Lady Penelope retired quite early leaving Sophia and Charles to conduct the conversation she had been dreading for a few days. Where have you been? A not unreasonable enquiry given the obvious but unspoken affect they had on each other in Paris a week ago, the one with the 3.00am phone call.

"And before that, why didn't you tell me you were about to go missing?"

Again the question was not unreasonable. And Sophia moved gallantly into the firing line, trading facts with one of finest detectives in London. Still, she could scarcely tell him the truth, that she had just popped over to Hong Kong to murder some Japanese rapist in cold blood, and then leave a scene of total chaos behind her.

"Charles," she said, "You might not believe this—"

"Very probably," he interjected.

But he underestimated her and the pure feasibility of her story gave him a proper interest in believing her. She told him how her best friend Kate Mildmay had called and told her she was going with her father and his highly-amusing horse trainer, Sir Mark Prescott, to the bullfights in Madrid for two or three days. They had four tickets and Kate wanted her to take a short flight from Paris and join them in Madrid. The truth was, the fourth member of the party, a friend of her father's had pulled out at the last minute.

"So, on the spur of the moment," said Sophia, "Since you had left me on my own for the weekend, I hopped on a cheap Easyjet flight for £75. It only took a couple of hours. Next thing I knew, I was in the Madrid bullring with Kate, Richard and Mark."

"You mean *Las Ventas, Plaza de Toros*—the home of bullfighting?"

"Well, I'd never been before," she said. "But I suppose I do. Just didn't realise I was in the presence of Senor Charles el Cordobes!"

Charles chuckled, as usual, but persevered with his questions. And who did you see? Sophia was ready for this one.

"Oh, the most graceful young matador, Jose Cortes," she said. "It had been raining and the surface was a bit muddy, and he still fought the bull in the centre of the ring. The crowd gave him huge applause."

"Do you know why?" asked Charles.

"Not really."

"Well, on a wet surface, any matador can slip, even fall over. Which is of course, lethal. And the centre of the bullring is the farthest place from help. It's the most dangerous place a matador can be, all on his own on very slippery ground, facing a killer."

"Wow!" she said. "No one told me that. But I did see Mark up and clapping."

"Did Jose kill the bull?"

"Oh, yes. One thrust of his sword, and the bull collapsed onto his knees."

"Clean kill. That Madrid crowd loves that. See anyone else?"

"Yes, the next evening we saw Juan Bautista who I believe is quite famous."

"I don't know him. I don't go often enough to know them. But I have always thought it is one of the most colourful sights, with unbelievably brave men."

"A lot of people don't like it, though. Richard told me bull-fighting is ending in Barcelona. They say it's all fixed—and not nearly as dangerous as some people make out."

"I'll bet they wouldn't say that if they ever stood in the bullring when one of those giant, fighting bulls comes charging through the gate, full of blind fury, trying to kill anyone standing in his way."

"I'll bet they wouldn't. I'll never forget being there."

"Perhaps we'll go together one day."

"I'd love that."

Without once raising the subject of the deceased Lord Fontridge, they talked for another half hour. And then Charles took her to her room, which was in fact right next to Lady Penelope's. For the first time, he kissed her, very tenderly.

It was the first time in her entire life, she had willingly kissed a man, the first time she had done so with trust, and respect. And as he closed the door for her, and walked up to the next floor, Sophia was gripped by the irony, that this man may be her only true enemy, as the manhunt for Fontridge's killer continued. Who else was going to arrest her? And here she was planning to go to the bullfights with him. "The bullfights," she muttered. "Or the ends of the earth."

*****

The following morning, the three of them met for breakfast at 8am. The DCS would leave at 8.30, and before that told Sophia he would meet her this evening in the bar at the Connaught at 7pm. He was of course referring to one of the oldest and probably best hotels in London, with a pricey, intimate bar, world-renowned among certain types of people.

Perhaps it was because it was right up the street in Carlos Place, less than four minutes' walk from South Audley. But anyway, Charles Barton made this small but grandiose hotel, named with Royal permission after Queen Victoria's son Prince Arthur, Duke of Connaught, sound like the Dog and Fox pub on Fulham Broadway.

Sophia had been to the Connaught a couple of times, but she had not been to the "little place around the corner" where, Charles suggested, "they might give us something to eat." He referred, of course, to Morton's, Berkeley Square, perhaps the most exclusive private dining club in London, beloved of members, beloved of invited visitors. And beloved these many years by both Charles's parents. The Bartons were quiet, very welcome members in here. Lady Penelope treated it like McDonald's.

Breakfast at South Audley was proceeding gently, until Hudson arrived with the newspapers. Charles ignored them, Sophia was too scared to look, and then Lady Penelope suddenly cried out, "Oh my God! That appalling little disc jockey who fell over the bannisters in Monte Carlo has turned out to be a paedophile."

"What!" said Charles.

"A paedophile. The *Daily Mail* says a Leicestershire school mistress found him in bed with a 15-year-old girl. And that's not the worst of it. It says here she was tied to the bed by both ankles and both wrists."

"A good looking schoolgirl of 15 does not constitute paedophilia," said Charles. "It's another kind of crime. It constitutes statuary rape, under 16."

"Thank you, Charles," said Lady P, adding, "I always knew there was something damn weird about that Hartley character. He looked ridiculous with that scraggly dyed hair. And I always thought he spent far too much time in hospitals and schools for under-privileged children. Now there's couple of women here say he should have been charged with rape about 20 times."

"Well, why the hell didn't someone blow the whistle?" said Charles. "How did he get away with it?"

"According to this mighty edition of Jonathan Harmsworth's slightly tacky newspaper, it was all because he gave such generous gifts to the hospitals and schools. They relied on him for funds, and for years everyone shut up about his sexual antics with the older girls."

Sophia could have expanded on that with even more authority than the *Daily Mail,* but she was rooted to her chair, frozen to her cornflakes, so she left the reply to Lady Penelope.

"Oh, there's a little girl's mother here with a shocking account of the rape of her 15-year-old. Honestly, Charles I'm still amazed the police did not move in sooner."

"You can't really move on something if no one tells you it's happening," he replied. "Personally I think the *Mail* deserves enormous credit, for A) unearthing the disgraceful behaviour of a national icon, and B) even more credit for running it to ground, and then publishing it. And good for Jonny Harmsworth for allowing it."

And there was no denying the truth of this. Young Harmsworth had inherited this newspaper empire on the death of his father, Vere Harmsworth, the 3rd Viscount Rothermere, in 1998. Now, at the age of around 50, he was the 4th Viscount and well on his way to following in the footsteps of the giant press barons of the past: Beaverbrook, Kemsley, Camrose, Northcliffe, Thompson, and another Harmsworth by birth, the legendary Cecil King, Chairman and owner of the *Daily Mirror*, Director of the Bank of England.

And right now, it looked as if his *Daily Mail* had tossed the reputation of Sir Josh Hartley, straight over the bannisters with him, sent it thudding onto the racetrack below. Sophia Morosova was still terrified either Charles or his mother was going to draw her into the conversation. And she was basically too scared to speak. But Lady Penelope announced she was "bored sideways with that common little pervert," and, anyway, Charles was on his way out of the door, leaving the two principal ladies in his life to more pleasant meanderings. His driver was outside, and the *Telegraph* was on the back seat. He scanned through the news pages, ignoring an interview with Sir Josh Hartley's mother, and another with Jane Fontridge, who had told the writer even less than she told a couple of PC Plods from Lewes.

Nonetheless, the *Telegraph* newsroom was attempting to join the party in the biographic assassination of Sir Josh, now a certified sexual menace, on account of the volume of evidence being trumpeted to the world by the *Daily Mail,* which had everyone, as they say in the trade, on toast.

Charles skipped right by a story on the financial page about that billionaire found murdered in his hot-tub in Hong Kong, because no one was even guessing they had anyone under suspicion. He was not, of course, to know that if he had nurtured even an inkling of the truth about his mother's house-guest, he would probably have ended up with a Triple Pulitzer Prize for investigative skills beyond price.

It was only a short drive even in traffic, down Park Lane, through St James's Park, past Horse Guards and into Parliament Square. He was at his desk in less than 20 minutes. And awaiting him were two critical coroner's reports, one confirming that Lord Fontridge had died from cardiac arrest after a fatal knife wound to the heart. Verdict: murder.

The other was the Monaco coroner's report which returned a verdict of 'death by misadventure.' The coroner had decided that Sir Josh Hartley died from multiple injuries to head, neck and spine, which had killed him instantly, after a 100-foot fall from the balcony of the *Le Beau Rivage* apartments.

In the opinion of the coroner, the police had no evidence whatsoever that anyone else was in apartment 8G. He also declared that Sir Josh Hartley had fallen, and he could see no evidence, or even reason, why the British celebrity should have suddenly jumped to his death. The verdict was irrevocable—the death was an accident. The coroner signed off on: *Mort par Mesadventure*— Death by Misadventure.

The report about Lord Fontridge, did of course, shed an absolutely glaring light on the totally obvious. The one from Monaco would certainly save everyone a whole lot of trouble. Because the case was closed. Sir Josh had died by accident.

Of course, today's *Daily Mail* may have caused people to wonder slightly more about the possibility of suicide. But no one knew this morning's story was going to appear. Certainly they did not know anything two weeks ago. Monaco had it right. No reason to suspect anything.

In the opinion of Charles Barton, the papers could label Sir Josh a lifelong pervert, paedophile, rapist or whatever else. He was just pleased they were not dumping another murder case in his IN-Basket, especially one which took place 750-miles away in one of the world's smallest countries.

Meanwhile he had a meeting in 15 minutes with two officers from Scotland Yard's Digital Forensic Unit located on the third floor of the building, and populated by a breed of investigator known locally as the Super-geeks. They operated Scotland Yard's nerve-centre for cybercrime, and they were highly praised for work which basically no one else really understood. Although sometimes admitted only grudgingly.

They all had Degrees in Computer Sciences and Creative Technologies. Without that Bachelor of Science degree you'd never get in the door. Without the word 'Honours' attached to it, you were most unlikely to be hired. Their field was in the hidden recesses of big corporations—forming the first line of defence against cyber-attack, gathering obscure digital evidence against cyber-crime.

This degree in digital science is probably the most sought-after qualification in the world's biggest businesses, the creation of iron-clad security against brilliant but unseen marauders, the kind of characters who once breached the cyber-lines of the Pentagon.

In England many universities have a department for these future cyber warriors, and the acknowledged masters are the professors at the University of the West of England, Bristol. And they admit freely this carries the highest-demand of all the degrees they teach.

Their best brains will bear the word 'Honours' with them for all of their lives. And the finest of these are likely to end up at Scotland Yard, third floor. They are well-paid, but for them it's more than a job, it's a vocation. And their creed is simple: if any criminal, or even a suspect, leaves one single digital fingerprint, anywhere, on desk top, laptop or cell-phone, we will find it, no matter how cunningly it's hidden.

Chapter Fifteen
The High Priest of the Tokkotai

*Because Chief Barton now held the key, he knew what no one else had ever suspected—the secret code which led to the **Maidens in the Vale**—it was perhaps a criminal discovery which could split the very foundations of England's system of justice.*

Detective Chief Superintendent Charles Barton had handed over his most secret piece of evidence—Lord Fontridge's laptop to the Super-geeks. They'd been working on it for a few days, and now they were due in his office with their report. Charles anticipated their arrival with some trepidation, for they were men of literal mind. If a keenly thought-out piece of wit ever strayed into their laboratories, it would surely die of loneliness. Humour, they did not do.

But Charles understood this, and he admired them unconditionally. When his secretary announced their arrival, he told her, "Send them in, and bring them coffee and biscuits." Larry and his assistant, Jerry, were the type of guys who probably forgot to eat for three or four days at a time, so engrossed were they in the project of the moment.

And just then they came through his office door, Jerry holding the laptop Charles had personally lifted from Freddie Fontridge's secret compartment in the House of Lords.

"Morning, men," said the Superintendent. "Thanks for all you've done, and I'm sorry it proved so complicated."

"Not really complicated, sir. Just laborious, stuff that takes time, despite its elementary quality."

"Yes, quite," said Charles. Perish the thought he was suggesting something might be too difficult. Because that would be unthinkable.

"Anyway, sir, I'm returning the computer. But it's useless now. I removed the hard drive, just unscrewed the bottom, and took it out. We took a verbatim copy of everything on it. You really have to do that these days, sir."

"You do?"

"Almost every villain we encounter installs some kind of a code, which will boot-up and destroy everything on the drive the moment someone tampers with it, or even enters wrong data. We call them the fatal codes. It's what you might call a very clever booby-trap. And we can't afford to chance the damn thing catching us out.

"We just remove the entire hard-drive before we even switch it on, and immediately copy it. That way we have more time, and no one else has its contents. They are secure and safe with us, on a proper data base downstairs. That computer we brought back is just a shell, useless. It will never work again."

"You mean I don't have to return it?"

"Not much point, sir. We might as well dump it."

Charles was not entirely sure about calling Lord Fontridge a villain. Not yet anyway. But he accepted these two knew a lot more than he did, and there was plainly more to come."

"Anyway, sir, we found three critical things in plain view on the drive. All three were EXE files, and the first of these was the owner's search engine, that's the browser on the laptop. Now, sir, this is important. There was only one search engine. Not one of the familiar ones, the kind accessed by millions every day. This was a TOR browser."

"Ah, yes," said Charles, "I know something about that. It's the system invented by the US Navy Research Laboratory in Washington—must be almost 20 years. It was designed specifically for Naval Intelligence, a kind of anonymous web, so US spies working in deep cover could make contact with home-base without leaving a trace—what you'd call a footprint."

"That's correct, sir. It's still governed by the concept of anonymity. But whereas once it was strictly for US military agents, carrying out probably the most dangerous work in the world. Now it's for pretty well anyone. It's the sinister web for anyone wanting to stay hidden, to keep their shady activities untraceable."

"Do the military still use it?"

"We're not sure. They'd never admit it, or anything else. But one thing is accepted among the science community as absolutely gold-plated certain. No one would install a TOR system on their computer unless they had something very definitely to hide. It has no other purpose. It was designed for anonymity, for secrecy. Nothing else."

"You mean like uranium 235?"

"Sorry, sir…?"

"Various countries buy uranium and spin its main component, uranium 238 into 235. Takes about seven years and there's always a lot of blather about 'defensive purposes'.

"But it's all rubbish," said Charles. "Uranium 235 has no other purpose except to make an atomic bomb."

"Exactly, sir. The TOR system also has but one single purpose, and that's secrecy. Whoever owned your computer was up to something he badly wanted to be hidden, and stay hidden."

Charles quietly thought that applied to the computer itself, which had been, after all, sealed in a secret compartment, in a locked cupboard, in a private office, deep inside the House of Lords.

But Larry continued, "Sir, I am sure you know, but over the years the TOR system has become the gateway to some very dark places. It's a search engine for paedophiles, white-slave traffic, prostitution, even murder, You can go into what's now called the Dark Web and see people being killed … it's about depravity, ghoulishness and sadism, not to mention the internet highway for arms dealers."

"Christ!" said Charles, "Sounds like British television!"

Neither Larry, nor his assistant Jerry, even cracked a smile. They both looked kind of quizzical, as if the Superintendent had lost track of the conversation.

In fact Charles Barton knew a lot more than he was letting on. He just liked to coax people to tell him more, to fill in the gaps. It was probably a subconscious technique, one which had powered his astonishing rise to one of the high peaks of his profession.

He had personally helped smash a crime ring which was bringing truck-loads of terrified young girls from South America to Yorkshire for a short life of prostitution. And he knew perfectly well that on the Dark Web it was possible to buy a combat-ready battlefield tank.

He also knew that TOR's US Navy founders had designed it for two-way traffic, not just for Intel back and forth from their own brilliant network of agents; but also from the darkest of the dark, their foreign agents, working in hostile countries, trying to send encrypted and untraceable signals back to Washington, right under the noses of their own governments.

Larry decided to stick to the point. "Sir," he said. "I don't mean to be repetitive, but whomever owned this computer, was up to something highly clandestine. There is, as you say, no other reason to have a TOR system installed, except complete secrecy."

"Thank you, Larry," said Charles. "And you, Jerry. Thank you both very much indeed. Is it yet possible to have a look at what was on the hard drive."

"Absolutely," he replied. "Much more to tell you."

"Shoot," said Charles.

"Well, the TOR router deletes all sensitive search history and data, which in itself is a smoking gun of suspicion. But we recovered a lot. And after the search engine, the next thing was another EXE file, headed simply *Maidens in the Vale*. We got it out, and found two short videos, one of a near-naked man with what looks like a whip-thin leather belt striking a very beautiful, sobbing young girl wearing only a school tunic.

Another was film of an equally young girl being summarily raped, trying to fight the man off. They are bloody nasty, sir. Do you want to see them?"

"Afraid so," said Charles, reaching out. And then, "Jesus Christ!" He'd seen a few wicked things in his police career, but these were among the worst. And the thought that was smashing its way into his brain was that the man in the pictures might just have been Fontridge himself.

Mother of God! he breathed. The guy's an Appeal Court Judge. He's a Privy Counsellor ..."

It was one of few times in the life of the DCS when he literally did not know what to do. Instead of picking up the phone, he simply yelled to his secretary, "Matty! More coffee for all of us, before I go into shock!"

Larry and Jerry once more had not a smile between them. But Larry pressed on.

"We found a third EXE file. It was called 'Membership.' But we had no idea why, and never found anything to clear that up. However, the file had six names on it. All pseudonyms, each one followed by an email and a cell-phone number. We went straight into that, but the emails were all hidden under false names.

"We have applied to all the web-mail providers for all the email contents. I have informed them, on your behalf, this is a Scotland Yard enquiry at the highest possible level. Non-cooperation, I told them, was inadvisable in the extreme.

"The cell-phones were also dead, just pay-as-you-go sim-cards, which were very easy to get back then, with no ID required. But there was one exception— just one number still in use. We did not try it, of course, but the country-code, 54, was for Argentina."

Charles nodded. "Okay, boys," he said. "Did you bring me transcripts of the names, as well as these awful photographs."

"Right here, sir," said Jerry. Handing over a slim folder. "And we're still probing that hard drive," he added. "We don't think there's anything else. But you never know …"

"Just one more thing," said the DCS, "Why is that browser called TOR?"

"Sorry, sir, I thought you knew that. The Americans named it, The letters TOR stand for The Onion Route."

"The what!"

"The Onion Route."

"You mean like pickled, Spring and Spanish."

"Yes, sir. Because anyone trying to solve this kind of search had to peel away layers of data, one at a time, like trying to get into the interior of an onion."

"Trust Washington to come up with something shockingly direct, which sounds esoteric. They're good at that."

"Yes, sir. We'll be back in touch, just as soon as we have something."

As soon as they were gone, Charles took a long careful look at the six pseudonyms written on the print-out. None of them meant anything much to him, but he made brief notes.

Birkenhead: shipbuilding town on the banks of the Mersey, opposite Liverpool.

* *Sweet Charity* : Neil Simon's Broadway musical.

Divine Arima: God knows.

Tilden: US tennis player 1930's. A small photograph next to this one.

* *Beauregard:* Southern General in US Civil War.

* *Florida Garden*: No idea. But it has a possible Argentine phone number.

These were the non-too-impressive notes Charles wrote against the six pseudonyms. Even he was profoundly unimpressed with his reasoning. But he kept thinking and arrived at two conclusions. There was some kind of a thread, just beginning, and it might end anytime.

This very morning he had been presented with two specialists in juvenile sex—1) Sir Josh Hartley, 2) very possibly Lord Fontridge—if indeed that was him, almost naked and trying to ram himself into the body of a schoolgirl. And again whipping a slightly younger girl with a leather belt.

Was there a connection between these two unspeakable perverts, and the hard-drive on that computer? Plainly Fontridge was involved in something, because it was his bloody computer. But was Hartley one of the six names, carefully hidden like everything else to do with Fontridge? Did one of those pseudonyms conceal the identity of the dead disc-jockey?

Charles Barton had a feeling about this list; not one that he could explain, but Fontridge plainly had a darned good reason to hide it as thoroughly as anything could be hidden. It wasn't tucked into a secret compartment deep in the Upper House for nothing.

He decided on a methodical internet search. Birkenhead seemed the easiest, but he found nothing. Next he went to Tilden, which at least was a famous person, even though, he, Charles, knew little about lawn tennis. It took him a while since he found it hard to reconcile the fabulous record of this truly great player, with the fact that he had barely heard of him.

Seven times US open Champion, three-times Wimbledon Champion, Big Bill Tilden was described by the New York Times, and in an Associated Press poll, as the greatest tennis player who ever lived. Charles could not find anyone arguing. Bill Tilden's winning percentage at the US Open, over 90%, put him ahead of both Federer and Pete Sampras.

A 42-win match-streak from 1922-26 put him ahead of Federer and Ivan Lendl; his win-loss percentage in 1920 was 78-1—better than John McEnroe or Jimmy Connors ever did. Only Federer and Nadal, have matched Tilden's achievement of reaching 10 finals of one single Grand Slam event.

But then Charles Barton found another fact which made the hair on the back of his neck stand on end. Big Bill Tilden was a paedophile. Twice he was arrested—once on Sunset Boulevard in 1946 by the police for having sex with a 14-year-old boy in a moving vehicle; again three years later on a similar charge with a 16-year-old boy. He served jail time for both, and was ruined by it, shunned by the world of tennis in which he was once a god.

Who was on Fontridge's list of six, who might have used the name Tilden as a pseudonym? Not sure about that, murmured Charles. But I just might be getting somewhere.

And he returned again to the work done by Larry and Jerry, the Super-geeks who could peer into the darkest recesses of the Dark Web, and from whom no secret was safe, and who might yet pave the way to a criminal discovery involving a High Court Judge and Royal Advisor. If so, this would be a criminal discovery which would split the very foundations of England's system of justice.

Right now he did not have much of a handle on any of the six pseudonyms. But he had a meeting with George Kenny who was in London for the day, and of course they had many reasons to touch base. Sir George came up to the office and Charles had coffee and a couple of sandwiches brought in. But before they got around to the total lack of leads in the Fontridge murder, the Sussex Chief of Police had a quick joke he'd been reserving for Charles.

"It's about F.E. Smith, who you know was England's greatest trial lawyer in the early years of the last century. Well, he became a very senior judge, and one morning a newish judge came to his office and asked him for a professional opinion on sentencing: 'What would you give a chap who was prepared to let men bugger him?'

"'Oh, probably a pound,' said F.E. 'Maybe 30 shillings, depends what you've got with you really!'"

Both men were laughing at the jest, recounted at the expense of the former Lord Chancellor of England, but George swore it was true. "I've just read a biography, it's in there. He did say it, and a lot of other very funny things as well. His closest personal friend was, like him, a copious drinker, Winston Churchill. But the PM was tougher. FE died at 58, of cirrhosis of the liver!"

"He must have had one hell of a brain," said Charles, "Wasn't he Attorney-general, Solicitor-General and God knows what else?"

"Absolutely," replied Sir George, "He was the youngest Lord Chancellor for more than 200 years. They didn't make him the first Earl of Birkenhead for nothing—that's where he was born, up near Liverpool."

Charles Barton's head swivelled around so fast he nearly popped a couple of vertebrae. Birkenhead! Another Law Lord! Was that Fontridge's pseudonym? A name designed to conceal his involvement with a London Vice Ring?

He decided not to tell anyone about this at present, not even George, who anyway was about to leave. And once more the facts clamoured to be sorted out. Charles right now had an obvious, even probable, pseudonym. Fontridge had selected one of the finest legal minds in British history. And the two words clattered through his brain … *Law Lord … Law Lord … Law Lord.*

These were extremely rare people. One person in perhaps every million. And Freddie Fontridge, a vain man looking for a pseudonym, was a Law Lord himself. He had gone for the word 'Birkenhead'—the name of a fellow Law Lord, not to mention one of the immortals of English justice.

So far as Charles Barton was concerned this was it. The first name on that list, on his own computer was Fontridge himself. In the idiom of another sexual deviant, Big Bill Tilden, that was game, set and match. Lord Fontridge was 'Birkenhead.' "I wonder who the hell murdered him?" muttered Charles. But I might be a bit closer to the truth.

He found the list of six somewhat disquieting. He was quite sure it was a group of sexual deviants, and he felt a compulsion to identify the people on it. But he only had the pseudonyms to work with. Also his task was to find out who murdered Lord Fontridge. At present, nothing else.

But completion of the list might very well give him the clue to which person hated Fontridge so badly he was prepared to ram a stiletto into his chest and then dump the body in a lake.

And there was only one other word shouldering its way into his thoughts. And that was 'charity.' His mother had been talking about Sir Josh Hartley and how the work he did for charity was the key to his association with royalty and other high echelons of British society.

And, like a thunderclap, Jonny Harmsworth's newspaper had informed an unsuspecting world that the saintly Hartley had a driving preference for sex with very young girls. Some of them too young. Far too young. Against-the-law too young.

And then, no sooner was he settled into his office than Jerry Super-geek had strolled in with the list which was critical to this investigation, and the second word on the second pseudonym was 'Charity.' Coincidence? Charles Barton did not think so. Hartley and Fontridge were perverted weirdos, and it looked to Charles as if they were both on that list.

That gave them two things in common—1) a twisted desire for sexual gratification from under age females, 2) they were both dead. Charles accepted the Monaco police could not find anyone who might have shoved Sir Josh over the bannisters, as his mother had phrased it. But this did not mean no one had. It meant only that the Monaco police could not find anyone, and had given up looking.

In Charles's mind, Sir Josh very well could have been heaved over the rails to his death. And if he had, this meant the first two names on the pseudonym list would have been murdered. And right there, thought the DCS, we might have the start of a hunt for a serial killer: a serial, perhaps sex-vengeance killer.

With all this clattering around in his brain, he hit the keyboard on his desk-top computer, and asked Wikipedia about *Divine Arima*. Nothing. Then he tried just *'Arima'*—and, to his mild surprise, there were a couple of clues—one being a fairly common house plant in Mozambique, the other the last name of a Japanese 'Kamikaze' pilot in the Pacific in World War II.

The latter was quite a way from the Glyndebourne Lake, and the houseplant was bloody ridiculous. But Charles pressed on with the pilot, who it turned out was quite well-known in the Land of the Rising Sun. Admiral Masafumi Amira was in fact the first-ever 'Kamikaze.' On that first, and by definition, only mission, he had come in from a great height, aiming his fighter/bomber hard at the deck of a US aircraft carrier, overshot, plunged into the ocean, and died anyway.

Legends had grown up around him; how he cut the decorations and insignia from his uniform before taking off, and announced he did not intend to return. Japan has never forgotten him, and since this is a nation of many secret societies, his death is still commemorated in some of them. Admiral Amira was inventor of the phrase 'Divine Wind'—which is still used in some circles, to lionise, 75 years later, the 'Kamikazes,' Japan's selfless heroes who were prepared to deliberately lay down their own lives for the glory of The Emperor.

"Christ!" said Charles, "I'm looking for a perverted patriot—someone with a devotion to a dead Japanese hero."

The Wikipedia account gave a link to some of the Secret Societies of Japan, and Charles clicked it. There were not that many listed, only eight, and it looked as if half of them had died with their members. Three of them were well known, the ultra-nationalist *Gen'Yosha* (Dark Ocean), the rabid right-wing military *Sakurakai* (the Cherry Blossom Society), and the *Kokuryukai* (the Black Dragon Society). But the one that interested Charles listed several young pilots who had 'died so valiantly for the cause.' It was the *Society of the Tokkotai*, that being the collective word in Japanese for 'Special Attack Units."

165

One of them was a 24-year-old Pilot Officer of the Imperial Japanese Navy, who was promoted to Rear-Admiral before he took off for the last time. He died on April 6th 1945 in a fireball on the deck of the 2,500-ton, heavily-gunned US destroyer, *USS Colhoun*, in the Battle of Okinawa. Before she went, the *Colhoun* blew three Japanese aircraft clean out of the sky, and it took four Kamikazes to sink her. The last of them crashed into the bridge and blew it apart.

The name of this pilot was Yunto Takahashi, which rang a distant bell in the mind of Charles Barton: a bell which would have sounded like Big Ben on steroids if he'd properly read any of the reports about the Japanese tycoon who was murdered in his bathtub a few days ago. Still, it was there, a very small bell, tinkling with insignificance.

But Charles was not seriously into Asian murders, not when the pressure was mounting on him to produce results concerning the murder of an English Law Lord in nearby Sussex. But he found the subject of Kamikaze interesting. Particularly in the way a section of Japanese society was determined to keep alive the stories of the 2,800 men who committed suicide for the Emperor.

He read more about the *Society of the Tokkotai*, which had several benefactors in Japan and beyond. They had a museum, and spent their money on full-sized statues, portraying in bronze the lifeless stares of an almost forgotten generation of extreme warriors.

To Westerners this would seem unnecessary, commemorating, so fervently, dead combatants from a war so shatteringly lost. But the *Society of the Tokkotai* apparently lives on, and its Board of Directors meets regularly, and tears are still shed by families who attend the secret dinners; tears for young men who died hopelessly. Tears indeed, for the misbegotten.

Charles pressed on, pulling up more details on the Society. He found a list of their Directors, 10 of them, and he scanned down the names, each one having a specific area written after it; there were five from Tokyo; one each from Osaka, Nagoya and Hiroshima; one from the north-western Honshu seaport of Niijgata. But it was the name of the Deputy Chairman of the *Tokkotai* that stopped Charles Barton in his tracks: Yunto Takahashi (Hong Kong). And suddenly the little tinkerbell began to chime.

I know that name, he muttered. But the guy's been dead since 1945. How the hell can he be vice-chairman of anything? And then he spotted it, two small Roman numbers. He was Yunto Takahashi II, the probable son of the young Rear-Admiral who died in the Pacific fireball.

And the tinkerbell kept chiming, and suddenly Charles tuned into that as well. Yunto Takahashi was the name of that Hong Kong tycoon who died in the hot-tub. And Charles zipped out of the Kamikaze section, and re-directed his laptop to the vice-chairman's name—and one of the headlines in the *Telegraph* re-emerged before his eyes : **Yunto Takahashi found throttled in his hot-tub.**

And another major national figure joined this morning's Parade of the Perverts. *Divine Amira*, the obvious pseudonym of one of the Japanese patriots who admired the Kamikaze most of all… a high priest of the *Society of the Tokkotai.*

Well, that meant Charles had identified three of the six names on Fontridge's secret list, very possibly all murdered. And he was not precisely sure what he was supposed to do now. There was automatic connection, since they were all on the Law Lord's computer under assumed names. He just wondered if the first two, Fontridge and Hartley, knew each other. Because if they did, this meant things were really heating up.

And the new information might throw up one or maybe more people who would gladly have killed them both. Then the hunt for the Law Lord's murderer would come to life. Meanwhile, the question stood stark before him: Did the same person kill all three of them? Charles actually thought that unlikely, in such a short time, on account of the 20,000-mile round trip to Hong Kong required for such a mission. All three deaths had occurred in well under three weeks.

Once more he summoned the Super-geeks, and gave Larry a piece of paper with names and details of Fontridge and Hartley written down. "Check pictures of all London society balls and dinners, and see if you can find pictures taken of these two standing or talking together. Go back as far as you need."

Larry left without a word. Nothing much to say really. Either he'd find them or he wouldn't. Whatever he located would be an absolute. Yes or no. In his world, discussions beyond that were widely considered a total waste of time. He just nodded and left, preparing to run the two names through literally thousands of possibilities.

It took him about an hour and Larry came up with two definites … a very clear shot of Fontridge and Hartley chatting amiably at the Berkeley Square Ball in London. And another of the same two working as part of the black-tie charity committee at Queen Charlotte's ball, the 240-year-old traditional 'coming out' evening, now for England's modern debut girls. It was named for the wife of

King George III, but the girls, aged around 19, no longer curtsy to the reigning monarch.

"I'd have thought they were far too old for Hartley and Fontridge," remarked Charles Barton, wryly.

Larry looked totally bemused by this, and just said, "I suppose so, sir," and once more left without cracking even a remote excuse for a smile, which Charles found, quite frankly, disappointing.

With the Super-geek on his way back to the third floor, Charles did some research of his own—checking murders and killings involving questionable sex. The data was sketchy, many of the crimes had never been solved, but he found one statistic that interested him; that of known victims striking back at their former tormentor.

It looked as if there were a few, not that many. But there were hardly any angry relatives, brothers, even parents. Historically, so far as Charles could see, the only people sufficiently bold to pull the trigger were usually the victims themselves.

But there were so many unsolved crimes against sexual predators it was impossible to get a decent grip on the frequency of such homicides. Charles decided it did not produce a statistic sufficiently relevant to the Fontridge killing, but he resolved not to dismiss the thought if a victim of the Sussex peer ever broke cover.

He did fire off an email to the Commissioner of the Hong Kong Police Department requesting information on any suspect they might locate in the case of Yunto Takahashi, particularly after their announcement that his murderer had been a 'Western woman.'

He sent it more in hope than optimism, since it was already apparent that not one member of the 34,000-strong HKPD had the first inkling about the culprit, despite placing the Island into 'lock-down' for four days, with no flights, no rail and no road, either inward or outward, permitted.

That bird, thought Charles, had flown the coop. And with some reluctance he faced up to the fact that despite three very high-profile probable killings in under three weeks, despite Fontridge's oh-so-revealing list of sexual deviants, he was not much further advanced than Hong Kong. Despite everything, the three deaths had one melancholy quality which applied to them all:

Fontridge: no clues.

Hartley: not enough clues even to make it suspicious.

Takahashi: no clues.

"Bloody dreary," said Charles Barton to no one in particular. "But something, or someone, has to break soon."

*****

He and Sophia had a wonderful last night in London, and their dinner at Morton's was all that either of them had ever anticipated. It was, however, slightly edged with sadness because of Sophia's departure the following morning for Paris, where she was meeting Uncle Rudolf for a family conference. And this might mean a journey back to Russia for both of them, since her mother, his sister, Veroniya, was in a condition of obvious decline.

Neither Charles nor Sophia was certain when they would meet again, and on Thursday morning they clung to each other for more than four minutes in the foyer of the South Audley Street house, before Sophia somehow tore herself away, and ran outside to the waiting taxi back to Heathrow.

She was relieved to be telling Charles, by way of a change, the truth about her forthcoming travels. Well, it was the truth, and, she supposed, nothing but the truth. But it was not the whole truth.

Sophia was taking the cab to Kensington Palace Gardens, to pick up a Russian Embassy car. Her flight to Paris was not until 2pm, and she had a small task to complete before she left. Her family meeting was not until tomorrow in Paris, when she and Rudolf Masow were meeting to plan the next step of their mission to eliminate the vicious brutes who had ravaged her and her sister more than seven years before.

The black SUV and driver were awaiting her in the driveway of the Embassy, and the journey down to Henley, against London's notorious rush-hour traffic, took a little more than an hour. Sophia had the car stop around the back of the Leander Club, because she preferred to walk alone along the River, as she had done in happier times with her mother.

She reached the low, stone-wall surrounding the Church and walked in through the iron gate. The morning was bright, but as usual the graveyard was in shadow, beneath the pines, and the grass was still damp and dark green, and there was no one around. Little Sasha had a peaceful last resting place, but it was never peaceful here for Sophia, who saw not the ancient bell tower of the church, but again the stark and evil residential tower in West London from which her sister had jumped.

And she saw again the terrible whip of a leather belt with which Fontridge had virtually punished sweet-natured Sasha to her death. Sophia had tried for years to stop blaming herself, for not fighting back, and she'd tried hard not to recriminate herself for cowardice. Fontridge was too big and too strong. They'd both been helpless, and there was no help. Not from her step-father.

It always seemed to Sophia that the end had come when Fontridge had ruined Sasha's Sunday school dress, the dark green one. She was never the same after that. Sophia had never heard any living creature scream like Sasha did when she saw the marks on the dress. And for days the blameless young girl kept saying she was scared she'd go to hell.

Which was why the words had been chiselled onto the grave beneath Sasha's name: **A Tragic Child of God.** Sophia knelt at the grave as she always did, and prayed that eternal light will shine upon her. She reached out and put her hand on the cold headstone, and once more an eternal light lit up her own thoughts. It was a piercing, crackling bolt of pure fire which signified only Revenge.

She stood up and stared for a few minutes at the flint from the Glyndebourne Lake which now jutted out from the stone, and she very quietly said, "Don't worry, darling Sasha, this is not over yet."

Chapter Sixteen
A Warrior Princess Enters USA

"Your ancestors fought and beat Napoleon, they fought in the streets of St Petersburg in the1917 Revolution. Your great-grand-father was a Russian General, your family fought and died storming the Winter Palace. You're more Russian than I am!"

The essence of the Roman Catholic faith is very possibly stronger in Russia than anywhere except Italy—particularly among families whose ancestors celebrated Mass for centuries past, and whose faith had withstood various outright bans by the Bolsheviks.

And for two young girls such as Sophia and Sasha it was especially difficult, and held together only by the unquestioning devotion of their mother Veroniya. Drummed into the girls from an early age was the one biblical phrase which must never be questioned … *Thou art Peter, and upon thy rock I will build my Church* … the unforgettable words of Jesus Christ, as he uttered the very bedrock of Roman Catholicism, the first Christian religion.

And not Judas Iscariot, Henry VIII, Karl Marx or Joseph Stalin could shake them from Veroniya's soul. And, as a result, Sophia and Sasha were, and would always be, lifelong, devout, God-fearing Roman Catholics. Which was an impossible complication as they tried to reconcile young lives in which they suffered enforced prostitution, with the strict regime of the most important Catholic girls school in England.

St Margaret's Pangbourne saw itself as a special branch of the Vatican, occasionally with very much higher standards, at least sexually. Never, down all the years, had there been a scandal of any kind, either involving staff or former pupils. Which was a sight more than anyone could claim about the modern Catholic Church and its most trusted guardians.

There were four school dormitory Houses, in which the girls lived. The upper two floors in each House were devoted to private study rooms which two senior girls shared. Sophia and Kate Mildmay occupied one for their two years in the sixth form. Sasha never reached such seniority.

The St Margaret's Houses were named Sepphoris, Magdala, Saint Agnes and Saint Agatha; Sepphoris, of course, being the birthplace of the Holy Mother. In turn Magdala was the birthplace of Saint Mary Magdalene, the most important witness to both the crucifixion and the resurrection.

The two venerated virgin martyrs, Saint Agatha and Saint Agnes of Rome occupied immensely influential parts of the St Margaret's curriculum, especially St Agnes, the patron Saint of chastity and virgins. She was but 13 when she died, beheaded by a Roman soldier when the flames of execution parted and refused to harm her.

Sasha Morosova was in Saint Agnes House, and prayed to her each night before bed. She also prayed to Saint Agatha, not just each night, but to her dying breath.

Veroniya Morosova brought up her daughters in both the liturgy and the history of her faith. When they were all at home they attended the majestic, Gothic edifice of St James's Church, which stands in splendour on George Street W1, less than a mile from the house in Maida Vale.

This 19th century structure has deep catholic roots, as a former church to the Spanish Embassy. When they held a Requiem Mass in 1908 for King Carlos I of Portugal, King Edward VII and Queen Alexandra became the first British monarchs to attend a Catholic Mass since James II was banished from the English throne in 1688. The removal of England's last Catholic King is known as the 'Glorious Revolution.' Veroniya and later Sophia shared no such enthusiasm.

To suffer as the Morosova girls had suffered, sexually, emotionally, and personally, was obviously magnified 100 times over by their religion, their upbringing, and by St Margaret's Pangbourne. Sasha found it intolerable. Sophia possibly more so, but she may have been more of a Russian in her soul than her sister ever was. Rudy, at any rate, was certain of that. He actually thought Sophia was a throwback to the fierce and loyal Obolensky Imperial officers, Bodyguards to Peter the Great.

Perhaps she was. But now she was a sad and beautiful lady of 24, and sometimes she longed for the certainty and closeness to the Holy Mother that St Margaret's provided. It was a discreet and thoughtful place set in almost 300-acres on the Berkshire bank above the River, most of it beech woodland, some of it parkland, and all of it pervaded with a sense of piety and the utmost respect for Reverend Mother Anna McAuley. This devout and holy lady ruled St

Margaret's with strictness and kindness—but always with complete devotion to the Church.

Both girls were in awe of her. Both of them believed she was one of God's chosen representatives on earth. Just to see the great lady walking across the school lawns distinctive in her black habit, her hands clasped before her, her eyes cast downwards in prayer, the blessed cross of Jesus on a long chain around her neck. It was a memory Sophia would treasure all of her days. And there were times in Sasha's final weeks of overwhelming agony when she would awaken in the night, and cry out Anna McAuley's name, in both hope and terror ... *Anna ... Anna ... help me, Anna!*

St Margaret's was situated just 18-miles upstream from Remenham where Sophia now stood—eighteen miles and about a thousand light years from the sure but pious guidance of the Reverend Mother. Sasha had died without that guidance. Sophia swore to God she would seek it when her Crusade of Revenge was complete. She would confess her actions, as she always had, to the only true Sister of Mercy she had ever known, Reverend Mother Anna McAuley.

And now, she left the grave of her sister, having delivered one last assurance ... *this is not over yet, my dear. They will not walk away from this as long as I am alive ...*

And she made the sign of the cross in the Catholic way, and then her fists clenched. And, for the first time in eight years, she did not weep as she walked back towards the river. There were a few tiny trickles running down her cheeks. But Sophia Morosova did not weep. Not this time.

*****

Her driver dropped her at the airport on the way back to London, and she made good time to Paris, arriving home shortly after 4.30 in the afternoon. She unpacked, made a bundle for the local laundry and dry cleaner, phoned and requested a pickup, then called the Russian Embassy over on Boulevard Lannes.

They connected her immediately to Rudolf's phone and she told him she'd be there by seven o'clock. Always on time, he met her in the courtyard, right after she'd dismissed her taxi. He was thrilled to see her, and could scarcely wait to hear about her adventures in Hong Kong, and had Ivan been helpful?

"He was wonderful, Rudy," she said. "I could not possibly have done it without him. The escape plan was flawless. I think I was on a boat and chugging out to the South China Sea before the Hong Kong police even knew Takahashi was dead."

"Perfect," said Rudolf. "Ivan and I are very old friends. I'd trust him with my life."

"I just did that," smiled Sophia, and then sung a line from the Edith Piaf classic: *"Rien, je ne regrette rien!"*

Uncle Rudy clapped, but then he grew very serious. "My dearest Sophia," he said. "I must tell you, we'll get a drink, but I'm extremely worried about this next mission. You'll be operating a long way from help, and I cannot be certain you can make your kill in one comprehensive swoop."

"You speak as if I am a matador," she said, "Out there in the middle of the bullring, fighting the bull alone, on his territory, as far as I can be away from the *banderilleros* who must run out, and save me if I fall."

"That is precisely where you will be. And I am the chief *banderillero*, and I will be 4,000-miles away, worrying myself senseless while you tempt the bull to charge forward to his death, with a graceful flick of your muleta, before you strike, hard, fast and deadly."

"OLE! Uncle Rudy. And how d'you know so much about the *corrida de toros?*"

"I was stationed in Madrid a few years ago, around the time those Al-Qaeda terrorists were trying to blow the place up… remember they hit the train station, killed nearly 200 people and injured 1,800 more. My government had an interest in maybe six of that Islamic gang. And I was ordered to take care of it. Actually, a couple of them got away."

"And where were you, Uncle Rudy, when they escaped?"

"Can't quite remember—probably at the bullfights! I used to love it."

"I've always wanted to go. But I've never been in the right place at the right time. And now I'm getting ready to put my own life on the line again."

"I know, my dear. I know. And you are just like a matador. As Hemingway said, in *Death in the Afternoon … It's the only art-form where the artist risks death every time he takes part.* And that's why I want to talk to you."

"You do? I mean, about the plan?"

"Yes. About the plan. I don't want you to do it. It's too damn dangerous. Sophia, let me get it done for you. Please? I couldn't bear it if I lost Sasha, *and* you."

"Rudy, every time I look in the mirror I see the scar right below my hairline. I know he disfigured me, and then raped me while I was still lying on the floor with blood streaming down my face. It took twelve stitches to close the cut. And that brutal American ape just laughed at me.

"No, Rudy. There are some things you have to do yourself. And I am going, just as we had planned. I've been dreaming of this for such a long time. That ape is going to die. And he'll die at my hand. I have to go, I promised myself. And more important, I promised Sasha."

"Jesus Christ!" replied Rudy. "You're more of a fucking Russian than I am. Is there any point in discussing this further?"

"None. I'm going. I'd rather be caught and executed, than not go."

"You really are a Russian of the blood," added Rudy. "On your mother's side you're a Masow. But on your real father's side you're a pure-bred Obolensky, senior combat officers for centuries in Russia's Imperial Guard, the Bodyguard regiment to the Emperors of all the Russians—the Romanovs.

"Your ancestors not only fought and beat Napoleon's troops, they fought in the streets of St Petersburg in the October Rising. They were an elite Corps, your great-grand-father was a Russian General, your family fought and died during the Storming of the Winter Palace. You're a warrior princess by birth, darling Sophia. I can't very well expect you to ignore the disgusting insult and rape by this second-rate, tennis-playing oaf."

"Rudy, we're agreed he must die."

"Yes. I just hoped we could discuss who pulls the trigger."

"The discussion's over, Uncle Rudy. I'm going. As you say, I'm a direct descendant of Prince Obolensky."

Rudolf Masow knew, in any argument with Sophia, precisely when the game was up, that finely-balanced point in time when further protest was futile. And he reached into his briefcase and pulled out a black pistol, manufactured by the 170-year-old Massachusetts gunsmiths, Smith and Wesson. It was the very latest model of the M and P Bodyguard 380, beloved by both the police and the military as a simple gun to conceal, and lethal when fired.

Its steel barrel is a little over 5-inches long. It's lightweight, with double action fire control (second strike compatibility). Its heavy-duty ammunition packs a serious wallop, at 1,000-feet per second, rapid fire, five shots a second.

"This little handgun is identical to the one you will use to kill Buck Madden," said Rudolf. "One shot to the head should do it, but this thing will give you two shots real quick, and that will very definitely do it."

Sophia took the gun and wrapped her relatively small fingers around it. "It's comfortable, Rudy," she said. "Compact and lightweight. But I'm not sure you know. I've never actually fired a pistol in my life."

"Judging by your recent record, wouldn't be much need" chuckled Rudy. "But you're going to need to fire straight for this mission. Which is why I'm taking you down to the range in the basement, right now, before dinner."

"Okay, I'm ready," she replied.

And they headed to the elevator, down to the second basement where the Russians trained and treasured what they believed was one of the front lines of their defence system. Rudolf kept his niece working for an hour, ramming in the magazines, taking her sight lines and firing the .38-calibre bullets into a steel target. At first she missed the target all together, not having grasped the recoil of the little gun as it fired. The Bodyguard 380 had a very minor kickback, but just enough to throw off the aim of a slim-wristed girl.

But Sophia soon got the hang of this, and within a very few minutes, guided and encouraged by one of the weapons experts of the world, she grew accustomed to the process, pulling the gun from her pocket, kicking off the safety catch with her thumb, and then levelling it at her target, all in one movement. Both hands, rock steady on the aim, and smack into the target every time. And Rudy informed her, once more, that a Bodyguard 380 would be awaiting her in Washington DC.

Sophia was a quick study. "Must be the fancy school you went to," said Rudy. "Among its many achievements, they also produce a pretty good gunslinger. We're all done. This fucking rapist can probably count his time left on this earth in hours. I'll tell you about the bullets over dinner."

The dining room at the Russian Embassy in Paris was fairly busy this evening, the food as usual was good, as long as no one went for anything too elaborate. Uncle Rudy betrayed great concern about the long journey, the entry into Canada and the USA on a British passport, the long train ride down America's east coast to Washington DC.

He assured her he'd covered all bases at the Russian Embassy on Wisconsin Avenue. Her transportation deep into the Blue Ridge Mountains was organised, and, if necessary, there was an emergency route of escape. "Your bullets for the

Bodyguard gun were specially made in Russia for this type of work—the very latest flex-tip which actually explodes on impact. Target survival chance: Zero."

They each had steaks for dinner and shared a bottle of burgundy. And all through the evening, Uncle Rudy kept impressing upon Sophia the urgency of knowing if anything had gone wrong, if someone had detected her. Even if someone did not trust her.

"Look for the little signs, the suspicious looks, and never be afraid to bail out. I have organised things for you. But they're only good if you're right on top of your game. Remember, Sophia, God is on your side, you have the moral rights. It is 100 percent correct that this Buck Shithead should die. Just don't lose your nerve, and do something unscheduled. Stick to our plan, okay?"

"Okay, boss," replied Sophia. "I won't weaken and I won't stray from the plan. Three days from now that bastard will be receiving service on the outer ring of the Seventh Circle of Hell, the one for murderers—mind you, it's probably not that far from the Inner Ring, and he'll have a few comrades down there, I expect. According to Dante, the Inner Seventh is for Sodomites and other perverts."

"Christ, Sophia, they didn't teach you that stuff at St Margaret's, did they?"

"Not exactly. But I've known about it for so long I can't quite remember where I first found it. Actually I think it was from Sunday school. After Sasha left. She never went again after the dress. Too scared."

"Did you have her in your mind as you executed our enemies?"

"She's in my mind most days, Rudy, and every night. 'Specially now, this tennis bastard was very cruel to her, insisted on having sex with her when she was only 15, a virgin. It was awful, and she could not stop crying, sometimes for two days. And she couldn't understand what she'd done wrong. She just knew it was a mortal sin.

"I hope, Rudy, you never have to see a child that age weep for that long. It nearly broke my heart—maybe it did break it. I couldn't get over it, especially after she died. But it might be getting a bit better now."

"It will, my dear, I know it will. Perhaps not completely, but a little better after this mission, I'm certain of that."

Sophia brightened. "I have a chance, especially when I think of him dead. Did you know the residents of the outer ring of the Seventh are surrounded by boiling blood?"

"Can't say I did," he replied. "And if that's true, I am not particularly anxious to dwell on it, given my line of country!"

"Don't be silly, Rudy. You're not a murderer. You're a Crusader like Richard Coeur de Lion. Just carrying out the sacred wishes of your country's government, on behalf of the people. Buck Madden helped to murder Sasha, for sheer lust, and he's going to pay the price. If not yet in the eyes of God, then by the hand of Justice."

"Delivered by whom"

"By me, of course. Who d'you think?"

"Jesus, Sophia, you're more Russian than Ivan the Terrible."

"Unsurprising. I'm related to him!"

*****

The following morning, Sophia arose and began to pack her small lightweight suitcase. She felt rather sad, because she was going on a long journey, and her path would lead her into unbelievable danger. Mission Four was nailed-down, planned and organised. Following that she was wandering into the unknown, Mission Five, searching for a person about whom she had almost no clues, save the memory of a metal lapel badge, and a total inability to pronounce the word 'chair.'

She was preparing to leave Paris, which she loved, and which had become her home. Uncle Rudy had already left for London on the early Eurostar. But worse than all this, a whole lot worse, was that Charles Barton was disappearing from her life. In the next couple of weeks she could not speak to him. He could know nothing of her whereabouts. She could make no phone call which would betray her location. She felt sorrowful now, and she had not even left. A week from now, she would, she knew, feel absolutely desolate without him.

She strangely hoped that Charles would be furious with her. But not too furious. She also knew she was leaving the apartment which meant so much to her. An entire life was somehow stacked into these very personal rooms. And she loved the street, and the people and *Deux Magots*. But the truth was, she may not pass this way again. The dangers of her mission were too prevalent. She could be shot, arrested, even imprisoned. But she could not fight it. She had to go, for cascading reasons, but one in particular. For Sasha.

The journey to Canada, and the pressure of a connecting train in the half-French City of Montreal had been a major problem. Because of the six-hour time difference, the regular flights all arrived mid-afternoon. The train was the easiest way to cross the US border, but it left Montreal in the morning. Sophia was trying to avoid a very long wait, possibly 17-hours, on a Canadian railroad station.

This proved impossible, unless she took a flight with a stop on the way. And she'd settled for that. Offhand she could not even remember the name of the airline, but she had her ticket on Air Eskimo, or something, and would land in Reykjavik on the southwest coast of Iceland for a three-hour stopover. They'd touch down at Pierre Trudeau International Airport sometime after midnight.

It was a long day, and when they flew over the north banks of the St Lawrence estuary, it was pitch dark. Immigration however was easy, and she sailed through a rudimentary check of Mrs Doris Farringdon's British passport, and picked up a cab right outside the terminal building.

It was a 15-minute ride to Montreal's Central Station, and she collected her online reserved ticket on Amtrak's Adirondack Express to New York, a 10-hour journey of nearly 700 miles, straight down the Empire Corridor, through the mountains of Vermont and into the Great Appalachian Valley, one of the most spectacular train-rides in the world.

The enormous silver, red-and-blue striped locomotive arrived on time and left promptly at 10.20am. Sophia tried not to sleep, but kept dozing off, until they reached the utterly unprepossessing Rouses Point station. Right here the Adirondack Express had just crossed the unseen line into the United States of America, New York State, Clinton County.

And before them stood a 130-year-old red-brick building with wide overhanging eaves forming a covered passenger platform. The old station was very tired, and run down when it was sold early this century for $5,000—a diminutive sum of money even in this lonely, undeveloped area of the country.

In any event, Rouses Point represents the first sight many travellers from the north have of the USA, and this is where the immigration process happens on the Adirondack railroad. It's nothing like so severe as international airport security, and the customs men boarded the train for a cursory, but doubtless expert, scrutiny of passengers and identification.

Sophia's passport was checked by an officer, who snapped it shut and wished her a safe journey. Mrs Farringdon was in, and on her way, down through the ancient vineyards of New York State, crossing the Hudson River at the State

Capital of Albany, and on down to the last 50 miles, with a sensational view of the ramparts of the 200-year-old United States Military Academy at West Point on the far side of the River.

Sophia was following this part on her guide map, which she bought at Montreal Central. She was a natural scholar, Cambridge-educated, and she understood the significance of America's military stronghold across there, on the west bank. "The Black Knights of the Hudson," she muttered, staring through the window. "How impossibly romantic."

And she looked again at her guidebook, at the men who had learned Command at this fabled place: Robert E. Lee, Dwight D. Eisenhower, Ulysses S. Grant, General Douglas MacArthur, General Patton.

"My God," she breathed. "There's nowhere like that, not in all the world. And I'm looking at it." And Sophia crossed herself, like a Catholic priest, and offered a short prayer, "Please, God," she said, "Make me as brave as they were. Let me come through this. I'm trying to be virtuous, just for my little sister."

The Adirondack Express came thundering into Penn Station deep in the bowels of Manhattan just before 9pm. She'd been on this train for more than 10 hours, and she was glad to get off, glad to stretch out, glad to find a really pleasant, well-staffed, little station café and buy herself a cheeseburger and fries for supper.

Her ticket took her right through to Washington DC, with a 90-minute layover here in New York, and another, shorter one in Philadelphia. The cheeseburger, in her opinion, was world-class, and coffee was outstanding. The new train was less busy, and she was travelling in the comfortable club car, with its uniformed attendant, a large, gracious black man, with a huge smile, which made his nose look as if it were playing the piano.

"Anything you need, Miss," he said, gallantly. "I'll be right here. And I'll call you when we're pulling into 30th Street Station, in the very great American City of Philadelphia. That's mah hometown. Yes, ma'am." Sophia thanked him, and noted that he did not sound one bit like the man with the metal bulldog on his lapel; the one who couldn't say 'chair.'

Sophia slept. She slept all the way under the tunnel out of Manhattan, all the way through New Jersey, racing parallel to the Turnpike, and was still asleep as they came rattling through the northern suburbs of Philadelphia. They ran just south of Germantown, birthplace of Bill Tilden, which may or may not have been slightly poetic. Either way, the exhausted Sophia Morosova was awakened by

180

the attendant as they pulled into the monumental 30th Street Station, one of the last such towering railroad edifices in the country.

The wait was not long, and they pulled out of the City of Brotherly Love before midnight, on the 140-mile journey into Maryland and then on to America's capital. They were still right on time.

Everything was growing quieter now, and rail traffic was light, and the Amtrak Inter-City flashed through the open country of Delaware, swerved around the city of Baltimore, and came in to rest at Washington's picturesque Union Station, the southerly last-stop of America's Northern Railroad Corridor.

Sophia pulled down her bag, walked outside and looked for a black SUV with darkened windows, standard issue for Russian undercover men. There was no need to look far. Hard against the sidewalk was just such a car, and, standing right next to it holding the rear passenger door open was a young man in a black polo-neck, with jeans to match.

"This way Mrs Farringdon," he called. "I've just been talking to Uncle Rudy in London, and, by the way, he's just got up! I'm Sergei."

With almost overwhelming gratitude, Sophia climbed in and sank into the backseat. "Thank you, Sergei," she said. "Thanks for meeting me. I hope you haven't been waiting long."

"Not at all," he replied. "The Inter-City from New York's never late."

By now, Sophia was well into her third day of non-stop travel, sleeping on planes and trains, eating at odd times, worrying about her forged passport in a foreign land. She was absolutely exhausted. But this Sergei, who spoke with an American accent and, she guessed, was in his mid-twenties, struck her as a particularly cheerful companion. He was a good driver too. Anyone could see that.

"Are we going direct to the Embassy?" she asked.

"No, ma'am," he said. "You're staying overnight at the ambassador's private residence."

"Overnight!" laughed Sophia. "It's a bit late for that. It'll be daylight in about 20 minutes!"

"Well, I thought you wanted to drive into Virginia this morning," he replied. "It's a hell of a long way—more than 100-miles."

"Sergei," she replied, "If you'd covered the miles I have these last couple of weeks, nothing's a long way."

"Well, Sophia, right here you're among friends. We do know your proper name by the way. I called you Mrs Farringdon just as a kind of code. Just so you knew you weren't being kidnapped by some friggin' towel-head or something. You call all the shots on your travel plans. I'm just your driver."

"You're coming with me to Virginia?"

"Yes, ma'am. I'm with you all the way."

"Are you an American?"

"No. I was brought up here after the age of about eight. We're Russians, from Saint Petersburg. My dad was a cultural attaché in the Embassy here in Washington. He and my mom never went back. They live out in Leesburg."

"And you went to university here?"

"Sure did. UVA. Read American History. Best years of my life so far."

"You'll have to forgive me, Sergei, but we Brits are not good at universities. We've got Oxford, and Cambridge and a couple of others, and the rest's a mystery. What's UVA?"

Sergei chuckled. "University of Virginia, founded by the immortal Thomas Jefferson. Its original Board of Governors included three US Presidents, Jefferson, James Madison and James Monroe."

"Wow!" said Sophia. "That's impressive."

"It's still one of the best schools in the country—some people think the best, 'specially now the Ivy League teaches tired left-wing politics which basically died with Marx and Lenin."

Sophia paused for a moment, and then said, "So, you're not just an embassy driver?"

"No, Sophia, I'm not. I'm a second-line Intelligence attaché, based here in the USA permanently. Actually, I'm your bodyguard. I'm under orders to look after you with my life. The ambassador's a good friend of my dad's, and of Uncle Rudy, so we better not screw it up, right?"

"No. We'd better not."

Just then, Sergei turned onto 16th street NW, and came to a halt outside number 1125, a huge Beaux-Arts mansion which, in its day had caused more strife in Washington political circles than any other building in the world, with the possible exception of Hitler's underground bunker around the back of the Reich Chancellery in Berlin.

Number 1125 16th Street is now the residence of the Russian Ambassador, but it was once the Soviet Embassy in the USA, a home from home for spies, defectors, con-men, agitators, and blackguards. JFK was so jumpy about the place he was convinced they kept an atomic bomb on the third floor, four blocks from the White House! President Kennedy took anything connected with the Soviets very seriously indeed, and it was this downtown mansion, in Washington's historic district, which kept him awake at nights.

These very arched doors, through which Sophia and Sergei were now walking, were once the entranceway of the grotesque, bearded John Anthony Walker, former US Chief Warrant Officer, as he embarked on the most damaging spying career in the history of espionage.

It was against his own country, and it lasted 17-years, during which he sold just about every major US Naval secret in the Pentagon to his Soviet paymasters. One million encrypted documents. "He almost certainly swayed the Cold War standoff in favour of the Soviets," was the opinion of the brilliant Sir Casper "Cap" Weinberger, President Reagan's Defence Secretary, and a rare American statesman to be Knighted by the Queen of England for his priceless assistance during the Battle for the Falkland Islands.

For $1,000-a-week, until 1985, John Anthony Walker made his international headquarters at number 1125 16th Street NW, Washington DC.

Robert Hanssen, an FBI agent, and son of a Chicago policeman, walked through these very same doors in 1979, and offered his services to the Russians. Thousands of classified documents later, in which Hanssen betrayed US agents all over the world, he was finally nailed when the FBI paid the Soviets $7 million to give them the name of the mole in the FBI. Hanssen remains incarcerated in Butner Jail, Colorado, reviled perhaps most of all by the families of the brave and loyal US agents, who were executed in distant lands, thanks to him.

Sophia Morosova stepped into this dark, and ominous old building, shortly before the sun rose above the Potomac River, happily ignorant of its shudderingly awful history. Sergei let her know he could zip around this old house in any direction, having been a regular here all his life.

He led her up to her room, dumped her case casually on the bed, and handed her a cell-phone. "Touch that button," he told her, "And I'm on the line. It's one of our special ops systems, untraceable. It'll also get you through to the main embassy here, and if necessary, to the London Embassy. That's Uncle Rudy— by the way. Half the staff here owe him their lives!"

Sophia thanked him again, and told him she doubted she would be up for the Virginia trip today. "I'm so tired," she said, "I haven't had a proper night's sleep this week. I'll get up late this afternoon, find something to eat and we'll leave mid-morning tomorrow."

"That's just fine, Sophia," he said. "The ambassador is Dmitry Kutnezsov. Very nice guy, wife's name is Raeza. I'll tell her we're going for a drive round the city later this afternoon, show you the sights."

"Perfect," said Sophia. "I'd love to do that."

At which point the lights went out for Sophia for the rest of the day. She took a long hot shower, and unsurprisingly slept without even stirring, from 6am until three o'clock in the afternoon. Raeza Kutnezsov awakened her with some tea, and told her, "It's the middle of the afternoon, my dear, I thought you might like this," adding, "Your Uncle Rudolf is an old family friend of ours, and he instructed me to look after you." ·

"Thank goodness," said Sophia. "I might have slept 'til tomorrow."

Mrs Kutnezsov, a slender lady in her mid-50s, added, "So far as I know the plan is for Sergei to take you for a drive around the city, and return here for dinner. My husband will be back by six, and we usually have a drink and then dinner at eight."

"Gosh, that would be lovely. I'll get up now and pull myself together. That's a very comfortable bed."

"My husband's looking forward to meeting you," said Mrs Kutnezsov. "He knew your real father, you know. He and Mikhail had dined together in the very week of the crash. He never quite understood why your name was changed— you had such a wonderful heritage. Just to think, you're really an Obolensky, and that's a name to savour … right there with Romanov, Galitzine, Dashkova and Saltykov."

"I often think about that," agreed Sophia. "It doesn't matter so much in England. To them, Obolensky was just a wing-three-quarter in a pre-war Rugby team."

"The English are so taken up with their own heritage, they don't really believe anyone else has one," replied Raeza. "And, I suppose, in this modern world they are more or less correct. But they're not correct about Russia. No, my dear. Not about Russia. No one has a greater heritage than us. Did you know this very house, one of the finest in the middle of Washington, was purchased by a Russian Emperor?"

"No. I most certainly did not."

"Yes, Czar Nicholas II paid $350,000 for it in 1913. It's been Russian ever since."

Sophia smiled. She always loved hearing about the nation of her birth.

"See you a bit later, my dear," said Raeza Kutnezsov. "Dmitry's so looking forward to it."

Sophia understood instantly that she really had landed among friends. And when Sergei brought the car around to take her sightseeing, he handed her a package, which he told her to open and examine. She sat in the front seat, tore off the outside wrapper and found herself holding the exact same Smith and Wesson P308 gun with which she had practiced back in Paris.

"I picked it up this morning, at the Embassy," he said. "You're to check on the bullets and the two magazines, make sure you know exactly what you're doing."

"When we pull out of the area, we must get rid of it at all cost. Dump it in a river, or a deep forest, somewhere no one will ever find it. Remember, if we get pulled over for speeding, we must not have a gun with us. That leads to questions, driver's license, names, addresses, stuff we do not need with the Virginia State Police. This gun goes. Okay?"

"Okay, Sergei. I'm with you."

"Also remember, if you don't use the cell-phone, I'll just take it back. If you do use it, smash it, and then get rid of it, like the gun, but not in the same place."

"Okay."

What followed was one of the swiftest, most efficient tours of Washington ever mounted. Sergei drove first out to Arlington Ridge Park especially to show her the United States Marine Corps Memorial, the enormous bronze which shows six Marines raising the US flag at the Battle of Iwo Jima in the Pacific, WWII. President Kennedy issued a proclamation that the Stars and Stripes should fly on that flagstaff in perpetuity, 24 hours a day, in formal memory of every US Marine who had died in the service of the country.

"Iwo Jima was a terrific victory for the USA," said Sergei, staring at the mighty bronze. "And capturing that island, forcing the Japanese surrender, was an historic triumph for the Marines. But the Americans had 26,000 casualties."

"My God!" said Sophia.

They spun around and headed out to see the world's largest office building, the Pentagon, headquarters of the United States military. Then they drove on to see the colossus of the Lincoln Memorial, and the Jefferson Memorial. Then the

555-feet high obelisk of the Washington Memorial, which by law must remain the tallest building in the capital. Sophia saw the White House, the Capitol Building, and the Smithsonian. And that did it. Sergei swerved into 16th Street NW. Back to the former Soviet Embassy.

Dinner at the home of Ambassador Kutnezsov was an absolute treat for Sophia, just speaking to this enormously-important man about her father was a joy, and the vodka they served chilled, from a decanter, was like nectar.

There were only three of them at the dining table, but the food was delicious. Little *blinis* with cream and caviar to start, then the most superb *koulibiac*, a traditional Russian dish, fresh salmon lightly-baked in puff-pastry. For desert the Kutnezsov chef produced an exquisite *Pavlova,* meringue-based, with cream and fresh strawberries, named, of course after Anna Pavlova, Russia's immortal prima ballerina.

They said their good-byes after dinner, since Sophia and Sergei were making an early start in the morning, and the ambassador had a breakfast meeting with a Pentagon official at Wisconsin Avenue. Dmitry's last words to Sophia were: "Remember I was close to your real father, and I'm just like an uncle to you. So you have two uncles, both Rudy and myself. Promise me, you will do exactly as Rudy instructs on your next mission."

"I promise, Uncle Dmitry," she smiled.

"We will meet again," he said, graciously. "Au revoir, Sophia."

She walked up the wide staircase with Raeza, and they made their farewells outside Sophia's room. She slept soundly until her 7.30am call, and Sergei had them on the road before Ambassador Dmitry had finished his eggs at the Embassy.

Chapter Seventeen
Get Me Out of Here

*"Sergei, DEFCON 2—go to Operational Plan B right now.
I've overplayed this. I think he knows—40 minutes, Virginia
Tennis Camp. Latitude 38.05; longitude 78.84. Floodlit tennis
Court."* **Uncle Rudy 106** *...NEVER be afraid to bail out.*

Sophia and Sergei drove out to Route 95 and headed south on this famous US Interstate highway, which basically runs non-stop from Maine to Miami, a distance of almost 1,900-miles. As it happened, they only needed it for 50 miles, down to the city of Fredericksburg, which Sergei pointed out was perhaps the bloodiest cradle of the entire American Civil War.

"Right here," he said, as they crossed the bridge above the town, "That's where Major-General Burnside's enormous Union army stormed across the Rappahannock River and ran into the terrible fire of General Lee's Confederate troops, entrenched on the heights, up there."

Sophia stared for a moment at the hills above the town, from where the Southern marksmen had fired down on Burnside's brigades. "It was an absolute massacre," said Sergei. "Yet another futile frontal assault by the armies of the north. They had twelve-and-a-half thousand casualties that day. It was one of the most one-sided battles of the War.

"Even when Burnside ordered his 'Grand Division' to swing left and attack the southern defences, it was all hopeless. They ran into the steel-willed regulars commanded by General 'Stonewall' Jackson, who initially fell back through the marshes. But they regrouped, and Jackson's renowned 'foot cavalry' thundered forward again, with that chilling Southern war cry, and battered the Union troops all the way back to the river. Union losses were disastrous. General Burnside was later fired."

"Sergei, how do you know all this?" asked Sophia.

"I told you, UVA, American History. That's me!"

The car sped up, swung right off the highway, along Route 3, heading for Charlottesville, into the foothills of the Blue Ridge Mountains. Sophia saw a sign after a few miles, for the Chancellorsville Battlefield, and asked, "What happened there, Sergei? Anything major?"

"Sure was," he replied. "That's where General Jackson was accidentally shot down by his own side after winning the battle. He died on that riverbank down there, a few days after they amputated his left arm. It was one of the saddest moments in the entire War. General Lee never got over it..."

"How awful." said Sophia, with a very slight tremble on her upper lip. "What a terrible thing."

She actually looked to Sergei as if she might shed a tear these 150 years later for the fabled Southern Commander. And he decided not to mention the unforgettable words, written in General Lee's log-book ... *Lieutenant-General Jackson lost his left arm today. I lost my right hand.*

They took the long looping Route 29 all through the sloping foothills of the Blue Ridge Mountains and into the Shenandoah National Park, passing through some of the most beautiful scenery east of the Mississippi. Sergei swung off the road leading into Charlottesville, a quick right-hand turn and headed out along a country road towards Afton.

"Excuse me," asked Sophia, "But how can you possibly know this area well enough to duck and dive along back roads without even turning on the GPS?"

"General knowledge question coming right up," he said. "Ask me the precise location of the very great University of Virginia, Home of the Presidents?"

"Okay, give me the precise location of the very great University of Virginia, Home of the Presidents?"

"No problem. Charlottesville, Virginia. I spent four years here, speeding along these very roads. I know 'em like you know Paris. How's that?"

Sophia was compelled to laugh, now that she was over holding back her tears over the death of Stonewall Jackson in 1863.

Sergei kept going, and after one particularly daring swerve left, and then immediately right, Sophia was obliged to ask him, "Did we just go straight through someone's garden?"

"Funny you should mention that—it's an old short-cut, mostly late at night. Saves us three miles. Friends of mine own the house."

"Sergei! You don't know if they still own it."

"I can't deny that. But they definitely owned it five years ago. Guess I just rolled the dice. Don't come this way that often!"

Sophia rolled her eyes heavenwards. "It would just be so nice if we could reach our destination without getting arrested on the way for driving across someone's front lawn at 80mph."

"Seventy," said Sergei. But before the young Russian could elaborate, they both saw a roadside sign which read:

Royal Virginia Tennis
Club
Professional—Buck Madden
2-miles ahead

Sergei swung left, straight up a long, winding mountain road until they reached, on the right-hand side, two stone pillars and a wide open gate. A very large sign confirmed they were indeed at the tennis courts owned by the former Wimbledon doubles semi-finalist, and US Davis Cup team member, Buck Madden.

The drive up to the main court area was very steep, up the side of a mountain really, about another half-mile of twists and turns, through deep pine forest. But the view from the top was spectacular, to the West rose the high peaks of the Blue Ridge, back to the east were the rolling foothills, all the way down to Charlottesville, and, somewhere beyond that, the Virginia vineyards, and Monticello, home of America's third President, Thomas Jefferson.

"Well, old Buck surely knew how to buy himself a piece of land," said Sergei. "This place must be priceless."

"Old Buck didn't have a whole lot to do with it," replied Sophia, who had read every last word ever written on the Internet about the Madden family. "Old Buck's daddy just dropped it right in his lap," she said. "He had a fortune when he died, made it all from coal-mines in West Virginia.

"Daddy was a good ole boy, from Up-holler, as they say around here. That means he was a mountain man, born in the hollows made by ancient mountain rivers, rushing past some of the greatest coal-seams in America. He left everything to Buck's mother, and she's still alive. But the old Forehand King still did pretty well."

"Did Daddy own this land?" asked Sergei.

189

"Definitely. And one hell of a lot more. From what I read, he thought West Virginia was a coal-mine and he, old Bobby-Joe Madden, was the very right man to hack it all out, and the heck with the beautiful views.

"Young Buck never did care about anything 'cept hitting a tennis ball. And he was pretty darn good at it. So Momma Madden upped and sold all the coal-mines for an absolute fortune just before that discredited black President, Barrack-room, or whatever his name was, closed 'em all down in the interests of clean air. Put thousands out of work. My own dear Russian Daddy said he wouldn't have given him a job running a flower shop."

Sergei did not notice Sophia just touching the scar that was still visible below her hairline. Neither did he see, on this left-hand drive vehicle, her right hand slide into her jacket pocket and tighten her grip on her P308. And he certainly could not read her one single thought … *You wicked, unspeakable bastard … don't worry, Sasha darling … we've got him now…*

Buck Madden was never an absolute top-flight tennis player, not around 1980 when he was approaching his prime. It was the era of John McEnroe, Borg, Connors and Lendl; the twilight of Stan Smith and Jan Kodes. By 1986, Lendl was still No. 1, but here came Becker, Pat Cash and Stefan Edberg.

Buck could not beat them, but it was the era when the very top guys, chasing, for the first time, enormous prize money, had largely pulled out of the doubles, concentrating on the Big Bucks (that's dollars, not the local Virginian rapist).

Which left the way clear for the top doubles players of the era. And Buck Madden crept right in there, owing to the shameless manner in which leading players told the world's Davis Cup selectors they didn't really have time for that old-fashioned love-of-country team stuff. In fact they often said, to hell with all forms of patriotism.

Buck Madden got his chance, played and won two doubles ties for the USA against Czechoslovakia and Brazil. And the big, handsome Virginia Tech 'Hokie' has been lionised in the State ever since. Especially as he took another local boy, fellow 'Hokie' Jack Lehman, to Europe with him to play on the Wimbledon grass-courts and the red clay of Paris. And once they very nearly reached a final.

So there he was. Buck Madden, out there on the court, giving a lesson to a couple of young girls. Sophia could see him through the darkened SUV windows. But he could not see her. She checked her phone with Sergei, checked it worked perfectly. She checked her gun. She checked the time, 2.00pm. Then she told Sergei to spin around and get them to the nearest hotel which had a halfway decent restaurant and bar.

Sergei made for the main local town, Waynesboro, named for Brigadier-General Anthony Wayne, General Washington's ferocious Light Infantry Commander in the Revolutionary War. It was around 25-minutes from the Madden courts, and they settled for the new Dorchester Heights Hotel on the Afton side of the town.

It was three-star, $250 per night, best restaurant in town. Which did not actually say a lot, but it was a very pleasant, softly-lit room, where you could probably buy an acceptable bottle of wine. Sophia booked herself in for a single night, and for dinner for two at around eight.

She and Sergei had a late lunch there, just salad for her, a fourteen-and-a-half pound steak for him, at least that's what it looked like to Sophia, and it needed a kind of oblong china plate the size of a chessboard to hold it.

The Russian Intelligence officer gave it a good old college try, but failed within sight of the line, leaving about one quarter of the strip sirloin on his plate. Sophia thought it looked like enough to feed a pack of foxhounds.

At around 4pm she set off, alone, for the tennis courts, arriving just before 4.30. She parked and switched on the GPS, making a note of the co-ordinates, latitude and longitude. She cut the engine, just in time to see Mr Buck Madden walking away from what looked like a rather grand residence. With Sergei probably asleep back at the Dorchester, Sophia felt slightly exposed, but understood precisely what she had to do.

She walked towards the low building next to the main court with the big sign, OFFICE, on the door, arrived there at approximately the same time as the big tennis pro, who held open the door for her.

"Thank you," she said, "Might you be Mr Buck Madden?"

"That's me, ma'am. How can I help?"

"Well, I am trying to book four children into a tennis camp for August, and I have been given a very strong recommendation for this one."

Buck smiled. Sophia could have willingly killed him right then and there. But he just said, "Okay. Are they beginners?"

"Oh, no. They are aged between 8 and 11, two are mine, and two belong to a close friend. All four have played the game on and off since they were very young, and two of them are on their junior school team."

"Sounds pretty good to me. Do you have any idea what that will cost?"

"I imagine comparable to most other tennis camps run by professional players."

"We might be just a little more, on account of my wide international experience, and I assume they will all need full board, and concentrated tuition, regarding technique, and match-play training. Guess you'd like 'em to come out of here fit, and ready to play, and win, right?"

"Well, that would be excellent."

"Okay, that would be around $2,000 a week, per child. That's the cost of a medium priced hotel for the week with no food, and no hittin'."

Sophia suspected Old Buck had used that line many times in his life, and he smiled that lop-sided grin she remembered so well from those far-lost, nightmare afternoons when he'd raped her right in front of her 15-year-old sister, Sasha. Again she could have gladly killed him, right then and there. Also she could see him stealing little glances at her legs, as she sat across from him, her skirt swept just a shade too high.

"That's more or less what we expected," she said, "Around eight thousand a month each. Thirty-two thousand dollars for all four. Extras?"

"That's it. That's our rate for August. We don't worry about the extra days, in fact we throw in a couple of nights in September in case parents need a little more time to get here to pick 'em up."

"Very sporting," said Sophia. "I think we can get this sorted out today, if that's okay with you?"

"That'll be just fine," he replied. "I expect you'd like a little tour to see our facilities, dormitories, dining room, and stuff. And then we'll take a look at the gymnasium, and the courts, maybe watch a couple of my assistants coaching. Now the evenings are staying light, we have kids hittin' out there sometimes until 7pm—if they want to."

Sophia told Buck she would very much like to look around, and they took a long tour, inspecting the immaculate premises, right down to a good-sized swimming pool for the students. "August can get kinda hot up here," said Buck. "But mostly we get nice cool evenings after about 4pm, and early in the morning. We tend to give them time off if it's too warm after noontime."

"What's the biggest problem you have with the students?"

"Oh, that's easy. Gettin' 'em out of bed in the morning. I try to tell them, if any of you guys ever become a professional tennis player, and I really hope you do, you have to get up early, and hit the ball with your playing partner. Because tournament play is almost always in the afternoon. And you don't want to be tired. You just have to be used to early morning practice."

"I never really thought of that," said Sophia, smiling.

"Not too many people do. It's just real good to get 'em a little discipline early on—don't encourage them to think it's easy money out there. It's a lot of money. But it ain't easy money, no sir. You need to be real good. And highly disciplined."

It was way after 6pm by now, and Sophia knew she represented a very sizeable hunk of cash for the Royal Virginia Tennis Camp. They strolled back to the office companionably, and Buck asked a few questions, just routine stuff, where Mrs Farringdon lived? Massachusetts. Addresses for all the girls. Full names, schools, next of kin, guardians. Agreeable to paying a deposit?

And then, "Are you British, Mrs Farringdon?"

"No, I'm Canadian. I've been to England a few times."

"But you sound British."

"My husband was British. We're divorced now. He worked in Massachusetts. That's why the girls and I still live there."

"Did you come down here especially for this?"

"No. I was visiting friends in Washington. So I drove down to try and sort out my summer plans."

"Okay, Mrs Farringdon. If you're happy, I'm happy. We do like to take a deposit if we're reserving places for a couple of months into the future."

"Oh, I quite understand. How about $10,000 now, $10,000 when they arrive, and the balance when I pick them up."

"That'd be just perfect. Now, to seal our little arrangement, how about a walk over to the house for a drink, before you leave?"

"Buck, I cannot think of anything nicer. This has been nothing but a pleasure. And I'd like you to call me Doris."

The interior of the Madden house was as lavish as Sophia expected. Classic fabrics and drapes, carpets from the Middle East and antique furniture. Buck produced a bottle of cold Virginian white wine which was surprisingly crisp and steely. They clinked glasses and sat down.

"Well, this is very different from my original vision of a tennis academy," she said. "And the grounds are just beautiful. It must be a real pleasure for you to play on these courts every day of your life."

"It sure is, Doris. It took me a lot of years to get it running perfect, and these days we've had some very good results. Just hope I can get one of your little ladies to make it to the junior rankings."

"That would be wonderful. And I think you'll be pleased with their level of play right now."

"Which ones are yours, Doris?"

"Oh, the two youngest. I'm only 28-years-old, but I was married very young."

"I wouldn't have put you at even that age, not a day over 23 if you asked me!"

"That's very kind of you, Buck. And I must say you're a very well preserved man yourself."

"I'm kinda mid-fifties," he said, "But a lifetime of sports, at a very high level, keeps you young. I can still play a hard three-setter, and mostly still win 'em!"

"What about those very athletic assistants of yours—they look tough."

"They're tough to beat alright, but they still gotta play their very best to take the money off old Buck."

"I'll bet you're up to every trick in the book—drop-shots, lobs, backspin, with a real hard serve just when they're expecting a little kicker."

"I'm a devil against a left-hander," he grinned. "In my day I always fancied my chances against young Johnny Mac. We played coupla times, but he always just got me in the end."

"Not many people could claim to have stepped on the court with him," said Sophia, "Never mind having a shot at beating him. How many majors did he win? Six?"

"Seven," said Buck. "And he always played doubles, won five times at Wimbledon. If it hadn't been for him, me and Jack Lehman might have landed a title."

"Lovely memories, though," said Sophia. "This is a really nice conversation—and since I have to go back to my hotel to get you a check—how about having dinner with me at the Dorchester. I'm on my own."

"Why, Doris. I can't think of anything nicer than that. It'd be a real pleasure."

They both checked wrist watches and said, almost together … better get going, it's nearly seven.

Outside, Sophia said, "Would you ride down to Waynesboro with me? I don't want to miss that turning. Then we can drink a little wine together, and my driver can bring you back up here if I'm not feeling up to it."

"Can't argue with that," said Buck, glad of the opportunity for a good evening out, and no driving. Plus the fact, Miss Doris had the most enticing figure, beautiful long legs and the night was young.

An adult lifetime of predatory relationships had left him single, but ex-Wimbledon tennis star Buck Madden still saw him himself as a smooth, potent lover of pretty ladies, and, occasionally very young girls, though not as often these days. Real star quality never fades, he told himself.

They reached the Dorchester in about 20 minutes, and Sophia deposited him in the bar and went to the desk for messages. Then she took the elevator up to her room, and took out Doris Farringdon's check book and wrote one out for $10,000 to the Royal Virginia Tennis Camp.

She quickly called Sergei who was downstairs in the television lounge, and told him she was on schedule. "The car will be outside in the drive. I'm leaving the hotel at around 9.30. Don't move, I'll call you soon. Bye…"

When Sophia reached Buck in the bar, she had her light travelling bag slung over her shoulder. Buck noted that, and thought the stars were aligning for him, which was only appropriate, he thought, being one himself.

He smiled at her and handed her a glass of wine, and she in turn handed him the check in an unsealed envelope. "Why, thank you, Doris," he said, and slipped it in his jacket pocket.

And what followed was a very flirtatious evening. The dinner was pretty good and they talked a lot about tennis. Sophia had always followed the sport, and right now she was glad she did. Just before it was time to go, she made a suggestion which Buck almost fell over himself to accept.

"Now, I'm going to ask you a big favour," she said, smiling the smile of the true fraud. "I'd like to come up to the camp for a nightcap, but we'll go in a taxi, and I'd like to stand on one of the floodlit courts, and play just a few shots with you. Just to know what it's like to hit against a real Wimbledon maestro. Would you do that for me?"

"Of course," he said. "That would be real fun. I've had about four glasses of wine. You'll probably beat me. Perhaps we could have a little wager? If I win, I get a real nice goodnight kiss."

"Oh, Buck," said Sophia, smiling just a tad coquettishly. "I don't think you need to win a tennis match for that to happen."

Buck beamed. Actually Buck preened. Temporarily, he slammed his eyelids down, thus shielding from Sophia his irises which had just lit up like a couple of high-intensity light bulbs. At which point he nearly died of happiness. That ole tennis stud charm. Never misses. And that old overnight bag Miss Doris was carrying; that was sure as hell a critical sign. Hot Damn this is a good day.

But, all at once the thought flashed across his mind that this unimaginable sexy encounter with this beautiful high-class lady, who'd just given him $10,000, might be just a bit too good. Too good to be true? Too good to be real? Jesus, could this be a setup? Plus, he'd been thinking for some time, there was something remotely familiar about her. Of course, he accepted that was impossible. But there was something in her look—something cold, in direct contrast to her flirtatious demeanour.

Buck Madden might be a rich, spoiled boy, blessed with good looks, and an easy talent, but he'd inherited a fair slice of real up-holler coon-cunning from old Bobby-Joe. *Just not quite sure what in the Sam Hill's goin' on ... that's my problem.*

Then, quite suddenly, he said something surprising. "Miss Doris, I'm detecting a little accent that wasn't Canadian and not British at all. Am I missing something here?"

"Not so far as I know, I'm Canadian, born and bred. But Montreal's a very French city, and it's not hard to pick up an accent. So many people speak only French—I wouldn't be surprised if I say certain words like them."

"Aha," said Buck. But Sophia sensed he was worried. There was a small frown on his tanned forehead, and for the first time he'd stopped looking at her legs. Had she imagined the slightest flicker of recognition? As they stood up from the table, she said, "I'll just slip into the ladies' room, and see you on the forecourt. That taxi out there is ours."

"Okay," he replied and headed right to the men's room. Her telephone conversation behind the locked cubicle door was alarming: "Sergei. I may have been rumbled. Please put Plan B into operation and get me out of here—40 minutes Virginia Tennis Camp—that's latitude 38.05; longitude 78.84. Floodlit tennis court. Sergei, I may have overplayed it. I think he knows."

As she clicked off the cell-phone, the words of Uncle Rudy echoed back to her ... *the slightest suspicion, never be afraid to bail out.*

They regrouped in the taxi, and set off for the tennis camp, up through the pines, around the steep contours of the mountain. Buck held her hand and she made no objection, aware that he might be just trying to stop her shooting him.

Back at the courts, she dismissed the taxi, which would be included on her hotel bill, and told the driver, "I have your card. I'll call in about an hour, when, and if, I need you."

Meanwhile, Buck had gone to the court and switched on the lights. He called over to her, "There's a couple of my rackets here, and a box of balls. I'll be a few minutes, just going to the house. Better start practicing, but I don't wanna lose my kiss, no sir!"

Buck was serious about that. If this was no set-up he did not want to screw it up. He should keep playing the infatuated dude, like always, since he was Virginia junior champion 45 years ago. But, once in the house, he called the Waynesboro Police Department. And if Sophia had heard Buck's conversation she'd have fled right now.

"This is Buck Madden, tennis academy, can I speak to the duty officer." Then, "Right here I might be in real danger. Like I'm with someone who might be trying to murder me."

He then explained to the officer about a private society he had been in over in England. "And two other members had died in the last couple of weeks, one of them murdered, the other in suspicious circumstances in France or somewhere."

The officer said, "Mr Madden. You mean right here we might be dealing with a serial killer?"

"That's what's scarin' me."

"Is the person with you right now?"

"Yup."

"Armed?"

"I don't think so. She's a lady. A real lady, matter of fact. Seems kinda harmless."

"Okay, Mr Madden. But you never know. We better get right up there. I got a couple of teams out west tonight. It'll take about 15 minutes to get 'em back. I'll send them both out to you. Look for us in 30 minutes."

"Thank you, officer. I appreciate it."

But the real action had taken place in cast-steel secret before they'd left the Dorchester. Sergei was terrified by Sophia's phone call … Jesus, if anything

197

happens to that girl, there'll be a goddamn uproar … and he hit the emergency button, direct connection to the switchboard at the Russian Embassy in Washington.

He spoke in encrypted code only: DEFCON 2 (US military scale of threatened disaster—**Defence Readiness Condition)** Order immediate emergency take-off Lewisburg helipad Augusta AW9S. Destination: Fifteen-love floodlight. 78.84 Long. 38.05 Lat. ETA: 35mins. *Emergency. Emergency! Emergency!* Alert RA1 Immediately. Do you copy?

And now the $8 million Russian-owned Augusta Westland AW109S helo was up and thrashing its way east over the Blue Ridge mountain range, piloted by the decorated former Soviet gunship driver in Afghanistan, Lieutenant Pietr Markovitch. He was aged 56 now, and hammering his way over the peaks at 180mph assisted by 1st Officer Nikolai Kaverob. This was a converted ground attack helicopter driven by two 735hp Pratt and Whitney turbo-shaft engines, under a 36-foot rotor span.

Both men were wearing night-vision goggles as they skimmed the long ridges of the Appalachians, using split-second skills perfected high in the Hindu Kush, where they feared every escarpment was shielding Afghan's fighting tribesmen, armed to the teeth with President Reagan's lethal 'Stinger' ground-to-air missiles.

Contrary to all US national air navigation laws, the AW109 was showing zero navigation lights. But both Markovitch and Kaverob were getting a real kick out of this potential high-pressure rescue, and the helo was travelling like a bat out of hell, straight towards the historic Shenandoah Valley.

Markovitch to base. Air speed 180 … 79 degrees east-northeast … ETA 19…

*****

Sophia Morosova was an interesting sight, practicing her serves, wearing her jacket, and her thin white leather driving gloves, all by herself on a tennis court in the Blue Ridge Mountains, Virginia. Buck Madden came over to join her and observed that he'd seen a couple of real zingers go well into the service court.

He walked to the other side of the net, and took up a stance close in, ready to return volley her ground strokes. They hit the ball back and forth three times, until Sophia sent him a high, but short lob. Buck went up for it, hitting the overhead shot with casual ease, right over his opponent's head, and laughing quietly.

However, when he landed, and looked over the net, he stopped laughing very quickly. Because he was staring straight into the muzzle of a short Smith and Wesson P380, clasped in both hands by his opponent. Buck Madden summoned instincts honed over a lifetime on a tennis court, and tried to twist away.

But Sophia had squeezed the trigger hard and the 680mph flex-tip bullet smashed into his left-eye socket on the diagonal, and blew his head almost in half. He catapulted backwards, but before he landed, she fired again, slamming one more of these deadly high-velocity slugs directly into his heart. "That one's for Sasha," she gritted. "Just in case you're wondering, you sonofabitch."

But even as she turned away, Sophia heard the distant howl of police sirens, as the two patrol cars from Waynesboro came racing up the mountain road. She couldn't see them, but she could hear them clearly, and guessed they were about four miles out. Maybe eight minutes climbing the slow turns and gradients of the heavily wooded Blue Ridge.

She was trapped now. And she knew it. But she'd done her duty in the eyes of God, of that she was certain. And she walked quietly to the electrical boxes, and switched off the court floodlights. Her options were limited, a life on the run, up in the forest, until she was caught. Or, more probably, a lifetime in jail. She decided on a third option, the one almost everyone has, and, standing alone in the dark, she drew her gun for the second time that night.

She took one final glance at the dead tennis pro, lying in a pool of blood in the darkest shadow of the net. Then she checked the gun's magazine, decided there was no point calling Sergei, and raised the weapon to her head. "I'm coming, darling Sasha," she muttered. "Don't worry, I won't ever leave you alone again.

The police sirens were still howling, the white Dodge Chargers with their wide blue stripe, roaring around the chicanes of the Blue Ridge. But suddenly there was another sound, a loud throbbing, clattering right towards her, out of the mountains. Sophia momentarily lowered the gun, but could see nothing, and the police sirens were growing closer. So was the deafening night monster screaming over the tree-tops, and unleashing a sudden, outrageous beam of light, which split the darkness over the tennis courts.

She raced to the side netting, and clamped her hands over her ears, trembling all over. It was like a sci-fi movie come to life. She understood it was a

199

helicopter, that or a space-ship. But it had no lights, in this mountain blackness, just the beam of a searchlight, which threw no shadow.

"DEAD AHEAD, PIETR!" yelled Nikolai, sitting rigid, white-knuckled in the co-pilot's chair. "But goddamnit, the lights on the court just went off. Go straight for the tennis court anyway. We got a firm landing area, even in the dark, and I got the beam fixed dead ahead."

Lieutenant Markovitch lurched the AW109 almost to a standstill, 30-feet above the court, balancing the three-and-a-half ton aircraft with fingertip precision, while his first officer tried to keep the overhead searchlight on the net. The slashing rotors were the same length as the baseline, 36-feet, with six-feet clearance either side. Baseline to net: 21-feet, nine-feet clearance at the back.

All Sophia could hear was that shattering *BOM-BOM-BOM* of the blades above the scream of the turbos. And she closed her eyes, her head pressed against the side netting, as the Russian helicopter slowly descended.

"STOP LEFT!" bellowed Nikolai. "Come in straight down the centre line— *WATCH THAT FUCKING WIRE DOWN THE TRAMLINES!"*

"For Christ's sake! The name's Markovitch not Djokovic! Gimme clearance—*COMING IN NOW!"* called the pilot ... *"TWELVE FEET!"*

"Easy, sir, we might be on the wrong court."

"I know… I know … but there's blue and red lights on the drive…"

"LOOK OUT, SIR ... THERE SHE IS! ... I CAN SEE SOPHIA ... DEAD AHEAD!"

"WELL, OPEN THE FUCKING DOOR—FOR CHRIST'S SAKE OPEN THE FUCKING DOOR AND YELL!"

Nikolai stamped on the big red button at the doorway, the one every First Officer hits if the Navy has to ditch in the ocean. The door slammed back. Nikolai jumped the last six feet, ducked below the rotors, yelling … *SOPHIA! SOPHIA!* And then he grabbed her, half-running, half-dragging his petrified passenger.

"GET IN!" he shouted, *"GET IN!"* She certainly knew enough to obey that command, and with language to make a drill sergeant blanch, she smacked her knee, bashed her head and rolled into the cabin.

"Nice job," said Nikolai, helping her into a seat. "Uncle Rudy will be pleased!" And then, bellowing, *"THAT'S IT, PIETR ... GO! GO! GO!"*

And the mighty British-made helicopter, engines screaming, lifted off from the service line, drifting right, as Nikolai finally slammed the door shut. With the throttles wide open, the rotor-blades cutting into the thin mountain air, Lieutenant Markovitch launched her away, tipping forward, and rocketing west now, straight up and over the mountain, climbing out across the Valley, towards the State Line of West Virginia.

Their only passenger, Miss Sophia Morosova sat in the back, and wept uncontrollably, from sheer gratitude. In front of her were two very gallant Russian pilots. But, for the moment, she saw only the hand of God, which she was certain had delivered her from the wrath of Satan.

Pietr had them across the first ridge, 180mph, and well out of sight, before the two police cars arrived outside the Buck Madden courts. The AW109 still carried no running lights. Lieutenant Pietr Markovitch had his NVGs strapped on tight, and there was a little smile on his face, as they flew across the Shenandoah. It's known in his trade as *Mission Accomplished.*

Markovitch to base. Casualties zero.

Roger that, sir.

Chapter Eighteen
A Bulldog from the Bayous

*"In my experience," he said, "Playing things strictly by ear
is the best possible formula for ending up dead ... plans,
Sophia ... accurate, ruthless, properly thought-out plans.
I know of no better procedure for staying alive. Understand?"*

The two police cars from Waynesboro came bursting over the summit of the hill where the Madden courts were situated. Their headlights lit up the area and the four patrol cops jumped out of the cars immediately, shouting, "Mr Madden? Are you out there?

They were greeted by stark and widespread silence. The place was deserted. No lights were on anywhere, except in Buck Madden's residence. All four of the officers ran to the front door, banged and then entered, searching upstairs, downstairs, everywhere. There was no one at home.

Back outside, they scanned the place with flashlights, then swung the patrol cars around so the headlights beamed over the tennis courts. Which was when they located the dead body of the professional, lying close to the net. A few tennis balls were still on, and around the court. There were two rackets, one dropped near the baseline, the other still clutched in Buck Madden's hand.

Two of the officers continued the search on foot, the others returned to the patrol cars and reported in, summoning an ambulance. They checked out the last call made by Buck Madden to Police HQ, the one where he had assured the duty officer, that the person of whom he was afraid, was indeed a woman, actually "a real lady, kinda harmless."

"Yeah, looks like it," said one of them, giving a sidelong glance at Buck's brains spilling out of his head, onto the deuce court, surrounded by blood.

"Any other injury, aside from the gun-shot wound to the head?" asked the senior officer.

'Do I have your permission to move him? Turn the body over?"
"You do not. Better wait for the doctor."

The time was 10.45pm. And whoever did this was long gone. The howl of the sirens had blanked out any chance the police had even of hearing the departing helicopter. And there had been nothing visual, especially as the Westland AW109 was a mile away over the ridge, and well on its way, before the police even arrived. No one saw anything, and anyway the helo displayed no running lights.

In time, the ambulance arrived, and the doctor confirmed that Mr Madden was indeed dead, and this should be confirmed at the University of Virginia Hospital. They placed the body on a gurney, strapped it in, and had it transported to Charlottesville.

They taped off various sections of the grounds and declared them a 'crime scene'. Two officers were left on duty, and the other car returned to Waynesboro, where a state-wide murder hunt was already in place, with spot searches being carried out on the highways, and helicopters deployed to search the woodland around the Madden camp, mostly using thermal and infrared techniques to try and unearth anyone who might be hiding out in the forest and on the mountain-side. Not even the station sergeant at Waynesboro considered the slightest bit of good would come from this.

Someone had indeed shot Buck Madden dead, but that someone was no longer in the area, which was a serious mystery, since no one could have escaped down the road to Waynesboro, not with two big police cruisers, high, wide and handsome, blocking the road, and travelling fast in the opposite direction.

And there was no other way out, nothing suitable for road transportation. So, either there was someone out there on foot, walking through the trees, in which case they would be found within 24 hours. Or someone had been airlifted out of there, which was regarded as impossible since no one had seen anything, or indeed heard anything. Stone-silent, invisible air transport had not yet been invented.

Which meant that Buck Madden had been murdered by a spook, or, as one officer put it, by "a fucking extra-terrestrial." Whatever, the silence on the mountain was rapidly giving everyone the creeps. Was it even possible that right here near Waynesboro, there was some kind of a homicidal maniac roaming around with a pocket-full of dumdum bullets, and a powerful little gun with which to fire them?

It all seemed bizarre, but tomorrow morning there would be questions asked and answered. The tennis pro's assistants would be on duty, there would be students packing up and leaving, members of the ground staff arriving. It had seemed pointless to question the kids in the middle of the night, and anyway there were very few in residence this early in the season, all aged about nine.

The Police Department had done its collective best in the middle of the night, but investigation was somehow 10 times as difficult in these remote country areas, compared with the problems in the city.

Surrounded as they were by hundreds of square miles of virgin forest, impossible mountain gradients, and narrow roads, concealment was too easy. At least it was initially. But most of Waynesboro's 50-strong staff understood that criminals usually break cover in the end.

The biggest problem tonight would be the media. Right now there were probably 20 people who knew someone had arrived at Buck Madden's tennis camp and shot him dead on Court One, blown his brains out with a .38 calibre handgun.

Within an hour, say by midnight, that number would have trebled, with the main leakage coming from the hospital. Someone on the University of Virginia public wards would have notified the night desk of *The Daily Progress*, at Charlottesville. Same from the police or ambulance departments at Waynesboro, where the night desk of the *News Virginian* stood ever ready to leap all over a controversial murder. The *Fredericksburg Free Lance Star*, and the *Culpeper Star Express* would also be in the hunt. But there were not many local television stations likely to hit the airwaves during the small hours.

The first enquiries came in shortly after midnight. After that it was non-stop. The local reporters had a source of income that was very quiet, assisting the networks in a big breaking new story. And they were swiftly into this one. In fact the local police chief in Waynesboro was truly surprised at the interest in the death of the 59-year-old tennis pro.

Virginia's Big-Hitting Tennis Great
Shot Dead On The Court

Buck Madden Murdered in late-night Slaying

That was the drift of all the Tuesday morning papers, and in a heartbeat it was all picked up by the grown-up writers of daily journalism. Then by the cruising vultures of the internet, the jackals of Facebook, the hyenas of YouTube, the scavengers who live daily off the newsrooms of the pros, the Big Boys of print journalism.

Some of them tried to put Buck's achievements into better perspective, but the news of the handsome unmarried old-timer swept across the nation, making it strongly on the front pages of the *New York Times, Post* and *Daily News*. From the *Washington Post* to the *Los Angeles Times*, from the *Boston Herald* to the *San Francisco Chronicle*. Front pages all the way...

Television came trundling along behind, and by lunchtime there were reporters and cameramen all over the place. They stationed themselves in Waynesboro, and had the Dorchester Heights Hotel under siege, as they tried to interview the waitress who had served Buck and an unknown young blond for dinner the previous evening. This thing got better by the minute. For reporters, you simply cannot get better than *"an unknown young blond."*

*****

Sophia's ride home was complicated by the fact that she no longer knew where home was. Also she had not the slightest idea where they were going, nor did she know who Nikolai was, nor indeed his cheerful cohort who was at the controls. It was pitch black outside, and hard to speak inside, such was the roar of those big Pratt and Whitney engines.

She could sense the two pilots were speaking in Russian, and she understood they were flying very fast in a dead straight line. She was encouraged by Nikolai's mention of Uncle Rudy, but essentially she had no idea whether they were remaining in Virginia or going to Vladivostok.

Sophia ventured to ask Nikolai what was below them, and he just said, "Five thousand feet. Shenandoah Valley." This meant absolutely nothing to her. Except that Sergei had told her that Stonewall Jackson had marched his Confederate army up and down its entire length three times, claiming victory after victory.

At this point, Nikolai asked her for the gun, and both magazines, which she duly handed over. Then he wanted the phone Sergei had given her. He put that on the floor and smashed it with the heel of his flying boot. And then he slid back a small sliding window, and tipped the whole lot, one by one, out into the night, scattering gun, bullets, and cell phone into the stratosphere high above the dense pine forest.

"Uncle Rudy's orders," said Nikolai. "Leave nothing behind. Make sure not one shred of evidence can ever be found. Destroy everything."

"I'm pretty certain no one will ever find any of that little cargo," said Sophia. "Not for several hundred years."

"That's the plan. Just so long as everyone knows. When Rudolf Masow says do it, that's do it. He's got a long reach."

"Does he know where I am?"

"He knows where everyone is!"

Eventually she asked Nikolai exactly where they were going, since she could already sense they were losing height. He told her, "We are landing at Lewisburg, over the border in West Virginia. It's a small private airfield for helicopters only."

"Are we staying there?"

"You are Miss Morosova."

"Have I been kidnapped?"

"Don't be ridiculous. It's Russian. It's an adjunct of the Embassy. Ambassador Kutnezsov set it up a couple of years ago. The Lewiston Air Base has the same diplomatic protection all embassies do."

"But what's it for?"

"I cannot tell you exactly. But it's very hard to fly in and out of Washington in helicopters, it's too busy, and impossible to land without clearance from the main airport controls. You just can't put an aircraft like this down on the roof of some city building—you might hit the Smithsonian by mistake! And it all interferes with the President's security systems."

"Do other embassies do this?"

"No, just us. Because we are always bringing people in, and flying them out. Usually short distances from city airports, Boston, Newark, Philadelphia, Atlanta. It just suits us better to have our own air connection."

"It suited me pretty well tonight," said Sophia.

"It definitely did. Pietr made a fabulous landing in very tight lines. By the way that's a slight bruise on your forehead."

"Not as bad as Buck's." she thought.

By now the AW109 was descending steadily. Sophia could see lights outside, and two landing officers holding coloured light sticks, signalling them in. They touched down gently, and Nikolai opened the door, helped her out and handed her the shoulder bag.

One hundred yards away, was a discreetly lit, low ranch house, and beyond that Sophia could see fenced paddocks. It looked like a very sleek operation, typical of the cattle-breeding heartland of the Mountain State, where there's close to 380,000-head grazing every week of the year. This medium-sized ranch, set to the northeast of Lewisburg, was the only one in the entire state, the only one of 23,000 breeding ranches, which did not own a single cow.

This, instead, was Russian East Coast Air Command, where the men from the old Soviet Union monitored coming and goings of both foreign and domestic air traffic, military and civilian. To the right of the old cattlemen's bunkhouse was a windowless room which contained more LCD (Liquid Crystal Display) screens and satellite link-ups than Cape Canaveral.

The view of the US government was sanguine. Since the Russians were going to do this somehow, somewhere in the US of A, they may as well do it somewhere "we know darned well what's going on, keep an eye on 'em." It was not of course beyond the realm of possibility that there was a similar command station, in some small corner of the Russian Tundra, which would be forever America.

Sophia was shown inside by an 'executive secretary' named Olga, and taken to a really pleasant ground floor bedroom, with a photograph on one wall of the world's first outer-space cosmonaut, Yuri Alekseyevich Gagarin, and the Vostok 1 spacecraft which took him there in April 1961. On each of the other two inside walls there were spreads of longhorns, and a couple of Indian tomahawks in memory of the Shawnee who once roamed these mountains.

The walls were wood-panelled, and a writing desk, with a desk-top computer" was placed in the window to the right of a king-sized bed, covered with a large quilt featuring a buffalo the size of Yuri's Vostok 1. Sophia crashed onto the bed fully-dressed and was asleep before the rotors of the AW109 had come to a halt outside her bedroom.

She slept for the rest of the morning and was awakened by Olga shortly after lunch, who brought her some coffee, a toasted English muffin with smoked salmon, and a couple of sugar-dusted Russian pastries. "That really is very sweet of you," said Sophia, smiling at the attractive, slim, 30'ish official who plainly had rank in the Russian Air Force. She'd noticed both pilots showed her obvious respect, flying officers to a senior officer.

"Miss Sophia," said Olga. "Around here, the beloved niece of Rudolf Masow is entitled to any darn thing she may want. Your uncle is a legend, and the most trusted friend of the President. His work on behalf of the Motherland is beyond price. I do hope you'll be joining us for dinner … just the two pilots, the director and myself."

"That would be lovely," she said. "Also I'd like to have a look around these paddocks, if possible. Looks like a beautiful farm."

"Of course, you may. I'll take you myself, say around 3pm. But don't be too disappointed there's no livestock. I'll tell you why later."

Sophia ate her lunch thoughtfully. It was all delicious, but there was something on her mind which would not go away—the abiding mystery of Mission Five. Just who was that awful American who could not pronounce the word 'chair'?

She'd never forget him, and she'd very definitely never forget the way Sasha absolutely dreaded his arrival. Sophia, much older now, still could not imagine the horror of any teenage virgin being forced into every kind of sex act at the age of 15 with some brute of an elderly man.

The thoughts still tumbled through her mind, over and over, and sometimes she thought Sasha was haunted by the memory of that weird American, right until the moment she jumped. And still her own brain was in a turmoil, just thinking.

It was bad enough for me … but I was more than two-years-older and a bit more savvy. But Sasha had no idea what was happening. There was one time she was so scared she was physically sick when she heard his voice on the stairs talking to our step-father.

And now Sophia had set herself a task: to find this pervert somewhere in this vast country in which she was a stranger, but appeared to have heavyweight backup thanks to Uncle Rudy, who was even more upset about the death of Sasha than she was.

She actually had two clues. Nothing else. One was, she knew he spoke in an accent heard only south of the Mason-Dixon line. She'd once attended a showing of *Gone With Wind* at the St Margaret's School Film Society, and several people spoke like the man who couldn't say 'chair.'

Strangely it was Scarlett O'Hara herself who captured Sophia's attention, and she later learned that the English actress Vivien Leigh had apparently worked tirelessly to perfect an accent straight out of the great Southern State of Georgia.

Must have been pretty good, thought Sophia. They gave her an Oscar for it.

Anyway, that narrowed it down to about 150 million Americans, which represented a start. And she had one other clue—the mysterious sexual deviant from the USA always wore, right on the lapel of his jacket, a small metal badge. You see them everywhere in the States, usually just a plain Stars and Stripes.

However the badge worn by this character was different. It displayed a gruff-looking English bulldog wearing a black and red cap with a "G" on the front. And she recalled one evening at the Mildmays, there was an American guest from a bank in the City. His name was Jefferson. She remembered that too.

And after dinner she'd asked him if he had any idea what that badge she remembered might represent.

"Bulldog, with a big G? Hell, that'd be someone from the University of Georgia. That's their emblem. Their football team's the Georgia Bulldogs—the whole State of Georgia comes to a complete halt when they play.

"If they win, everyone has just one phrase *HOW 'BOUT THEM DAWGS!* They are, of course, nuts," added the Princeton-educated Jefferson.

She'd then asked him how big a school was UGA?

"About 30,000 students, I guess," was his somewhat discouraging reply.

And now, years later, she had to give it some serious thought. She was in the right country, she was pretty sure she knew which college he had attended, and pretty sure he came from way down there in the Deep South. Her only lead was the University of Georgia, and she was not sure they could be that much help, given that probably 1.2 million students had been there in the last 40 years! But, nevertheless, she was here and she had to try.

Sophia asked Olga how to fire up the desk-top computer, and logged into the University of Georgia. She then telephoned the Alumni Association and found herself trying to explain a roughly 60-year-old man who wore the bulldog badge.

"But, my dear, there have been so many bulldog badges over the years. Could you send me a photograph, then I can tell you roughly the time it was made?"

"Well, actually, It's only in my mind. But I remember it very well."

"My dear, why don't you come down for a visit. I can show you all the metal bulldogs for the last hundred years, and perhaps you will recognise the right one?"

Sophia copied down the lady's name, and the Alumni address in Atlanta. And decided to check in with Uncle Rudy in London, where the time was 7.30pm

She thanked him profusely for getting her out of the tennis camp in one piece, and then explained precisely what her plan was, going to Atlanta, to find the Alumni lady, and playing it strictly by ear after that.

"In my limited experience," he said.

by ear is the best possible formula for ending up dead."

"What do you mean?"

"Plans, Sophia. Accurate, ruthless, properly thought-out plans. I know of no better procedure for staying alive."

"Well, I'm just checking things out. Trying to locate our target. Get his name, and address and local habits. I want to know where he lives, and I want to be familiar with the surrounding country."

"I don't have a problem with any of that," said Rudy. "And I still believe that not one of your six targets deserves to live. But when you've done your reconnaissance, you come right back here to London.

"And bear in mind, you just had one very close call. I know all about it, Sophia, and I do not want you running risks like that ever again. The slightest suspicion, you bail out. I've told you that so many times. And you did have a suspicion, and you still went right ahead with your plan, and damn nearly ended up in prison for the rest of your life.

"Do what I tell you, Sophia. Do your recon and then get back here to make a plan. Hear me?"

"Yes, Uncle," she said, demurely.

Olga came for her shortly after that, and they took an afternoon stroll around the farmland. It was a glorious day, not a cloud in an azure sky, with a light southwest breeze right off the Appalachians. The Russian officer explained to her guest the basic workings of the Lewisburg Base and why there was no room for cattle.

"This is a secret place, Sophia," she said. "With direct lines to the GRU in Moscow Centre. Any time we want to bring in Intelligence field officers to work in Washington, we fly them into Boston or Philadelphia, and fly them out here under cover of darkness. That way they enter the US Capital unsuspected and unknown.

"Same method for getting people out. Keeps everyone well away from Washington Airport Security, which I have to say is very hot, and we think it's been getting worse every year since 9/11. Actually, that's the way you got in here this morning. Slightly high-pressure, but a classic Russian entry nonetheless!"

Sophia liked this Russian officer, and was grateful for the frank and fearless way she had explained the set-up, guessing correctly that if Uncle Rudy wanted someone protected, then "Uncle" Dmitry, Russia's senior envoy in the western world, would issue orders, which could not be countermanded.

Nonetheless, she did think Rudy was being particularly bossy towards her, patrician, she supposed. But a bit bloody pompous all the same. He was of course perfect, but she still felt a tiny bit piqued at being patronised to quite this extent. Even after she owed her life to him, about four times? *Yes, even after that ... I'm not a child, after all.*

She and Olga walked quietly back to the ranch house. There were so far no flights in or out today, but there were a half-dozen surveillance operators working in the control room.

"Any idea how long you'll be here," asked Olga.

"Well, I hope to leave very soon. I need to be in Atlanta like tomorrow, but I'm not sure how to do it. I don't suppose you run commercial flights from here, do you?"

Olga laughed, "Not hardly! But we do have to make that Atlanta run quite often for various Russian trade delegations. And I'm afraid there's only one way from here; being out in the boondocks as the locals like to say."

"Break it to me."

"I'll give you the good news first. It's an easy helicopter ride from here, less than an hour to the railroad station at Charlotte, North Carolina. From there the fast train to Atlanta takes about six hours. Right through the mountains. Very pretty. Nice train."

"And the bad news?"

"The train leaves Charlotte at two o'clock in the morning!"

"Oh, gosh! That's pretty early. Will Pietr and Nikolai take me?"

"Certainly. They've done it many times. We land just outside the city. And we'll have a car there to run you into the railroad. Leave around mid-night."

"I'm glad I'm not doing this without help. I'd never get there."

Sophia repacked her shoulder travelling bag carefully, especially the hidden leather compartment in its base, where she kept her $10,000 for the journey. She secured it with a Russian military security system that would have defied Albert

Einstein, and caused the entire bag to explode if anyone tampered with it who was not named Sophia Morosova. Rudy's idea.

They took off at the midnight hour. Pietr Markovitch at the helm of the AW109, Nikolai co-pilot. And in 10-minutes they were up and over the West Virginia State line and into North Carolina, flying at 180mph in the pitch dark.

They flashed over the City of Winston-Salem, birthplace of America's greatest tobacco fortune, R.J. Reynolds, which was situated just east of the fortuitously named Great Smokey Mountains. A half-hour later Pietr put them down as quietly as humanly possible in a flying machine designed, essentially, to awaken the dead.

The AW109 was on the ground, rotors pounding, one hour and 15 minutes after take-off, and Miss Sophia Morosova stepped out on to the tarmac of North Carolina for the first time, Wilgrove Air Park, on the far eastern outskirts of Charlotte, the biggest city in the Carolinas.

Wilgrove was a very unobtrusive place, and there was a taxi waiting to drive her 11-miles directly to the Amtrak Charlotte railroad station on Tryon Street. And there she would pick up her ticket and board the mighty high-speed Amtrak Crescent for a part of its 1,400-mile journey from Midtown New York to the Union Terminal Station in New Orleans, thundering through 11 US States en route, riding that American magic carpet made of steel.

Sophia wanted only the middle part, the 260-mile stretch between Charlotte and Atlanta, which put her in Peachtree Station right after 8am. She stopped at the station coffee shop for a cappuccino and a croissant. The quality of the latter probably would not have caused *Deux Magots* to close down.

And, just before 9am she picked up a cab outside the station and took a five-mile ride north up to Lenox Road, to the splendid nine-story building which is home to the 300,000-strong University of Georgia Alumni Association.

Sophia blinked at the sight of it, staring in the morning sun at a building, which might have been the world HQ of a Fortune 500 corporation. Beige, with heavily-tinted glass. Somewhere in there was Mrs Betty-Anne Jones, head of the Alumni office, the lady who had been so helpful on the telephone.

She was escorted up to the inner sanctum of the Association where Mrs Jones assembled a thousand lists of the Bulldogs down the years. "Well, I'm real pleased to see you," she said, in a Georgia accent that might have stepped right out of the great hallways of Tara. "But I don't believe you ever told me your name?"

Sophia was ready with the name in the new French passport she would use to exit the USA and touch down in Paris. "Yes, I'm so sorry. My name is Janine Belleau, we're from Provence."

"Okay, Janine, I'm guessing we have a pretty long search in front of us, I think we better sit right down and you tell me all you can remember about this man."

"It's not really very much," replied Sophia. "I'm sure I'll remember that bulldog badge when I see it. But I've never known his name, although he might have had a wife called Katrina. I heard him tell my step-father once he was really glad that bitch was gone out of his life!"

"Did he say anything else about her?"

"Yes, he also said she was real trouble."

"What year was that?"

"2006."

Betty-Anne smiled. "Janine, I think you might find Katrina was a hurricane not a person."

"A hurricane?"

"You were probably a little too young to take much notice. But down there in Louisiana they had a Category Five with 135mph winds in 2005, killed close to 2,000 people, flooded half the State, including the city of New Orleans, the levies just plumb let go and that water came right on in. That hurricane was named Katrina.

"And there weren't a whole lot of people had a good word to say about that. I'm not surprised your man was glad to get rid of that bitch, so was half of Louisiana. The destruction was terrible … and if he lived right near the water, well, he'd be glad she'd gone too. Real glad."

"Wow!" said Sophia. "That explains a whole lot. But I'm not sure where it takes us."

"Tells us one thing, though," said Betty-Anne. "If your man was that angry about Katrina, he probably came from New Orleans, or somewhere down in the bayous—Katrina wiped out entire parishes."

"I'm just not sure where that takes us," said Sophia.

"I'll tell you where—it takes us a whole long way. This university is 84 percent made up of students from our home State of Georgia. And nowadays there's probably six percent or so from overseas.

"That means there's 10 percent of our places left for all the other states in the USA. And we're looking for a student from Louisiana, who was an undergraduate right here. Janine, if your memory's good on that ole bulldog badge, I'd say we were hot on the trail!"

Chapter Nineteen
The Fears of the Soviet Assassin

His opinion took time but then it was clear ..."My niece is
behaving like a schoolgirl... but I can't just sit here and
do nothing ... because in the end you have to follow your heart
and if anything happened to her, it would surely break mine."

Sophia was thrilled to have a new helper, someone who knew precisely what she was doing. And she smiled happily as Betty-Anne Jones walked over to her desk and came back with two sheets of white paper, with lines and lines of photographs of the Georgia Bulldog lapel badges. All different. Different wording. Different coats of arms, different shapes, and very different bulldogs.

"Now you take your time, Janine. Look carefully and try to find one which matches your memory."

The entire process took less than three minutes. "Here he is," she cried, triumphantly, pointing to a very growly looking dog, his college cap set at a rakish angle, with the big 'G' right on the front panel."

Oh, my!" said Betty-Anne, "We haven't made that badge since about 1920."

Sophia's face fell. "Oh, gosh," she said, "That's awful. We'll never find him."

"I wouldn't be too sure about that. How old is this character?"

"When I knew him he'd have been about 50. That makes him almost 60 right now."

"Then he graduated from here roughly 40 years ago. Say 1976-1980."

"Yes, I suppose so," she replied, "But Mrs Jones, what was he doing wearing that very old badge? I never saw him without it. Maybe he just found it, didn't go to University here at all."

"Miss Belleau," replied the Alumni Chief, "I need to explain to you the significance of that badge. First thing to remember is, this is the oldest formal University in the country. I know a couple of places try to dispute that, but I'm talking 1785, so don't pay 'em no never mind.

"This is the oldest. Period. They were teaching high education here four years after Lord Cornwallis surrendered his sword to General Washington at Yorktown, less than one decade after America became a nation."

"That's pretty old," said a gracious Sophia, whose own nation had thrived under a four hundred-year-old monarchy, two hundred years before that.

But a nerve of the purest devotion had been touched. "That old bulldog badge might not mean a whole lot outside the State of Georgia," said Mrs Jones. "But right here that badge is not much short of sacred. People only wear them if they were educated at UGA. And if we have a man wearing a very old one, probably made before he was born, that badge belonged to either his Daddy, or his granddaddy. I'd be sure of that."

"Is that good?" asked Sophia.

"That's real good. Because it means we're looking for a two or three generation alumnus, which is on a separate list, from the State of Louisiana. And that narrows it right down. If the college graduated 25,000 per year around 1980, there's only 2,500 from out of state.

"Maybe 50 from Louisiana, but how many were third generation? Maybe a half-dozen. And now I'm going to let you look at those yearbooks, we have them online. And you can sit right there and find the man who wasn't married to Katrina!"

Sophia sat and looked at the photographs, and she found her man in the Class of '81, after a 15-minute search. It was a serious picture of him, and underneath was written his name, Hunter de Villiers III, from a family residing down in the bayous near Houma. He was about 22 at the time. Sophia would have recognised him if he'd been six years old.

The notes confirmed his grand-father had attended the university at the turn of the last century. His parents had decided on the established permanence of the 115-year-old University of Georgia, rather than the University of Louisiana, which was not founded until 1898, and then mostly as an industrial school.

Sophia asked Mrs Jones to look at her findings, and it was very obvious she was very startled. "Hunter de Villiers!" she said, "Oh my good Lord!"

"Who is he?" asked Sophia.

"Who is he? Why Hunter de Villiers is one of the most important men in the South. He's run for Governor of Louisiana twice, and last time darn nearly got it, and he's not even a proper politician.

"That's one very important family. And that's going to make it a lot easier for you. And I want you to sit right down there at that computer and bring old Hunter up there on Wikipedia. They're very big down here, and you'll find out all you need.

"I'll give you 10 minutes." And then Betty-Anne smiled, and made her last observation in the unique phraseology of the Old South. "Right about then, mah dear, you're gonna be walking in t-a-a-all cotton."

Sophia laughed, despite not knowing quite what this meant. And tapped in a request for Wikipedia to find Hunter de Villiers III, who popped right up, third generation of a considerable Louisiana fortune, started on a 5,000-acre cotton plantation, and developed by his father, de Villiers II, into an enormous natural gas operation down in the bayous south of the city of Houma.

The family home was situated on the outskirts of tiny Montegut, a village on the banks of the Terrebonne Bayou, the main waterway through Terrebonne Parish, running down to the sprawling wetlands of Louisiana. There were hundreds of square miles of water down here—lakes, streams, bayous and rivers all flooding together in readiness to meet the deep salt waters of the Gulf of Mexico.

It was these great waters which provided Terrebonne Parish with its principal income down all the years, the bounty of oysters, crabs, shrimp, crawfish and fish, which still make the parish the 20 percent provider of all Louisiana's fishing state product. There were times when oil and natural gas made the entire area a boom town on the water.

But the days when oil was king were over. It was still important, and families like the de Villiers invested heavily in the new offshore drilling industry. But it's not what it was. And those old fishing boats, chugging out every day to harvest the wildlife of the sea, still play a profitable part in the local income.

The young Hunter followed in the footsteps of his forefathers directly into the study halls of the University of Georgia, and right after that he followed them some more, straight into one of the biggest fortunes in the State.

Hunter de Villiers III was a quiet-spoken man, who loved the quiet bayous and the near silent sport of fly-fishing. He was excessively rich, and a total stranger to the word No. Most everyone said Yes, right away, to the man who had inherited de Villiers Natural Gas. And he stood as one of the biggest donors to charity south of the city of New Orleans.

He'd never married, but was usually escorted to society events by a succession of very beautiful, high-born southern belles, none of whom had ever tempted him towards the altar. He was just a rather solitary person, although there was always local gossip about him.

But in the end he stood tall in his Colonial plantation home, high on the wide garden staircase, which resembled nothing if not the long, rising approach to the breath-taking desert Temple of the female Pharaoh, Hatshepsut, who ruled Egypt for 20 years in the 15th century BC.

Hunter de Villiers liked grandeur, and in a life based on total self-indulgence, found it mystifying to comprehend anyone else's point of view. That's often the way with men who have too much money. Which is why he spent much time with his sole companion, private secretary and bodyguard, Russ Lambert, former offensive lineman for the Rajun' Cajuns, the University of Louisiana's football team.

Russ was 40-years-old now, still heavily-built and handsome, with long, blond, curly hair, slightly unkempt. And he appeared to have no other life except inside the Plantation house. He accompanied Mr de Villiers everywhere, whenever he stepped anywhere outside the mansion, including fishing on the bayou right outside the door.

His boss had only one other permanent companion—and that was the little metal bulldog badge, pinned on the lapel of every jacket he wore. Old Hunter never left home without it. Just as Betty-Anne had stated: "That little old emblem is kinda sacred."

Sophia printed off a couple of pages, scribbled a few notes, and wished Mrs Jones a heartfelt goodbye. She could never have located her target without her. "Well, I'll say goodbye now, Miss Janine. I hope you find Mr de Villiers, and I'm glad to have been of some help … anyway y'all come back and see us again now, y'hear."

Sophia walked outside and found a cab waiting, and decided to head back downtown. There was no train to New Orleans today, not until 8am tomorrow, same train on which she had arrived. So she found a supermarket and bought herself a pay-as-you-go phone, with $50 worth of untraceable calls (at least they would be after she'd spoken to Rudy, smashed the phone with the heel of her shoe, and dumped the pieces in a trashcan).

She sat in a small park, under a wide dogwood tree and contemplated the call to Uncle Rudolf. It was still only 11am (4pm in London)—the middle of the day in a busy embassy.

So she decided to give it another half hour, and killed time by reading the Atlanta guidebook she'd bought in the train station. She would not be in Georgia's capital for long enough to need detailed information. But she knew from *Gone with the Wind* that the Northern General, William Sherman had burned down the City in the 1860's.

Which was probably why she liked the Great Seal of Atlanta, which shows a Phoenix rising up from the fire and ashes, beneath large curved letters which spelled out the Latin word, *Resurgens*—Rising Again.

Somehow it appealed to her highly developed sense of both justice and revenge, and she looked around this mighty, gleaming, prosperous American city, an everlasting symbol of the wealthy South, getting its own back, every day, on the old enemy from the North.

She gave it another 30-minutes, and then called Rudolf in London, who it must be said, was a bit cool towards his beloved niece. "Hello, Sophia," he said. "I was wondering when you'd check-in."

"I've had a very good morning," she replied "I've found him. His name is Hunter de Villiers III, very rich, oil and gas fortune, lives down on the bayous in Louisiana. He's done a few things which made the headlines, but the biggest was when he backed a movie with a lot of money, *Cottonwood, Mississippi.*

"Hey, even I've heard of that," he said. "Well, you'd better get back here right away and we'll work on a plan."

"To be honest, I was planning to press on right now, take the train to New Orleans in the morning and do what I've got to do, as soon as possible."

"That is not a plan, so you can forget all about it. This man will be a high-profile hit, personal bodyguard, security, and every other danger you can imagine. You may consider yourself forbidden to do any such thing. Get back here."

"Uncle Rudy, I've made up my mind. I'm going to Louisiana as soon as possible. And I'm going to carry out my mission."

"How are you going to achieve this."

"Shotgun."

"A shotgun! Are you crazy? You could never fire a 12-bore accurately."

"Well, I learned to fire the pistol. I can learn to fire this."

"And who's going to teach you?"

"The people in the shop. It says in their advertisement they have quick lessons for beginners."

"Jesus Christ!" said Rudy. "How many people will know that a very beautiful young lady walked into a gun-store on her own, purchased a brand new 12-bore shot gun, and a day or so later one of the most important men in the State of Louisiana gets blown away just a few miles down the road."

"Oh, I'll be in disguise," she replied. "And I'll vanish into thin air."

"You'll vanish into the Louisiana State Penitentiary, that's what. Come back to London right now."

"Uncle Rudy, I thank you for everything you have done for me. But in this instance, I have made up my mind. I'm going to Louisiana in the morning and I'm going to carry out my task. This one's 'specially for Sasha. My God, you know how she hated him."

Rudolf Masow, professional assassin, officer of both the KGB and the GRU, completely ignored that. "Sophia," he said, "May I remind you that I am your legal guardian. I am responsible for you in the eyes of the law. I forbid you to embark on this hair-brained, crazy venture. You are to return to London, now."

"Uncle Rudy, I can't. I just can't. I owe it to Sasha and to myself."

"I assure you Sasha won't know, or care, whether you go to Louisiana or not."

"That, I am afraid, is where you're wrong. She will know. She's with me every minute of every day. I'm sorry, Uncle Rudy, I'm going."

And with that, she clicked off the phone, took out the sim-card, and ground it into the concrete path. Then she smashed the rest of the phone, carefully picked up the pieces and dropped them into a trash-can on her way to find a small, unobtrusive hotel; somewhere Rudy would never find her, no matter how many calls he made.

*****

Rudolf Masow sat quietly in the office, deep in Kensington Palace Gardens, and considered the proposed moves his niece was making. And he arrived at two irrevocable conclusions: 1) was certainly the most likely; she would somehow screw it up and get herself arrested and then serve a 12-year sentence for attempted murder.

2) was rather more simple. She would get shot dead by de Villiers' security detail, or the armed Atlanta police, or even by de Villiers himself.

"Jesus," he thought. "How would I feel about that? If Sophia was killed and I had not raised a finger to save her? If I just sat here and assumed she was just an ungrateful little brat?"

His overall opinion took a little time to formulate, and when it did, he found himself whispering to himself ... *You can make all the professional rules you like ... and you can tell yourself over and over she's behaving like a silly schoolgirl ... but I can't just sit here and do nothing ... because in the end you have to follow your heart ... and if anything happened to Sophia, it would surely break mine.*

Rudolf Masow hit the button to summon his secretary with such force he nearly slammed it straight through his desk and into his top right-hand drawer. Katya Bolotnikova thought the building must be on fire, and came running into the room to find Rudolf Masow in a plain state of dire emergency, but, strangely for him, with very obvious tears streaming down his face, tears he was unsuccessfully trying to wipe away with his shirt-sleeve.

"Book me on the nine o'clock flight to Boston tonight," he snapped, not quite politely. "Then get Ambassador Kutnezvos on the line, then get every Wikipedia detail you can on a guy named Hunter de Villiers III, down in Louisiana in the American South. And hurry up!"

Katya spun around and walked right out, telling her assistant to book the flight tonight for Mr Masow, first-class to Boston. Then she dialled the number for the Russian Ambassador in Washington, waited until she was through, and told his assistant, to stand by for Rudolf Masow in London, urgent.

She left the office door open, in case the boss yelled out another order. And she picked up mere snatches of the conversation with Dmitry ... Yeah, New Orleans ... mostly because she's nuts ... that would be just great ... sniper I guess ... a vehicle from the consulate ... perfect ... hey, Dmitry, you're a true friend ... no, I'm okay, I'm alright ... just couldn't bear it if ... love to Raeza ... and you, stay safe ..."

Katya Bolotnikova knew how to turn six pages into one, and she crammed detail by detail onto a separate sheet, including the de Villiers address, which was more than even Sophia had.

*****

At this exact time, 5pm on Wednesday afternoon, DCS Charles Barton was finally catching up with the London daily papers, and thus far nothing very startling was jumping out at him. Every news editor was fed up to the teeth with Sir Josh Hartley's grotesque record as a practicing sexual deviant with teenagers. Having shredded his reputation and tossed the remnants in the bin, today for the first time there was no mention of the deceased disc-jockey and human benefactor.

Lord Justice Fontridge was also off the news schedule, but for different reasons. With no suspicions, no motive and no clues, people were just bored with the subject. The nation had uttered a long sigh of acute disinterest. They had not spoken but the message was clear, call us when something breaks. Until then we've all got better things to think about.

Charles kept going, scouring the news pages for something interesting, as usual keeping the *Daily Telegraph* until last. The front page was very routine, an attack on the Foreign Secretary after a row with Italy, a particularly grisly murder in Yorkshire, and an NHS scandal in Northampton. On the right, just below the fold, over three columns with a photograph, was the story of another murdered man—an American tennis player, found shot dead on the service court.

"Where else?" muttered Charles, unsympathetically. He checked the name, Buck Madden (never heard of him). But noted he'd played at Wimbledon for 10 years, on and off, won a couple of Davis Cup doubles matches, and once reached the semis of the men's doubles at Wimbledon.

The *Telegraph* was London's most serious lawn tennis newspaper, its correspondent for 30 years, the charming and erudite Lance Tingay, wrote the brilliantly perceptive official *One Hundred Years of Wimbledon*. The newspaper treasured the memory of their International Hall of Fame tennis writer, and strived every year after his death, in 1990, to stay out in front with all news involving the sport he loved.

And here they were, strolling down Memory Lane again, reminding British tennis fans that the tall, handsome Virginian was no more. They pointed out that he died with his racket in his hand, doing what he loved most (well, one of the two things he loved most).

But by now, Charles Barton was no longer reading. He was staring at the photograph, six-inches deep, over two columns, showing Buck in his prime, volleying at the net, like the lean power-hitter he once was.

"Now where the devil have I seen that face before?' he wondered. And then, within moments, he remembered. *"Mother of God!"* muttered Charles, "It's Pseudonym Four. It's 'Tilden.' The fourth one on that list. And, since the *Telegraph* says he was shot in the head and in the heart, he was murdered like the first three. Especially like Freddie Fontridge."

He went to his computer and pulled up the images on the list. There was only one with a photograph, 'Tilden,' and the pictures match. "I'll have them compared scientifically," he muttered. "But there's no doubt. This Buck Madden was 'Tilden,' rapist. And he's on the Fontridge list, along with Hartley, and Chiang Kai Chec or whatever his fucking name is."

It seemed to Charles that every time there was a critical piece of news, or a coincidence, or a shocking development, the entire conundrum grew more complicated than ever. At this moment he knew an enormous amount about Fontridge's secret, available teenage girl network, he understood there had been four fairly obvious murders, and Fontridge's secret list shed unimaginable light on so many things.

But he was concerned only with Fontridge, the one classic murder which was actually committed on British soil, the one from which he was experiencing increasing pressure from the men to whom he must ultimately answer. There were not that many of them, but from the PM downward, they were becoming extremely jumpy. Results, they wanted results. Who murdered an English law lord and dumped him in the Glyndebourne lake?

It sounded simple, And in one sense it was. Yet Charles had to admit he did not have a clue who did it. Yes, he'd uncovered a bitterly unattractive little group of bi-global sexual deviants, criminal rapists towards adolescent schoolgirls. And he did have some gruesome idea of where Fontridge and the rest stuck their daggers. But he had no idea who stuck one in his heart.

It seemed to Charles that the more he found out, the more murky the waters became, the ones which surrounded Lord Fontridge that is, both evidentially and indeed, metaphorically.

He retraced today's scenario in his mind. Yes, Pseudonym Four had been located, shot dead. But so what? The Virginia Police Department was offering no information yet. But even if they named their murderer, would that likely be the same person who ended the life of Freddie Fontridge? Charles doubted it—a shooting 4,000-miles away, in the gun-toting outback of the US of A, out there in Indian Country, Shawnee at that, tribal warriors for a thousand years.

Same with Chiang Kai Chec. What the hell did that have to do with anything? Friggin' Japanese sex-fiend, throttled in a Hong Kong bathtub? It was all too spread out. And although Charles understood that the first two names he found, Fontridge and Hartley, were plainly deviant and plainly knew each other, so what? How could that take him any closer to Fontridge's murderer? The entire sackload of evidence he had so far accumulated, took him no nearer to his principal task … Who killed Lord Fontridge?

And speaking of mysteries, where the hell was Sophia. She'd vanished completely, and he did not even have a phone number for her. He'd even telephoned Rudolf Masow at the Russian Embassy, and the cultural attaché had been as mystified as he was himself. "She's just disappeared," he'd said, "And all I know is, she was very worried about her mother, and told me she was going to Russia right away to see her. She's a bit headstrong, Superintendent, you may not have noticed."

Charles Barton had noticed many things about Sophia, but the headstrong part had passed him by. The fact was, after only three or four intimate meetings with her, he missed her terribly. And every day he made some attempt to find her. But it had been almost two weeks now, and she was becoming at least as elusive as Freddie Fontridge's killer.

Elbowing his way into Charles's thoughts was the increasingly obvious truth, that of the six pseudonyms on the list, four of them were dead, all probably murdered in the past month. And as ever, the questions mounted up :

1) Is this a big operation, involving many people, hired assassins to wipe out that list of weirdos? Hired by whom?

2) Or, is it just one person, a deranged serial killer, perhaps the 'mystery western woman,' as seen and recalled by the Japanese tycoon's bodyguard? Female serial killer? Almost unknown in the Free World.

3) If so, was this some sort of organised vigilante killing-spree by one woman, backed by a group of well-organised world-changers determined to frighten the life out of all sexual predators.

4) Or was it one of the two remaining men on the *Maidens in the Vale* List, men who desperately needed to hush the others up? Perhaps bad blood? Or fear of exposure? Which meant the four were not only victims of homicides, but the other two would be serious and dangerous criminals themselves: which was a new and utterly unwanted door of investigation. Especially as it was mostly abroad.

Charles Barton's thoughts were interrupted by a knock on the office door and his secretary announcing arrival of Larry Super-geek, a man who was ever welcome in the inner sanctums of Scotland Yard.

He walked in, bristling with excitement, as Charles's mother might have put it. "I have something, sir. And I think you might find it important."

For Larry, this rated as an outburst of joy and wild optimism.

"Lay it right on me," said Charles.

"Remember you wanted to know details of the email content concerning the six communications on Fontridge's list? We have them all, written down right here, five sheets of paper."

He handed them to Superintendent Barton, on each sheet being written only two or three lines. All of them carried the same subject-line: *From Freddie With Love.*

"You will notice, sir, only five sheets. We obviously do not have one from his Lordship, since he sent them, and anyway they are password-secure from the website-server. And the only person who can tell us that is dead. But don't give up, sir, I think we'll have it in the next 24 hours."

Charles looked up, eyebrows raised, and asked, "I see all these emails came from Maidens in the Vale. But what are all these numbers right below the email content lines?"

"Sir," said Larry, "These represent the heart of the email. All five of them received it, all exactly the same."

"Is that the numbers?"

"Yes. It's an encrypted code, a book cypher. Same system as the Third Reich used for all their agents in the UK. It actually goes back hundreds of years— from Genghis Khan getting lost on the Silk Road, to Helen of Troy after her first row with Prince Paris.

"Are you making this up, Larry!" laughed Charles, who was truly astonished at the Super-geek's first ever known attempt at humour, but he put it down to the excitement at effectively cracking the mystery of the Maidens in the Vale.

"Nearly making it up, sir, but it's based on truth!"

"Okay, Larry, give me the codes."

"This is a simplified code. Which is probably why we cracked it so easily. You see the grouping of numbers? That's Page, Chapter, followed by the words. So here we have page …"

"One-three-eight," said Charles.

"Correct. Now the Paragraph …"

"Six … then 27…"

"That's the 27th word, sir … and you'll see that's four groups—with three sets in each."

"So all we need now, is the book? Because each of the five must have been sent the same identical book, same edition, otherwise they'd be in the dark as much as we are."

"And now it's rather up to you, sir. We can break the code, we can get you into the Maidens of the Vale site. That book solves many puzzles and it gives us the password which solves everything… But we cannot solve the puzzle. The *book* has to be identified, then we can see what Fontridge wrote to them."

Chapter Twenty
Concealed Money—Liechtenstein Calling

"If you will not reveal the account number, I'll have the Prime Minister speak to the Chairman of the IMF. As you wish. You will now conduct all future UK transactions, directly through the Bank of England, where cooperation may, of course, be limited."

"From Freddie With Love," said the DCS Barton, absent-mindedly humming the theme song from the second James Bond movie, *From Russia with Love*. He was not quite so melodic as Matt Monro, and neither did he give it as much thought. Which was probably, with hindsight, a misjudgement.

He told Super-geek Larry he understood, thanked him for everything, and sat down thoughtfully to assess the situation. If he could find the book, then the password would be excavated via the code. And that password would let Larry into those emails, and all the secrets would emerge, very possibly leading to the killer.

And since there's about a hundred zillion books all over the country, that might prove difficult. However Charles was clear-sighted about such matters. He knew that somewhere Fontridge and his buddy Hartley owned an identical book. They all owned it, in order to decipher the code.

He doubted if Hartley owned a substantial library, and thought his very proud mother would allow them in to have a look. The police in Warwickshire knew her well, and he asked them to go and search his home, where mum still lived. If necessary they could get a warrant, but it might not be required.

The library at Laughton Towers would be a more testing problem, but that was irrelevant until they'd taken a thorough look at books owned by Sir Josh. Charles wasn't sure of the timeline here, but he needed that book and without it he was powerless. He spoke to the Chief Constable of Warwickshire, and received an assurance they'd get right on it.

There were two or three officers who knew Mrs Hartley very well and he was certain they would receive full cooperation. "If he has very few books, which

I suspect," said the DCS, "See if we can borrow them all—if it's only a couple of boxes—and get them down here to me asap."

It did not take the Warwickshire boys long at all. The Chief Constable called Charles in person at 10.15am the next day to tell him Mrs Hartley had been very helpful, and two boxes of books, most of them about motor racing and pop singers, were on their way to Scotland Yard in a fast squad car, which was currently heading down the M40 motorway in Buckinghamshire, roof lights flashing.

Charles could hardly wait, but he did, until shortly after 1pm when a couple of Warwickshire constables turned up bearing gifts, direct to his office. The DCS thanked them profusely, and asked them if they'd like a couple of sandwiches and some coffee, and asked his secretary to get three orders. And in the next two hours he paid attention to their account of Mrs Hartley, and worked his way through the books.

The Warwickshire boss had been right. Sir Josh had been heavy on motor racing and pop music. There were biographies on Jackie Stewart, Stirling Moss, Graham Hill, Nigel Mansell, Michael Schumacher, Lewis Hamilton and several others.

The pop-singers' names were a complete mystery to Charles and anyway he thought it most unlikely that his Lordship would have sent a book on that particular subject to anyone, never mind his friend, Sir Josh Hartley.

Only one book out of the cache of around 50 caught his eye as even a possibility. It was a paperback amid a golden sea of glossy hardbacks. It was obviously a women's romantic novel by an unheard-of author named Camille Borchetta, and it had a title which might have been written by a 14-year-old lovesick fourth-former: *Heartstrings Along the Grand Canal*. It's second-deck sub-title was worse: *A 19th century love drama in Italy's City of Bridges.*

But Charles was struck not by this literary wasteland which he assumed would continue inside the book's jacket. But by its sheer lack of place in the very insignificant library of Sir Josh Hartley. Here was a man who possessed not one book outside his own interests—either his work (pop singers) or his hobby (motor racing).

And yet right here was a profoundly trashy novel, in paperback, detailing a 200-year-old sex fantasy which apparently took place in Venice. What could a millionaire, petrol-head, like Sir Josh possibly be doing with such a publication?

In Charles Barton's mind, if there was a book, hiding a secret code in the home of Sir Josh Hartley, this was it.

He picked up the telephone, spoke to someone in Sir George Kenny's office and asked if a couple of patrol-men could take a run down to Laughton Towers and check whether there was a book in the library, entitled, *Heartstrings Along the Grand Canal.* There was no need to borrow it, read it, or comment on it.

He told them, "It was a paperback by some author called Camille Borchetta. I expect Lady Fontridge, or her staff, will be cooperative, but if not, get a warrant, and tell the clerk I'm responsible. Murder enquiry. Remember don't do anything. Just tell me whether that book's in his possession."

Charles sat back and considered the astonishing lack of progress he had made. He was no nearer solving the murder than he had been the night it happened. No suspects. And even if the code into the Venice book revealed a full, frank and fearless resume of the six-man Pseudonym List, well, that might or might not lead him to the killer.

However, in his experience, the clues to all murders lay within the dead person themselves, their secret lives, the unknown enemies, their way of life, and the seamy pathways which led who knows where. And just as an exercise he decided to treat the book as it if were indeed the key to the code which would unlock the website.

He studied his sets of numbers and went to page 138 of *Heartstrings.* Then to paragraph six. Then to the seven letters which locked in with the numbers. Four minutes later he was looking at …

T-I-C-K-E-T-S. Which was not particularly dramatic, but not rubbish either. He pressed on to the second set, Page 138, paragraph six … and only three letters this time: F-O-R.

He tried the third set, three letters again … T-H-E. Then he went to the last set: seven numbers … spelling out G-O-N-D-O-L-A.

There was a Venetian connection here, but why or how only the writer really knew. And once more Charles found himself humming his own Venetian love song *From Russia With Love*, recalling again a magical weekend, long ago, with Emma Stuart, the daughter of a belted Earl from the English shires who fondly imagined an exciting future with the young Scotland Yard detective.

It was, perhaps, the only love affair Charles truly remembered with joy and happiness. He and Emma riding in a gondola down the canals. And that song *From Russia With Love* would forever bring back memories.

Just for amusement he punched in the letters and zoomed to YouFilm, and to the closing moments of the movie, James Bond and his spectacular girlfriend, the Italian actress, Daniela Bianci, smoothing along the canals. The waters looked so familiar to him, as did the words of that haunting theme song, beautifully sung by the former Shoreditch bus-driver, Matt Monro.

"What a voice," murmured Charles. And while he realised Daniela had it all over Emma Stuart for pure sex appeal, he always thought he'd give 007 a run for his money in the brains department. And while he might have been less accurate with Bond's standard Walther PBK 7.65mm, when push came to shove, he, Charles, was still pretty handy with a 4 X 2.

From Freddie With Love. Charles wondered all over again what the subject-line meant. Was it perhaps a clue to the city of Venice? A nearly obvious indicator to the Bond movie—and its Venetian background? And how about the gondola tickets? Must be Venice, right? All of it springing to life after the EXE file the Super-geeks found on the secret computer, *Maidens in the Vale.*

"They don't even have vales in Italy," he muttered. They're all in Wales. And then, by some blinding flash of brilliance, he cast a glaring light on the obvious. This has nothing to do with Italy, he thought. This has to do with London. West London. "If I'm not very badly mistaken, that's Maida Vale, right down the road from Little Venice, right by the Regents Canal.

"The Sex-Ring code is Maidens in the Vale; Fontridge writes in code under From Freddie with Love; and the deep code into the TOR Website is: *Tickets for The Gondola.* None of which tells me who murdered his Lordship. But it spreads a deadly light on something. A Venetian light. Not least that an English Law Lord, operating at the highest level of the Legal System is the head of a London Teenage Sex-Ring. Nice. Especially when four of the six names are now murdered."

Certainly Larry and his men would punch in the code, **Tickets for The Gondola**. And this would unearth all kinds of filth from the Dark Web. And it just might throw some light on who hated the Judge so badly he decided to stab him.

But Charles was aware that another potential line of investigation was elbowing its way into the picture, and that was money. He did not consider it a coincidence that all four of the dead men were extremely wealthy, neither did he think that long sexual sessions with teenagers were free. No, in Charles Barton's mind, someone was paying top-dollar for these dubious privileges.

And whereas he may have found the cypher links on the Dark Web, he now believed the way to the murderer was through the money. Because big money had been paid. And it had to come from somewhere. And, money being money, it had to leave a trail.

The phone rang sharply on his private line. George Kenny reporting in from Sussex. "Hello, Charlie," he said cheerfully. "You were right. The boys found the book at Laughton Towers in about five minutes. It was on a table under a reading light, not in the shelves, which was just as well because there were about seven million books in that library."

"Did they confiscate it?"

"No, you said not to."

"That's good. I'm trying to keep our heads well down on this. And I don't need another copy of *Heartstrings*. I just needed to know he owned it."

"Well, he did. And the boys never even told Jane Fontridge what they found. Very subtle. But they did take a picture showing the book with a library background. Just in case."

Sir George rang off, and Charles hit the button to summon Larry. The book held the key to the dark web, and he had cracked the code for the password... He told Larry to punch in the four words, **Tickets for the Gondola**, and see what happened.

Ten minutes later, Larry was on the phone, "We've got something here, sir. It's not pretty. Matter of fact it's disgusting. But it's important. I'm sure of that. Will you give us another half-hour?"

"Hurry up, Larry. Remember, I'm the codebreaker!"

"We all understand that, sir. If I may say so, very well done."

"See you in 30, Larry."

That 30 passed very slowly. The Superintendent drummed his fingers on the table, tried to call Sophia in Paris, where there was no answer, and once again debated calling Rudolf Masow. Where was she? A simple enough question, without one single answer.

And he tried to stop himself thinking that whatever his personal feelings may be, Sophia Morosova was the one person who could indeed have killed Lord Fontridge: she had the opportunity, she was in the exact right place, at the exact right time. And he was not at all sure she had ever returned to her seat after the interval.

Rudolf said she did, but Johnny Fairchild said she didn't. The little butterfly earrings. Charles could just tell the Brighton jeweller was not happy with the story that Sophia had changed these little adornments out there on the lawn. Men of his type are often super-sensitive to the wiles of the female.

And Fairchild's uneasiness at Sophia's story, had bothered Charles right from the start. It still did. The one thing that absolutely exonerated her, however, was the acute lack of motive. There was no motive. Neither she nor Rudolf had ever even heard of Lord Justice Fontridge. But now Charles Barton was wondering, really wondering, why Sophia Morosova had vanished from the face of the earth.

But could he really imagine, the beautiful, gentle Sophia, plunging a fucking dagger into the heart of Freddie Fontridge? Answer: No. Not in a thousand years. And Charles prided himself on his ability to spot a criminal. Any criminal.

Larry and Jerry took exactly 26 minutes and 43 seconds to make it up to Charles Barton's office with the print-outs they had selected, six sheets of horrifying photographs which would have shocked Caligula himself.

They had also blasted their way into another of the clandestine corners of cyber-space—the anonymous email service provider, Info4-TOR. This was a top-secret facility, deeply hidden, with an ability to dive in and out of the Dark Web, without leaving one single digital fingerprint. What it did leave was a floodlit pathway to the elusive money trail which Detective Chief Superintendent Charles Barton had always anticipated.

And what a trail it was—detailing the sums of money transferred via offshore accounts and shell corporations, from five of the six pseudonyms to just one other, the ringleader, whose wealth rested to a considerable extent on the sunlit shores of Grand Cayman Island. And the ringleader was beyond dispute. It was Lord Justice Fontridge, Appeal Court Judge, Adviser to the Royal family, Life Baron and high-goal sexual predator.

The Super-geeks had nailed him, once and for all. The sums of money paid never varied. There were emails detailing the accounts, detailing account numbers, the routing numbers, the SWIFT numbers. And the sums involved were always £10,000, always into a Cayman Corporation, controlled through a Trust owned by a Sussex family named Fontridge.

The money was being paid to enable these appalling men to find sexual satisfaction in the deviant world of very young girls, child/women—the one that ravages those under 16, schoolgirls, prefects and netball players at their school.

And those £10,000 cheques were always consolidated into a £50,000 wire transfer, direct to a numbered account in Liechtenstein.

"Sir, I'm sorry but you'll have to personally put the arm on that bank for the name of the account holder," said Larry. "We tried, but they said they would not reveal it without a request from either the British Government or from Scotland Yard. Me and Jerry weren't important enough. You are."

The emails which the Super-geeks had cracked were damning, all of them hidden behind the password **Tickets for the Gondola** "... I have wired the money ... and I shall require both little girls for two hours ... *Tilden.*"

"Money gone to *Birkenhead.* Please ensure the girls are naked when I enter the room ... as always ... *Beauregard*

"One hundred and fifty thousand Hong Kong dollars forwarded to Cayman—I hope elder daughter very good with Fuji camera—ha ha. Very fine record of juvenile fuck Ha Ha Ha ... *Divine Amira.*"

"Arriving 6pm on 18th. Money paid. Two hours. I need time with the little one. She's very beautiful. *Sweet Charity.*"

Larry had not exaggerated the horrific quality of the photographs. Charles was stunned by the explicit sexual nature of the pictures. If anyone was ever identified in any one of these pictures, in the opinion of the DCS, they really would throw away the key to the jail.

Larry summoned the whole collection, and uploaded them onto Charles's computer. After thanking them both for their heroic efforts, Charles settled down to scan the photographs as swiftly as possible, looking for pictures of the first four pseudonyms, the ones for whom he had positive ID.

Only one picture stopped him in his tracks. It showed a young girl, lying on the floor, blood streaming down her face, mingling with her tears, the photo having been taken by the very obvious person who was about to rape her. But there was something about the little girl's face, distorted as it was, by sobbing, blood and tears. And yet there was something—something familiar to him.

He stared at it for what seemed like several minutes. No it couldn't be, but by God it had an eerie effect on him, starting with the memory of a scar just below the hairline on the forehead of his vanished girlfriend. Charles had long ceased to worry about using that epithet about her—because as long as Sophia Morosova existed, he understood he would have eyes for no other woman, wherever that may lead.

The scar was forcing the unthinkable into his mind. If it was really the face of Sophia, then she had almost certainly stabbed Fontridge to death. But he refused to accept the logic of this, which was one of the few times he had refused to accept logic in his entire life. But it couldn't be, could it? Nonetheless, Charles downloaded that picture, and pressed on with almost indecent haste to the next set of shocking images.

It took just a few more moments for him to abandon his perusal of the most disgraceful photographs he had ever seen. And he called out to his secretary to get him the chief executive of the Liechtenstein City Bank on the line. She moved with alacrity on this one. Scotland Yard rarely puts in a call to the tiny Alpine Principality wedged between Switzerland and Austria, without a fairly urgent reason to do so.

And even those calls were never anything to do with the network of historic, fairyland castles which decorate its rolling landscapes. They were always to do with its network of very, very secretive numbered bank accounts. These are less protected now than they were a few years ago, before various governments began wondering where their taxation income was being hidden.

The Banks of Liechtenstein were dragged kicking and screaming into the modern tax-dominated world by Governments which would threaten any bank with outright ruin if they failed to betray their clients. This was almost exclusively because those governments wanted to go on spending and borrowing and lying their nations into bankruptcy, and if they had to kick the tiny tax-havens to death—well, I guess that's show business.

Charles Barton's secretary summoned the President of the Liechtenstein City Bank to the phone, and the Superintendent introduced himself, then requested the name of the owner of the Numbered Account 23082826-BOL41.

"Sir, I don't have to remind you that under our agreement with the British Government we are not obliged to reveal any account unless there is compelling evidence to suggest you are investigating a criminal act of some description."

"I understand that," replied Charles. "In this case we are investigating the death of a very senior Lord Justice of the Court of Appeal, and an adviser to the Royal family who was found murdered, stabbed to death in a lake."

"Yes, Superintendent, I remember reading about the case."

"My enquiry into this bank account is very closely tied to the possible arrest of the murderer. I'd be obliged if you would facilitate that for me."

"Sir, may I ask if the holder of this account is the person under suspicion?"

"I'm afraid you may not. But I do think we will solve the case when we have this account number. If you do not wish to reveal it, I'll have the Prime Minister make the request through the Chairman of the International Monetary Fund. As you wish. Meanwhile we will instruct you to conduct all future transactions involving the UK, directly through the Bank of England, where cooperation may, of course, now be limited."

The CEO of the Liechtenstein Bank had heard quite sufficient of this one-sided battle, and he said, "Just a moment, sir."

When he returned, he said, "Superintendent, my directors acknowledge the importance of the request, and are perfectly willing to provide you with the information. Bank account—23082826-BOL41—is held under the name of a person we contact only at a PO Box in Moscow. His name is Boris Morosov.

*****

Sophia waited in a bus shelter throughout a fairly warm shower of rain sweeping across the city of New Orleans. It was carried on a south wind right across the wetlands of Louisiana on its way up the Mississippi towards the Great Plains of Oklahoma. It was currently hurling down a lot of water.

She was dressed in trousers, a white blouse and boots, with a rain slicker she had just picked up in a convenience store. And she was reading a free newspaper, full, cover to cover, with classified ads, one of which was sending her to her destination.

That was Al's Used Car Dealers and Repairs, set in the uniquely undesirable neighbourhood of Dixon, right there on Chevlon Street, the heart of Dixon's parking-lot wrecks, many of them so low in the bargain basement they were not even on the chart.

When the bus turned up, Sophia boarded and asked the conductor to let her off in Chevlon Street, a journey of about three-miles. Her objective was a 1978 Chevy Blazer truck—'priced to sell—good running order.'

She told the conductor where she was headed, and he dropped her off right outside the forecourt, which had the unusual distinction of being without concrete. It was a rough old dealership, in a rough old neighbourhood, on rough old ground, tatty cars, most of which had been in accidents, and piles of trash, which suggested the place had last been swept around 1947.

The garage itself was an old wooden shack of a place, dark green in colour, last painted around 1847. Al's masthead, a sign nailed shakily above the entrance, had been painted by no less a graphic artist than Al himself. And colour-blindness had not deterred him.

"And what can I do for you, young Lady?" he called from deep beneath an ancient Ford Mustang. "You here to buy a vehicle, or get one fixed. Whichever that is, I'm your man. I'll be right with you."

"I'm here to buy," replied Sophia.

And Al shot out from under that Mustang like a Mark 48** torpedo from the guidance tube.

"Right, ma'am, now you just tell me what you're looking for."

"I'm answering your advertisement right here in this newspaper for a '78 Chevy truck."

"Well, ma'am, I have to tell you I just sold that one, but I have a better one across the lot." And he led her out to a truly tired-looking, battered old Mustang.

"No, Al," said Sophia, "I want a truck not a race-car." She definitely did not alert him to her recent record with that type of vehicle.

"Okay, ma'am," he said, "What about this one. Dun't look much, but this here truck has a classic engine, probably run forever. Only got about 80,000 on the clock."

"Well, it's at least 30 years old, so that's pretty light mileage."

"Sure is, just one owner, an old lady lives right around here. Serviced this vehicle myself all its life."

Sophia decided that no former pupil of St Margaret's Pangbourne could tolerate this level of bullshit, from this ludicrous old conman, and she told him, "Al, stop giving me a load a rubbish. All I want is a truck that will not let me down for 500 miles."

"Then I have the vehicle for you," he said, which Sophia did not consider a major surprise. He led her to a different Chevy truck, old but not battered, black but not shiny. "You understand I can't let this one go for the same price as the one in the paper," he added.

"How much?" asked Sophia.

"Well, ma'am I couldn't release this one for less than $700."

"How about the tires?" asked Sophia. "The front ones I mean."

"They're not too good, ma'am, but for $700 bucks you're not gonna get tires which are perfect. Even retreads cost about $80 a piece."

"What about the battery?"

"I can't answer that," he said. "Might be old, might be new."

"Okay," she said, "I'll tell you what, if you get in the truck, and it starts first time, I'll buy it. And then you'll put two new retreads on the front wheels, then you'll fit a brand new battery. And put some new number plates on it. Old ones, not registered. Then I'll give you a thousand bucks. Cash."

"Done," said Al in very nearly world-record time, climbed into the truck, and it did indeed start first time.

"It's just that I'm going to a lonely part of the country," said Sophia, "And I don't want to get stranded with a puncture or a flat battery."

Al said he understood that, told her he had a pair of plates last used on a covered wagon heading west through Apache country! And he shouted for someone to bring the big car-jack. A half-hour later Sophia had new front tires, a fully charged battery, dodgy number plates, and freedom to roam the bayous of Louisiana. The proprietor of Al's Garage took the 10 one hundred-dollar bills, and told her, "Now y'all come back here and see me anytime, y'hear."

Sophia promised and roared off, heading south to Gert Town, a fabled area of New Orleans high-crime, where gang warfare, shootings, murder and robberies raised not one single eyebrow among the locals.

Chapter Twenty-One
The Shadow Tracking the Killer

The ex-Soviet Union military binoculars had leather grips,
bearing the crossed swords which confirmed the Russian
infantry in combat, But nothing was moving in these endless
swamps, except for a few venomous cross-bred water snakes.

Gert Town was always poor, but when the levies let go in 2005, Katrina decimated the place, flooding the streets, end to end. It never really recovered, but Sophia worked out it was probably a helluva place to buy a gun, no questions asked, and that was her plan. In fact her little free newspaper carried an ad for a pawn shop which sold unclaimed guns. Sophia, who had never actually seen a real ghetto, pressed right on to what she hoped was her personal armoury.

She had the address and she found it, noted the three brass balls hanging above the door, parked right outside and went in. The owner was a thin, weedy-looking guy, bald and 50-ish. When he heard she was trying to buy a shot-gun, he immediately told her, "Ma'am, I'm gonna find you a real lightweight weapon. On account of some ole shotguns have a kick like a wild boar."

He returned with a second-hand 12-gauge Mossberg over-and-under, break action with a 28-inch barrel, a pound or two lighter than the heavyweights. He also fetched a box of .00 buckshot.

"What do you need it for, ma'am?"

"I've got a rat to kill, a big one."

"A rat! This thing will bring down a goddamned grizzly."

"Sounds perfect," said Sophia, listening carefully as he told her there were only 12-shots in a three-inch shell, but they would form the same pattern as a regular duck gun—10 pellets over a 36-inch circumference at 20-yards, like being shot at with 12 rifles all at once.

"Can I still miss?" she asked.

"Not hardly. But you'll need a bit of practice."

"Can I do it here?"

"Hell, no. If we loosed off a couple of those shells around here, there'd be about 17 cops outside the door in five minutes."

"Forget the practice," said Sophia.

Five minutes later, the shotgun securely wrapped, and, light another $150, Sophia fired up her truck, and headed for one of the Crescent City Connecting bridges over the Mississippi River, after which she found the main road, Route 90, along the river, and down to the city of Houma, 50-miles west of New Orleans, a one-hour drive.

*****

As Sophia crossed what locals sometimes call, 'That Big Ole River,' one certain Mr Rudy Masow, having landed Jet Blue from Boston an hour before, was checking into New Orleans' five-star Windsor Court Hotel, on Gravier Street, no more than a mile from Sophia's scruffy old truck, hammering its way towards Route 90.

"Now where the hell is that girl?" growled Rudy to no one in particular, as he strode towards the Reception desk. But before he could answer that question, he received his first surprise of the day. The girl behind the desk said, "Ah, Mr Masow. We've been expecting you, these are the keys to that SUV out front, which arrived a couple of hours ago."

Rudy smiled and thanked her, and she added, "There's a gentleman sitting over there in the lounge, waiting to see you."

The big Russian assassin thanked her again, signed the pre-prepared, pre-paid check-in form, and walked over to meet the stranger who'd arrived from God knows where.

He offered his hand, and the young man stood up and said, "Hi, Mr Masow. I was sent by my boss, the Ambassador in Washington. My name's Sergei, and I do know your niece, drove her in West Virginia."

"I'm very glad to meet you, Sergei," replied Rudolf. "Can I presume you understand the mission?"

"You can, sir. I'm told we have to save her from doing something really stupid, because if we don't, all hell's gonna break out."

"That's more or less accurate," confirmed Rudy. "I have an address. We ready to hit the road?"

"Yes, sir."

"Let's go," said Rudy. "By the way, are we armed?"

"Oh yes, silenced sniper rifle, telescopic sights, hidden in the vehicle, diplomatic plates, driven here overnight Houston Consulate General."

"Where's the driver?"

"Gone, sir, back to Texas by air. I'm the official driver, official assistant, official second-in-command. Not bad for a Cultural Attache, right, sir?"

"Not bad at all," said Rudolf, laughing. "I know the feeling well! By the way, the name's Rudy, not Sir."

*****

Sophia Morosova gunned the old Chevy along Route 90. It rattled a bit at over 80mph, so she kept her speed down to 70 on the Interstate Highway, which was high-quality thinking because the last thing she needed was to be pulled over for speeding, with a loaded shotgun in the back, and dodgy number plates.

After 40-miles, she swung south to the near-deserted four-lane highway 182. This was lonelier than a Bedouin dust-track through the Sinai. Sophia never passed a vehicle, either way. Never even saw one. She could have tested her new gun in the middle of the road and no would have ever known.

As it was, she kept going for seven miles, and then crossed the highway and turned off onto a dirt track, where to her amazement there were no Bedouins either. She found herself trundling along a lonely path right alongside the bayou. She stopped and looked around. Nothing. Then she pulled the gun out, unwrapped it, and took aim at a huge tree about 40 yards away.

However two things happened, both of which Lady Penelope would most certainly have found particularly disagreeable. When she pulled the trigger, the kickback landed her flat on her back, and she missed the tree by about 5O-yards. Sophia climbed to her feet, uttered a word which would have appalled the headmistress of St Margaret's, and re-loaded.

This time she took a lot more care, gripped the gun much more firmly, and came up from a slight swing, bringing the barrel up in line with the tree. But once more the kickback surprised her, and she fell back against the truck, feeling a whack, in the lower-jaw and shoulder, from the hard jolt of the stock. That was the bad news. The good news was she hit the tree, square on.

She reloaded, both barrels, and resolved to master this damn thing, right now. Again there was good news. She hit the tree both times. But on the second shot she'd mastered the kickback, never felt a thing.

She slipped the shotgun back behind the seat, And stood for a moment listening to the all-pervading silence of the Louisiana bayous. In the distance she actually heard a car travelling very fast, south down 182. Never gave it much thought, because the vehicle was making little noise. Those black Russian Ford SUV's always ran very quiet.

Sophia turned the truck around, drove slowly back to the highway, a couple of miles more down 182, to the city of Houma, in the very watery Parish of Terrebonne, a place where the land has always struggled against 850-square miles of Arcadian swamp. Houma is a city of Cajuns, descended from original French settlers, among whom the phrase *n'est ce pas* is heard a lot more often than *I was like Wow!*

Sophia stopped at a roadside motel on the outskirts of the city, where the nightly rate would not have bought you a sleeping birth in a broom cupboard at the Windsor Court. She pulled up among two other vehicles, parked and checked in for three nights, paying in advance, cash $150. She decided to remove her valuables from the truck—the shotgun, the box of .00 cartridges, and the second-hand binoculars she had also bought at the pawn-shop. She carried them all into her room up on the second floor.

She debated a trip this evening down to Montegut, but decided she was just too tired, all she wanted was a shower, and something to eat, and an early night. She intended to be on duty, in Montegut, bayou-side, at first light.

*****

Sergei drove at the limit of the speed laws on the long road through Terrebonne Parish. Houma flashed past in a blur, and they were on their way down Highway 57 directly to the little town of Montegut, home of the de Villiers family. This was to be one of the fastest recces in recent memory. Rudy wanted to make an instant survey of the land around the house.

He had the address and he intended to make this a half-hour stop, just to spy out the territory, assess the lie of the land, and gauge where Hunter de Villiers might take up his hobby of fly fishing. They pulled into the little town moving so fast they nearly overshot it and wound up in Lake Barre.

However, Sergei screeched to a halt on the shores of the Bayou Terrebonne. He flicked on the satellite GPS, punched in the de Villiers address, and had to flip the SUV round and head back to a small lake on the eastern shore of the wide bayou. And, right in the northeast corner was a very grand house with a wide back staircase, very wide at the garden end, wide-ish at the top, close to the back door, a bit like a Pharaoh's temple in ancient Egypt.

"That's it," said Rudy. "Right there, that's where he lives."

"Well, why don't we just pop in there now?" said Sergei. "Did you bring a couple of hand-grenades? It'd save us a lot of trouble!"

"To be honest, I forgot them," said Rudy, laughing. "I was already bringing four atom bombs!"

"Short-sighted," chuckled Sergei. These two really liked each other.

Sergei pulled out a pair of ex-Soviet Union military binoculars, the leather grips displaying the crossed swords which confirmed they had been used by the Russian infantry in combat, probably WWII. He handed them to Rudy who scanned the shores of the lake carefully, looking for some kind of betrayal of the presence of his wayward niece.

Inch by inch he surveyed the verdant shores of this beautiful lake, from which grew two enormous bald cypress trees, the hall-mark of these endless southern swamps, which down here run off quietly into the convergence of no fewer than six separate bayous. Along the shores grew cottonwood trees, gum-trees and glorious southern oaks with fronds of Spanish moss.

Rudy kept looking, but found nothing, not one single sign that Sophia had ever been here, not as much as a parked car, not even a boat cruising these tranquil waters above the green, submerged aquatic plants, and the less attractive venomous cross-bred water snakes.

She's not here and has not been here, was the verdict of Rudolf Masow. And he kept the binoculars trained on the house, scanning down to the private dock upon which was moored one small outboard fishing boat named *Beauregard*. Neither of them knew what to make of it. But this was where Sophia was headed. Of that Rudy was certain.

But for now they pulled out of the operations area, and continued their journey south through the heartland of Louisiana's coastal plain, a 30-mile drive ahead of them, to the world-weary fishing port of Cocodrie, which was full of aged trawlers, and bronzed, lined seamen, rewarded poorly for decades of brutal hard work in the Gulf.

Cocodrie is probably the leading shrimp-boat harbour in all the world, and nothing in all the world would ever tempt these rugged sons of Louisiana to do anything else. Rudolf could see a little group of fishermen sitting on a low wall drinking coffee. He had no intention of entering into some kind of seminar, but he wanted a boat, a good captain and good first-mate, and a semi-reliable trawler which would make it to Cuba and back, 1,200-miles.

It was, he already knew, a difficult time for the shrimp boat men, very late in the season, closed completely inshore to the west, limited supplies and opportunities offshore to the east. None of them was making even £1,000 a week, not even the captains.

From a distance, Rudy could hear them griping and moaning. But one of them kept laughing. He was a kind of white-skinned black man, handsome in his way, with a French accent, a mop of tight ginger curls, a perfectly cut goatee beard, and, incongruously, a pair of two-toned evening shoes, which made him look like a matinee idol from the Old Testament. Rudy swiftly discovered this was Captain Art Dubois, a Louisiana Creole, who very nearly signed pro for the New Orleans Saints as a Tulane University running back. But then his father died, and he inherited a really nice boat, which he was forced to take over, just to keep the family afloat.

The Dubois family had been harvesting these waters for several generations. But Art liked the shrimp nets, and at times had made a lot of money. He had a mystical knack of finding huge shrimp catches in these warm, murky waters. He had become an acknowledged master of his craft.

His younger brother who was not as savvy, was his first mate and mechanic. They were a good team, but right now even these two were feeling the pinch. It was a quasi-off-season, and the DuBois boys were short of cash for the repairs the boat needed. Art somehow kept smiling.

"That's my man," said Rudolf. "The joker over there with the orange hair and the big smile. Stay here Sergei. I'm going to hire us a boat."

Rudy walked quietly over to the area where the deep-sea men were talking. He caught the eye of Art Dubois, and gave a little smile and a nod. The big Creole fisherman came over and held out his hand. Rudolf told him his requirements, Art showed him one of the better-looking boats in the harbour. And Rudy explained he wanted Art and his boat on standby for tomorrow and Saturday, fully gassed up and ready to cross the Caribbean at a moment's notice.

"Well, sir," said Art Dubois, "I could sure arrange that. No problem right there. But it'll cost you quite a bit of money, a few days for me and my crew, coupla thousand for gas and running costs. Could run you $6,000. Easy."

"I guess it could. And that's a lot of money," said Rudy. "But I want a reliable man, who's going to take that standby duty very seriously. I'll pay a little extra for that kind of loyalty. Now how much for all that?"

"Sir, I don't really know. But I guess I'll know it when I hear it."

"Ten thousand dollars, five now and five when we set sail."

"I just heard it, man," beamed Captain Dubois. "Right here on this dock, I heard them magic numbers. I'm real happy with that."

"And that makes you my right-hand man 'til Sunday morning, right? That's our latest time of departure."

"You got it, sir. We'll be right here in the Port of Cocodrie, Louisiana, just waiting your commands. Yes, Sir."

They both smiled and shook hands, and Rudy handed over 50 brand new $100 bills, fresh out of the cashier point at Boston Airport, Bank of New England. Then Art Dubois took his new charter client on a swift trip around the boat, a smallish outrigger, equipped to drag three or even four 'rock-hoppers' over the ocean floor. That's nets rigged with wheels on the underside strut, allowing them to climb over impediments. The boat had a nearly new 'beast of an engine,' a for'ard wheelhouse and an aft working deck.

Art was rightly proud of his working craft, and he smiled cheerfully as he walked Rudy over to his car. He gave him a couple of business cards with his cell and home numbers, and promised he'd be right here, waiting for the call. As he walked away Rudy noticed him do a little Irish jig, clicking his two-tones together quite gracefully, which made him look like Fred Astaire with ginger whiskers. He also had five thousand bucks in his pocket, which he did not have 15 minutes ago.

Rudy and Sergei drove back up the highway, sped past Houma, and arrived back at the Windsor Court at 6.30pm, well in time for a couple of vodkas, and then dinner. Sergei too was booked in. And over a very reasonable bottle of French claret, they talked tactics, mostly about how to prevent Sophia from doing something absolutely ridiculous. Assuming, of course, they could find her.

*****

Friday morning dawned, a hot, Delta day. It had rained intermittently all through the night, and high cloud still hung over the wetlands, casting a flat grey light which turned the waters the colour of pewter. As a point of principle, it was still raining. And in July the brackish swamp water was extremely warm. One way and another, it was a perfectly lousy day for fly-fishing along the bayous, as the big redfish travelled north in search of cooler pools.

Sophia stood by her motel window, staring glumly at the raindrops running down her truck windshield. It was not much of a day for killing another human being either. And she consoled herself by recalling that the sexual monster down in Montegut had no right to include himself as even a country member of the human race.

She also knew no one would believe her if she tried to explain what the revered Hunter de Villiers had done to her, and her little sister, when they were but 15 (just) and 17 respectively. Him and his friggin' bulldog badge. She'd put that in the lake with him …, as they mention down here … *yessir.*

But the light of dawn, cold, grey and uninspiring as it was, shone a new awareness upon her, that she had to be darned careful. And she remembered the real concern in Uncle Rudy's voice, when he had categorically forbidden her to undertake this mission.

And that concern was for all the obvious reasons … a weapon with which she was unfamiliar; a strange new place; an unknown enemy who may be armed or even have an armed bodyguard; and, of course, the acute likelihood of ending up in Louisiana State Penitentiary, 'The Alcatraz of the South,' America's largest maximum-security jail, situated on a big bend in that Big Ole River, only two miles short of the Mississippi line.

The possibilities of even the most elementary errors of judgment were accentuated because she was entirely on her own, with no help close at hand, no backup, no proper plan, and no well-organised exit route. This was not even similar to her other four exploits. This one was absolutely toxic.

But just then the everlasting image of the terrified, sobbing Sasha jostled its way into her mind. And she swung around, and seized her second-hand shot-gun, gripped it tight, and said through gritted teeth … I'll get you, you bastard, if it's the last thing I ever do, I will get you …

She glanced at her watch. It was a little after 6.30am. She 'broke' the shotgun as she'd learned in the pawnshop, and loaded two cartridges into the breach, one over, one under. She cleaned the lenses of her binoculars, pulled a few hundred dollars out of her secret compartment, and reset the special security system in her travelling bag.

She was glad she'd brought lightweight, waterproof boots with her, and her other clothes were much like yesterday—trousers, white shirt, and rain slicker. She debated a black beret she owned, but rejected it on the grounds it made her look too much like the half-crazed Cuban freedom fighter, Che Guevara, which was not the image she was currently nurturing. She carefully fitted on a new Parisian blond wig, and her dark sunglasses.

Then she packed everything in the bag except the shotgun, left the room and returned her key in the 'early box' outside the office. She slung the bag on the passenger seat, and carefully slipped the gun on the floor behind her. Then she fired up the ancient engine with the powerful new battery.

Sophia drove slowly across the desolate forecourt, knowing she would never pass this way again: even though she had not the first idea how she would get away. Get rid of the car and catch a bus, she supposed, trying not to think of precisely how contemptuous Rudy would be at such a half-hearted, amateur, hit-or-miss, potential disaster area this line of thought actually was.

"Still, I'll have to go somewhere," she muttered, "Just to get out of Louisiana. It's either road or rail, right after I've dumped the gun and bullets in the stupid bayou." She could vividly imagine the deep theatrical groan of a rabidly disapproving Rudolf Masow.

She now turned the truck in a southerly direction, heading further south in this country than she'd ever been before. It was 15-miles to Montegut, down Route 55 to the last proper town on the Bayou Terrebonne. She made it in 25 minutes.

There was no one around that Sophia could see, except the mailman, and she asked him to tell her the way.

The mailman knew full well that locals were not permitted to reveal the exact homestead of the wealthiest man in the town, but he surmised this pretty lady in a gardening truck had a real educated voice, and could not possibly be a threat to anyone. He told her exactly the way to the house, the track he'd used himself that very morning.

Which gave Sophia Morosova an instant insight into the property and all of its surroundings. Thus, long before the patriarch stirred on this lazy, rainy Friday morning, his arch enemy from Maida Vale knew every yard of his country estate.

She knew the shape of the land that swept down to the dock where the *Beauregard* was moored. She'd circled the lake, spotted the precise entry point from the bayou, she'd made a note of the track which ran right around the shoreline, and she'd picked out at least three spots from where she could watch the house, and see when he left to go fishing in *Beauregard*.

The lake was almost a half-mile long and 200 yards wide, and it was surprisingly shady, with cypress and oak along the banks, and a few huge trees jutting right out of the water. This was by design. The shade helped keep the water cool, which was perfect for game fish, attracting them on their journey, precisely as Hunter de Villiers liked it.

Sophia needed to rent a small boat, just an outboard for a couple of days. Like the fighting bulls of Madrid, she intended to strike when her victim was as far from help as he could be, well offshore, somewhere in the middle of his private lake. She understood this could not be done from the shore. She needed to be out there, firing from close range.

It was not difficult to hire boats around here. All the way along the bayou she had seen signs offering boats for hire, although she was not certain she could find a sufficiently small one. So she decided to buy herself some fishing gear, a couple of rods, lines, and some ready-tied flies, with a landing net. That way she'd look like a pro.

And that would enable her to park her truck well out of the way until the deed was done, and then she could vanish across the lake and down the bayou in her getaway vessel. A bit like 007 really, except Miss Morosova had no intention of flying at high speed across someone's lawn.

Temporarily, she drove away from the de Villiers lake and set off south for a couple of miles, stopping finally at a long wooden structure, roadside, with a large red and yellow painted sign announcing Alderman's Sport Shop. Another two even bigger signs offered, BAIT.

Lined along the outer wall was a row of wooden planks. A local shipwright was repairing a 40-foot coastal dragger, raised up on piles between the sport shop and the highway. At the back, the bayou flowed past, washing its way south, although it slowed up here, owing to the wreck of an old oyster longboat.

This had somehow managed to sink amidships, rather than bow or stern, and was now resting on the bottom surrounded by bullrushes. It looked like it had been there for years, somehow smashed in half, or, as the Navy would say, "with her back broken.'

It also looked as if it had been hit by a ground-to-surface guided missile, and basically gone to the bottom with all hands. Anyway, Sophia stared at this maritime wonderland, and then went inside to buy her fishing gear. The proprietor looked like Blackbeard's First Mate, a big, heavily-bearded former seaman, covered in tattoos, with a nice line in second-hand rods on display behind the counter.

It took a half hour, but she came out well equipped to spend time out there on the lake, like a native, quietly testing her two rods, trying to land a big redfish, or even a largemouth or spotted bass, the big game-fish which haunt these waters year round, swept in on the hard southerly flow of the Red River, or the Mississippi itself.

The fish spend weeks running down to the Gulf of Mexico, all along the bayous, streams, lakes and waterways. They are always out there, helping to cement Louisiana's perennial nickname, The Sportsman's Paradise.

Sophia drove on down the road which tracks the bayou. All along there were trailers, belonging to fishermen, and even local families who kept boats moored alongside on both banks. She decided to go for two miles and then look for something for hire. This was not difficult, there was plenty of choice, and she finally pulled over next to a sign which read, "Small craft for hire, Boston Whaler 17-foot, Yamaha."

Right next to this was a local man sitting at a desk with a pencil in one hand and a fishing rod in the other, "You interested in the boat?" he asked.

"Yes, sir," replied Sophia.

"It's 100 bucks a day, including insurance. Gas extra."

There was a deliberate economy of words here, and Sophia decided not to extend it. "Sounds fine," she said. "Can I have it for three days?"

"S'long as you got 330 bucks, that's okay by me."

Sophia handed over the money, which he counted carefully. Then he gave her the key and told her she had a full tank. "Where is it?" she asked.

"Straight down the road, about 200 yards, moored by itself on a cement wharf, green cover. It's a good boat, take care of it now, y'hear."

"Does it have a name?"

"Hell, no."

"I'll bring it back Sunday."

"If you don't, gonna cost you another hundred."

"Okay, I'll have it back here. By the way, what's the insurance for?"

"Just in case you steal it … or kill someone."

Sophia smiled, gave him a little wave, climbed back into her truck, and drove on down the bayou. She did not answer that last part.

Instead, she drove on south until she found the whaler with the green cover, moored on the concrete jetty slightly apart from the dozens of power fishing boats, which also made their home on this lonely stretch of this part of the Bayou. Across the street was a fishermen's parking lot with probably two-dozen vehicles. Locked and parked for owners who had already set sail in search of Bone Fish, the steely, lightning fast guardians of the shallows. Sophia parked her truck in the middle of the lot, shoulder bag, rods, nets, and shot-gun. She locked the door and ran across the road to board the whaler.

And the words of the Whaler's owner remained obstinately in her mind…The insurance? "That's in case you kill someone."

Chapter Twenty-Two
A Shrimp Boat to Havana

*The ex-KGB man squinted down the gun-sight, checked
the bolt, fixed the stock into his shoulder, and began breathing in
strict rhythm with his own heartbeat, just in case he needed a
long shot. It was the pure professionalism of the trained sniper.*

Sergei had Uncle Rudolf well under way from New Orleans, by the time his
niece located the Whaler, unclipped the cover, and worked out which button to
press in order to lower the Yamaha engine into the water. She knew how to drive
one of these, thanks to St Margaret's.

The school kept a couple of outboards next to the boathouse on the Thames
at Pangbourne, and it was not entirely unknown for a few of the senior girls to
'borrow' them from time to time. This was strictly forbidden, especially with no
lifejackets, but everyone knew where the keys were kept.

And as Sophia chugged softly north, through the rain along the bayous, the
black SUV was rapidly approaching Houma, about 10 miles out, dodging
through the rush hour traffic on Route 182, which amounted to 14 trucks and a
couple of cars.

They pushed on south towards Montegut, and ducked down a shaded track
they had surveyed the previous evening. It was at the far end of the de Villiers
lake, where there was the total seclusion of a substantial clump of trees and
bushes, into which Sergei steered backwards, in case they needed to leave, fast.
At which point he came to a halt.

"Good boy," said Rudy. "Now let's check out that 'hide' we found. It was a
bit closer to the house, but still a couple of hundred yards away, and impossible
to detect. "The tree's like a step-ladder," he said. "We'll take turns watching the
house and the dock.

"As soon as we spot Sophia, we'll try and get her over here. As soon as the
de Villiers character leaves the dock, I'll take prime position on the tree. We'll
leave the rifle, loaded, up there on that wide branch we saw yesterday."

Quietly they went about their tasks. Sergei got the packed sandwiches out of the trunk, and left the cooler on the back seat. He also brought out a couple of spray cans of mosquito repellent, since the place was a swamp whichever way you cut it. Rudolf checked every inch of the rifle, which had come with the car on its long drive into the bayous from the Houston Consulate.

It was a firearm with a deep history, originally developed in an armoury founded in 1712 by Peter the Great, the old Tula Arsenal, which is still manufacturing modern weapons of war at its original site, 200-miles due south of Moscow at Oblast, along the road to the Ukraine.

The specific weapon was the Vintorez VSS, a suppressed sniper rifle that uses a heavy subsonic 9 X 39mm SP6 armour-piercing cartridge which leaves the 8-inch barrel at 650mph. That's 300-yards-per-second, which was the area which most concerned Rudy. Its 400-yard range was accurate with a special telescopic sight.

Rudy was an expert with this old Soviet Union military rifle. He'd used one of them for years on more missions than he cared to count or remember, all over the world. He'd always relied on it, and today he'd do the same. However all the other missions, down all the years, were to do with brains and duty and patriotism. This one involved his heart. Because if anything happened to Sophia, and he failed to stop it … *Don't even think about it, Rudy, it's unbearable.*

Meanwhile, where the hell was she? No one knew that, but the Russian assassin somehow knew she was not far away. He could not explain it, nor indeed think very hard about it. But Sophia was near, and she was about to put her life, or at least her freedom, at dangerous risk.

Rudy aimed the rifle sights way down the lake, out into the waterway which led to the main flow of the bayou. There was nothing much to see and it was still raining. Sergei pulled one of the big golf umbrellas out of the trunk and rigged it up in the branches above the boss.

They both leaned into the tree and looked back at the de Villiers dock. Nothing. Not a movement, either outside or inside the house, nor through the only window through which they could see. It was 11am. No Hunter. No Sophia. Wet rain jacket, "Fuck," said Rudy, poetically.

The reason neither of them could see Sophia was her choice of observation point. She had scoured the left bank of the bayou looking north, and had found a spot overhung with cypress branches, and somehow manoeuvred her boat though them, into a mooring area in the middle of this watery undergrowth.

She did a bit of general housekeeping, broke off a few thin twigs and branches until she had an uninterrupted view through a gap, from a sitting position in the boat, straight across the bayou and up the short waterway into the lake. She could see the de Villiers Plantation house, very clearly through her binoculars. She could also see the dock and the *Beauregard.*

She found a way to hook the boat's green tarpaulin cover to the lowest branch on the tree, and let it fall back behind her, into the aft area where the fuel tank was set. This gave her complete cover from the rain if she pulled the cover over her head and shoulders. With her loaded shot-gun, and binoculars, she was invisible from the outside. It was a near perfect hideaway for a patrolling killer. Sophia waited. It was not yet 11am.

Time went by slowly; for her because she had nothing to eat or drink. For Sergei and Rudy because their shelter from the rain was nothing like as good as hers. The hour of 2pm came and went, the rain had ceased only once all day for about a half-hour. Then it started again.

By 4pm Sophia was about ready to swim or wade ashore and run to a store to buy water and food. Or even just to stretch her legs. But that was impossible. The other two were not hungry, nor thirsty, just wet, and Rudolf Masow was about ready to throttle Hunter de Villiers with his bare hands, just to get out of this hell-hole in the swamp. Again impossible.

By five o'clock they were still waiting. And quite suddenly the rain stopped. The sun peered out from between clouds, in Sophia's hideaway the silence seemed strange as the raindrops stopped pattering on the tarpaulin. She never took her eyes off the distant dock.

Which was just as well, because 20 minutes after the rains had ended, the back door of the de Villiers mansion opened, and out stepped the former Rajun' Cajuns offensive lineman, Russ Lambert, identifiable by his long, slightly unkempt curly hair. Sophia had not the first idea who he was. Rudolf Masow, however, knew exactly who he was, detailed Russian Embassy internet Intelligence being somewhat superior to Sophia's total lack of pre-knowledge.

"Action stations," snapped Rudy.

"I'm on it, sir," replied Sergei, crisply. "Long-haired asshole headed for small boat!"

Half a mile away, Sophia Morosova was peering through the cypress branches like a hunting coon-dog. Through her binoculars she too watched Russ

Lambert walk along the dock, step aboard *Beauregard* and sit down in the driving seat.

She could not hear him start the engine, but he made no attempt to pull away. Sergei did hear the outboard kick over, and reported to Rudy, "I'd guess he's starting the electric pump, throw some of that water out."

Five minutes later, the back door of the mansion opened again, and through it came Hunter de Villiers. Rudy recognised him from a dozen photos. Sophia would have recognised him if she'd been blindfolded. And her heart missed several beats, as she fired up the Yamaha and began to inch her way forward, out through the cypress branches, pushing them away from her face.

Russ Lambert unhooked the stern-line, then the one on the bow, leaving both on the dock. And slowly they made their way out into the lake, Hunter organising his rods, Russ had the wheel, and was already scanning the surface for redfish which often feed after the rain.

They moved about 100-yards away from the dock, and Hunter made his first cast, whipping his lure far back and then flashing it forward, hoping that fly would flick the water right in front of a big game fish. Neither of them noticed a Boston Whaler chugging up the inlet from the bayou, the calm stretch which led into the private lake, out of bounds to the public.

Hunter came up light, and cast again. In the huge low branches of his tree, the hidden Uncle Rudy spotted the incoming boat, and said, "Steady, Sergei. This is her, right out there in that whaler. I know it's her."

"Christ! I can't see who's in that boat. It could be Vladimir himself and I would not get it. Are you sure?"

"Flesh and blood, Sergei. I'm sure."

"What do we do?"

"Well, we can't shoot anyone. That's for certain. Just wait. See what develops."

Sergei held out his hand for the binoculars, simultaneously passing up the rifle, which was 100 percent primed. Rudy squinted down the gun-sight, checked the bolt, fixed the stock into his shoulder, and began breathing in strict rhythm with his heartbeat, just in case he needed a long shot. It was the pure professionalism of the trained sniper.

Sophia slowed right down and took a hard look through her bins. She could see Hunter de Villiers plain as day. And she put down her glasses for the last time. And with one hand on her shot-gun, she increased speed only slightly for the start of the last 150-yards into the lake. She knew exactly where she was headed, and she knew she would make a gentle turn to her left side, for the final approach, and then she would cut the engine, aim and fire, right opposite the *Beauregard*. Couldn't miss.

The nameless Whaler kept coming and Sophia made her turn. Big Russ stood up and waved her off. Sophia was now only 30-feet off their starboard quarter. Again Russ waved her off. But Sophia stood up, aimed and fired, slightly misjudging a little turbulence, and the shot-gun's kickback which knocked her flying back into the boat.

She'd missed de Villiers altogether, winged Hunter with a single pellet to his right arm, and caused both men to grab for their own rifle on the floor of the *Beauregard*.

But Sophia Morosova was nothing if not a born Obolensky fighter. And she recognised both the screw-up, and the danger. And she fought with all her strength to get ahold of her gun, fought to get back into a kneeling position, knowing she had only one cartridge left.

But as she looked up, sobbing with the effort, she came face to face with the rock-steady barrel of Russ Lambert's rifle, which was pointed directly at her forehead. It was too late to surrender, too late for everything. And Russ Lambert smiled—his last ever action on this planet. Uncle Rudy blew his head apart with one of those 9 X 39mm armour-piercing shells.

The suppressor ensured just a light pop from the rifle, and a 35-yard inch-perfect shot left a very small hole in Lambert's forehead, with absolutely nothing left behind it. The armour-piercing shell inside his brain exploded his skull asunder, a tirade of bone, blood and brain splashing into the lake.

But this was not over. Hunter de Villiers grabbed again for the gun, and stared across at Sophia, raising the weapon into the firing position. Sophia was in shock, unable to move, and there was an unmistakable leer on the face of the man she had hated every minute of her life these past seven years. She never even ducked as he lined up against this helpless, defenceless figure, in the cross-hairs of his rifle-sights.

And right then one of Uncle Rudy's subsonic 650mph bullets slammed into Hunter's temple, shattering his brains even more comprehensively than those of his bodyguard. He cannoned back from the force, slammed into the engine and collapsed over the side. And clear over the water, there rang out a shout which chilled Sophia's blood. She was so petrified.

"GET OVER HERE, YOU PRECIOUS LITTLE IDIOT!"

If she had not known better she would have thought the oak tree was shouting at her, but this was a voice she'd never mistake, and she broke down with fear, gratitude, and overpowering sorrow for the innocent bodyguard who died because of her. Sophia was too scared to steer the boat and her tears cascaded down her face.

"GET OVER HERE—UNLESS YOU'RE DEAF AS WELL AS STUPID!"

The tree had yelled again. "Oh my God," groaned Sophia. "It's him. Oh, my God!"

She pulled herself together, nearly, and steered for the shore. It wasn't far and Sergei grabbed the painter and hauled her in. "Get the stuff out of the boat, fast," snapped Rudy, "Bag, gun everything."

Sergei did it for her, since his old buddy Sophia was rooted to the spot. She was stunned by his own sudden appearance, not to mention Uncle Rudy's, and appalled by the happenings of the last five minutes. Out on the water, Hunter's fishing boat, engine in 'dead slow,' was just trundling towards the far end of the lake, where a stand of wide Cypress trees jutted 60-feet high, out of the water, each one fully draped with hanging Spanish moss. The *Beauregard* was headed for six of nature's great sentinels of the Louisiana swamps, enormous in surface circumference, forming a gigantic Indian tepee, and probably the best cover a boat can get.

Back ashore Rudy was still yelling. "See that black vehicle over there?" he shouted, *"Sophia, get in the backseat, shut the door, and shut up. That's all."*

To Sergei, "Grab the rifle, there's four slugs left, armour piercing. Punch all four through the deck of Sophia's boat, start the engine, and shove her down the lake. There'll be a big very big hole in her hull. She'll be under the surface in three minutes."

Sophia ran to the SUV. Rudolf Masow cleared up the left packages from the cooler and shoved them in the back seat with Sophia. He put both rifles and binoculars in the way-back. And watched her boat chug away empty, sinking lower and lower into the water.

Sergei climbed in behind the wheel, and Rudy in the passenger seat, told him to stop after five miles, to get rid of the hardware in some deep swamp with a lot of snakes.

"Okay, boss, straight down to Art, right? Here's the phone and his card."

Rudy hit the numbers, and said succinctly, "Okay, Art, on my way. Start the engines when you're ready, 30 minutes, two passengers. Straight to Cuba."

"Roger that, boss," replied Art, who was immensely proud of that sharp acceptance of command, once explained to him by a member of the Royal Navy's submarine service, a young officer on a fishing trip right here in southeast Louisiana.

Rudy turned around and faced Sophia for the first time, but he came at her in a sideways manner. "I really hate to smash up someone's boat, like your Whaler. Where did you get it?"

"It's okay Uncle Rudy. It's insured."

"What for?"

"In case I killed someone."

"Some hopes of that," he replied, his deep voice encased with irony.

Sophia blushed, and looked away.

Sergei drove with a new urgency. They headed back to Montegut and set out down Route 56, the faster and direct road down to Cocodrie, where Captain Art Dubois awaited them. Sophia sat quietly looking out the window, in a combination of sulk and self-recrimination, aware at last, that once more she owed her life to Uncle Rudy.

Rudy, sensing this high-octane female emotion simmering right behind, went on the offensive: "How many times did I tell you? Nobody undertakes a black operation like that, with a second-hand shot-gun bought from a ghetto, without even one day's practice. Who do you think you are? Wonder Woman?

"Don't answer him, Sophia," Sergei called back. "On your best days you'd leave Wonder Woman standing."

"Yeah, and on your worst it'd be very quiet," added Uncle Rudy. "Because you'd almost certainly be dead, like you would've been today—shot dead by a bodyguard trying to make a name for himself. A guy looking for a big pay raise by taking out the assassin who tried to kill the boss."

Sophia held up her head, and stated formerly, "Thank you, Uncle, for saving my life. I know you did. And you have my gratitude. But I can't keep mentioning it for the rest of my life."

"No time limit on your gratitude. Just don't ever forget your imbecile defiance. I'm still your guardian, and I'd still lay down my life for you. I just want to make sure you don't get us both killed. That's all."

Sophia Morosova was marginally humbled by that. And Sergei, sensing again that this could go the wrong way, flicked on the car radio, spinning the dial to the main New Orleans country music station, and right there was Louisiana's very own Hank Williams putting the finishing touches to *Honky Tonk Blues*, and steaming right into *Hey! Good Looking*. He'd just got to, *How's about cookin' somethin' up with me*—when Rudy flicked the radio off completely.

"I'm not actually cookin' nothing up with nobody," he said, single-handedly committing his third murder of the day—the strict grammatical law which governs every aspect of double negatives in the English language.

"Not even me," said Sophia, primly.

"*Specially with you,*" he yelled. "*And I can't help you, on account of you can't fix stupid!*"

"Harsh," she said, giggling.

"Not as harsh as a rifle bullet in your head," he muttered.

"And not as gracious as 'Darling, Sophia, how glad I am I saved your life—what a joy that we're still together as family members.'"

"There are times," he confessed, "when I know precisely why I loved you and your sister from the day you were both born." And then, "*THIS IS NOT ONE OF THEM!*"

This reduced Sergei to helpless laughter, and he felt he could just remind the boss of Sophia's courage under fire, the way she'd gone down, then regrouped, fought back against her enemy, gone for her gun a second time. "That's a brave character," he said. "In another life she'd have been with Stonewall in the Valley."

"Brick-wall in the cemetery," added Rudy. Which made the other two laugh even more, partly in relief, partly in admiration for the craggy old Russian spymaster.

At this point they were speeding down Little Caillou Road, that's Louisiana 56, with the Terrebonne Bayou to their left, and all along this rural outpost of North America there were little docks, wooden shacks, a few houses, many of them built on piles, elevated in case of flood. The land was flat, right across these wetlands, the highest point in Terrebonne Parish being about 3ft 6inches above sea-level.

Five more miles and they found a shaded swamp out to the right, surrounded by trees, some coming out of the water. Sergei said he saw an alligator, Sophia shuddered, and Uncle Rudy hurled the shotgun, the rifle, the ammunition, both sets of binoculars, into the middle of the murky green Jurassic water.

"You want to find those," he muttered on his way back to the SUV, "Good luck with that. Not in this century." The vehicle had not left the blacktop, and again they set off at high speed, the last 12 miles flashing by. Which was, of course, highly desirable with a couple of mass-murderers on board.

Soon they passed a sign that alleged Cocodrie Harbour was only three-miles farther. And they pulled in, opposite the moored fishing boats just before 7pm. Captain Dubois was right there to greet them, waving from the freshly washed and scrubbed decks of *Vagabond,* his diesel-powered shrimp boat, which was as seaworthy as any trawler in the harbour.

"All set, Sir," he called, "Come right aboard."

The arriving team said goodbye to each other. Sergei was going straight back to New Orleans to wait for the Houston driver who was on his way back to the city, in order to return the SUV to the Consulate. It was of course, minus its permanent sniper rifle which Sergei had already explained, "Rudy gave it to an alligator for its birthday!"

That was their last joke. Sergei and Rudy shook hands and promised to meet again, somewhere—London, Washington, Moscow?

Rudy then pulled Sophia aside, and told her sternly, "You are M'selle Janine Belleau, from Provence, France remember. We're boarding an aircraft soon, and you'll use your French passport all the way home."

Sophia kissed Sergei goodbye, and waved to him as he spun the SUV around and headed north. She did not kiss Rudy, who was still scowling as they walked up the gangway to board *Vagabond*. Rudolf Masow introduced his niece by her French name, and told Art Dubois to call him Pierre.

"Ready, Pierre?"

"Let's go, Art. Next stop Cuba."

*****

Detective Chief Superintendent Charles Barton asked the president of the Liechtenstein bank to repeat the name, then spell it. Except for the female 'ova' in the Russian style, the name was unmistakable. Boris Morosov. Sophia Morosova. Coincidences bored Charles, sometimes severely. But not this one.

The mastermind behind the astounding Vice-Ring he'd uncovered was the step-father of Sophia. The young girls who had been sexually ravaged by paying strangers, were Sophia and her little sister. The short list of facts which had pointed the finger lightly at Sophia—time, place, and opportunity—were now boxed, secured and slammed into perspective by one solitary word … motive.

She'd never had one. And certainly he'd never found one. The only person tip-toeing around the truth was the limp-wristed Johnny Fairchild, who never missed observing little sapphire earrings … *Just the same as you, darling, with dead bodies.*

Of course Sophia had killed Lord Fontridge. Charles now knew that. He also knew that with the aid of a brilliant barrister, no jury in the United Kingdom would ever find her guilty of anything, especially if that jury contained six women. Because every last one of them would be weeping uncontrollably in the courtroom at the pure horror at what had happened to these two darling God-fearing schoolgirls.

If the victim was a high-court judge, the highest court at that, so much the worse. By the time this trial ended, those female jurists would be all done with courts, judges, and murder charges. The only lasting images in their minds would be those of the raped, sobbing virgin-teenagers. The victim deserved everything he got, judge or no judge.

And the closing words of the defence counsel would ring in their ears for the rest of their lives: *"Just imagine, ladies and gentlemen … (pause) … just imagine, if these outrages, brutal and without mercy had happened to your own daughters … I am asking you … no …(pause) … I'm begging you … to save her from a lifetime of incarceration… she does not deserve it … God knows, she's suffered far too much for one lifetime …"*

And what prosecutor could bring himself to utter the words? "Ladies and gentlemen of the jury, I ask you to find the accused Sophia Morosova guilty of the premeditated murder of Lord Justice Fontridge, and to recommend she spend the rest of her life in jail.

YOU HAVE TO BE JOKING!

"Mother of God!" whispered Charles Barton. "There's not a QC in England who wouldn't give up a year's fees to defend this case. It's called a career-maker: can't lose, and you walk off with a reputation as the Queen's Counsellor with a heart, the man who saved darling Sophia from those awful English Judges, who ganged up on her, both in death, and in life."

Chapter Twenty-Three
State Police Dragnet for a Dead Man

Patrol cars were driving in. Relief police helicopter pilots were arriving. Miss Martha paced her kitchen, sometimes climbing the stairs to Mr Hunter's bedroom, just in case it was all a ghastly dream, and the boss was ready for his breakfast.

Her voice echoed and re-echoed all the way through the twilight of the bayous and southward down the long private lake. A couple of cruising alligators abruptly changed direction. "Now you come right back here, Mr Hunter! I don't know what's goin' on, but you ain't never been late for dinner, and I'm growing *anxious,* y'hear?"

It was 8.45pm and Martha Le Roux was positioned high on the top step of the garden staircase. In the fast gathering darkness, she made an imposing sight, a walking hurricane buoy. Miss Martha was built on the classic lines of a life-size Aunt Jemima cookie jar, and she had a considerable voice when she raised it.

Right now she exuded high confidence in her status as a fourth generation member of the de Villiers household, and she'd been waiting for more than 90-minutes to serve Hunter de Villiers a carefully prepared evening meal of his beloved Cajun *jambalaya*—baked andouille sausage, small chicken chunks, and shrimp baked with canola oil. It was a real spicy Creole production, based on Spanish *paella*. Miss Martha's voice betrayed a profound frustration with the continued absence of The Boss.

"Now where the hell is that boy?" she demanded of the deserted garden. *"Cain't hardly hear even the* Beauregard's *motor—don't make no sense to me—mah good Lord! He's gotta be hungry—NOW YOU GET THAT BOAT BACK HERE RIGHT NOW, MR HUNTER—AND YOU, RUSS, TURN THAT DARN THING RIGHT AROUND, RIGHT NOW, HEAR ME?"*

Miss Martha could have been heard halfway across the Blue Bayou—but for quite a few hours now Mr Hunter was not hearing anything. For that matter neither was Russ Lambert. The *Beauregard* was rammed into the overhanging fronds from the great stand of cypress trees jutting from the water almost a half-mile from the house. Hunter de Villiers was still on board, in a sense. His right arm was flopping over the side of the boat, the remains of his head unrecognisable, his faithful bodyguard gone forever, the boat invisible.

At 9pm Miss Martha walked down to the empty dock, confirmed to herself that the boat was still gone, and let fly with another tirade of frustrated demands that Mr Hunter get right back here for dinner. And again her voice echoed noisily in the soft muggy darkness, although the inscrutable silence of the lake swiftly enfolded her words.

At 9.30pm she walked back up the long staircase, and telephoned the Terrebonne Parish Police Department, breathlessly informing the duty officer that one of the richest and most important men in the State of Louisiana was missing, now for almost three hours, lost in his small fishing craft on his own private lake right down there in the lonely village of Montegut, hard by the Terrebonne Bayou. *Ain't heard sight nor sound from Mr Hunter since he pulled away from that dock nearly five hours ago.*

Thus Sam Pritchard, the late-duty officer in the Sheriff's HQ in watery Terrebonne was considering precisely the same conundrum as Sergeant Bob Hammond had tackled a few weeks ago in leafy East Sussex, 7,000-miles away in southern England.

"This de Villiers dude is a major deal but I expect he'll turn up. However, if he don't turn up, and I didn't even raise the alarm tonight, there'll be all hell to pay—and I'll be looking for a new job. This crazy housekeeper Martha sounds hysterical, but I'm still going right ahead and calling the Chief, yessir."

Hunter de Villiers/Lord Fontridge, different worlds, same vibrations when death comes to call … get on the case before someone gets on yours. It's more or less the same the world over.

And Sam sent a top-priority message ripping across the wires, which grabbed the undivided attention of the Big Chief of all Louisiana police departments, Colonel Paul Barrington, Superintendent State Police, Baton Rouge. And he instantly began to cover all bases. Jesus, if anything's gone wrong with Mr de Villiers, we need to be *seen* to be doin' something, not just talking … *Alert road, water and air patrol search troops right away, and get down to Montegut, real quick. That's everyone!*

By, now, of course, it was pitch dark and Miss Martha had not called back with news of Mr Hunter. And this meant the huge fleet of Louisiana Sheriff's water patrol was essentially wasting its time, and its gasoline, roaring around Bayou Terrebonne any time before first light. Two fast patrol boats were on their way to the Montegut private lake to try a search in the dark.

But the real action was high above, where three Bell-OH58 Sheriff's helicopters were making 100-knots from different directions, crewed by Louisiana's finest, trained search-pilots on call 24/7. The first of them touched down on the de Villiers lawn above the dock shortly after 11pm. The other two were in the area by midnight, by which time there were 14 State police patrol vehicles circling the lake and two fast police boats moving slowly along the shore line, searchlights probing, engines chugging, officers yelling.

One of the three helos took up air-traffic control duties, and the other two stayed aloft, everyone wearing night vision goggles, with the forward infrared radar cameras scanning the dark waters. By 1am, there was the shattering racket caused by the helos, the flashing blue and white lights of the police vehicles and boats, the occasional *whoop-whoop-whoop* of the sirens, plus the general tumult and the shouting, all illuminated by the piercing beams across the water of the Night Sun Searchlights from the Bell-58's. It was a bit like the Mekong Delta in the middle of the Tet offensive. Missing was only the gunfire, and, hopefully, the death.

But all the deep resources of the LPD could not find Hunter de Villiers. And a tearful Miss Martha had called in two extra maids to help ferry jugs of hot coffee to the troops. But by 2am they had found nothing, no Hunter, no Russ, no *Beauregard*. That giant stand of high, billowing cypress trees, with thick fronds of moss stretching to brush the water's surface, had shielded their master well.

By 4.30am all three helos were on the lawn. A police fuel tanker had arrived to refuel them and the patrol boats, as well as any vehicles which were running low. The hose lines stretched across the property, engines were running and the lights were still casting beams all along the shoreline. But the search was temporarily halted, as more than 75 police personnel waited for the dawn.

When finally the eastern skies began to turn the colour of spent fire, and slim, blue cloudbanks, a mile long, could be seen beyond the horizon of the bayous, the operation rose wearily back into action. The rotors began thudding as the fireball of the sun rose above the flat, shallow waters of Louisiana's lakes, streams, bays, and rivers.

Replacement troops were coming in to relieve those who had been up for most of the night. Patrol cars were pulling out of the estate, others driving in. Relief police helicopter pilots and navigators were arriving. Miss Martha paced her kitchen, sometimes climbing the stairs to Mr Hunter's bedroom, just in case it had all been a ghastly dream and the boss was ready for his breakfast.

But this was no dream. Hunter de Villiers, Russ Lambert and the *Beauregard* had apparently vanished from the face of the earth. At least that's what it seemed like to the men conducting the manhunt. And it seemed that way until almost 8am, which was when the helicopters' high tech probes sent a lancing beam straight through the cypress trees down at the south end of the lake and picked up the glint of either an engine or a steering console, tucked away deep in the mossy low branches.

By 8.05 they had hauled the little fishing boat out, and stared at the decapitated corpse of Hunter de Villiers, spread-eagled backward, blood everywhere, his shotgun still clasped limply in his left hand. In those few shocking minutes, the *Beauregard* ceased to be the objective of a police manhunt. Colonel Paul Barrington had himself a murder hunt on a scale rarely seen in the great southern state since the Baton Rouge Serial Killer, Derrick Todd Lee, went on a rape and murder rampage from 1992-2003.

This ended in a death sentence, after a 10-year on-and-off police manhunt, which was mostly frustrated by their certainty that Lee was a white-man, until irrefutable DNA showed he was 85-percent African. Lee went down for eight local rapes and murders. But the 47-year-old renowned Peeping Tom, cheated the executioner by dying of heart disease in a hospital near his cell on Death Row, Louisiana State Penitentiary.

He was suspected of dozens of other rape-and-murder crimes, and Colonel Paul Barrington hoped to hell his own detective squad would locate the killer of one of Louisiana's most eminent citizens before the case became a *cause celebre* attracting world-wide attention, and focusing public attention on the hopelessness of the State Police.

Captain Barrington had been a Division Commander back then, and he remembered, first hand, the media flak flying, as the police vainly sought the white-skinned rapist who was, in truth, a violent black lifelong convict from the nearby town of St Francisville. The Todd Lee case had been hideously embarrassing for the LPD, and the prime thought in the mind of the Chief was to keep the lid on this thing—as long as possible.

Too late. This was off the charts by 8.30am. The murder of Hunter de Villiers leaked worse than Sophia's Boston whaler which was currently parked 40-feet down on the lake floor. The news had escaped through the kitchen, through the police department, and through the mouths of a thousand locals who at 2am had heard the uproar, and there were US Navy veterans who wondered if the Viet Kong were crossing the delta.

KUHR—*Voice of the United Houma Nations,* out of LaFourche Parish east of Terrebonne, was first on the air announcing that a massive police search was taking place over at Montegut where it was believed Mr Hunter de Villiers had been found dead in his fishing boat. They confirmed that foul play had not been ruled out, but the police had stopped short of announcing a murder.

By 10am the item was on a couple of dozen stations, including KMRC, the redoubtable Morgan City broadcaster, featuring *The Swamp Dog,* and KLEB out of LaFourche, *The Rajun' Cajun.* Within two hours the media 'heavies' were out there and up there, a half-dozen helicopters circling above the Montegut lake where the searchers were wrapping it up.

Nonetheless NewsWatch Channel 15 out of New Orleans had a helicopter up there, so did the CBS affiliate WWL Channel 4, and *This Morning.* The Fox affiliate WVUE was flying 100-feet above PBS 12 and *ABC's WGNO 26.* All the networks were active. The death of such a man as de Villiers was big news, especially if someone had shot him last night.

And the hard news men, with their ravenous eyes, were on their way, photographers and cameramen, backing them up, shortly to be demanding the police get out of the way. Reason? *The public has a right to know!* The age-old mantra from these unelected, commercially-driven media men, posing as quasi-philanthropists, who were acting purely in the public good.

Colonel Barrington did not buy any of that, and had made it clear there would be no statement for the media, until he was good and ready. He then summoned all of his top investigators to Baton Rouge for a conference designed to establish the search area and its outer parameters. The pathologist had already ascertained that Mr de Villiers had died between 4pm and 9pm the previous day. No later. And he had not been in the water.

The LPD's number one suspect was Mr Russ Lambert, bodyguard, who was currently missing. But the police would search for him through every yard of the waterways, leading south to the Gulf. He'd plainly made his escape in a different boat, and every boat-hire company in the area would be questioned. If he'd already left in a motor vehicle, he would have an unassailable 12-hour start on the police, and visions of the Baton Rouge Serial Killer already stood stark before Paul Barrington's eyes.

But at least Russ was white. His famously handsome face, and unruly mop of hair was widely known by every Louisiana football fan, thousands of whom had thrilled to his Olympic starting block technique in the Cajuns' defensive line. They loved his rocket burst forward at the snap—four seconds to reach and hit the quarter-back …42,000 fans at Cajun Field were up and cheering every single time he slammed into the man with the ball.

Russ, of course, was only a suspect—and the police chief understood it would be real tough for him to hide out in his home State. That fact alone gave him confidence. He was not of course to know that Russ Lambert was already dead these past 18 hours, gunned down defending his boss, by the same sniper who would hit de Villiers himself.

The two men had died at around 6pm and it was now almost 11am—17 hours into the getaway of the ex-KGB assassin and the former right-wing for the St Margaret's Pangbourne hockey team. The hit squad were driven fast by Sergei, and took only 30-minutes to drive south and board Captain Dubois's pride and joy, the dragger, *Vagabond*. They were now close to 300-miles into the Gulf, heading south, slicing easily through a light swell on their way to Havana or thereabouts.

The skipper had been correct. *Vagabond* had a nearly new 'beast of an engine,' and Rudy sat next to Art in the for'ard wheelhouse, content that he and his niece had made an utterly unexpected escape. They'd be halfway to Cuba by one o'clock.

Colonel Barrington was of the opinion that Russ Lambert was hiding out in New Orleans, and he was beginning to position his troops, every last one of them hunting a dead man, while the real culprits raced farther and farther away to another country, indeed another world. Colonel Paul or Rudolf Masow? Right now, any London bookmaker would give you 100-1 about the Louisiana police chief.

*****

Colonel Barrington was in fact a two-time loser on this muggy, overcast, Louisiana Saturday morning. Up all night, he faced a blank sheet on the whereabouts of Hunter De Villiers' murderer. And the media, which had been driving him mad for many hours, was about to blow the story of the crime, despite his wishes and demands to keep the entire thing under tight wraps.

The culprit was the *New Orleans Advocate.* An afternoon newspaper and online wizard of hard news, the *Advocate* had been at it for over 100-years and today would be one of their biggest triumphs.

New Orleans' Billionaire
Benefactor Shot Dead
State-wide manhunt launched
for de Villiers killer—Police baffled.

The *Advocate* newsrooms in Lafayette, Baton Rouge and New Orleans were electrified with excitement, because this was a scoop by any standards. A couple of other publications suspected the truth, but no one else had the guts to actually splash it across the front page. When the newspaper finally hit the street at around 3pm, Colonel Barrington's office was under siege. The big news agencies from Washington, New York, Chicago and LA were on the line demanding answers. By 3.30pm the story was all over the world.

In London, shortly after 10pm, nobody cared. But in the newsroom of the *Daily Mail*, the deputy night editor was on his feet and shouting, waving a hard copy print-out from Reuters.

"Hold everything!" he yelled, "This dead bastard in New Orleans is the guy that put up $40 million for *Cottonwood, Mississippi*".

"What the fuck's that?" shouted a junior.

"Only the biggest movie of the year—four Oscars! There's stock pictures of this de Villiers character talking to the Queen and Prince Philip at the Royal Premiere." The night editor turned swiftly to the junior, "That, my son, is why I sit in the big chair." And then, under his breath, "Ignorant little prick."

No publication on earth slips into pure professionalism as swiftly as the *Daily Mail*. It took less than 20-minutes to reset the entire front page, with a picture of de Villiers and the Queen.

It was midnight. The presses were running. The new London front page would be on sale by 5am. Like the *Advocate*, the *Daily Mail* had the opposition by the ears on this one.

The Queen's Great Friend
Shot Dead At Louisiana Home
-Cottonwood tycoon's body discovered
in private fishing boat *Beauregard.*

******

A couple of miles east of the *Daily Mail's* editorial headquarters it was precisely 8am in the big house in South Audley Street. Lady Penelope was quietly eating a fruit salad and sipping her coffee. The place already set for Charles by Hudson, who had delivered a bone china plate containing three pork sausages, two rashers of bacon and a couple of fried eggs. The silver toast rack was full of crispy whole-wheat slices. Exactly the way the young master liked it.

Charles Barton walked into the breakfast room and wished his mother a good morning. He was less than halfway through his first sausage, before she told him, "I say, Charles, that very nice American we met at the film premiere has been found murdered!"

"What do you mean murdered?"

"Well if you insist on the grizzly details, someone blew his head off while he was fishing."

"Thoughtless!" replied Charles, "Had he caught anything yet?"

"How the devil do I know! And how could it matter?"

"Well, it matters a lot, fishing, in all its forms, is a cerebral pastime and shouldn't really be interrupted by gunfire."

"You sound like your grand-father. He once had a poacher arrested and jailed for rustling the bushes just as he was landing a salmon."

"Quite correct," said Charles, "A man and his rod ought never to be disturbed."

"Well someone certainly disturbed old Hunter de Villiers—and it looks as if they probably murdered his bodyguard as well…I always thought there was a certain lawlessness in America below the Mason-Dixon line—and I'm not sure it's much improved to the north."

Charles, with some reluctance, put down his fork and reached out for the *Daily Mail.*

He scanned across the front page, stared at the photograph of de Villiers with the Queen, and then almost froze at the sight of one single word—*Beauregard*—the fifth pseudonym on Freddie Fontridge's list.

Uncharacteristically, he pushed away his breakfast plate and took a gulp of coffee, shouting, "Thank you, Hudson, I wasn't very hungry this morning."

Lady Penelope who had noted Charles' world-record pace with the first 'banger,' said, as only a mother could, "Whatever is the matter, Charles? Have you just read something which startled you?"

"Oh nothing, Mum," said Charles absently. "Just debating whether I'm in love with a serial killer."

He had not really meant to say anything. But the shock was overwhelming. And he'd just blurted it out. Sophia had again been missing at the time of this latest murder. And the fifth pseudonym was inescapable. It was a tortuous moment. *Beauregard.* The word was unmistakable. And the pressing nature of the murder enquiries now collided with his personal feelings. For the first time in his brilliant career, the Chief Superintendent stood in the dark shadow of his own heart.

"I cannot understand what you are mumbling about, Charles," said Lady Penelope, shaking her head. "You're going on about being in love with a mass-murderer or something!"

"I suppose I am," he replied.

"You mean Sophia!" she retorted, "Don't be ridiculous. That darling girl makes the most delicious thin cucumber sandwiches. And you think those same beautiful hands could also have wielded a damn great shot-gun and blown someone's head off, 6000-miles away!"

"Well, put like that, I suppose that's a new height of absurdity. Of course, she could not have done it. I was just thinking aloud, not to be taken seriously."

"Well, you looked pretty serious to me."

It was perhaps at this very moment that Charles Barton realised he had been bottling up too much data for too long. Yes, he did think Sophia, with good reason, had killed Fontridge. But there was no proof, and he'd never allowed himself to dwell on the other pseudonym murders, scattered as they were all over the world.

For the moment, they both fell silent while Charles read the details of the story, including the paragraph lifted directly from the *Advocate*: "Identification was simple because of the boat, the initialled finishing rods, and, of course, the clothes. Facial recognition was impossible, since the bullet had blown apart the entire head and face of Hunter de Villiers. Most of the skull was missing, presumably overboard."

"Hmm," mused Charles. "That was no shot-gun, because, if it was, you'd have a skull peppered with pellets, like a downed pheasant. This was something very different—almost certainly a high-powered rifle with probably a high-velocity bullet that exploded on impact." He brightened for a few seconds and then muttered, "Well, one thing's obvious, Sophia could never have fired a rifle like that, not in a thousand years… thank God."

"Charles, you're mumbling again."

"Steady, Mum," he muttered. "Give me a second here. I'm under a lot of pressure. I'm afraid today's murder fits into a pattern of events I do not like."

"Well, why don't you tell me what's been driving you mad these past few weeks. You are obviously seething inside about something—and it's high time you spoke to someone about it." Lady Penelope dismissed Hudson. And then walked over and closed the door behind him.

"Now you can explain yourself to your mother. Remembering this has worked quite well in the past."

And so Chief Superintendent Charles Barton of Scotland Yard unburdened his soul not to the head of the Metropolitan police, but to Lady Penelope Barton, aristocrat, socialite, and Mayfair *bon vivant.* He told her of the Fontridge murder, and he told her of the only person in all the world with a proper motive for the killing. He told her he had possession of Fontridge's laptop. And above all he told her of the lethal list of sexual deviants, all of whom were identified by a pseudonym list. Five of whom were already dead. Four of whom had plainly been murdered.

"How very devious," said her Ladyship.

Charles listed the pseudonyms, and then mentioned the last remaining name—"*Florida Garden.*" Said Charles, "God knows what that means."

"Since Florida is well south of the Mason-Dixon line, it's almost certainly lawless."

Charles stood up and paced the floor, "Mum, this case gets more and more nasty. Sophia's villainous father sold the bodies of his step-daughters when they were very young. We have traced huge sums of money via Liechtenstein, and they all lead back to Fontridge.

"Sophia's little sister jumped off a 200-foot tower block in west London. Which leaves Sophia the possible killer of five people, and the surviving victim of the men who ravaged the girls. And you wonder why I have been worried?"

"And with one more to go," said Lady Penelope, "I suppose we're just waiting for someone to blow the brains out of *Florida Garden*, whoever that might be. And, from what I know, he most thoroughly deserves it."

"Accurate, Mum," said Charles. "Accurate as always."

The conversation had lasted for almost 40-minutes. Lady Penelope had demanded answers to every question. She actually demanded answers when there weren't any questions. At one point Charles had asked her if she'd ever thought of getting a job with the Spanish Inquisition!

"No, but I most certainly should have. I thought they were frightfully slack about Catholicism from time to time. Imagine putting that ridiculous Ferdinand in charge. I wouldn't put him in charge of a Sunday School outing." Charles appreciated his mother as catalyst, despite her searching interrogation of both him and his methods. He also appreciated her arched and somewhat acerbic wit, and he felt lighter for having told her.

She understood the intense need for discretion and the consequences of any breach of family security. As a teenager, he actually saw his mother make the decision when his father was unable to decide whether to buy a city bank. She was formidable, and when necessary, as secretive as the Old Lady of Threadneedle Street herself.

He gathered up his briefcase and papers. And his mother accompanied him to the front door, beyond which was a black Scotland Yard sedan. Unmarked, engine running.

"Have a good day Charles," said Lady Penelope. "And don't go worrying yourself with stupid possibilities like your gorgeous girlfriend being an international killer." But Charles was all too preoccupied even to acknowledge his mother's friendly farewell. In fact he slumped into the rear seat without a word, still staring at that front page, still staring at the word *Beauregard*. The driver had seen the boss in such a mood before. And, silently, he gunned the car towards Park Lane.

Charles, equally silently, wrestled with the problem, which he quickly divided into four sections.

1. Sophia could not have made it to Hong Kong, and certainly could not have made her escape, with the far eastern fortress of finance in total lockdown.

270

2. The French did not believe Josh Hartley was murdered

3. The Virginia tennis pro *was* murdered. But Sophia could never have got there, and certainly not got away, on a single-lane road, which was anyway jammed with police cars.

4. de Villiers—Sophia could never have lifted and fired a big sniper rifle. Impossible.

5. The last one, really. Fontridge. Poor darling Sophia. Guilty as charged. But probably unprovable.

The truth was, the scowling Charles understood that in a sense this was Sasha's revenge. And he believed beyond doubt that somehow, either by Sophia's own hand, or with the aid of an accomplice, this *'Florida Garden'* must also die.

"Fuck me," mumbled Charles. "How can I possibly deal with this. Also I don't have the faintest idea where the hell she is."

The car sped down the eastern border of Hyde Park. But Charles's thoughts were anchored on the west side of the park, where it joins Kensington Palace Gardens and the guarded avenue beside Russia's London Embassy. The smiling face of Uncle Rudy stood stark before him.

Because Charles had ten-million feelings of love for Sophia. And each one drew him to the same conclusion … *if she had committed any of these global crimes, then she had professional help. And in this there was only one suspect— and that was the Ex-KGB assassin who loved her as much as he did.*

The sight of the great wall that surrounds Buckingham Palace reminded him of his vows to serve Queen and Country without restraint. And he tried to cast aside the thoughts of his girlfriend's colourful life.

But these thoughts would not go away, and in his heart Charles Barton understood they probably never would.

Distraught, and almost beside himself with concern for the whereabouts of Sophia, he closed his eyes and tried to think logically. But right now there was only one phone call he could possibly make for information. And that was to the private line of the Russian Cultural Attache, who doubtless would assure him that his niece had thoroughly enjoyed the final act of *Rigoletto*. And that they had shared a companionable return journey back to Kensington Place Gardens … probably had a nightcap with the Ambassador.

Nonetheless, Charles took out his cell-phone and dialled Rudolf's number; with no great hope of a reply. He was right about that. The number rang…and rang…and rang.

Chapter Twenty-Four
In the Stateroom of Czar Vladimir IV

The first three Czar Vladimirs were on the Russian throne about a thousand years ago, and they wielded about 100th of the power of Comrade Putin. This also applied to Peter the Great, Catherine the Great, Ivan the Terrible, and Boris the Unsteady.

Exactly 4,783-miles away from Buckingham Palace, in a light ocean swell, and heading due south now, Uncle Rudy was dipping his lobster claw into hot melted butter. Which rendered him unavailable to accept a call from anyone, and that would include his London neighbour, Her Majesty, or indeed Vladimir himself.

And in this gastronomic endeavour, the lovely Sophia Morosova was playing her part, eating the lobster (a great deal more delicately than Uncle Rudy) and reheating the butter on Captain Art Dubois' small galley cooking range.

"Nicely done," said the skipper.

"Another lobster tail!" yelled uncle Rudy.

"Christ, he's already had two!" said *Vagabond's* Commanding Officer.

Sophia, thought privately, that your average Eastern-bloc assassin probably had a gargantuan appetite, most likely stress-related.

They had already crossed some of the deepest ocean waters in the western hemisphere—the 6,000-foot deep Gulf of Mexico Basin. But now they were in the legendary shallow fishing waters north of Havana, home of the big marlin and gigantic sail-fish, the predators of the deep that so riveted the attention of Ernest Hemingway, whose great masterpiece, *The Old Man and the Sea,* was created right out here where *Vagabond* still chugged onward.

A patrolling pilot boat now joined them, as expected, and began to lead them through a long left-hand turn. The Communist skipper gave a couple of sharp hoots on the coastguard horn, and Captain Art responded to this pre-arranged signal. Escorted passage into Castro's empire had cost one phone call and a couple of hundred bucks for the officers. Corruption in Cuba has shallow roots.

It was almost dawn, and the rising sun cast a rosy light on the crumbling stone buildings of this Communist outpost. Moving east now along the coast, with Havana off the starboard quarter, they were heading for the quiet marina of Tarara, a storied harbour in Cuban history.

Overlooking these quiet waters stood the huge edifice of the Communists' Paediatric Hospital, once the private home of the Titan of Castro's Revolutionary commanders, Che Guevara. But later it was the final home for many of the 18,000 Russian and Ukrainian children who were evacuated here after the Chernobyl nuclear catastrophe. The place will ever be shrouded in mystery—the truth unknown. Too many ghosts roam here even to be counted.

Captain Art took over the helm now and steered *Vagabond* past the coastal town of Alamar. Four-miles later they glided smoothly into the placid, sheltered waters of Tarara Marina. The Russian-born Sophia Morosova, niece of one of the most powerful men in the Kremlin's Foreign Service, was safe at last. For now.

Captain Art smoothed the big fishing boat into the harbour waters where there was no movement whatsoever, either afloat or ashore. He was in the process of making a complete about-turn when a large black limousine swept into the driveway and made its way slowly along the old stone wharf.

"Better pull over to the other side," said Rudy, quietly.

"There are some things you can leave to me," said Captain Dubois. "This is one of them." And he steered *Vagabond* towards the big Russian limo, and cut the engine seconds before they bumped the jetty. At this point Sophia noticed, across the deck, Uncle Rudy had taken a small dark red ribbon from his pocket and pinned it to the lapel of his jacket, presumably ensuring the personnel in the limo would properly understand, they were indeed dealing with a Hero of the Russian Federation.

Immediately, four uniformed Cuban/Russian guards exited the vehicle and waved to the docking American boat, as it drifted gently into the wharf. The first mate slung the bowline and then ran aft to launch the heavy stern line to the waiting guards.

They recognised the coveted insignia before they recognised him. And, with due deference they sharply saluted Rudolf Masow, and welcomed him ashore. The slightly shocked London diplomat returned the salute and introduced his niece to the escort. By this time two more embassy staff cars had arrived. Uncle Rudy shook hands, and said good-bye to the *Vagabond* crew, while Sophia was helped into the rear seat of the second limo.

Within five minutes Captain Art had cast off and was moving slowly out of the harbour into calm seas. The little motorcade, with the Cuban flags fluttering port and starboard, made its way out onto the communist highway with its new black-top surface.

No foreign arrival had ever entered the People's Republic of Cuba more discreetly. There were more staff in the Russian Foreign Service who knew about this dawn landing than there ever were among the Cuban populous. The Russian driver headed straight back to Havana's Old Town, and the *Hotel Florida* on the corner of *Calle del Obispo.*

The *Florida* brought an entirely new dimension to the words *faded glory.* It still stood resolutely (just) in an historic tangle of narrow streets and crumbling buildings. It would have not been the biggest shock in the world if the whole area caved into a pile of rubble.

And yet there was a magic about the *Florida,* a certain grandeur, despite the constant presence down all the years of Castro's feared Secret Police; men trained exclusively by officers from the Lubyanka. In its heyday, and long before the Revolution, the *Florida* was the world headquarters of the two literary giants, Hemingway and Graham Greene, author of *Our Man in Havana, The Third Man, The Heart of the Matter* and *The Ministry of Fear.* The latter being loosely based on the philosophies of A. Hitler, but with many passages most certainly familiar to J.V. Stalin, and his latter-day disciple F.A. Castro.

Inside, the old hotel still looks like a grand Spanish palace with marble floors, stone columns and majestic high, cloistered arches. The long polished mahogany bar, named for Hemingway himself; is an elegant memorial to one of literature's most heroic drunks: a bearded near-permanent fixture, night after night, in the hard drinking section of the *Hotel Florida.*

Uncle Rudy and Sophia said good-bye to their driver and personal escort to the hotel, and after some coffee and toast, retired to their rooms, for a long sleep. They'd been more than 30 hours on board the *Vagabond,* riding the gentle, but endless, ocean swells which carpet the deep-waters of the Gulf of Mexico.

Happily, neither of them were sea-sick, and arranged to meet at 6pm in *Hemingway's Bar,* where the diplomat ordered a very agreeable bottle of Spanish *Rioja,* a crisp elegant white *Macabeo.* He also addressed Sophia, for the first time in two days, with something less than total exasperation.

Uncle Rudy asked the waiter to send the remaining *Rioja* through to the dining room, to which he rather elegantly escorted his niece, who couldn't believe how nice he suddenly seemed. Rudy never once called her an idiot, or a halfwit, all the way across the marble floor, and he rather suavely assisted her into her chair with a slight bow, like some flunky from the court of Czar Nicholas.

The waiter poured the *Rioja* and the Russian diplomat asked for a new bottle, still *Rioja*, but this time a deep red from Benjamin Rothschild's Macan vineyards.

He smiled at Sophia for the first time in three weeks, and said, "If there is one lesson you must learn from the Louisiana disaster, it is the crucial nature of the plan, and in particular the getaway, because *that* is the difference between life and death.

"Just assess your track record so far. Glyndebourne—beautifully planned, no one knows whether you were there or not for the second act; Monte Carlo—you were gone, the wrong way, on a mountain train before anyone even suspected anything; Hong Kong—you were in a *sampan* heading into the South China Sea before Takahashi's body was found; Virginia tennis courts—my staff had you out of there before the police even arrived.

"Louisiana, as you well know, required my personal intervention, and a 4,500-mile journey, in order to save you, to make your escape."

Sophia fluttered her eyelashes and blew him a kiss. "I suppose," she said, "I should acknowledge that I owe you my life. But that would be superfluous."

"I suppose it would," replied her uncle. "But luckily for you, as I approach retirement, I can still shoot straighter than most. Meanwhile, those two words, *plan* and *getaway,* should be engraved on your heart. It just happens that I don't want you to die."

"One more to go, dearest uncle. And I promise never to forget those two words, *plan* and *getaway*."

"If it makes you feel any easier," he replied, "Also remember the operational creed of our mission—*some people are just too evil to live. God is always on our side.*"

Sophia raised her glass and Rudolph Maslow said softly, "A toast... To us."

They retired early after what Rudolph described as "A Cuban dinner under about half a ton of cabbage!"

****

The *Plaza de San Francisco* at 5.30 in the morning stood in the half-lit shadow of the Cathedral of San Cristobal. Here in the heart of Old Havana the silence was undisturbed by the usual horse and mule carts of Cuba's metro-tourism. Because this morning, the entire Plaza was sealed off. There were 27 armed Cuban/Soviet security troops blocking all streets, in and out. The quiet was already broken by the shattering *BOM...BOM...BOM!* of an approaching Russian helicopter attack gunship.

The MIL-MI-24, nicknamed by a generation of infantrymen, the 'Flying Tank,' was in full camouflage, dropping down with a deafening roar beneath its 56-foot rotors. It was landing specifically to pick up six apparent VIP's.

Complete with Borzov Gatling guns, and twin-barrelled auto-cannon, the gunship touched down, and immediately its six passengers began to walk towards the huge rotors, led by Rudolph Masow and his niece, who made an innocuous addition to this early morning fantasy by climbing the helo's steps in Jimmy Choo high-heels. Four stone-faced Russian diplomats followed her and her uncle into the cabin, which was originally designed to carry heavily-armed Soviet and Russian infantry into global warzones. Not Jimmy Choo, or for that matter, his finest shoes.

The door slammed shut behind them and the MI-24 took off instantly, sweeping high above the Cathedral, and clattering east on a 300-mile voyage to one of the most secretive military bases on earth—*Lourdes SIGNET*, still the haunted face of the worst years of the Cold War.

Re-opened with clandestine care, this most private Russian military operation still runs heavy transport in and out of Lourdes. But there's no holy water here; just a forest of antennae and satellite communications. It all stands just across the rough ground from the two-mile runway, from which untold evil against the USA has come and gone. Lourdes covers 28-square-miles of Cuban land—and that's a fair indication of the scale of spying and cyber-stealing conducted down the years from the crumbling buildings on this sprawling Russian Base.

Today there was yet another Russian flying fortress at rest on the renovated take-off and landing highway. This was unusual in the extreme, because the waiting aircraft was the IL-96-300PLU Airliner known colloquially in the eastern bloc as the 'Flying Palace.' It was indeed the aircraft in which Vladimir Putin flew to Helsinki to meet President Trump.

The flagship aircraft, wide-bodied and designed for a long haul, cost $700 million to build. Its cabin is lavish with tapestries, gold accents and marble floors. The furniture is in costly neo-classical style. It has a gym and the bathroom taps are gold-plated. It was built by the Voronezh Aircraft Production four-hundred miles due south of Moscow, straddling the Voronezh river, eight-miles upstream from Russia's mighty Don River.

The huge, gleaming white 630mph jetliner made a stark contrast to the rest of the aircraft fleet parked nearby. This consisted of eight or nine ancient Soviet MiG fighters, which probably did not have an airworthy certificate between them. Plus a half-dozen decrepit-looking Cold War rejects, Karnov 27 and 28 attack helicopters, two of which did not have rotor-blades, and were in residence purely as providers of spare-parts. The parking lots were almost deserted, save for one 1940's Douglas DC-3 with a faded red star on its tail wing.

The IL-96, resplendent in its Russian livery, had its front door folded back, with a boarding staircase, complete with red carpet.

The helicopter touched down 40-yards away and all six passengers disembarked, hurriedly, walking across to the President's runabout. Sophia's Jimmy Choo shoes led them up the staircase, and, within three-minutes of the helo's touchdown, the IL-96 was howling down the runway, en route to the Atlantic Ocean, and North Africa.

It was a short hop to the western tides of the Atlantic as they rolled towards the Bahamas. From there it was a straight shot 3,500-miles due east across one of the widest expanses of the ocean. More than 38,000-feet below them the water was not as rough as in the north, but neither was it as calm as the south. Winds were light and the Russian pilot made over 600-knots towards the distant, still mystical Kingdom of Morocco.

Sophia and Uncle Rudy settled into the elegant stateroom normally used by Vladimir himself. The diplomats, to whom they had never been introduced, rode somewhere up front. Spies tend to be unsociable creatures. The entire journey took six and a half hours, and with the Atlas Mountains shielding a gigantic view of the Sahara Desert, they made their way high above the trans-Algerian railroad before their long curve into Sidi Slimane Airbase, headquarters of the Royal Moroccan Air force, close to the capital city of Rabat.

As the IL-96 came smoothly to a halt, in a gusty, sandy, southwester, two refuelling trucks bearing the insignia of the Fifth Wing, Moroccan Air Base, were racing along the runway for the final refuel before taking off for Russia.

The airbase personnel were all Moroccan, but the jet fuel was Russian. Putin and King Mohammed VI were old friends.

Indeed Russia provides great assistance for the nuclear energy operations being constructed in the desert kingdom. And Russia treasures its strong economic and military ties, and staffs a busy Embassy in Rabat and a consular office in Casablanca, just around the corner from Rick's place. King Mo's Embassy was right in the middle of Moscow.

There were more than twelve uniformed engineers piling jet fuel into the IL-96. What with the total closure of the *Plaza de San Francisco*, the extraordinary luxury of the Russian President's aircraft, and the urgent, efficient nature of the men from the Moroccan Air Force, Sophia Morosova was just beginning to accept the obvious importance of her uncle, who was still wearing the small, but most coveted, decoration awarded by the Kremlin in modern times. Never mind the fact that he had just saved her life, and shot dead two Americans in the process.

"What a man," she whispered. "And, plainly, I'm not the only one who understands this."

They were in the air within one hour on the opening 2,000-mile stretch, east along the Med, high above the ever-shifting sands of the Sahara. The Russian pilots flew virtually a straight line until they crossed northern Libya and banked sharply to starboard at the Egyptian border. From here they flew north, across western Turkey, 38,000-feet above the Bosporus, the Russian navy's warm-water-highway into the free world.

Leaving their old colonies of Bulgaria and Romania to their port side, they pressed on for 120-miles up the Black Sea to their traditional navy operational areas around Odessa. It was then a strictly overland flight, across Crimea and bypassing the Ukraine, all the way to Belarus, and then over the chilled, barren landscape of north-east Russia.

They had effectively flown the two sides of a vast right-angle triangle rather than the shorter overland hypotenuse. And before them was the great waterway city of Saint Petersburg, disputed by Moscow, but nonetheless still the cultural capital of Russia, and indeed of what's left of the Russian Empire.

Sophia was unaware of the shutdown of Pulkovo airport, which stands 15-miles south of the City. But not an aircraft moved, and not a terminal door opened as Vladimir Putin's aircraft came lancing into dark and empty skies, above the runway. Putin might have inherited his own colonial kingdom from the detested, high-living Czars, but he sure as hell knew how to emulate their rarefied ways.

And his personalised jet came to a halt close to a VIP entrance to Terminal One, the private getaway for Czar Vladimir IV. The first three Czar Vladimirs were on the throne about a thousand years ago, and wielded about one-hundredth of the power of Comrade Putin. This also applied to Peter the Great, Catherine the Great, Ivan the Terrible, and Boris the Unsteady.

President Putin's Guard of Honour routinely greeted arriving VIP's on the presidential aircraft, even at midnight, which it now was. And the guards now awaited the arrival of Rudolf Masow and his niece, Sophia. For them there would be a warm salute of welcome to the former Imperial Capital, which stands elegantly on the Baltic Sea, a very far cry from its previous incarnation as the war-torn Soviet City of Leningrad, being systematically smashed to pieces by the invading Nazi thugs of the German army.

With its 100 tributaries and canals, and a total of 800 bridges, Saint Petersburg is a breath-taking sight today, a symphony of architecture, palaces, theatres, churches, museums, and a majestic waterfront on the broad, slow-flowing Neva River. It is indeed, the Venice of the Baltic.

Rudolf and Sophia took the salute, and hurried into a waiting limousine sent by the Hotel Europe, Saint Petersburg's finest, centrally located within walking distance of the Winter Palace. It was now 1am on Tuesday morning. And after a nightcap of coffee and brandy in the lush hotel foyer, they retired to bed, both of them exhausted after their long flight from Cuba.

"You are perfectly safe now, my little one," he told her. "Tonight you may sleep the sleep of the righteous."

Privately Sophia wondered at the dimension of the pure anachronism that was Rudolf Masow—this kind and considerate uncle, was, in his way, a bit of a poet, and a lover of the opera. And yet a ruthless killer, whom she had seen, three days ago, cold-bloodedly blow the heads off two quite important Americans.

"I'll sleep," she told herself. "But I'm not so sure about the righteous part. But I am sure he was right about my safety. We left no clues behind."

****

The level of bewilderment in the headquarters of the Louisiana State Police was still very high. The truth was no one had the first clue who shot Hunter de Villiers, unless it was the missing Ragin' Cajun line-backer, Russ Lambert.

And the most damning evidence against that was probably uttered by Miss Martha Le Roux who told several police officers, *"Russ! Kill Mr Hunter? Why, that's easily the most stoopid thing I ever did hear—and that includes my nephew who's eight and kinda backward. Where the hell do you get your detectives? East Louisiana State?"* (which is, by the way, the best-known local mental hospital).

The first dent in the armour of Sophia's ill-thought out master-plan occurred in a northern suburb of Atlanta where Betty-Anne Jones and her husband were watching the last couple of innings of the Atlanta Braves, who were 8-4 in front of the New York Mets. At least Mike Jones was watching. His wife Betty-Anne, head of the Alumni association at the nearby University of Georgia offices, was actually reading a lurid account of the murder of Hunter de Villiers in the Sunday Atlanta newspaper.

The baseball game was winding down, the Braves' closer was nailing the Mets to the wall. And there was an air of complacency in the packed stadium, and indeed, all over the city.

Except for the tree-lined house in a quiet street where nothing much would move until the Braves won the game.

"Oh my good Lord!" exclaimed Betty-Anne. "I'm damned if I didn't spend all last Thursday talking about that man."

"What man?" asked Mike. "You talking about our third baseman that just made that catch?"

"'Course I'm not," she replied. "Right here, I'm talking about that Mr Hunter de Villiers III—one of my alumni. Hell, he's a Bulldog, and someone done blown his head off all the way down there in the bayous."

"Well, I never did. But how come you spent all that time talking about him on Thursday?"

"Well I can't rightly tell you the answer to that one, but it
just occurred to me I might have been talking to the murderer."

"What murderer?"

"I'm talking of the murder of Mr de Villiers, class of 1962. I spent two hours in my office, talking to a tall French lady called Janine Belleau, told me she came from Provence, in France. And she had just one thing on her mind—the precise

281

location of Mr Hunter de Villiers III of Louisiana. And I found him for her. And now he's dead...*Oh my good Lord? What have I done?"*

The Braves' closer struck out the last New York Mets hitter. Mike Jones switched off the TV, and turned to his plainly anxious wife.

"That sounds to me like information that ought properly to be communicated to the State Police. I mean, that's a real big murder with a huge manhunt going on. Betty-Anne, I want you to walk right to that telephone and talk to the duty-officer about what you know. It might turn out to be a pain in the ass, with a whole lot of documents to fill out. But it's your civic duty."

****

The duty officer at the Atlanta Police HQ, down on southwest Peachtree, took the call from the Bulldog Alumni Chief at precisely 5.40pm. And as Betty-Anne spoke, his eyebrows raised. Everyone south of the Mason-Dixon line was talking about the Hunter de Villiers disappearance, and, *hot damn!* Here was a lady who sounds like she had afternoon coffee with the murderer; 'a mystery blond' who came in search of the billionaire from the bayous.

He kept her on the phone for 25-minutes, because any trained policeman would be riveted by her disclosure—Janine Belleau from Provence, was clearly in relentless search for Hunter de V, who was shot dead within 24-hours. *Holy shit!*

The message from Atlanta Police HQ hit all three of the main offices of the Louisiana State Police—Baton Rouge, Lafayette and New Orleans. Colonel Barrington very nearly shot black coffee (no sugar) straight down his nostrils, so astounded was he at the revelation; and, of course, the obliteration of his 48-hour belief that Russ Lambert had killed the boss.

And now thoughts cascaded through his mind. *Am I really looking for a lady killer? They are so rare—but this highly respected Atlanta lady was very certain, and she had, not only an excellent description, but knew her name and where she came from.*

The Colonel had no intention of releasing one word of this to the media, because he did not want to scare the suspect, perhaps causing her to take flight. Instead he called an all-State emergency meeting in his office, first thing on Monday morning. That gave him the whole evening to give this matter very

282

serious thought, and possibly a couple of phone consultations with his top detectives.

However, at 9.15am the following morning yet another bombshell was thrown into his whirring brain. The message came in from Houma Police, from where another devastating piece of information was exploding. A boat owner called Jed Barrow was reporting the possible theft of a 17-foot Boston Whaler, which he had rented to a tall, blond lady, with a slight foreign accent, for cash, on Friday morning. About eight-hours before the murder, just four miles up the road.

According to Jed, the boat was due back Sunday afternoon, and if no one had found it, there would be a substantial insurance claim. Jed wanted a police report document. But much more importantly, his description of the lady who took the helm of the Whaler was virtually identical to that of the Bulldog Alumni boss.

The colonel hit the urgent button for his meeting to start instantly. It was the biggest Louisiana State manhunt for years, and right now Colonel Barrington was the central figure, the man with the irrefutable evidence.

Except for a set of somewhat difficult circumstances—his quarry was thousands of miles away in northern Russia. The name was false. The description was absurd, the blond hair was a wig, there was no record of her even entering the USA. Her passport was a forgery. There was no departure record.

She was English, spoke with no foreign accent, and did not escape by public transport, which meant there were no CCTV photographs, and no ticket, customs, or passport stamps. Also she had not actually murdered anyone. At least not in Louisiana.

Right now, anyone would give you a 1000-1 against the success of the Louisiana Police chief, whose name and rank counted for precisely zero in the Russian Federation.

Chapter Twenty-Five
Middleweight Barton's Killer Right Hook

"I think that will do nicely for one day, Charlie Boy."
And a big smile lit up the trainer's craggy boxer's face
when he added, "Coming in here, causing chaos,
flattening my assistant... it's like training King Kong!"

Police departments, like governments the world over, are very leaky places. The motives, however, are different: pure cash for a young detective's good media tip-off; revenge, self-interest, fake-news, treachery and re-election for on-the-make politicians, these days despised by the public even more than the media.

And 29-year-old, newly-married Lieutenant Tom Chapman, sitting in on the Colonel's staff meeting, knew the insertion of a 'mystery blond' into the de Villiers manhunt was worth $500 of anyone's money in the tabloid media world.

He quietly phoned the *New Orleans Sentinel* and informed them of the two dramatic breaks in the case, the double sighting of the French blond and the weight of corroboration behind the evidence. He even named Betty-Anne and Jed Barrow—the *Sentinel*'s news editor thought $500 was cheap.

Lieutenant Chapman was not new to this game, and the extra $500 was very useful.

The front page exclusive splashed on Tuesday morning's paper, reflected the news editor's enthusiasm in end-of-the-world-typeface. It proclaimed:

Police Now Seek Mystery
Blond In De Villiers Slaying
Sensational UGA Tip-Off and Missing Boat—
Police closing in

There were two photographs accompanying the story, one was a long view across the lake towards the mansion, the other was a candid shot taken straight from the film set, from *Cottonwood Mississippi*. It showed Hunter de Villiers in his brand-new producer outfit, bush-jacket, white jeans, Gucci loafers and a wide straw Stetson.

He was pointing across at the tall, blond, famous French actress, Francoise Radan. Rumours of their affair were never confirmed. But this picture, the third mention of a tall French blond, was gold dust to the newspapermen.

Colonel Barrington almost had a heart attack when he saw the *Sentinel*, naming his two sources, Betty Anne and Jed. However the reaction in the old *Daily News* building on New York's 42nd street was entirely different. Joy and excitement pervaded the glum corridors where so many foreign newspapers maintain an office.

Unsurprisingly, an outstanding London journalist led the pack. He was a 42-year old feature writer from the scurrilous British tabloid, *The News-Dispatch*, and he added two and two together to make about 784. He filed a story, which proclaimed the Louisiana movie tycoon had probably been murdered by a jealous lover!

With all manner of trans-Atlantic shouting and fact-checking, the *News-Dispatch* announced, splash lead, Wednesday, with pictures:

Movie Tycoon Slain
By Jealous Lover?
Interpol quiz Francoise Radan

They had somehow purchased the film set photos of de Villiers, which they ran alongside the story, above a caption which read; ***Dressed to kill****: the Producer calls out to his girlfriend in a 2014 scandal that rocked Hollywood.*

The story began on the front page and then ran inside, in a two-page spread *… The mystery blond in the de Villiers murder in Louisiana has been identified by the United States Police and media. French screen-goddess, Francoise Radan has been helping Interpol with their enquiries—but a spokesman last night stated, "She is not a suspect, and is voluntarily assisting us with background checks."*

There was a suspicion of truth in all of this, but the *News-Dispatch* editor was nevertheless happy with that unbreakable tenet of English Law that states, **You cannot libel the dead.** He was not so certain about Miss Radan's legal position, but decided to keep his head down on the grounds that she was not resident in England.

A publication like the *News-Dispatch* would never find its way into South Audley Street, never mind the home of Lady Penelope Barton. And her son did not catch a glimpse of it until he reached his desk at around 8.30am.

****

Charles, still stunned from the sight of the word *Beauregard,* realised his heart was pounding as he checked the credentials of the legendary Confederate General Pierre Beauregard. The man was Louisiana through and through, born there, lived there, died there, buried in New Orleans. He was the man who ordered the opening cannonade against the Yankee fleet at Fort Sumter, South Carolina, the opening volley of the entire American Civil War.

Beauregard ... Beauregard. It was not the grotesque aptness of the name for a boat owned by a Louisiana billionaire. It was the appalling truth that he did not know where Sophia was, and he had no way of contacting her. Phone calls to Rudolph Masow remained unanswered. But this was about to get worse. Charles Barton picked up the *News Dispatch f*rom the media pile on his desk, and did yet another double-take at the sight of another front page.

The headlines were indeed astonishing. But the opening words stopped him in his tracks. At least they would have, if he'd been walking.

As it was, he shot backwards in his office chair, transfixed by the words "Mystery blond,"—because, he'd seen them before, right there under the heading *Tilden,* the fourth murder on the pseudonym list. Actually the words of the waitress at the Dorchester Heights Hotel had specified 'an unknown young blond,' who had dined with the tennis pro, Buck Madden. Same thing. And here today was yet another reference, pin-pointing yet another 'mystery blond.'

The third killing in Hong Kong featured a police search for a western woman. And his beloved Sophia was the only suspect in the killing of Freddie Fontridge.

Charles actually thought he might throw up. He walked to Scotland Yard's executive bathroom and paced the floor, asking himself over and over, could my Sophia possibly have committed four, maybe five, ruthless killings?

There was a yawning gap deep inside his stomach, and his heart was still racing. He stood in front of the mirror, splashing water on his face, but the acute anxiety of the situation seem to dominate his entire body. And Charles did what he always did in rare high-stress moments like this. He told his secretary he would return by lunchtime, and asked her to summon his staff car. And he ordered the driver to exit Scotland Yard onto the embankment, and to head directly to London's East End.

"The Club, Sir?"

"Thanks, Fred."

They drove in heavy rush-hour traffic past Blackfriars and to the City financial district. From there they kept going east until they ended up four miles from Trafalgar Square in the earthy East End district of Bethnal Green, former stamping ground of Jack the Ripper.

Here they swerved into a red-brick courtyard in front of a Victorian converted warehouse which announced in curved stone letters above the entrance, *Helston Boxing Club.*

It's frequently wondered why a London fight club should be named after the most southerly town in England, Helston, which stands at the north end of Cornwall's Lizard Peninsula. The answer lies in antiquity. Helston was the birthplace of Bob Fitzsimmons, Britain's first heavyweight champion of the world—he knocked out the legendary 'Gentleman' Jim Corbett, America's reigning champion, Carson City, Nevada, St Patrick's Day, 1897. Fitzsimmons, who actually floored Gentleman Jim with a thunderous body blow, was rated the eighth hardest puncher in history, by the fight-game's Bible, *Ring* magazine.

A wealthy Irish fan from Helston, Pat McMahon, who had journeyed by train across America to see the action, was so excited, so proud, he returned to London and opened the Helston Amateur Boxing Club. He did so in 1901 and immediately borrowed the motto of the nearby Repton Boxing Club, **No Guts, no Glory,** which is also engraved on the cornerstone of the club.

Fred drove across the courtyard, and swung around the back of the building into a small unobtrusive space, unseen from the road. The long-time club Head Coach and ex-amateur middleweight titleholder, Mick Pearson, considered the sight of a Scotland Yard staff car not good for the club's image—"Not in this part of the world, son."

But when the Chief Superintendent walked through the door, the coach greeted him with a warm smile, "Morning, Charlie. I suppose you're suffering from some kind of fucking stress. That's the only time we see you these days."

The two unlikely old friends gave each other affectionate bear-hugs. Charles Barton had secretly been a member of the Helston Club since first the Metropolitan Police had sentenced him to four-years pounding the beat in the notoriously dangerous streets of the East End. In those days the Metropolitan

Police were not armed, and Charles, who had been coached as a boxer at Eton college, decided he'd better learn to throw a professional left-hook, rather than a schoolboy one.

He had popped into Helston one day in his lunch-hour, and Mick had gloved him up, and put him through a few paces. Charlie was a white-collar boxer, but he could box, and he had a left-jab that could really rattle your cage, and a straight-right that would knock you spark out, if it landed.

Mick, who had once served a couple of stretches at Her Majesty's pleasure for armed robbery, swiftly saw the potential in the young Etonian, and occasionally advised him there was a career in pro—fighting, big money just waiting for him. But Charles was a detective, in his mind the heir to Sherlock Holmes, and the call of the prize-ring faded before the *Shangri-La* of 221B Baker Street.

Helston was a gritty, spit-and-sawdust kind of a gym. Generations of amateur champions had trained here. Mick Pearson in his third decade at Helston had worked them hard, and tried to give them heart, courage, and character. He worked them mercilessly on the heavy bag, and in short, one-minute, controlled sparring sessions.

He ordered them to bed early, banned alcohol and insisted that any fighter preparing for any title fight must report to the gym at 6am: *"That's the life of a pro, son, might as well get used to it."*

Charles emerged from the locker room in boxing shorts, boots and head-protector. And Mick started him off with the light skipping rope to the music of *Night Train,* just like ex-heavyweight champion Sonny Liston, prior to having his ears boxed off by Muhammad Ali.

Like all good fighters, Charles was a master of the fast rope, alternate feet. The rope was a mere blur, the throbbing rhythm of *Night Train* echoing among the punch bags. After five minutes, Mick shouted to double the pace, and the rope became invisible, an unseen whirring gyro, as Charles pounded on the balls of his feet through this demanding discipline for 10 minutes. It was 10 minutes that would nearly kill a normal mortal, and Fred the driver stared, as he always did, in pure amazement as the sweat streamed down the grim face of the Scotland Yard Chief.

Mick put him on the fast, light bag for five minutes, battering the age-old boxers' punching machine, which requires such inordinate control, before the killer right-hand concludes the sequence. Then it was the heavy-bag, with Mick standing guard, barking instructions, *"The left... the right...remember your combinations... the jab, the hook...let me see you lead off your right foot...easy now, Charlie Boy..."*

Mick called for his young black assistant, Ronnie, to step into the ring with Mr Barton, and he himself climbed up onto the apron and leaned over the top rope.

"...Gimme five rounds...one minute...with a one minute break." And the old trainer watched inscrutably, as his assistant danced gracefully around the taller, heavy-hitting fighter from Scotland Yard, occasionally popping a light left-hand onto the Barton nose.

Charles was doing a lot more work than Ronnie, and by the fifth round he was plainly frustrated, not just by his highly-skilled sparring partner's evasiveness, but by the sheer impossibility of Sophia Morosova. The missing murderess he loved so dearly.

Ronnie ducked left, clipping Charles with a left-jab twice as he went, and those fast, but light punches, on this particular morning, infuriated him.

Charles lurched back onto the ropes, and stuck a hard left hand into Ronnie's face before slamming him under the heart with a right hook—the punch that Mick thought could take him into professional boxing. Ronnie went down clutching his ribs and gasping, "Fuck you, Mr Barton, this is sparring, not a fight to the death."

Mick Pearson was through the ropes instantly, throwing his arms around his old friend and shouting, *"That's enough, Charlie Boy, what the fuck are you doing!"*

Mick actually thought Charles might wait 'til Ronnie climbed to his feet, and then hit him again. He manhandled him back to a corner, appealing for calm. "I'm sorry Ronnie," shouted Charles "It's just …I got a lot on my mind…all bad."

"If you don't mind me saying so sir, that was hell of a fucking whack. I wouldn't be a villain in your neck of the woods. Screw that!"

And Mick added, "I think that will do nicely for one day, Charlie." But a big smile lit up his craggy boxer's face when he added, "Coming in here, causing chaos, flattening my assistant… it's like training King Kong!"

Charles did not look like a killer. He was tall for a middle-weight, with broad shoulders. And there was a spring in his step as he headed for the showers. He actually felt better than he had done since his detective eyes had locked onto the word *Beauregard*. Mick said good-bye to the two policemen and Charles gave him £50 towards the Helston charity foundation, which helps retired fighters, with another £25 tip for Ronnie.

"See ya soon, son," said Mick, "And you're wearing 20oz gloves in future … you were dangerous as a kid. You're a lot worse now!"

Fred turned right out of the courtyard, and a couple of blocks later swung by York Hall, reputed to be the home of modern British boxing, a fabled East End fight venue, where Britain's peerless world heavyweight champion Lennox Lewis cut his teeth, years before he extinguished the psychotic rage of 'Iron' Mike Tyson, knocking him senseless in the eighth round of their title fight in Memphis, Tennessee.

All of his life, Charles had been a student of boxing history, and the names of the East End greats always sprung into his mind as he rode through the streets of Whitechapel or West Ham. There was the light-heavyweight champion, Ron Barton, his namesake; the Olympic gold medallist Terry Spinks; and 'Smiling' Sammy McCarthy, the sweet-natured British featherweight champ, who unhappily ended up in jail three times, once for armed bank robbery.

The East End breeds them tough, but in Charles' memory they were artists, with skills beyond words. And the cries of his old corner men echoed through his mind …*'Stick and jab, Charlie!…Stick and move, son… combinations…left jab, right hook…be first, son!'*

There were perhaps only two people in modern day London who understood how hard Charles could hit when riled. One was Ronnie, whose ribs still ached. The other was the armed villain, whom the young cop from Mayfair had slammed with a 4x2. Even the judge did not understand the burglar spent a month in hospital, with a badly fractured skull.

Fred drove the boss back to New Scotland Yard, and Charles spent the rest of the morning pondering the absence of his girlfriend. He was haunted by the possibility that she may be in the United States and heavily involved with two high profile killings, one in Virginia and one in Louisiana. She had told him very clearly she was actually going to Moscow to visit her mother, but could he any longer believe a word she said?

His workout at the Helston Boxing Club had undoubtedly calmed him down. Slamming the heavy bag and then chasing Ronnie around the ring had sent his heart rate skyrocketing. But when it returned to normal, it stayed there. Helston had a way of removing all kinds of mental aggression except for that in the immediate vicinity, which was mostly wearing 12-oz gloves.

Charles kind of punched it out of himself, and no longer felt at war with the entire world. That particularly applied to Uncle Rudy, whom he knew was avoiding him. But one way or another, a spell on the heavy bag, and then poleaxing Ronnie, he found it oddly cathartic. He usually did at infrequent times like these.

And now a much steadier Charles Barton was alone with his thoughts and he could not get the vision of that Pseudonym List out of his mind—*Birkenhead; Sweet Charity; Divine Wind; Tilden; Beauregard.* All identified. All dead. Probably murdered. With one more to go, there was the sixth and final codename, *Florida Garden,* whoever the hell that might be.

There was only one question that refused to go away. Exactly where was Sophia Morosova? And the thought of her drove all else from his brain. She occupied every minute of his time in the office. *Was she really in Moscow? Or was she packing up her gun in some Louisiana swamp?*

Finally, recognising that he was approximately useless on this day of thuds, sweat, and fears, Charles decided to take off early for home, and have a chat to his mother.

He did not much want to drive himself, and called Fred to bring a staff car around to the main entrance. From there they drove into Parliament Square, along Birdcage Walk and into Mayfair. Fred was ducking and diving in the traffic, and scooted into Berkeley Square from Dover Street.

Almost immediately, Charles looked up at the most fashionable dining club in London—Morton's where he and Sophia had spent their final, unspeakably romantic evening before she left for Russia *(I think).* Fred was just driving up the west side of the square, past the old *Annabel's* and the *Clermont* private gaming club, when his cell-phone suddenly rang.

He glanced down, and could hardly believe his eyes; an incoming call from Russia, an unknown number in Moscow and a so-familiar voice demanding…*where are you, Charles? I've been trying to contact you for days…what's the matter with your phone, or are you now thoroughly fed up with me?*

The Scotland Yard Superintendent shouted *"Sophia! Where the hell are you?"*

"Well, right now I'm on the south side of the Kremlin, staring out over the Moscow River and wishing I were in South Audley Street with you."

"Well I'm right outside Morton's pondering the fact that you are very, very late."

Before Sophia could even reply, the mind of Charles Barton was racing. *Was she really in Moscow? I suppose she must be, otherwise the phone would have revealed where the call was being made…could she have got from Louisiana to the Russian capital in the short time since the de Villiers murder?*

"I'm afraid my mother is very sick and I'm going to be here for another couple of weeks," she said. "I think she's on the slippery slope now, and barely recognises me. You know she's Rudy's sister and he arrived here three days ago. He'll stay with me until the end. The funeral will be in Moscow."

Charles pulled himself together, after the pure shock of Sophia finally making contact. He said how sorry he was and asked if he could call her on the weekend. Surprisingly, she said this was sometimes difficult in a Moscow Hospital but she would call the house in South Audley Street on Sunday morning.

However, Charles did not miss that suddenly evasive edge to her voice, but he was not to know she was using Uncle Rudy's cell-phone, which was patched through from his principal office in the Lubyanka, HQ of Vladimir Putin's Secret Police.

This would have been an entirely inappropriate place to direct a call from New Scotland Yard, and anyway, the Superintendent was feeling a lot more relaxed now, and Sophia was indeed staying in touch, and the cell-phone locater could scarcely be lying.

The phone call served its purpose. Sophia Morosova had once more surfaced and ended by saying, "Wait for me Charles. I'm coming home." And all was once again well with the lovers. Which was something of a miracle since Sophia was 400-miles northeast of Moscow on the shores of the Baltic Sea. She'd never been anywhere near Moscow, nor her mother. And even though Charles Barton might wonder about this, he'd never know the truth. Sophia and Uncle Rudy had not yet completed their mission, as *Florida Garden* would doubtless find out.

****

Sophia had never been to Saint Petersburg, and was transfixed by the beautiful city, around which Uncle Rudolph was escorting her. At this particular moment she was strolling in Palace Square, staring up at the 155-foot high Alexander Column, built to commemorate Russia's resounding defeat of Napoleon's Grande Armee.

This monumental Square was the actual scene of the October Revolution in 1917, in which Sophia's Obolensky ancestors had fought and died. The mighty Column, which towered above her, was hewed from an enormous single piece of red granite weighing 660-tons. It had been transported by sea from Finland, carved and decorated to the order of Czar Alexander I, before being hauled upright by 3,000 men.

There were no modern cranes, and they did it in less than two hours. The Emperor personally made certain the wording carved into the base of the Column reflected his importance; **To Alexander I from a grateful Russia.** High atop the Column stands an angel holding a cross. Its elegant face is more or less identical to that of Emperor Alexander I.

Czar Alexander is, of course, forgiven anything by the Russian nation, for it was he who stood firm against Napoleon's colossal army when it marched into Moscow in 1812. And it was he, mounted on his battle charger, who still stood defiant when the French were turned back.

By the time their long, frost-bitten retreat back to France was over, Napoleon had lost 380,000 men, more than 200,000 horses and 1,000 heavy artillery pieces. There are countless tributes to that famous retreat, but behind Sophia was the most famous one of all. That's the Military Gallery, inside the Winter Palace, which contains one of the most revered collections in the world—the 332 portraits of the Russian generals who defeated Bonaparte in the Patriotic War of 1812.

Czar Alexander commissioned them all, and it's a fabulous artistic memorial to the men who saved their country. Many of the paintings were done by the superb English artist, George Dawes, who lived in Russia for many years while completing the work. He was the first Portrait Painter to the Imperial Court of Russia.

Curiously his supreme portrait of Arthur Wellesley, the first Duke of Wellington, is included in the collection. He is posed in dress uniform before the still smoking battlefield of Waterloo, which was effectively, Napoleon's Last

Stand. Uncle Rudolph told Sophia, "That's a typical generous Russian gesture to the somewhat arrogant foreigner who finished the French Emperor."

And he led her into the Military Gallery's barrel-vaulted hall, past the single armed guard from the Russian Army. And he steered her towards the portraits of four Russian commanders—General Yakov Kulnev, Peter Volkonsky, Adam Ozarowski and Count Mikhail Miloradovitch. "Remember their names, my little one," said Rudy. "All of them had connections to your own family. I have spent much time researching our ancestors—these four generals make it worthwhile."

He then took her to another portrait. That of the 67-year-old Field Marshall Mikhail Kutuzov, a royal prince of the realm who, with immense heroism assumed command of the Russian Army and led them to the village of Borodino to face Napoleon for the very first time.

It was a monstrous battle, the bloodiest of the military clashes in Russia's War of 1812. Of the 250,000 troops who started, more than 70,000 men were killed or wounded. The French, probably, won, but it was closely fought with deadly courage and murderous consequences.

Historians have forever praised the determination of Field Marshall Kutuzov who faced an unknown quantity led by a brilliant French general. That aspect of the conflict sets Kutuzov apart, because he alone, of all the Russians, did not understand what he was confronting. But he never flinched and he refused to give up.

The Field Marshall survived the war, but died the following year and Uncle Rudy pointed out to Sophia, "He's buried in the Kazan Cathedral, right here in Saint Petersburg. We'll visit his grave tomorrow." They spent the rest of the afternoon in the Hermitage Museum, which has been for 250 years, the world's landmark for the collection of fine art—over three million paintings, the bedrock of which was assembled by Catherine the Great in the 18th century.

Sophia was mesmerised by the great masters. She stood for 10 minutes before Rembrandt's huge *Return of the Prodigal Son*, a masterpiece bought by Russia's ambassador to France for the Hermitage, 1766.

Uncle Rudy steered her to the 15th century *Madonna Litta,* one of the great masterworks by Leonardo da Vinci. He showed her priceless paintings by Rafael, El Greco, Van Gogh, and Titian. Sophia was over-whelmed, having spent her young life in an English boarding school which had convinced her London alone was the centre of historic art.

They returned to the hotel, and as a special treat Uncle Rudy took her to the Four Seasons Hotel, just around the corner from the Hermitage for dinner. They dined at the in-house Italian restaurant, *Percorso,* and retired to their rooms early, since tomorrow Rudy's plan included two cathedrals and a look at the Mariinskiy Theatre, home of the Kirov Ballet, *alma mater* of Rudolph Nureyev and the immortal Russian prima ballerina, Anna Pavlova.

The following morning it was raining and they borrowed a couple of umbrellas from the concierge and strolled over to the Kazan Cathedral. They found the ornate gravestone of Prince Mikhail Kutuzov, Russia's towering commander in the Battle of Borodino.

They took a cab across the river to the Cathedral of Peter and Paul, and stood before the tomb which contains the remains of the murdered Romanov emperor—Czar Nicholas, his wife Alexandria, and their children. Despite his long allegiance with the ruling Bolsheviks, Uncle Rudy always found this small gallery in the baroque church overpoweringly moving. And Sophia noticed a tear run down his craggy cheek as he stood there, perhaps recalling the words of the late President Boris Yeltsin—*"the most shameful page of Russian history."*

Late that afternoon they went down to Theatre Square. Uncle Rudy showed his niece the world famous auditorium where the great ones had danced and, according to him, the even greater ones had sung the operas of Verdi, Puccini, Rossini and Mozart.

There was no opera tonight, and they dined at a favourite restaurant of Uncle Rudy's. The following morning they took Aeroflot's direct four-hour flight to Paris, landing at *Charles de Gaulle* mid-day.

There was a near-permanent smile on the face of Uncle Rudy, who had caused impenetrable confusion among the Louisiana State Police; and laid down a route of escape from the USA, so impossible, it would have bedevilled a tribe of Apache trackers. They'd never have found Rudy and Sophia, not in a thousand years. There was no trail.

Chapter Twenty-Six
The Unarmed Assassin Loose
on the Pampas

Sophia had her back to the wall on this one. It's like trying to knock off the Duke of Norfolk in Arundel Castle, or even Putin's foreign minister in his Black Sea dacha...especially as I don't even have a gun, and I know almost nothing about him.

The taxi ride from the sprawling Paris airport was quiet, almost subdued. Rudolph thought it should have been a celebration, but it was no such thing. Here they were successfully through 80% of their tasks, on the verge of a brand new adventure, and Sophia Morosova had a face like a thundercloud.

She spoke not one word all the way in to St Germain, when she finally said quietly: "It's just that I hate lying to Charles and I've been doing little else for as long as I can remember."

"Well," said Uncle Rudy, "It's a very good thing you lied to him about the murder of Lord Fontridge, otherwise we'd both be in the slammer!"

"I understand that," she replied, "But it's the rest of it I'm talking about, the international stuff, the deceptions over my location, where I am, how to contact me, the usual shared confidences of people who care about each other. That's all been denied to me, and I just hope it changes soon."

The taxi moved slowly along *Rue des Beaux Arts* until it reached the apartment building. They both climbed out and carried bags into the foyer where Sophia introduced her uncle to Gaston the concierge.

"That was not because you're so automatically charming," she smiled at her uncle, "It was just that I did not want him, being French, to think we were involved in some torrid love affair!"

Uncle Rudy chuckled as the elevator took them up to the sixth floor and into Sophia's Paris residence. He left his small suitcase near the door and followed her into the kitchen where she put the kettle on before leading him into the living room.

She motioned to a rather elegant armchair and said, "I'll just get rid of my stuff and then I'm coming back to make you some coffee and give you some information which you will thoroughly dislike." She grinned when she said it, but that was pure deception. What she would tell Rudy was truly diabolical.

The kettle boiled, the coffee was made and Sophia was hunting for *le sucre,* which the Russian diplomat always spooned into his cup. When finally they were settled, Sophia told him she was about to reveal the sixth of her detested targets.

"His name is Eduardo," she said. "Edward Garcia-Romano. He is an inordinately wealthy Argentinian ranch owner, one of the biggest beef cattle farmers in the entire country—about 90,000 acres out near the western border with Chile, in the long foothills of the Andes. He was a top polo player."

She stood up and walked to the window, but kept talking. "He's one of the cruellest, cold-blooded men you could possibly meet. He was a friend of my father and for some enormous sum of money he paid to have sex with my baby sister. She was about fourteen at the time. He was very rough with her and liked to smack her back-handed across her face before he raped her. He always made me watch."

Rudolph Masow's knuckles were white as he considered this assault on his beloved little niece who had ended her own life because of men like this. Rudolf scowled. And just muttered the name, "Eduardo fucking Garcia or whatever the hell he's called." The subject of Sasha always upset him very badly, and Sophia could see the iron-tough ex-Soviet assassin weeping as he walked to the kitchen.

It took him five minutes to compose himself and when he came out and returned to his chair, he just said, "He deserves to die, and he will die, because we are Russians and we do not let people like that live among us."

Sophia considered the terrifying career such a man must have conducted—taking people out silently, and professionally, on behalf of an impatient and ruthless government. For him the removal of certain people was both a necessity and a well-deserved fate. Right at this moment Eduardo Garcia-Romano fell precisely into that category. For the second or third time in his life he asked her, "Do you want me to do it for you?"

And for the second or third time in her life, Sophia said, "Not this time, my dear uncle, not this time. I have to do this myself. He was the most appalling man. So cruel to Sasha with such a hard, violent demeanour. He terrified my little sister, it always took her hours to stop crying when he finally left. I just want to look into his eyes when he dies."

"And what about that bastard step-father of yours?" snarled Rudolf. "What the fuck was he doing while all this was going on in his own house?"

"That we will never know," she replied. "But he condoned it, even encouraged it, and he definitely took the money. I'm not sure which of them was the most evil. But they were friends, sometimes talking for a half-hour before he left. I'll never forget that Eduardo. He was a wicked, wicked man."

Rudolph gave the matter his consideration for about five minutes, sipping his coffee but holding it with a slightly trembling hand. Still angry, fit to kill at the appalling new facts he had been told.

"If he's that rich, he'll be protected. He'll be hard to get at. If he's a polo player, he'll be very fit and I would not even consider a knife attack or even poisoning…personally, I'd blow his fucking brains out. That way there are no mistakes."

"Well," said Sophia, "That's not the most subtle of plans, but of course I understand it's probably the only one."

"How do you intend to get near him?" asked Rudolph.

"I plan to telephone him and tell him I'm a niece of Lord Fontridge. I'll tell him my name and I'll tell him I'm working on a project for the University of Madrid, and that I'd like to come and see him on behalf of my family. We were, after all, old friends."

"What happens if he checks you out?" said Rudy, sharply. "What happens if he calls Fontridge's widow and checks up on this niece who suddenly arrives in the middle of the friggin' Pampas. What happens then?"

"That's a chance I'm willing to take," said Sophia.

"Not if I have anything to do with it," he replied. "That's not just a dangerous risk. That's lethal. You could find yourself in an Argentinian prison for making life-threatening statements to one of the most important men in the country."

Sophia fluttered her eyelids. "But what if I charm him?" she said. "What if I flirt with him? I've usually found those tactics work with men, and I imagine will work even better with this sex-crazed South American rapist."

Rudy laughed but continued, "How exactly did you run this little rat to ground?"

"First of all because I found a photograph of him wearing his high riding boots. So I guessed he was a polo player. I had already investigated Lord Fontridge, who was Chairman of the South Downs Polo Club, and from there I worked out, as a fellow sexual deviant, Eduardo probably played for his Lordship down in Alfriston. "I googled the South Downs Polo Club and then checked the team photo for the past half dozen years. Bingo! There he was, right there in the front row. Polished high boots, big smile, one of the nastiest, most vicious little bastards I've ever seen."

"He dies," confirmed Rudy, as anyone might say in his line of work. "But how did you trace him?"

"Easy," she said. "Only the best come to England in the Summer, so I googled the top-50 strata of high-goal players in Argentina during the past six years. And there he was again, the salivating Eduardo in his polished high boots clutching his hateful polo stick, which for me and Sasha would make an extremely nice change."

"Quite a little detective, aren't you?" said Rudy. "If you ever need a job I could fix you up with a good one, in the Lubyanka!" And before she removed the coffee cups, he gave her a somewhat illuminating discourse on polo in Argentina.

"Just remember," he said, "There is a sacred quality to that game all over the country. Down there, it's the Sport of Kings. The whole nation loves football, but polo is the royal game, with huge traditions, generations of the same families, representing almost every one of the high-goal players.

"The 10-handicap guys are the absolute best, the gods of the game, and for decades no other nation had even one. They were all Argentinian, men with fabulous skills, daredevil horsemen, with wrists of blue twisted steel. The biggest tournaments, the biggest crowds, the highest paid professionals. They are all found only in the Argentine.

"And I'm just alerting you. If this Eduardo character is a 10-goal handicapper—well, that's aristocracy in Argentina, especially if he's from one of those polo dynasties. Beware tampering with them, and remember they wield considerable power in all walks of life. If you even suspect a problem, get out, fast. Abort the mission. That is my order."

Sophia took both cups to the kitchen and poured some more coffee, with about a pound-and-a-half of sugar for Rudy. And then she said, "You see, I know how to get there, I know how to get to his house and I know how to kill him."

"There are two things you don't know," said Rudy. "You have no idea how to get hold of a gun in Argentina. You don't dare to take one through Immigration when you arrive. And you have no idea how to get away from the scene of the crime. This, as you know is my critical path. Because without that you may as well blow your own brains out, or else settle for a long spell in the National Penitentiary in Buenos Aires. You don't even know how to get into the country without leaving a trail."

"Well, I admit I have not gone into the areas of micro-management you and your colleagues are accustomed to," she said. "But I have found out how to get into the town of Mendoza, 20-miles from the ranch, without being much noticed. I am flying into Santiago in Chile, and then taking a bus straight across the Andes on the main road down to the Argentine wine-growing country, where Mendoza is situated. I understand the Immigration frontier, on the way down the long hill from the peak of the Andes, is fairly easy-going…"

"You need a Spanish passport to make it even easier," said Rudy. "I'll get you one—same details, new name—don't worry about it."

"All I lack now is a gun," she said, "What do I do about that?"

"I'll have someone meet you in Santiago and you can hide it in your bag, then shove it in the luggage hold in your trans-Andes bus. I doubt they'll bother with that."

"Seems I'm all set," said Sophia, "And I know you have to get back to the Paris Embassy, so let me see you out and I'll call you before I leave in the next couple of days."

"Stay in touch," smiled Rudy. "You know my number 24/7. Just stay as your charming self, and when the crunch comes, don't miss. I'm going to make a couple of phone calls, and do some serious thinking. Just trying to cut mistakes. I do not want any more of that Louisiana bullshit…"

"Of course not, Uncle Rudy," replied Sophia, with false politeness. "I'll follow your orders."

"You'd better," he said. "That way you'll probably keep breathing."

****

Sophia decided to spend the weekend relaxing in Paris but the following morning she took a cab over to the white-stone Russian Embassy on Boulevard Lannes, one mile from the Arc de Triomphe. The place always gave her the chills with its high-black, iron railings and intense security checks. But Rudy was there instantly to bring her through and take her into the main lounge for coffee and pastries. Also for a stern lecture on the forthcoming mission in Mendoza, the first part involved the weapon.

And Uncle Rudy decided she should use the same pistol she had in Virginia—the Smith and Wesson Bodyguard 308, a deadly, lightweight, black revolver capable of firing an exploding bullet at a speed of 1000-feet-per-second with a double-action fire control, giving the shooter two shots real quick. She'd learned on a range below the Russian Embassy in Paris, and used it in combat on the tennis courts, in Virginia.

"I don't think there's a better gun for you, both lightweight and packing a heavy-duty wallop. I've arranged for someone to meet you in Santiago and hand it over. Let me know as soon as your flights and onward transport are definite."

He told her over and over every minute detail of her journey and travel to her final destination. He added that he could not yet finalise her getaway but right now he was favouring a helicopter, a night-landing to evacuate her directly off the endless grasslands of Argentina.

While Uncle Rudy talked, Sophia wrote rapidly in her travel notebook, amazed as she always was by the thoroughness he exercised on every aspect of her coming journey. Before they finished their meeting Uncle Rudy presented her with a Spanish passport with a new name, Dr Isabella Fernandez.

It carried the old photograph of Sophia in her blond wig which she would wear for the duration of this mission. Uncle Rudy also gave her a faculty card from the University of Madrid, confirming she was on a research expedition to study anthropology in South America.

He concluded by giving her a large bundle of Argentinian pesos. God knows, she thought, where he came up with that. And right there she slid the bank notes into the secret compartment of her shoulder bag, and locked it. She assumed this was ultra-safe since it was especially made for her by Uncle Rudy's colleagues in the Russian Secret Police.

They had a light lunch together at the Embassy and she left early afternoon to allow Rudy time to pack his bags and fly on to London. Her roof garden on this sunlit Parisian afternoon was paradise for Sophia. No interruptions, no need for wariness and no fear. However, she steered her mind away from the upcoming assassination in the foothills of the Andes.

She'd need to be at the top of her game to pull this off but she never forgot her promises to little Sasha. She'd pulled it off five times, or at least she and Rudy had pulled it off five times. She would let nothing stand in the way of her sixth success.

On Monday morning, carrying only her shoulder bag, she locked her apartment and took a cab to the main Paris airport. She was travelling Air France, as she usually did. But this was a particularly interesting flight because it was one of the very first overseas flights the airline ever made. The principal difference between 1933 and now was the airliner would no longer stop to refuel 15 times on its way to the capital city of Chile, Santiago, way out there on the Pacific West Coast of South America. However, it's still Air France's longest flight, (7,400-miles, 14-and-a-half hours).

Sophia, who paid cash for her ticket at the airport was travelling, for a change, in the back of the aircraft but it was not full, and after a quiet, but endless journey right across the Brazilian rain forest and then the world's longest mountain range, the Andes, she was awakened as they began their descent over some of the most rugged snow-capped peaks on Earth.

They came in to Santiago International Airport early in the morning around 7:30am local and her new passport bearing the name Dr Isabella Fernandez, a resident of Madrid, was perfect. Sophia slipped through immigration with only her light travelling bag and took a taxi to the bus station—the special one in Santiago which runs a service directly through the mountains and over the border into Argentina.

She quite enjoyed the ride across the ancient neo-classical city with its astonishing and grandiose Spanish architecture, fitting for a modern metropolis which dates back to 1541 and is named after Saint James, patron saint of Spain. Nearly seven million people live in Santiago.

It occupies almost the entire valley of the fast flowing Mapocho River. And all around are the high peaks of the Andes and the Chilean Coastal Range to the east.

But the bus station was not just a place to jump on a ride over the mountains to the Pampas—it was the secret rendezvous for Sophia to meet an unknown messenger from Uncle Rudy. A Chilean, Russian agent, who would bring her the Smith and Wesson P308.

In Rudy's opinion, there would be no heavy searches on the bus ride over the Andes. He was as sure as he could be if he shoved it to the bottom of her travelling bag it would not be discovered—"but don't go anywhere near an airport."

Sophia's bus was to leave at eleven o'clock. She bought her ticket for the 250-mile, seven-hour journey to the Argentinian city of Mendoza with a handful of her pesos, and settled down to wait. Her instructions had been simple, "A man in western dress, no poncho, will approach you carrying a small, expensive gift-wrapped parcel which looks like perfume or something," Rudy had instructed, "Probably pink with decorative flowers. He will say 'Welcome to Chile, Madam, this is from your sister.' You will reply, 'I am grateful, Senor.'"

Sophia knew the man would recognise her because she would be sitting outside on one of the green benches and holding a copy of the French magazine Paris Match.

Ten o'clock came and then 10.30. By 10.45am Sophia was becoming worried. Ten minutes later she was at her wits' end. The bus was filling up, the driver had started the engines and the doors of the big air-conditioned vehicle were due to close.

Sophia had to make up her mind one way or the other, to go to Mendoza unarmed, or to miss the bus and wait right here in the hope that the tardy messenger would show up in the end. *But what if he had been apprehended? What if his captors now came for her right here at the bus station?* Sophia made her decision. She slung her bag over her shoulder and boarded the bus, perhaps one of the first unarmed assassins in history.

Passengers were ordered, without explanation, to leave their baggage in a cordoned-off area near the front and they set off towards the northern edge of the town. They took Freeway-5 up to Los Andes where they swung right, along the major Route-57 to the Argentinian border at Los Libertadores where documents and passports were required for the border guards.

Immediately they stopped, officials came in and removed all the luggage in the bus, and set each bag on a baggage beltway which carried each one through an x-ray system. Passengers were not required to disembark and the officials politely and carefully returned each bag to the bus when it had cleared the x-ray.

"Jesus!" muttered Sophia. "If I'd brought that gun it would have stopped the x-ray machine dead in its tracks, and they'd be marching me off to Los Libertadores Jail. That was Rudy's first mistake. Thank God, it all went wrong."

Still unarmed, Sophia sat quietly as they rolled on past the second highest mountain peak in all the world, the 23,000-foot mountain, Aconcagua, which is right up there with Mount Everest. The scenery was truly spectacular, although barren all along dry desert plains, which had a stark and dramatic atmosphere. They stood, after all, in the shadow of the enormous snow-capped, red mountains of the Andes.

They passed opaque blue and probably bottomless mountain lakes. They even passed a couple of old Andes railroad stations but the real star of this unique road journey was Freeway-7 which cascaded rather than stretched down the hundred mile long gradient of the main highway from Chile in to the cattle and wine country of Argentina.

At one stage, there were 28 successive hairpin bends twisting across the face of the mountain, so steep was the gradient. From its high point to the Argentinian flatlands, there was a drop of 3,000-feet which made the construction of Highway-7 something close to the engineering marvel of the western world. Maybe not quite to the brilliance of the Panama Canal, but as ingenious as any other man-made construction.

They drove through the rolling vineyards of north-western Argentina and arrived in the urban sprawl of Mendoza, with its wide tree-lined streets and modern buildings. Sophia took a taxi from the bus stop to the modest two-star hotel she had booked, and moved into her new home for the next two or three days.

There was a phone directory on the bureau and she tried to find a gunsmith but then thought better of it. Instead she took a stroll along one of the wide avenues and settled on a small, anonymous-looking restaurant where she sat outside and watched the world go by.

She decided that since she was in South America's greatest beef-producing land, she had better order a steak for dinner, which was accompanied by a delicious local Malbec red wine. Sophia spoke to no one since she was preoccupied with the words of warning from Uncle Rudy, regarding the structure of Argentina's aristocracy.

She was certain Eduardo Garcia-Romano belonged to that elite class of millionaire sportsmen as outlined by her uncle. She knew he was a ten-handicap player who was paid a fortune to play in Sussex every year. And, judging by the amount of land the internet had told her he owned, she had her back to the wall on this one. *This is like knocking off the Duke of Norfolk in Arundel Castle, or even Putin's foreign minister in his Black Sea dacha...especially as I don't even have a gun, and I know almost nothing about him.*

She decided that her first stop the following morning would be the *biblioteca*—Mendoza's Public Library down on San Martin's Avenue. The one thing she definitely knew was her need for some heavyweight details on the man

304

she planned to murder. She also realised, if she called Uncle Rudy, he would tell her to abort the entire thing, and get the hell out of Argentina.

But Sophia was made of stern stuff, even if she couldn't shoot straight, and she resolved to finish her debriefing with a long session in the library. She turned up there at 10am the following morning and swiftly ensconced herself at a small private table with three books which contained long accounts of Argentinian noblemen and military leaders

After an hour, she had written down two or three particularly interesting notes, the first being Eduardo's honorary membership of a secret military society of Argentinian officers who still believed that the Malvinas (Falklands) should be recaptured from the British.

This clandestine organisation had existed long before the War of 1982 and indeed it was there that General Leopoldo Galtieri and Admiral Jorge Anaya, with their most loyal, patriotic supporters planned their attack on the British Protectorate, which, in turn, led to the most shattering defeat and humiliation.

But they never quite got over it, and they still met for several decades afterwards, not just to lick their wounds, but to plan a terrible revenge, and wipe out the memory of their destruction by Admiral Sandy Woodward's Task Force.

They still called their secret club the *Agencia de Patriotas Argentinos.* Meetings were sporadic and yet almost permanent in memory of their old optimistic days before 1982. They gathered at the Buenos Aires coffee house, the *Florida Garden,* situated right off the busy shopping district of Florida Avenue.

It was not really a coffee house. It was a rather grand restaurant with a sweeping central staircase, glass walls and copper-covered columns. There was a curious Officer-Club atmosphere about the place with a special table reserved for the secret patriots.

Some weekday nights there were very few, but on Friday and Saturday nights there were usually a dozen or more—and they would discuss the glories of Argentina. And when the coffee and pastries evolved into bottles of Argentina's finest wines, they would sing the great songs of Argentina.

The notes of the stirring military marching song, *San Lorenzo,* contains lyrics to celebrate the Regiment of Mounted Grenadiers at the battle which bears the name of the famous song. Such tales of heroism from the Argentine War of Independence still echo among the strong wooden tables of the *Florida Garden.*

It took place more than 200 years ago now (1810-1818), and when those deep baritones of the modern Argentinian front-line begin to sing on a Saturday night, the ghastly memories of defeat by the British in the *Malvinas* seem utterly impossible.

And what seems especially ghastly to them is the all-too-vivid memory of Woodward's sudden, brutal sinking of the Argentinian battle cruiser, *General Belgrano,* on the evening of May 2nd, 1982 with the loss of 320 men. That essentially cleared the Argentine Navy off the high seas, but overwhelming sorrow still resonates.

The great warship was named for General Manuel Belgrano, the principal Argentine land commander of that far-lost, but still glorious battle for Independence from their Spanish masters. And the officers stand when his name is mentioned. And they drink a toast both to him personally, and to those lost on the ship that bore his name. The little ceremony ends the same each time, with the dying words of General Belgrano … *Ay, Patrio Mia! … Oh, my country.*

The history of the *Agencia* recorded that all meetings of eight or more military officers at the cafe, even an informal occasion, must end with the haunting 200-year-old National anthem …

> *To the great Argentine people, hail!*
> *Or let us swear with glory to die …*

By the time Sophia finished reading about the *Agencia* and Eduardo Garcia-Romano's membership, it became obvious that members of his family had fought and died for their country, and that he occupied an important place in these gatherings. Eduardo really mattered here, both in the wide cattle-lands, which he owned, and in the very heart of patriotic Buenos Aires.

Generally speaking, Sophia did not consider she would be very highly applauded for shooting this much-revered man. In fact her long and beautiful neck might easily find its way into a hangman's noose, an implement not unheard of in the secretive Argentinian Halls of Justice.

And as for a suitable site for the coming execution, Sophia decided this may very well be a two-step operation—one for reconnaissance, and two for the actual deed itself. And one thing was very definite. Eduardo might turn up unarmed to meet his fellow patriots at the *Florida Garden,* but she would not be making an appearance there.

Because that fabled café, which was reputed to serve the finest coffee in the city, represented a plain and obvious short-cut to the gallows. The mere production of a revolver in that room…well, your feet would not touch the ground.

She closed her notebook and returned to her hotel and, impetuous to the end, she checked the phone number of *Rancho Garcia-Romano* and waited to be thoroughly vetted by some secretary.

To her amazement when she asked for the Senor he replied, "Speaking…and who may I ask is this?"

Sophia gave him her well-prepared speech, how she was Dr Sally Scott-Martin, of London University, and a niece of Lord Fontridge, her Uncle Freddie, who had so sadly passed away. However, he had always spoken so fondly of his polo colleague, Senor Eduardo, and she decided she must at least give him a call while she was taking a course in anthropology in Argentina. She told him she had no idea where he was, but if it was at all possible, perhaps she could come and visit him. She would make her own way there.

Senor Eduardo said he was very close to Mendoza, and would be delighted to see her and show her around the ranch, perhaps tomorrow, *which would mean you could drive over later this afternoon for dinner, and we could make an early start.* He added he was so very sorry about Uncle Freddie, and looked forward to speaking with her about his final years.

Sophia rang off, smiling. But what Senor Eduardo had not told her was that he also knew of the deaths of Sir Josh Hartley and Buck Madden. Although their connection to him was secretive in the extreme. He was, understandably, very cautious these days.

He opened his laptop, and sent an immediate email to Lady Fontridge, all the way to England and down into deepest Sussex, where Laughton Towers and its farmland represented approximately one-forty-fifth of his own *Rancho Garcia-Romano.*

My dear Jane, he wrote, *I recently had a telephone call from your very charming niece, Sally Scott-Martin, who lives in London, and would like to visit. I, of course, invited her, since she is staying in Mendoza, a town very close to the ranch. However, I did so on the understanding that she was a genuine member of your family.*

I thus ask you to send me back a confirmation of this. I know you are busy, and if I don't hear from you I will assume you know precisely who she is. As I have mentioned, so many times before, I am still, deeply distressed at Freddie's passing.
Fondly,
Eduardo.

Chapter Twenty-Seven
Three Gunshots in an Ocean of Grass

*"He would have been better with some Latin blood," Eduardo
laughed. "It's different down here in South America. We treasure
life, living, enjoying companionship with beautiful women—
the kind I have now." And he touched her hand again.*

Rudolph Masow remained incandescent with fury all the way from Paris to
London. He had known for years that Boris Morosov was an absolute bastard
and totally the wrong man to have married his beloved sister, Veroniya. The
tragic break-up of that family had long mystified him. But Sophia's revelations
had cleared up many questions.

Now, he merely wanted to murder Boris. And in Rudolph's case that was not
a simple figure of speech. It was an ice-cold declaration of intent, made by a
professional on an unsuspecting (he hoped) fellow Russian. A man whom Rudy
considered had been directly, and totally, responsible for the death of poor,
darling Sasha.

And now, as he sat glowering in a Russian Embassy staff car on his way to
Kensington Palace Gardens, he decided to trace Sophia's father. And this might
prove difficult since the leader of the London teenage vice-ring had gone missing
immediately after Veroniya had half killed the Japanese tycoon, Takahashi.

Boris had not been seen since. Sophia thought he may have returned to
Russia, but Rudolph discounted this and considered he'd vanished into very
foreign parts and would be seriously difficult to trace. When he returned to his
office, he texted a few of his agent friends in various world capitals, requesting
a search for the absent Boris Morosov. He ended his short communique with the
words: *You will have my eternal gratitude if you can locate this unspeakable
man.*

Thus, as Sophia prepared to find her way out to *Rancho Garcia-Romano,* a
worldwide network of Russia's secret policemen was slipping into action,
checking the internet, checking local newspapers, checking the police, checking

airports, immigration officers, anything to please the massively-regarded diplomat, Rudolph Masow.

Nothing much happened for two or three days and that was also true of Jane Fontridge's study at Laughton Towers. The room remained closed and her Ladyship was too busy to check her emails, an oversight which, silently and unnoticed, would save the life of Sophia Morosova.

****

The prospect of a hire car for Sophia was out of the question, the paraphernalia of contracts, insurance, credit cards and licenses would leave the kind of trail she could not afford. Neither did she want to buy a car, and she especially did not want to take a taxi, because right there would be a single Argentinian driver who would know precisely where he dropped her off, and equally precisely what she looked like, her demeanour and the hotel where he collected her.

No, she had to do better than that, and she walked through Mendoza's shopping area back to her hotel, and tackled the receptionist.

She requested some member of staff, who finished about 4pm to use his own car and drive her out to the ranch, around 20-miles, for which she would pay US$100 cash. It was possible she might need a return journey for which she would pay another $100.

The receptionist smiled, and hit a button on the in-house phone system and said, "Antonio, will you come here a moment?"

Through the door came a handsome young man of around 22, wearing the white jacket of a waiter. The receptionist reminded him he would be off duty at 4pm, and would he care to provide transport for this lady, a guest in the hotel, out to the *Rancho Garcia-Romano*.

"Actually," he said, "I am very busy this afternoon, I am afraid that is not possible…"

"She'll give you $100 US in cash," said the receptionist.

"I'll be there," he said. "What time?"

"You'll use your own car?" asked Sophia.

"Of course, madam. It will be my pleasure."

Thus was arranged Sophia's anonymous ride to the home of the man she had absolutely detested for more than seven years.

Antonio backed out of the staff garage, and drove his second-hand Toyota to the front entrance of the hotel, where Sophia was waiting. They set off in a south-westerly direction along a reasonable secondary road. It was typical Pampas country, miles and miles of grassland, occasional herds of cattle, enormous numbers with, it seemed, just a few hard-riding gauchos steering them in the right direction.

It seemed to Sophia that everything here happened in the far distance. It was that kind of land, vast stretches of prairie beyond the imagination of any European farmer. The wind made waves in the grasses like the ebb and flow of ocean water.

There was a remarkable, remote beauty about it that almost captured Sophia, but in the end her European roots of picture-postcard green hills and valleys kept her a captive of a distant cooler place, and rendered the Pampas of Argentina a strange and wild land which was completely foreign to her.

They rattled along at a decent speed, passing the occasional wandering cow or steer. There were no fences out here. The cartography of the Pampas covered such outrageous distances, it would have taken almost the national debt to pay for the post and rails. Argentina, by the way, has a national debt which often made officials at the International Monetary Fund gasp.

The journey took about 50-minutes before they arrived at the tall, open gates of the *Rancho Garcia-Romano*. The house was so remote it could not even be seen from here, and they set off up the mile-long drive, which was lined by tall hedges, and the ranch house stood before them in a shallow valley. It was a classic two-story building, like a giant log-cabin, with powerful gable-ends and a huge double front door, obviously of solid oak, with black iron fittings.

Her host, however, had seen her coming and he walked across to the car to greet her. She climbed out, and his face lit up at the tall, blond beauty before him. There had been no communiqué from Jane Fontridge, at least not yet, and he took her right hand and softly kissed the back of it.

"Welcome to *Rancho Garcia-Romano*," said Eduardo, smiling. "I am indeed honoured to meet the niece of my great friend, Freddie Fontridge, may he rest in peace."

Sophia was nervous to look him directly in the eye, lest he should recognise the schoolgirl whose younger sister he had ravaged. But she still would have recognised him anywhere, the haughty look in his dark eyes beneath the small flat-topped gaucho Stetson. His springy, confident walk befitted a man who owned the land as far as the eye could see.

Still, Sophia remembered, he had that springy step when he walked across their bedroom. The egos of certain men, especially predators, she guessed, really had no limits whatsoever. He walked like a king, and he had the instincts of an alley-cat. At least, that was Sophia's opinion.

She was certain he did not recognise her, but she would have spotted him a long way out and needed little reminding of the vicious way he had slapped her and Sasha around. The way he had threatened to rip off her clothes before he forced her to watch his disgusting sexual antics.

Sophia was uncertain she could contain her hatred even on the short walk to the house. But she knew that she must contain it. And somehow she believed that, although she was alone, Sasha was watching, and Uncle Rudy was thinking of her.

The house inside was like something from a film-set, Indian rugs, the walls decorated with historic artifacts from this wild livestock empire. There were huge mounted horns from the various breeds of champion bulls which had roamed these prairies, increasing the size of the herds at their will, for almost a century. Every one of them bore the *Garcia-Romano* cattle brand.

There were antique guns, paintings of fast horses and tough men—gauchos with whips, a magnificent oil of a stampeding herd about eight-feet across, by an artist who was unknown to Sophia, but plainly regarded with great affection here in the Pampas.

Eduardo informed her he had three or four of this man's works, and was very proud to have them. It really was the most beautiful collection. They decorated the house because the owner loved them. No set of bulls' horns could have looked more magnificent than the ones mounted into the stonework, above a great fireplace in the main room. This was indeed the central building of a cattle kingdom.

A housekeeper named Anna appeared very suddenly, and Eduardo handed Sophia over to a lady he said would take care of her every need. He suggested she report to the fireplace at 6.30 when he would introduce her to the rest of his family, and they would all have a couple of glasses of wine before dinner.

Sophia, as a matter of course, assumed this would probably be a six-pound rib-eye each! But she didn't mention it, even though she stole a surreptitious

312

glance out of a big bay window and noticed about three million cattle moving slowly across a field like a giant cloud, as sunset approached.

Anna steered her up a wide wooden staircase, where artifacts and weapons of the indigenous Indian tribes of northwest Argentina decorated the walls and alcoves. There were superb examples of the warriors at war, ancient crossed axes, crossed spears, battle clubs and on beautifully-carved shelves, there was highly decorated pottery.

It was all interspersed with early sepia photographs of a long ago civilisation, which for hundreds of years preserved these lands for families like the Garcia-Romanos. Over the years the new settlers shaped and utilised everything for their own grandiose purposes. Sophia thought, as she had downstairs, this was a very beautiful house.

Anna took her to a big bedroom with a carved, wooden-framed double bed. There were two large Indian tapestries on the wall, and the most exquisite woven bedspread, which featured a running herd of cattle pursued by a hunting warrior from the ancient Indian people. A large spread of animal horns was erected on the wall in front of her. A couple of long antique spears crossed above it, were presumably to confirm the pecking order on a big Argentine ranch.

Sophia slung her bag on the bed and crashed for an hour, before making herself ready to meet the Garcia-Romano family.

At 6.30 she presented herself in the main room, dressed now in tailored black trousers and a white blouse with a ruffled front. She wore the emerald necklace Uncle Rudy had given her for her 21st birthday—just in case this strutting peacock of a farmer, Eduardo, considered her to be of the lower orders.

His two nephews, Andreas and Hugo, late teenagers, introduced themselves and said how delighted they both were to meet a member of Uncle Eduardo's polo families in Europe. Both boys were studying at University in Buenos Aires. They were very pleased to talk to her, not about the feeding of vast herds of cattle, but about pop music, sports and drugs, the latter one of which Sophia was not much able to help.

Eduardo came in wearing a large smile, dressed elegantly in a Spanish dress-shirt and still smiling broadly. Jane Fontridge had not yet answered his email. He was accompanied by his very beautiful niece, Gabriela, who was older than the boys, but still in her last year at university across the River Plate in Uruguay, where she was studying design under one of the South American maestros.

313

Sophia told her of her own hopeless quest to become a fashion designer in Paris, and wished her much luck, along with a warning that she'd have to go to Europe, probably Paris or Milan in order to reach the pinnacle of her new profession. Gabriela clearly approved of this final career move and mentioned, "I would love to, if I could afford it"…at which point she offered a sidelong glance at her uncle, who did not seem overly distressed by this veiled, and probably expensive application.

Another rather beautiful lady, 40-ish, joined them for dinner and Sophia never really got a handle on who she was, but by the end of dinner, as they finished the wine, she guessed this was some kind of a live-in girlfriend for Eduardo. Privately she thought the lady was rather too old for him. But then, she would have thought that of any girlfriend over the age of fifteen.

She was in bed by 10pm and rose early at around 7am when she heard the rest of the household on the move. She found her way downstairs, between the axes and the arrows, and joined the others at the same large table, now containing plates of omelettes and bacon, toast and coffee, with cereal and croissants at one end.

She settled for one of the omelettes, which was delicious, and after one cup of coffee, Eduardo summoned her to accompany him outside for a look around the stables and the flower gardens. He told her he would very much like to talk about her Uncle Freddie and suggested that perhaps they could drive out across the ranch, bring some horses and go for a ride out near Lake Potrerillos, on the edge of the property, in the shadow of the lowest range of the Andes mountains.

"It is very beautiful out there. I think you will be impressed and we can have a long talk about dear Freddie."

Sophia declined to inform him that the last time she had been near a lake with Uncle Freddie she'd stuck a seven-inch dagger into his heart, and then dumped him in the water. Instead, she said that sounded absolutely lovely, but she was afraid she had no riding clothes with her.

Eduardo turned around towards the back end of the house and bellowed "*ANNA!*" and when his housekeeper opened the kitchen door he shouted, "Please fix Dr Scott-Martin with some boots, jodhpurs and gloves. We're going for a ride."

They took a swift look around the heavenly Spanish stables, which represented an architect's vision of dark polished wood, brass, leather, painted tiles from Barcelona, and black steel grills. Sophia had never seen a stable block that lavishly built. She would never forget it.

They walked back to the house where she was able to change into her borrowed riding gear, and she wore a snazzy black Argentinian gaucho hat, which accentuated her flowing blond hair. Her expensive dark glasses gave her a distinct air of remoteness. She actually looked nothing like her real self.

When Eduardo reappeared he looked like a matinee idol. He wore polished boots with high heels and spurs, pressed gaucho trousers, a white silk shirt with a scarlet poncho decorated in gold.

His classic black Argentinian Stetson was slightly tilted back, and around his waist was a gun-belt containing two pearl-handled Colt pistols. The ensemble was completed by a crossed ammunition-belt from his left shoulder to his right hip. He looked like the alter ego of Emiliano Zapata, the god-like Mexican peasant king who rallied his nation to arms.

It was all Sophia could do to stop herself exclaiming, *Viva Zapata!* ... the distant cry of a down-trodden people on the march. As things were, she just said, "Eduardo, you look absolutely awesome."

The Argentinian sportsman smiled confidently, as one accustomed to receiving heavy compliments would. He did not and never would, recognise the pure hatred in the eyes of his riding companion. "Do you like my guns?" he said blithely, easing one from its holster, "They are Colt single-action US Army revolvers, the precise weapon used by General John J. Pershing when he led the Tenth Cavalry at the Battle of San Juan Hill in Cuba."

Sophia, of course, had no idea about the General, certainly not that he fought shoulder-to-shoulder with Teddy Roosevelt and the Rough Riders, in one of the most hard-won and decisive battles of the 1898 Spanish-American War. General Pershing had two pairs of display pistols made identical to the seven-and-a-half inch-barrelled weapon he carried with him at San Juan Hill—the only difference being the pearl handles on the revolvers. "I bought them at auction in New York," Eduardo told her.

"They are very beautiful. Do you wear them loaded?" she asked.

"Only for riding out across the Pampas. You'll occasionally see a snake out there. And I've never been crazy about the prairie foxes. But when you are far from home riding a horse, you never want to be unarmed."

Sophia agreed with that, and they walked to a waiting jeep attached to a double horse-box in which, were two good-sized steeds already saddled and ready for the journey.

Eduardo took the wheel and they drove down the long drive to the road and turned left for a couple of miles before taking a new track, which led, apparently, out towards the lake. With every turn of the wheels the low peaks of the mountain range seemed to grow nearer.

Eduardo stole a couple of glances at his iPhone and noted that still Lady Jane had not replied, and it was now almost twenty-four hours since he'd sent the email. Indeed with the four-hour time difference it was almost 2pm in Sussex, and he would most certainly have heard, were there anything awry about the presence of this very beautiful Dr Sally.

The ranch owner was now beaming with anticipation, and he touched her hand, as an opening gesture to the afternoon which lay ahead of them. Sophia smiled and made no attempt to distance either herself or her hand from her wickedly licentious companion.

Finally she could see the lake up ahead and it was everything she had expected.

"My gosh!" she said. "Uncle Freddie would have loved this. Did he ever come out here to visit you?"

"No. Always I tried to persuade him, but he was forever busy on the Queen's private council, running the English legal system, and organising the Polo Club. I told him he should take a break and come out here for a couple of weeks but he never made it."

"He was such a good man," said Sophia. "So conscious of his duty, so determined always to do the right thing and such people are rare…"

"He would have been better with some Latin blood," Eduardo laughed. "It's different down here in South America. We understand our duty but we treasure life, living, enjoying our moments of peace and freedom, and good companionship with beautiful women—the kind I have now." And he touched her hand again.

Sophia did not mention the very feel of him gave her goose bumps, not of excitement, but with cool revulsion to one of the most hateful men she had ever met. It was a journey of paramount deception; his predatory lies perhaps overwhelming her false interest in him. But Sophia's dislike was as deep as the enormous lake spread out before her.

For one shuddering moment she thought he might lean over and try to kiss her, but the old cattle-boss was too cool an operator to rush his fences. He just smiled, and drove on nearer to the water, eventually stopping, shutting off the engine and stepping out onto the grasses, in which his great fortune reclined.

He walked around to the passenger side, and held out his arms to his guest, helping her down and holding her just a little too closely. Sophia silently loathed the touch of him, but she held on to his hand and said, quietly, "Eduardo, this is just so lovely. And so kind of you to invite me."

"My dear," he said, "The pleasure is entirely mine. Now let's get the horses, and take a ride along this southern shore. I am certain you will enjoy it."

He walked to the back of the big horse-box, and undid the first ramp, expertly backing the dark bay hunter out, and turning him around. "Now, Sally," he said, "These are good sized horses, ex-hunter chasers from England. And this one, whose name is Sammy is yours for the afternoon. He's very strong, very fast if you want him to be, and very affectionate—much like myself!"

Sophia smiled shyly while Eduardo backed the other horse out. He was another fine bay gelding, with black points, and a somewhat dashing white blaze. Sophia took the reins of both horses and held them while her host walked quickly around to the driver's side of the jeep, and rummaged inside. But he was not rummaging, he was checking that iPhone again. Still there was not a word from Jane Fontridge.

Eduardo was delighted, and he took the reins of the second horse and helped Sophia get mounted, expertly holding out his hand for her left boot, and lifting her up, as she swung into the saddle.

He mounted his own horse, Denny, and they set off over this lonely *Garcia-Romano* land, riding for a half an hour before Eduardo turned to the lake and told her, "Right here up between those peaks, you can see the last mountain we have which still has snow…"

Sophia stared ahead and said, "Oh yes, I can see it, doesn't it look very mystical?"

"Everyone recognises the spiritual quality of the mountains," said Eduardo. "But now we will turn back, and re-box the horses. There is another beauty-spot I would like to show you, around 10-miles farther around the lake. We'll drive around there, and then take a ride into the foothills—where I'll show you one of the greatest views in the whole of Argentina, back across the lake, looking west. It's like a photograph from a travel magazine."

"Sounds wonderful," replied Sophia. "This a magical day for me, and I thank you so much."

"I am enjoying it too," said this *El Patron* of the Pampas. Later we must drink a private toast to Uncle Freddie with my finest wine … for bringing us together."

Sophia wasn't sure about any of that, especially the parts about "private" and the "together." But again, she feigned a look of joy, and whispered, seductively, "Perfect." Eduardo was almost beside himself with desire. And he increased Denny's speed as they headed back to the horse-box.

They arrived at their start-point about 25 minutes later, and quite suddenly, Sophia said, "I keep looking at those beautiful pistols … could I actually hold one?"

"Of course, my dear," he said, and drew the Colt revolver from its holster and, holding it by the barrel, handed it to her in what was unquestionably the biggest mistake he would ever make.

Sophia handled it lovingly. "Perfect," she said. She swung around towards him, and fired straight into his temple. And then again, same place, before lowering the barrel and slamming a third bullet directly into his heart.

Both horses shied, and Denny swerved away, causing his master to topple from the saddle, and land with a dull thud in the long grass. Sophia slipped out of the saddle to the ground, and gave both horses a light slap on the rump telling them to *shoo*, to walk away.

Denny came back to see Eduardo, the last time he would ever see him. He probably disliked the blood pouring from a gaping hole on the left-side of Senor Garcia-Romano's skull. The master of these endless prairies was dead, no doubt about that. Sophia had blown his brains out, as she had vowed to do. She was still wearing her riding gloves, and grabbed the second revolver. Strolling to the lake, she hurled them both, one at a time, as far as she possibly could into the water.

She walked back and unbuckled the ammunition belt, and hurled that too, far into the lake. For good measure, no real reason, she ran back to the Jeep, grabbed Eduardo's iPhone and flung that into the lake as well.

She then climbed into the driver's seat of the Jeep and drove it forward, until she came to a thick overhanging waterside copse. She crashed straight into it, smashing her way over the light branches, and hauled the horse-box, still with its ramps down, to a position where it could not possibly be seen from beyond the immediate area.

She had already noticed an electronic lever marked *Trailer*, and with the engine running, pulled it hard and felt the rear of the Jeep subside. When she arrived at the steel coupling it was no longer one unit, and if she unhooked the chain, the Jeep was free to go.

It was a very modern vehicle, and the GPS showed her precisely where the city of Mendoza was. And she set off across the Pampas, following the tyre tracks of their outgoing journey, and then swerving left at a wide, dusty road which had an old sign post reading *Mendoza 15.*

She turned left and accelerated, knowing that somewhere along this stretch she would reach *Highway 7,* the way to the Chilean Border. She found herself trembling, still dressed in her riding clothes, wearing her gaucho's hat. But there was only one thought in her mind, and that was to get through that Chilean frontier with one of her passports.

All six of them were in the secret compartment of her shoulder bag, which was still over the back of her seat, where she had put it when they left the ranch.

It was over 150-miles to the border, and Sophia still had work to do long before they arrived. She had made no notes along her inward route into Argentina, because, of course, she'd had absolutely no idea that this mission would even take place.

However, she did recall two or three public rest areas overlooking some of the most spectacular mountain scenery at the higher elevations. She drove for three hours on this smooth but twisting highway before she found one, a quite busy place with probably 50 cars parked, and many people sitting at picnic tables.

It was an outdoor restaurant set in front of a little shed, where the proprietor was serving sandwiches and hamburgers to American tourists. Smoke billowed out of a chimney, which was crooked, and looked like something out of a nursery rhyme. Nonetheless, trade was brisk, and families were enjoying one of the most spectacular views in the southern hemisphere, right across the valleys of the Andes, with the high peaks forming a jagged pattern against the sky.

Sophia parked in a space for three cars, and waited. It took 15 minutes, during which time she rattled around in the Jeep's toolbox until she found a screwdriver. And then, a car pulled in next to her. She watched a family of four get out, lock the door and walk over to the hamburger shed.

Swiftly she moved to the front of her vehicle, removed the number plate and then did the same to the newly arrived one. It took her five minutes to switch the plates. Then, she placed her bag on the ground behind the two cars and did the same again. But this time she could easily be seen, and she interspersed her task by occasionally groping around in her shoulder bag, hopefully diverting attention from her engineering exploits.

Then she climbed aboard the Garcia-Romano Jeep once more, and sped on up the highway, her transportation now replete with Chilean number plates, all ready for any border inspection.

It was another hour's drive and she kept going, principally on adrenaline, trying to cast aside the bullying thought in the centre of her brain which kept telling her she had just ended the life, in cold blood, of one of the most important aristocrats in this vast and beautiful country.

She had assassinated *El Patron,* cut down a member of the *Agencia*, and, not for the first time, started what might become a nationwide manhunt for the murderer of a very great man.

Chapter Twenty-Eight
The Dire Sequel to a Missed Email

Instinctively, she avoided the place, but that was where her
laptop lived, and she still kept it on Freddie's desk, as she
always had. Even on good days, the study made her sorrowful.
It was too stark a reminder of her brilliant, fox-hunting husband.

Sophia arrived at the frontier, understanding that now she would pass only through Chilean immigration. She used her English passport, the one in the name of Doris Farringdon. The immigration officer was simply conducting a car-to-car check on people travelling into the narrow, elongated Pacific State, which runs almost top to bottom of the South American continent.

The uniformed officer stopped at the driver's side of the Jeep, and politely asked to see her documents. She handed him her English passport with the photograph that matched her current appearance.

He gave it a cursory glance, had a look through the back windows of the vehicle and said cheerfully, "Okay Ma'am, you're fine." And Sophia accelerated away into the country she had designated for her getaway.

It was 4pm by now and she tackled the zigzagging roads through the mountains gamely, trying and failing to follow the buses which traversed these steep inclines and valleys; each one as if inspired by the spirit of Argentina's immortal Juan Fangio, a legend of the Grand Prix. They squealed around murderous bends and accelerated boldly along the straight parts, with a precipitous drop to their right.

Finally Chile's *Route 57* led them down to *Highway 5's* direct route into the city of Santiago.

Sophia slowed down and meandered into the centre of town, where she cited the brand new Savoy Hotel, a gleaming glass emporium of luxury with two uniformed doormen on duty outside beneath a lavish dark green and gold overhang.

Sophia drove right by and took the next left, where a neon sign announced the presence of multi-storey, public parking. She drove through the electric barrier, and set off down the slope to the lower level. There she found a corner around which she could see no cameras.

She turned off the engine and took out the keys, still with her driving gloves, which had left no fingerprint from the moment she drove out of Eduardo's ranch. And there, in the gloom of the underground garage, she changed out of her boots and jodhpurs into normal clothes.

With her light travelling bag slung over her shoulder she locked the car, crouched down in the narrow space in front, and removed the number plate.

Then she squeezed back to the rear of the vehicle and removed the back number plate. On her way out, she dumped both plates in a garbage bin, and, just before she exited, pulled Eduardo's key-ring out of her pocket, and slipped them, one by one into her hand. Then she dropped them all, plus her riding clothes, and high-boots, into another rubbish receptacle at the entrance. The actual key-ring, with its silver metal emblem showing a horse's head, she carefully placed in her wallet.

Sophia walked around to the hotel, checked in for one night and handed over a $600 cash deposit in pesos, and produced her Canadian passport under the name of Louise Cerdan, which last saw the light of day at the immigration check-point in Hong Kong.

She telephoned Air France directly, principally to enquire whether the flight to Paris tomorrow was full, and they politely informed her there were many seats, both in business-class and at the back of the plane.

Sophia elected to take yet another gamble on this trip and just show up at the airport tomorrow lunchtime, and buy herself a ticket. She put down the telephone, put the *Do Not Disturb* sign outside her door, double-locked it and took a long, luxurious, hot bath, using about a pint-and-a-half of bath oil.

When she finally emerged from the life-restoring soap suds, she found she was still trembling. But the deed had been done, she had carried out her pledge to her little sister, and the man who had driven Sasha to the most terrifying suicide, was now dead. Where he belonged. She had delivered all six of her step-father's clients safely to hell.

And so far as she knew there would not be one solitary footprint revealing her presence in South America—the way Uncle Rudy liked it.

It was 6.30pm now, and a quiet peace of mind eluded her. She escaped in a way which was highly conducive to all of her race in times of high stress. She

322

headed straight downstairs to the hotel bar and downed two large iced vodkas, inside 15 minutes, and felt a whole lot better for it.

Not wanting to set foot publicly in the streets of Santiago she retired to the grand and wildly pretentious hotel restaurant. She thought it unlikely the food could possibly attain the heights of the décor: the immaculate white table cloths, the great billowing velvet window treatments, and the deep pile carpet which looked as if it had been stitched privately for a couple of Maharajas. Her seat at the table was like an armchair. She had, however, been hasty in her judgment of the cuisine.

She stuck with steak, in tandem with the local wildlife, but only as a *carpaccio* starter. Then she ordered the grilled Chilean sea bass, with a lemon *beurre* sauce and parsley, on the basis that she was dining a few hundred yards from the world's largest ocean. It was probably the best fish she had ever eaten outside of Paris, and was an excellent *accoutrement* to a couple of glasses of the pricey *Bodegas Re, Velado, Casablanca 2012,* widely regarded as one of the princes of Chilean whites. Even Sophia, a naturalised Parisian devotee of Burgundy's Meursault, made a careful note that this wine could be purchased at *Berry, Brothers & Rudd* in London's toney St James's.

Unsurprisingly she slept soundly in her new headquarters, skipped breakfast, paid the balance of her bill, and took a taxi to the international airport, from whence she came.

Air France told her she could have an empty three-seat row, in cabin-class, which Sophia settled for, at around $3,000 cheaper than business class. But she had her unused Air France mileage card, which somehow gained her entry into the lounge. And there she stayed, reading magazines and sipping coffee, until flight AF 401, a twin-engine, long-range Boeing 777 came hurtling off the Santiago runway, bound for France's City of Light, more than 7,000-miles away.

Senor Eduardo had now been missing for approximately 30 hours, and in the household there was something approaching pandemonium. At first they had decided that the Senor had merely run off for the night with the English blond, Sally. But when morning came and there was still no Eduardo, and still no Sally, Andreas and Hugo, along with everyone else, began to feel extremely jumpy.

Eduardo missed his midday meeting with the ranch's senior cattle executive, and at 2pm Hugo called Mendoza Police HQ, and informed them Senor Eduardo Garcia-Romano was missing, and had not been seen for almost a day and a half.

"You mean the Big Man himself?" asked the quite senior, *Sarjento Primero.*

"Yessir, he's my uncle. And he's been gone since yesterday morning."

"Any idea where he was going?"

"Not really. He drove out with a couple of horses and a friend from England. They were going riding somewhere out on the property."

"Male or female?"

"Female. Young, early twenties. Very pretty. Blond."

"Jesus! You sure they didn't elope?"

"No. I'm not sure. But equally I'm not sure they haven't been murdered either. Nothing's come back, the horses are still missing and so is the horse-box."

"Well, if they'd run off somewhere, they would probably not have taken the horse-box. And I'm assuming you've tried his cell-phone."

"About a hundred times," said Hugo. "It's dead."

"You were right to call us, sir. I'll send a couple of cars out to the ranch, half a dozen officers. We have to start somewhere. Within the hour."

"Thank you, officer, we'll be here."

They arrived with blue lights flashing, shortly after 4pm, about seven minutes before Flight-401 thundered off the Santiago runway towards the peaks of the Andes, bearing the 'young, early twenties, very pretty and blond' horse-rider, the only person in this world who could possibly shed light on a mystery that would baffle the powerful Mendoza police force for many, many weeks to come.

The senior officer sat down with all members of the household, Andreas and Hugo, the housekeeper, two ranch managers, and the stud groom who had prepared and saddled the horses. It was obvious that none of them had the slightest clue what had happened to *El Patron*.

"This is such a hell of a big place to start a search," said the sergeant. "But I can tell from your concerned faces this is rapidly becoming a very serious matter, and we're going to need helicopters to search the Pampas, almost certainly with infrared beams. They might pick up heat on the ground, the kind of heat only a human, or big animal body, can reflect."

"The trouble is," said Hugo, "We don't even know which direction they headed. The damned driveway is so long you lose sight of the car completely, before it makes either a left or a right at the road. But I think you may assume, officer, that something really has happened. My uncle would have definitely taken his iPhone and made contact, whether he was going to elope or not."

"I am sure you are correct," said the officer, "Of course he would, your family has run this enormous operation for about 100 years. He would not have just left without a word, and not even turned up for his meeting with Raoul, the cattle executive. It's just totally out of character, and from now on we'll regard this as a hunt for a missing person, with foul play suspected."

Hugo assumed a loose command and asked, "Will you be driving out onto the prairie?"

"Oh yes," replied the policeman. "We'll take one car to the end of the drive, and turn to the left. The other will go right. It's just possible we might spot that darned great horse-box somewhere, and I shouldn't be surprised if a couple of the gauchos round up Mr Eduardo's missing horses. Meanwhile, I think we'll put out an alert—no point keeping this secret, the general public might turn out to be our best helpers."

The hours passed slowly on *Rancho Garcia-Romano*. By 10pm they had heard nothing. The police phoned in just before midnight to confirm they also had heard nothing. The late news on a local television station reported no sightings of the missing cattle tycoon.

Despite the story being very local at this stage, the report was on the wire services, including Reuters, but Europe was not much interested, while New York could not have cared less. The only publication to show any interest whatsoever was the *Argus*, in Brighton, England, where an alert night-editor was on duty at around 10.30pm. He noticed Reuters copy coming in with an account of a well-known, high-goal, Argentinian polo player going missing somewhere on the Pampas.

"Hey!" he called out. "Eduardo Garcia-Romano, one of the South Downs Club's best players has just gone missing on the Pampas. *Fuck me!* Looks like the Argentine police think he's been murdered. You don't often hear of one of those South American beef barons getting wiped out—Eduardo played *Number 3* for South Downs, and he was the tactical brains behind the team when they beat Cowdray Park, a few years ago—10-goal handicap, one of the best in the world."

The tabloid's editor who was often in the office late, looked up and commented, "Well, if he's really well-known down here on the south coast, we might as well be first with the news that he's come to harm. You sure he's that important?"

"Important! He's a fucking legend among polo fans. He used to stay at Laughton Towers during the season. A lot of people would be amazed if someone's murdered him. And if they have, this story's going national. We need to get this on Page One, Last Edition."

In the time-honoured manner of late newsrooms the world over, a traditional cry of urgency rang out … *Pictures of Eduardo Garcia-Romano! Fast—stills, posed and action—get them all, and lemme have a look.*

By Saturday morning, the *Argus* was on the streets, running a very sharp page one story. A head-and-shoulders picture of Lord Justice Fontridge, wearing his judicial wig, was set left into the headline:

South Downs high-goal polo ace missing on the Pampas
Eduardo Garcia-Romano
Believed Murdered

The story was set around a large picture of the Argentinian dismounting from his pony, and talking to Lord Fontridge. It pointed out the long friendship between the two, and detailed his many years of success with the Sussex club.

And it quoted a local businessman saying, "The death of Lord Fontridge was a huge blow to the South Downs. And this news about Eduardo is also very sad. He was probably the best player we ever had. I know it's all a very long way away, and we haven't seen Eduardo for a few years, but that does not lessen the loss we all feel."

The news gathered steam until it reached the local police headquarters in Lewes, where a young detective sergeant telephoned the chief constable of Sussex, Sir George Kenny. He told him, "Sorry to bother you so early, sir, but something a bit bloody weird has come up. Reuters are running a story about the probable murder of a guy called Eduardo Garcia-Romano.

"He's one of the best polo players ever to represent South Downs over at Alfriston. He's Argentinian, a high-goal handicap—and a really close friend of Lord Fontridge. He always stayed at Laughton Towers.

"A bit odd that, don't you think? Fontridge murdered, and now his polo mate possibly murdered, both within four or five weeks. I just thought you'd be interested."

"You got that right, old boy," said Sir George. "I'm very grateful for that. I will make a couple of calls on my own."

It was still only 7am, but he picked up his cell phone, and dialled the number of Detective Chief Superintendent, Charles Barton, in Mayfair.

"Yup, who's this?" muttered the Scotland Yard chief.

"It's me, George," he replied, and proceeded to tell Charles what he knew.

"Now, that is very interesting," said Charles. "Will you keep me posted? It sounds like the *Argus* is covering this fully, and I think we should find out everything we can about the missing man, especially if he and Fontridge were close friends. It is, after all, possible the same person murdered them both."

"Hold it, Charlie. We don't know if he's dead yet."

"No, but the Argentine cops think he might be, and when that happens the answer is almost always in the affirmative…Call me back."

****

Lady Fontridge was swiftly into her stride on this bright Saturday morning. South Downs were playing at home in Alfriston this afternoon, but she still thought it inappropriate that she should attend in person, with Freddie so recently deceased.

She was actually finding the big house very depressing these days, and although the dark-panelled rooms may have been wonderful for Freddie's grand-father, she was not absolutely certain they were ideal for her.

Increasingly, she was thinking of a major redecoration or, alternatively, a demolition and the building of a new modern house on the property. The 2,000-acre farming estate was still very profitable in good years, and anyway her friends were all in the area and she had always hoped to spend the rest of her life on the estate.

This morning, as she took a light breakfast in the only bright room in the house, the kitchen, she remembered she had not checked her emails for a couple of days. This was partly because she found so many of them acutely boring, but it was mainly because the Laughton study/library was one of the gloomiest rooms she'd ever been in—all wood panelling, lines of ancient books, many of them volumes about English law. The furniture had not been updated since Henry VIII was on the throne. Well, something like that.

Instinctively, she avoided the place, but that was where her laptop lived, and she still kept it on Freddie's desk, as she always had. Even on good days, the study made her feel sorrowful. It was too stark a reminder of her brilliant, fox-hunting husband.

Anyway, it had now been a couple of days and she walked along to retrieve the laptop. Back in the kitchen she opened the computer, entered her password and clicked on her *Inbox*. The messages were routinely tiresome, except for one—it had somehow whipped through cyberspace from the Pampas of Argentina, and she smiled at its final words, *Fondly, Eduardo.*

He had been such a very good family friend and both she and Freddie had loved having him stay at Laughton for the season. And what a player! In her mind she could still see him pounding across the Alfriston field, yelling orders to his three teammates, his mallet held high ready for the resounding whack which turned a polo ball into a howitzer. *Dearest Eduardo, she thought. And then she read the email.*

"Sally who?" she said out loud, to no one in particular. "Dr Sally Scott-Martin and who might she be, may I ask?"

Actually, there wasn't anyone to ask, but Jane Fontridge was faced with a very big question. Who the hell was this London University doctor, posing as a member of their family, and using that name to inveigle an invitation to the *Garcia-Romano Ranch?*

She racked her brains through a personal list of relations, both distant and close: cousins, uncles, aunts and all the accompanying nephews and nieces. There was not one single possibility of recognition. And no possibility of a mistake.

Jane Fontridge knew one thing for absolute certain. Dr Sally Scott-Martin was a liar, a fraud, and possibly dangerous. She picked up her address book and dialled *Rancho Garcia-Romano*. It was only 9.30am, 5.30am on the Pampas, but she thought this was sufficiently important to act now.

The number rang many times until an extremely sleepy voice answered, "Hello, this is the *Garcia-Romano Ranch*—Hugo speaking."

"Oh—Hugo, darling, this is Jane calling from England. I am sorry to wake you so early, but I had an email from Eduardo two days ago—and I've only just read it. I think it's important. Could you wake up and sit down? I need to talk to you."

"Aunt Jane!" he exclaimed. "Where have you been? We haven't seen you for so long, must be three years after Eduardo retired." And then he slipped into the modern idiom of speech, "Hey, what's up? It's really cool to hear from you."

Behind him, dawn was beginning to break, and suddenly the horror of the missing Eduardo came tumbling back into his mind, and he blurted out, "Jane! Something god-awful has happened. Eduardo has gone missing…"

"Jane Fontridge's heart missed about seven successive beats, and she just said, *"Oh my God!* What do you mean missing?"

"It happened on Thursday morning. My uncle went riding out on the property with an old friend from England. They took a couple of those big hunter 'chasers he loves and no one's seen either of them since. The police are on the case but they actually think something terrible has happened.

"And the chief detective down here thinks either one, or both of them have been murdered. Everyone finds it impossible to believe he would just vanish without even a phone call home. He never goes anywhere without his iPhone."

"Oh my God…!" said Jane again. "Oh my God…I cannot believe this."

Hugo could hear the lady he had called 'Auntie' for as long as he could remember weeping on the telephone, unable to continue the conversation. Hugo, who was now nineteen, and already slotting into a senior position in the family, was now an adult studying at the Law School of the University of Buenos Aires.

"Jane, Auntie Jane…Auntie Jane…please, you have to calm down—and I know you have called for something important. You would not have woken the household before dawn unless it was important…"

"Hugo," she said hesitatingly, "He wrote to me, he wrote to me on Thursday afternoon and he wanted to know about my niece, Dr Sally Scott-Martin…Hugo—I don't have a niece called Sally Scott-Martin. I've never even heard of her…Hugo, she's a fraud and she's a liar…and I'll never forgive myself for not alerting Eduardo."

"JESUS CHRIST!" he yelled. "I thought she was a very old friend. He just introduced her as Sally Scott-Martin from England…I assumed they'd known each other for years."

"Would you recognise her?" asked Sally.

"Well, I don't know, really, she was tall, blond and very pretty."

"Oh my God," said Jane for the 60th time in five minutes. "That damned roving eye of Eduardo's. He probably fell in love with her in the first 30 seconds—and after that cast care to the winds. But I should have read the email. I should have warned him. I just feel so badly about this…"

329

"Right now, I'm studying human rights," said Hugo. "And anyone has a human right not to read their fucking emails." He too had now cast care to the wind and was speaking to Jane as if she were one of his mates from University.

"I'm serious about that. Of course it's not your fault. But I do understand it will always be in your mind, that if you'd made this phone call a couple of days ago, there wouldn't be a police manhunt going on now out on the Pampas, with helicopters, and Christ knows what else."

"Hugo, I can only assure you this Sally Scott-Martin is a fraud. We don't have anyone even remotely connected with that name. Honestly, I do our Christmas card list every year, and I have never seen anything even close. We don't even have a Sally, never mind a Scott-Martin."

Hugo pondered this for a moment, like a lawyer standing before a courtroom witness box. "At the moment, the police have not yet dismissed the possibility that something may have happened to them both. Your message puts an entirely different light on it. This Sally woman is now a known conman, entering the family under false pretences, lying about her background and probably her name. I think the Mendoza police headquarters will now accept they are probably looking for a body, *and* searching for a murderer. That's very different. I intend to call them right now with an update."

Jane Fontridge said good-bye, and told Hugo she hoped with all her heart that Eduardo could be found alive, and this Dr Scott-Martin would be brought to justice.

"Let's stay in touch, Janie," he said, as he put down the phone.

****

Sophia glanced out of the cabin window, as the Boeing raced above the fields of France, the landing wheels coming down with a near silent 'clump', as it stretched out for the runway at Charles de Gaulle airport. As before, the flight was not busy and Sophia was out and through the airport with a quick wave of her Canadian passport at immigration. She picked up a cab and made it to her apartment in 40-minutes.

It was 7am, and her driving instinct was to go to bed and stay there for at least a day, but she had another instinct so much more powerful, and she decided to sleep only for five hours.

She awakened at midday, and packed a light suitcase, because the only thing she really wanted to do was find Charles Barton, whom she had not seen for more than a month. She could hardly believe what she was doing but she grabbed her suitcase, her raincoat and her shoulder bag and buzzed down for Gaston to find her a cab. It was only a short journey to the *Gare du Nord* train station, where she would jump on the next available *Eurostar* to London, which departed at 2pm.

She read and dozed all the way across France and through the Channel Tunnel. The *Eurostar* flashed through Kent, the Garden of England, before running into the sullen suburbs of South London. Sophia Morosova disembarked at St Pancras Station shortly after 5.30pm, without the slightest idea what she was going to do next.

She simplified her task by deciding she'd only come to London to see Charles, and since she could scarcely present herself at the desk of New Scotland Yard, like some detective sergeant, she'd risk going straight to South Audley Street. And there she'd throw herself upon the mercy of Lady Penelope Barton, Charles's acerbic, autocratic but essentially kind and generous mother.

It was, of course, the middle of the London rush hour. The journey would have taken about 20 minutes in the middle of the night, but right now it could take an hour-and-a-half.

As it was, the cockney driver swerved into South Audley Street in just over an hour. And Sophia, slightly dazed, and dizzy with travelling, attempted to pay him with Argentinian pesos, which caused him to say, poetically, "Come on now, darling! What's all this about? Pesos! What do you fink I am, a bloody bull-fighter?"

Sophia scrabbled about in the secret compartment, discarded about $5,000 worth of euros and finally located a few British pounds, which she gave him with a very generous tip. The young cockney thanked her, and with an East End flourish, drove off with his fist in the air, shouting, "Ole!"

She laughed, despite her tiredness, and with some trepidation, walked up to the door of Lady Penelope Barton and rang the bell, thinking to herself...*Gosh, she might not even remember me.*

The door opened and her Ladyship stood there with a beaming smile and exclaimed: "My goodness, Sophia! Where have you been? You do seem to make a habit of turning up at dinnertime. Let me get Hudson to take your case up to your room, and we'll go and have a drink."

To Sophia's surprise, she heard a so-familiar, adorable voice call from the drawing room, "Mum! Do you remember I'm dining out tonight?"

"Not any more, you're not," she retorted. "Trust me." And she led Sophia Morosova into the room where Charles was sitting in a deep armchair, reading a pile of documents. He looked up, and it was clear he could not believe his eyes. He stood, and opened his arms wide, as Sophia rushed across the carpet and flung her arms around his neck, as if she would never let him go.

"We'll be three for dinner, Hudson," called Lady Penelope.

"You can say that again," Charles mumbled, from somewhere next to Sophia's Parisian cut and combed, dark hair.

His mother made a discreet exit, leaving the Scotland Yard superintendent with 1,000 questions to ask the Russian-born girl, whom he loved.

"We've got, quite a lot to talk about I think," she said. "I've been so far away and I have missed you so much and Moscow was so bloody depressing and I'm finished with travelling, for at least a couple of months."

Charles asked her how long she could stay, and she replied simply, "About 1,000 years, if you like."

Charles Barton had not been this happy for as long as he could remember. Certainly not since that magical night at *Morton's*, which seemed a lifetime ago.

The three of them had a reunion drink together and there was so much to say, dinner was not served until after 8.30pm. They finished late, and each had a glass of 40-year-old port, and, generally speaking, behaved as if Charles and Sophia were about three steps away from Felix Mendelssohn's *Wedding March*.

Chapter Twenty-Nine
The Swoop of the Condors

The University had never even heard of a Dr Sally Scott-Martin.
There was no record of any Dr Sally Scott-Martin ever having
worked at the huge London College. In its 182-year history, not
even a student of that name.

Charles, however, had struggled valiantly to restrain a seven-ton Burmese bull-elephant, right in the middle of his mother's dining room. This particular Jumbo was private only to him, and it came in the form of a little bombshell of a memorandum, from the Big Boss of Scotland Yard, that very afternoon. And memorandums from the Big Boss were rare, the Commissioner believing that his senior detectives were world-class, and that every last one of them understood every last requirement of the tasks in front of them.

Also, tomorrow was Sunday, and while it was not entirely unusual for the Boss to turn up on the Sabbath, he must have an extremely urgent reason to do so, like a hot scolding from the PM or even the Monarch.

The memo read: *Charles, I am receiving intense pressure from our masters, to make immediate progress on the murder of Lord Fontridge. Is there any chance we can make an arrest and charge someone? If only to shut them all up. I know it's difficult when hard evidence is lacking, but I'm just afraid this thing could ride up to the PM. And we really don't need that. I'll be in the office for a couple of hours in the morning. Let's have a chat, and see if you can come up with something.*
Best,
Reggie

Sir Reginald Warren,
(Commissioner Scotland Yard)

No memorandum in Charles Barton's career had ever landed on his desk with so many complications. This was unimaginable. He accepted he was helplessly in love with this Parisian goddess. Never in his entire life had he met a girl of such allure, such fun and such droll intelligence.

The prospect of spending even an hour of his life with someone else was unthinkable. And now, it was a damned sight worse, because here was Reggie bloody Warren virtually ordering him to arrest her, and march her into some fucking courtroom, charged with murder.

The memorandum preyed on his mind or, phrased more realistically, tormented him. Here was Sophia, and despite this being his mother's house, he longed to sleep with her tonight, and every night for as long as he lived.

But that was out of the question. How could he? How could he finally cement this sublime relationship, knowing that tomorrow afternoon he might have to put her in handcuffs?

"Fuck it!" thought Charles. "They've got me every which way. I'll take Sophia to her room, but she must sleep alone tonight. And I'll have breakfast very early tomorrow and get to the office before she's out of bed. Mum'll look after her. But by Christ! The life of a policeman sure as hell has its drawbacks."

At this point, he cast aside the fact that, but for his occupation, he'd never have laid eyes on the fabulous Sophia Morosova in the first place.

****

The office of Sir Reginald Warren, situated in the penthouse area of New Scotland Yard, represented sacred ground to the hundreds of policemen who swarmed all over London every day. Most of them had never even seen it, through an open door. Most of them never would. And now Detective Chief Superintendent Charles Barton walked into the police kingdom's Holy of Holies.

"Morning Charles," said Sir Reginald, who was already seated behind his desk, wearing a frown that very nearly dug a trench across his forehead. "I do not wish to put too fine a point on it," he said, "But this Fontridge death is heading towards a right bugger's muddle. It's been several weeks now, and I can just tell the media are getting slightly agitated about our silence.

"One of those bloody tabloids came up with a *Why, oh why? Is Scotland Yard covering this up?* The very next evening, last Friday, I received a note from the

Attorney General, informing me that our political masters are demanding action and I must respond."

Charles nodded, he hoped, sagely. But he knew the game was up. He had to level with Sir Reginald, at least part of the way, without actually informing the old tyrant that he happened to be in love with the murderess.

"Sir," he said, "This is a very difficult case…"

"I know that, old boy," grunted Sir Reginald, "Otherwise we wouldn't be bloody well sitting here, would we?"

Charles shot him another sage-like nod, and then began, "I do have a suspect, sir. In my view, the only possible suspect. George Kenny down in Lewes and his team have interviewed every single person who attended *Rigoletto* the night his Lordship died.

"There's only one person who can't really explain herself, and I've even been to Paris to see her. Unfortunately, she's the niece of a senior Russian cultural attaché at the Embassy, here in London. And he's a very powerful and secretive presence. But she could have done it at the first interval of the opera, and the man sitting behind the four complimentary Russian Embassy seats actually wonders if she ever came back after the interval.

"Someone came back, but it might not have been her. The guy behind was a jeweller from Brighton, light of step, and a bit of an expert on the sapphire, butterfly earrings she wore—at least she wore them until that first interview. But when she came back, she was wearing pearl studs in her ears. Both I, and the light-stepping Brighton jeweller, consider it might have been a different person."

"And you are suggesting that's enough to arrest her and charge her with murder?"

"Of course not, sir, but there is more…"

"There'd better be," added Sir Reginald.

"Sir, she had a motive and a very powerful one. She and her little sister, as teenagers, had been beaten, raped, and ravaged by Fontridge, who, as you know is a Law Lord, Appeals Court, a member of her Majesty's Privy Council, and one of the most respected lawyers in the country."

"Holy shit," said the Commissioner inelegantly. And he asked Charles Barton, "Can you prove this?"

"I can," said Charles. "Although that still does not guarantee her guilt. She may have had the opportunity, the right time, the right place and one hell of a motive. But the cultural attaché of the Russian Embassy will stand alongside her in any courtroom, and swear to God he took his niece to the opera, where she watched the entire performance, and then accompanied him, in an embassy car, back to London. The jury would have to do a lot of thinking."

"The jury are not the only people who would have to do a lot of thinking," said Sir Reginald. "If some bloody barrister steps up to defend her, can we really permit him to savage the reputation of an English Law Lord, right in front of the entire country, as it would most certainly be?"

"I was pretty sure you'd say that, which is why I've been a bit reluctant to make a forward move on the case, and the suspect does live in a foreign country. She speaks perfect English, but I don't think she would ever admit to the murder. She'll plead *not guilty,* and the fucking case will go on for about a month, allowing tabloid editors in London to go berserk."

Sir Reginald then wanted to know why a Detective Chief Superintendent had taken so long to alert the upper echelons of England's judicial system of the complications of the case?

"Because I knew everything, but the motive," replied Charles. "And without that motive there's not a prayer of a murder charge. The motive, however, as you well know, changes everything...but brings with it a ton of problems, which, in my judgment may prove insurmountable. Anyway, I only just discovered it."

"Yes, Charles, I understand what you say. But I have to tell the AG something. I think I'll release a public statement, which says, *'Scotland Yard expects to make an arrest in the case of the murder of Lord Fontridge, sometime in the next few days.'*

"Although, quite frankly, I think we need advice on this, and the first step may be to talk to a senior barrister about the ethics of destroying the reputation of a deceased high court judge."

"I'll do that right away," said Charles, "And I'll keep you posted, maybe even late this afternoon."

"Good boy, Charles," said Sir Reginald, but before Charles reached his office door, the Commissioner asked him, "Tell me one thing, did you actually ask this lady whether she plunged a dagger into the heart of Lord Fontridge, and then shoved him into the Glyndebourne Lake?"

"Not yet, sir, but I will, if I have to."

"Good luck with that," chuckled the Big Boss.

Charles took the elevator down to his office, pondering to himself who should be briefed to defend Sophia. And he decided to put in a call to an old and trusted friend of his father's, Sir Roger Beaumont QC, one of the best trial-lawyers in London, whose dazzling successes had earned him an impressive, penthouse apartment in Lowndes Street, one of the finest addresses in the Belgrave Square area of London.

Charles had his private number, and the Titan of the

Old Bailey's Central Criminal Courtroom, told him to come over right away, stay for lunch, if he wanted.

And within 20 minutes the Chief Superintendent was ensconced with the tall, white-haired 60'ish barrister, whom he had known for most of his life. Lady Beaumont insisted he stay for lunch, while young Charles outlined the case against Sophia Morosova.

He started by suggesting that the truly shocking motive involved, was a double-edged sword, because, at once it pointed the finger of guilt sternly at the defendant, but at the same time it provided the most drastic, extenuating circumstances, which would almost certainly cause the jury to throw the case out.

"Charles," replied Sir Roger, "The motive is the bedrock of the case. If you want me to fight for the life of this young lady, you give me no alternative but to drag Fontridge's name through the deepest mud, and I have to tell you, I will not have the slightest hesitation.

"But the motive is also a grave problem—if I point it out at the very start of the trial, everyone will think she must have killed Fontridge. But I have to bring it up, because otherwise the jury may convict her, even without the knowledge of why she committed the murder."

And Sir Roger stood up, paced around the room and said, "The truth of this matter is, we are about to destroy the reputation of one of the senior Appeal Court Lords in the country, a member of Her Majesty's Privy Council—and that is inevitable.

"If what you have told me is even half true, the entire situation is an absolute disgrace. But much more important, the jury, which will probably be 50% female, will dismiss the case of the prosecution without a second thought. I should confirm, that when I have finished with this story, about these two precious young girls being sexually ravaged in their own home by this maniac, Fontridge, I will have half of the jury in tears.

337

"I might even have the whole of the jury in tears…I could actually have the entire courtroom in tears…And if you think for one split-second I'll lose my *not guilty* plea, then you don't know me very well."

"Of course," said Charles. "But we both know that's not the issue here, is it? Because when push comes to shove, we are talking about the reputation of English justice, and the men who administer it. That was Fontridge.

"And while it's not my decision, I cannot believe the rulers of this country could possibly allow a Law Lord to be hung out to dry in the tabloids, as some kind of a bloody fiend. English justice would take a long time to recover from that."

"I know, I know," said Sir Roger. "But if you appoint me to defend her against a charge of murder, which carries a compulsory life sentence, that's what you'll get. I will not allow her to go to jail for more than 20 years. And I'll carry the jury with me."

Charles gave one of his sage-like nods and replied, "Well, I guess that clears that up." And he asked Sir Roger to treat the whole matter in the strictest confidence, for the moment, because there were many people who must be apprised of such a tenuous situation, and not just the Attorney General, who was already involved.

Sir Roger replied, "So far as I'm concerned, Charles, this conversation never happened, but keep me posted. And you might inform this former victim of terrible depravity, that I indeed would be honoured to act as her Knight in Shining Armor …"

And with that, the most theatrical of all London's QCs, spun on his heel, and said, with high drama, *"Ladies and Gentlemen of the jury, you are good and true members of British society, and I would like to remind you … it is not always wrong to follow your heart in a court of law … and in this instance I would beg you to do so, and in the name of God … to set her free."*

Charles almost stood up and applauded. But he kept a tight rein on his own feelings in this heart-breaking saga, which would almost certainly affect him more than anyone. And he faced Lady Beaumont's roast beef with suitable grace, although he felt like a prisoner, before the hangman.

****

338

It was 10.30am on the Pampas, and one of the herds was wandering slowly eastward with a couple of extra visitors—two big English hunter 'chasers, saddled up and meandering through the thick grassland.

It did not take one of the gauchos long to round them up, take ahold of the reins, and lead them slowly back to the ranch, where the stud-groom and the police awaited them.

The groom confirmed to the policeman that these were indeed the two horses he had saddled up on Thursday morning, for Senor Eduardo to take out, with his English guest.

The Mendoza sergeant, now almost permanently on duty at the main house, told Hugo, in his opinion, this confirmed that something awful had indeed happened to *El Patron*. And it was now necessary to intensify the search. If the horses had been caught somewhere out near the lake, it was likely there were one, perhaps two dead bodies lying somewhere close by, in the long grass. Half-an-hour later the sergeant's cell-phone shuddered again, as another of the gauchos called in, to report they had found the horse-box, in thick undergrowth, but without the Jeep.

This signified two things, 1) They needed a new vehicle out there to tow the horse-box back, and 2) It was now almost certain this mysterious Sally Scott-Martin had killed Eduardo, and made her escape in his personal Jeep.

The Mendoza police put out an immediate alert for all stations to look out for the dark, green 4-wheel drive, and, of course, he communicated the number plates to everyone. As for Sally Scott-Martin, if she'd escaped some time on Thursday lunchtime, that gave her three days to disappear, to anywhere in the world.

The Argentine police had sealed off her exit from the national airports, but they had not yet communicated the flight of the female desperado, to the Chilean police. It was regarded as impossible that this English blond could possibly have escaped through one of the most rugged mountain ranges in the world, to another country.

The truth was, no one had even considered she'd unhooked the horsebox, and somehow made a bolt for the mountain passes in her host's wagon. The discovery of the lone horse-box, parked with its ramps down in the undergrowth, changed all this. And the Argentine sergeant thought, privately, this would probably end up with Interpol, since Dr Sally could so easily have come through Santiago International, without anyone noticing.

The Mendoza station requested the *Gendarmerie* of Chile to conduct a searching scan of all airport closed-circuit televisions and all outgoing passenger tickets on all airlines, on the off-chance that the English doctor had made it to another South American country. There were only a few international flights from Santiago, and even fewer in the evening, when she must have arrived, after the 350-mile journey across the mountains.

The Mendoza police force had done everything they could to close a gigantic net around the fleeing murderess—for they now considered it definite. But they were far from locating her; no nearer than they were on Friday morning, when Hugo first called them.

They knew roughly what she looked like. They hoped she wasn't travelling under a false name, and they knew that if indeed she was Dr Sally Scott-Martin, she was a thunderous liar, a cheat, a con-artist, and now, a killer.

A check with London University took about four hours to complete. And by late that afternoon it was confirmed that like Jane Fontridge, the University had never even heard of a Dr Sally Scott-Martin. There was no record of any Dr Sally Scott-Martin ever having worked at the huge London College.

There had never even been a student by that name in the 182-year history of the University. They did, however, have a Spanish-speaking student on hand, who translated, in minute detail, to a slightly baffled Argentinian detective. And now everyone knew the English doctor was a fraud from head to toe, and she appeared to have travelled out to the *Rancho Garcia-Romano*, with the specific aim of murdering the owner.

And that's how it would stay for many weeks, because Sally did not exist, and never would. Right now she was having a quiet lunch with her future mother-in-law at Morton's, in Berkeley Square, preparing to meet Charles Barton back at the house in a couple of hours. Morton's was a quiet, sedate place on this Sunday, which was a sight more than could be said for the *Garcia-Romano Pampas,* where you could hardly hear yourself think, above the four police helicopters, battering their way over the grassland.

Air crew were searching through binoculars, the infrared beams were lasering down, trying to pick up a heat-print from these desolate areas. It was a hugely expensive business and they came into land around 5pm, having been aloft, on and off for almost five hours.

The sun was beginning to decline over the Andes' peaks, when the gauchos spotted a clue the police had missed: four giant condors, the world's largest vultures, with their 10-foot wing spans, were circling, four of them right over the waterfront to the lake.

In the normal way, this would have raised an alert among the Argentinian cowboys, because it may have signalled a steer or a regular cow, had gone down, perhaps with a broken leg, or some injury which would not permit it to rise again.

The gauchos normally raced to put it down, and then get transport to haul the carcass in, to be frozen and transported direct to the butcher, or a pet food factory.

Either way, they did not want a big carcass on the Pampas, being torn to pieces by the vultures from the Andes, with all the attendant insect attacks that would ensue. It was usually a clean-up operation, but not today. Because the cowboy labour force knew to a man that Mr Eduardo was missing. And, if he was lying out there somewhere, it was their duty, to find him, no matter what.

The horsemen reached the lakeside area, and a couple of them let loose with a few gunshots at the high, overhead condors, to frighten them off. Then they formed a line and walked back and forth across the area, until they were almost at the waterside.

And right there was *El Patron*, lying dead with a large bullet-hole in his left temple, and his white, Spanish shirt, scarlet on the left side with his own blood.

They telephoned their report to the policemen at the Ranch House, and within 10-minutes could hear the perfectly unnecessary wail of the police cars, as they hammered their way across the prairie, blue lights flashing and dust flying. They reached the spot where the gauchos were gathered, produced a plastic body bag, and carefully lifted *El Patron* into position for his last ride over these sprawling acres. An ambulance was on its way.

****

Before returning home to meet Sophia, Charles drove back to his office and arranged for a private Monday morning meeting at the office of the Attorney General. This was a highly significant step. Her Majesty's AG for England and Wales, David Parkinson, was the chief legal advisor to both the government, and the Crown. The office has been in existence since the 13th century, and was formed to protect the King's interests in court.

It was unusual in the extreme, for even the most senior of policemen to call in the Attorney General, no matter what the circumstances. This is a high-ranking official who answers only to the Prime Minister. The AG superintends the

341

government's Crown Prosecution Service, the Serious Fraud Office, the government's Legal Department. He advises ministers on all legal matters, he answers questions personally in Parliament, and recommends certain cases of law to the Courts of Appeal.

The Office of the Attorney General has kept an unrelenting grip on power for 800 years. It has always provided the steady voice of good sense, its occupants carefully chosen to steady down over-excited members of Parliament. As recent as 2016, when the Cabinet began meeting to untangle the grotesque muddle of Britain's membership of the European Union, the Attorney General was right there in prime position, to advise Ministers precisely what they could, and could not do.

A request for a private meeting from a high executive of Scotland Yard was not quite irregular, but it was close, and David Parkinson understood immediately this was a matter which would probably demand his attention. He knew Charles Barton, and did not believe for one split second the Chief Superintendent would be wasting anyone's time.

Charles finally left his office and returned to South Audley Street to face Sophia, and, probably, the music. For surely now, he must finally tell her that arrest may be imminent, probably in a matter of days. Although, given the incendiary nature of the consequences, nothing was certain.

He finally arrived late afternoon, and he found Sophia reading, alone, in the drawing room. Hudson had brought her some tea, and her Ladyship had retreated upstairs to take a nap. After a long embrace on the sofa, Charles told her, softly, that unfortunately, high ranking members of the British judicial system now wanted to know who had murdered Lord Fontridge, and he, Charles, was obliged to make an arrest of the prime suspect, whoever it might be.

"And I suppose that might be me," she replied. "Will you visit me in my cell?"

The Scotland Yard chief refrained from telling her that he would, if necessary, visit her on the Seventh Ring of Hell, but he did say, with unmistakable concern, that he had a few questions to ask her, and they were extremely important.

"Now?" said Sophia.

"Afraid so," he replied. "And the first one is, if you are charged with murder, what will you plead?"

"Not guilty."

"And what if the prosecution says, you were at the scene of the crime, exactly the right place, exactly the right time, with obvious opportunity. And they have a witness sitting behind you in the opera house who believes you did not return after the first interval, when both you and Fontridge left the theatre."

"I shall answer by saying I was with my uncle, a highly-placed diplomat in the Russian Foreign Service, who will testify that I watched the whole of the opera with him, had a picnic supper during the interval, left with him, and drove back to the London Embassy with him. Two other Russian attaches were also at the opera, and both will testify to the veracity of that statement."

Charles smiled. He understood fully this was a prosecutor's nightmare. No witnesses to the crime, no one who even saw Sophia outside the opera house. There was a slightly unreliable witness to tell the jury about the small sapphire, butterfly earrings (*Jesus Christ!*).

It was a murder without witnesses, and it would be a charge on the flimsiest grounds. The difference was The Motive, because this would represent a savage blow to the defence. It nailed Sophia, sister of the tragic Sasha, as the plain and obvious perpetrator of the crime. She was the one person with a true and proper reason to stab Lord Fontridge to death.

However, Charles also knew The Motive was the one issue which could prevent the entire prosecution, because of the catastrophic damage to the public image of an English Law Lord, and, indeed, the entire English judicial system. This would be especially true when he produced the damning photograph of the stark naked, sexual deviant, Fontridge. He had kept it secret until now, but not for much longer.

He turned again to look at the lovely Miss Morosova and asked her, "Are there any circumstances, in which you, the accused, would consider pleading guilty, admitting everything and, in a sense, throwing yourself upon the mercy of the Lord Justice of the court?"

"I've had quite enough of English judges for one lifetime," she answered, "I will never plead anything but *not guilty*. And if anyone is in any doubt, I deny knowing Lord Fontridge, and I deny ever having heard of Lord Fontridge before the night that he died. I am not guilty. I admit nothing."

Charles nodded as sagely as he possibly could, but he wore a slight smile. Sir Roger, in his view, would batter the prosecution to death on the plain issue of whether Sophia Morosova had ever gone anywhere near the lake, or the dagger, or his Lordship. On the wider issue of The Motive, it was beyond

Charles's reasoning that the great legal powers of this government could possibly allow this spectacular scandal of a case ever to enter a courtroom.

He turned again to Sophia and he said, "I have a meeting tomorrow morning, which may have an important bearing on your future. I expect there to be another meeting in the afternoon, which may decide it. Just hold your nerve, darling Sophia, and do not leave the house under any circumstances. I won't be far away."

Chapter Thirty
The Eyes of the Iron Duke

The Prime Minister: *"My God ... cartoons of the Royal great-grandchildren*
hiding under the sofa, because the Queen
was holding a Privy Council meeting along the corridor—
with a wandering rapist from the Queen's Bench."

At 10am on that Monday morning, Detective Chief Superintendent Barton presented himself at the office of the Attorney General, in London's Petty France, right opposite the Ministry of Justice. The door was slightly ajar, and David Parkinson called, "Come in Charles, and upset my entire day, which I am quite certain you plan to do!"

Charles thanked him for seeing him and sat down to outline the case, which was being considered against the Russian-born niece of one of Vladimir Putin's most trusted diplomats. David sat quietly, listening to the oblique circumstances of the Glyndebourne murder, the lack of witnesses, uppermost in this former barrister's mind.

Charles proceeded to The Motive, and he recounted the story of the two young girls, both pupils at one of the most expensive boarding schools in England. He told David how they had been sold into under-age prostitution, as part of a vice-ring in West London. He told them how sexually deviant men had hurt and raped the two girls.

And he told how one of them was so agonised by her experience, she threw herself off the top of a tower block in Central London, to her death. David Parkinson's lightning-fast mind was already on top of this. "Are you about to tell me that one of the men, who beat and raped these two young girls, was Lord Justice Fontridge?"

"I am."

"*Christ Almighty!*" said the Attorney General.

Charles continued, "If this goes into a courtroom, I shudder to think of the damage, probably worldwide, it will do to the reputation of English law. I don't know how we can admit to having a sexually deviant Law Lord, in the highest court in the land, standing in judgment of other people."

What Charles had not told David Parkinson was that outside the door, waiting on a bench, was none other than Sir Roger Beaumont QC, preparing to enter the room and present the gist of his defence argument, in what Charles knew would be glorious Technicolor.

Back in the room Charles confirmed that if Sophia stood before a judge, essentially fighting for her freedom, a top lawyer would have no alternative but to slam the reputation of Lord Fontridge to hell and back.

The Attorney General then asked, "Charles, do you have any idea yet, who may defend the case?"

"I do, sir. The accused will be represented by Sir Roger Beaumont QC."

"*Christ Almighty!*" David Parkinson repeated, "This bloody thing is getting worse by the minute."

"I took the liberty of inviting Sir Roger to be available, should you wish to hear first-hand his intentions, should this go to a courtroom."

"Yes, I was certain you would not be wasting my time, and I absolutely agree that I should hear first-hand the strategy of the defence."

Charles walked to the office door, opened it and asked Sir Roger Beaumont to enter the private office of the Attorney General. The two men were old friends, and shook hands amiably. "I'll let Charles steer the conversation," said the AG. "I'll just sit here and continue shuddering, for as long as it takes!"

Charles interjected, with, "Sir Roger, straight question. If you find yourself defending Miss Morosova, on a charge of murder, do you intend to spare the reputations of any of the men who drove Sasha Morosova to suicide, and sent Sophia, and her mother, to the brink of insanity?"

"I do not intend to damage the reputation of Lord Justice Fontridge," he replied. "I intend to crucify him on the cross of decency. I will hit that jury with every last possible account of his wickedness, his brutality, his debauchery, and the disgusting moral corruption to which these two innocent and perfectly charming young girls had forced upon them. Fontridge is a terrible man, and deserves to hang, but I will not pursue my personal views on such a man. At least not here."

"Well I suppose that clarifies matters," said the AG. "If we go into a courtroom with this case, Britain's justice system is entering the valley of death."

At this point, Charles opened his slim briefcase and produced the photograph he had hijacked from the TOR, that secret internet system of deception, illegality, crime and perversion.

Charles solemnly handed over to the Attorney General the photograph of a naked man, whipping a cowering young girl—whipping her with a leather strap. As the Scotland Yard Supergeeks had observed, when they finally pulled the photograph from the depraved depths of TOR, "This is one of the most disgusting photographs we've ever seen."

AG Parkinson's eyebrows shot almost into his hairline. "Charles, are you telling me this is a photograph of Lord Justice Fontridge?"

"I am, sir."

"Could you prove it in court?"

"I most certainly could." And both men could see the perfectly wicked smile on the face of Sir Roger.

"Charles," said the AG, "This, I am afraid, is a bit too big for us. Plainly the case should be considered by both my boss, the Prime Minister, and by the Lord Chancellor himself. In the end it will come down to a simple decision of whether or not to prosecute, and we can't have Roger salivating through the next few days, in anticipation!"

"Certainly not," said Charles, drolly. And the Attorney General said, "Let me try and organise this now, while you are both here … just one thing, I'm not taking two Scotland Yard men into a private meeting with the PM. I'd prefer you, but what about Sir Reggie?"

"He said not, sir, but anyway he's away 'til Thursday."

The AG picked up a telephone and said crisply, "Get me the Prime Minister's office." Within four minutes he was saying, "Good morning, Prime Minister, David here. I need to see you today, on what I believe is a matter of extreme urgency. I intend to ask the Lord Chancellor and include a representative from Scotland Yard. I cannot see the matter taking less than an hour but I thought you might prefer we meet in Downing Street, at around 4pm…

"…Okay, sir. Assume that will be fine. We'll be there at 3pm and, for your own peace of mind, I am sure we can solve it without very much argument from anybody…

"Thanks very much, sir…See you then."

Very few prime ministers ever postpone a meeting requested by their Attorney General.

****

At 2.55pm, the gleaming black government Jaguar, bearing the Attorney General of England, swept through the tall, black, iron gates of Downing Street, and came to a halt outside Number 10, the historic 100-roomed residence of the Prime Minister of Great Britain.

From behind the Jaguar's dark-tinted windows stepped David Parkinson, and, on the other side, Charles Barton. Almost directly behind them was the government Jaguar of the Lord Chancellor of Great Britain, the highest-ranking minister in the land, a man who actually outranks the serving Prime Minister. The black door of Number 10 was immediately swung open, and the three men were led inside.

The appearance of the Lord Chancellor, Sir Randolph Carr, was a significant event. The holder of this Great Office of State is personally appointed by the Sovereign on the advice of the PM. He is a member of the Cabinet. By royal decree, he is responsible for the efficient functioning and independence of the British Courts of Law.

His arrival at Number 10 heralded a meeting at the highest possible level, probably involving some intricate, impenetrable issue of law, upon which the government must act. Or, perhaps even to untie some complex state secret, which would never be revealed beyond the famous black door.

Sir Randolph was a cautious man. Which was understandable, given his Office dates back to the Norman Conquest, 1066, and has been occupied by such historical giants, as the sainted Sir Thomas Moore, who was executed for failing to accept the annulment of King Henry VIII's first marriage.

All Lord Chancellors are normally seen in official dress, a black silk, velvet cutaway tailcoat, or the black silk Damask robe of state, with its gold trimming. Today, however, Sir Randolph wore a dark grey suit and a very worried expression. He followed the other two in, and walked on, to a small conference room, where the Prime Minister was waiting.

The chairs were arranged beneath historic portraits of four of the most powerful men ever to hold the office, William Pitt the Younger, the Duke of Wellington, the second Lord Melbourne, and Sir Winston himself. Each of them, down all the years, was still delivering an unsmiling, uncompromising, stare.

An armed police guard was on duty in the corridor outside. The PM welcomed all three of his guests warmly, and shook hands cheerfully with

Charles Barton, whom he had not previously met. They sat down, and David Parkinson politely asked the Scotland Yard man if he thought it appropriate that he, the AG, should outline the appalling truths of this particular saga.

Charles replied, "Absolutely, sir."

And the Attorney General proceeded to inform the leader of Her Majesty's government of the possible murder charge against Miss Morosova, and the unthinkable consequences, which would undoubtedly follow, if Sir Roger Beaumont was let loose on an Old Bailey jury.

The Prime Minister nodded, and said quietly, "Yes, I do see that. And our wonderful, loyal media would take the greatest delight in hanging us all out to dry, in front of the whole world."

The Lord Chancellor added, "Can you just imagine what would happen when the tabloids got ahold of this—the cartoonists, *Private Eye* and all the rest of the political reptiles that have such freedom in our nation?"

The Prime Minister shook his head, "My God! I could see cartoons of the Royal great-grandchildren hiding under various sofas, because the Queen was holding a Privy Council meeting in a room along the corridor—perhaps in the company of a wandering rapist from the Queen's Bench."

The Prime Minister had a colourful turn of phrase, which, had, on occasion, reduced the Leader of the Opposition in Parliament to a stumbling wreck. But now he had only a small audience, and while Charles and the AG were trying to suppress laughter, the Lord Chancellor, with all the crushing burdens of his Great Office, found no humour in any of it.

He said, with chilling authority, "This, gentlemen, is about as nasty, salacious and damaging a situation I have ever seen scheduled for an English courtroom."

"It's not actually scheduled yet, sir," said the AG. "But I have reason to think it might be, if we do not arrive at …er… a more sensible solution in this room today."

"May I assume," asked the Prime Minister, "That the account just given to me by David is more or less beyond reproach? I mean, we do know what an unleashed Sir Roger Beaumont will say? And we do know the Defence is in possession of this ghastly photograph, which, if it ever became public could bring down the entire edifice of the British Appeal Court system.

"Can you imagine! Some editor printing that picture, slightly doctored of course, alongside another picture of Lord Justice Fontridge, sitting in his judicial robes in the judge's chair of the Central Criminal Court."

"All too well," said the Lord Chancellor, "And while I cannot know the rights and wrongs of the case, it's a pretty good bet Roger Beaumont will get her off. He'll go on and on about the cruelty, the disgraceful conduct towards underage children, about the heartbreak, the suicide, the shattering effect on the mother, who ended up in a Moscow mental home. My God! Beaumont will have the whole bloody place in tears!"

"His words precisely", said Charles Barton. And the cold silence of dread hung over the table, for just a few seconds before the Prime Minister spoke.

"Okay, my keepers of the British justice system, what are our critical options?" It was a tried and tested question from this particular Prime Minister, himself a former lawyer. He always asked it, in matters financial, military and political. *What are our options?*

"Oh, that's fairly simple," said David Parkinson. "We march this girl into court and Roger Beaumont will persuade the jury to let her walk free, having in the process demolished the word decency in the annals of justice here in England. The other option is, of course, not to charge her."

"But how do we do that?" said the PM, "If we are being pressed by other forces, demanding justice for Lord Fontridge?"

"The matter is entirely up to the Crown Prosecution Service," said the Lord Chancellor. "They have much discretion. Much freedom to do as they see fit. However, David Parkinson is the Head of that department, and I may as well tell you that if he says no, that's no. And the case will not proceed.

"I'm not suggesting it's some kind of dictatorship, because it's not. But the ancient office of Lord Chancellor carries enormous weight. I have never before just stamped all over a prosecution before it gets off the ground. But I intend to let it be known tomorrow that I support our Attorney General very fully in this matter. You may assume our words will be heeded. And anyway I doubt that anyone would disagree."

"Without putting you on the spot, Randolph, could you now tell me formally that your personal decision, made here in this room in the spiritual presence of Wellington and Churchill, is final … of course, you may tell me to mind my own business, if you are so inclined?"

"I shall do no such thing, Prime Minister," he replied. "Of course, my decision is absolute. It is to spare the legal system I love, from this gross and shocking situation. David will be that much stronger with me onside.

"Remember, it is entirely due to the carelessness, stupidity and wantonness of Lord Justice bloody Fontridge. The man must have been out of his mind to be involved in this disgusting behaviour, when there was always a chance that the truth would come out, as it invariably does."

"Well, I'm with you entirely on that one," said the Prime Minister. "But, it is essential that the four of us have a united front which will never go beyond this room. And in that I must also formally ask David and the Detective Chief Superintendent."

"You may assume the Lord Chancellor and I stand resolutely together, with the Prime Minister," said the AG, "I would, however, like to issue a quiet warning that we may run into some flak from the media, demanding an arrest or at least a culprit for the Fontridge murder.

"It did, after all, receive more coverage in this country than any time since 1963, when Great Britain's War Minister was discovered sharing a girlfriend with a Russian naval attaché. Brought down the government, as I recall."

"Yes, I suppose that is true," said the Prime Minister, "But I would far rather have the media ranting on about no charge in the Fontridge murder, than ranting on about sex-criminal judges at the heart of the British legal system."

"I was merely pointing up disagreeable aspects of our actions," replied David Parkinson. "And I agree entirely with the Prime Minister's view. It is absolutely obvious to me that Sir Randolph and I stop this damned prosecution in its tracks. But we should bear in mind that the Chief Superintendent in this room is mainly concerned with criminal behaviour, and confirm that he too is on our side."

Charles Barton said quietly, "Of course I am. In my view it would put the whole legal system into a totally impossible position, defending behaviour, which was at best outrageous, and at worst massively stupid. I and my superiors would hate this prosecution to proceed."

"Gentlemen," said the Lord Chancellor, "This projected murder trial is essentially no damn good to anyone. Beaumont will win the case, no doubt in my mind. And running concurrently throughout the trial, will be the now public perception that not even our treasured traditions of unbiased justice is sacrosanct, protected from low and reprehensible conduct among its leaders.

"I have to say I believe we are taking correct action on behalf of this nation. I think even my illustrious predecessor, Sir Thomas Moore, would avow, that in the eyes of God we are correct, and that right is on our side. We cannot undermine a system of justice that has stood the test of time for 1,000-years.

"You may assume there will be no prosecution in this case, and I believe that in this instance we should stand and shake hands with one another."

The Prime Minister started off by looking hugely relieved, and he walked with them to the famous front door, before wishing them all good-bye for the moment, with a cheerful quip of, "Well done, gentlemen. Old Number 10 has done it again!" Even England's Lord High Chancellor chuckled. Although it was no laughing matter.

****

Lady Penelope Barton had a quiet breakfast in her room alone on Monday morning, and did not emerge until a little after 10am when she found Sophia curled up in a large, heavily-cushioned chair, sobbing as if she would never stop.

"I've been such a nuisance," she said, trying to wipe her eyes, "I've been such a trouble to Charles, and I never meant to be, and I love him so much. And now I'm afraid they might put me in jail…I'm so sorry…but I don't suppose you know my story."

Lady Penelope reacted with the automatic, unbending loyalty of the clans of Scotland's highlands. Her father was a duke, and so were her next four grand-fathers in line. Like most of her often dogged countrymen, she stood by her beliefs. Actually she stood guard over her beliefs. And when a threat occurred to one of her own, she behaved like a tigress defending her young.

And now, she took Sophia's hand and said, "Don't worry, my dear…I do know your story, and you have my word the Barton family will not desert you. I know Charles appears to be completely gormless at times…but he's a very good boy, and I've been told he's a very good policeman.

"He's told me more than once, he will protect you and save you, and nothing will happen to you without his permission. He's such a curious dichotomy, in some ways so silly, in others so unexpectedly tough."

Lady Penelope reminded her future daughter-in-law *(she hoped)* that there were people in Scotland whose loyalty to the ruling Stuarts had lasted for almost

300-years. And they still believed one of them should be on the throne of England!

"That's Charles," she said. "I mean, we named him after Bonnie Prince Charlie. He has loyalty in his DNA. He will look after you, my dear, and I am able to promise you that."

Sophia cheered up. She wiped away her tears and said, "With all the trouble I'm in, do you really think Charles can actually save me?"

"That's very simple," said Lady Penelope. "If he says he will save you, he will. He's that sort of man. And you may assume, he is absolutely devoted to you. I have never known him to be so smitten with a young lady. And I am obliged to say, for the first time in his life, he has shown excellent judgment."

Sophia smiled through the remainder of her tears, but nonetheless spent the rest of the day fighting back the fear and worry which assailed her for most of the daylight hours, and all of the night-time ones.

She had no idea that Charles was out there with the Prime Minister of Great Britain and the Lord Chancellor, fighting for her freedom, fighting to keep her out of an English courtroom. She also had no idea that he was actually winning, that no one was going to charge her with anything.

****

Charles arrived home late in the afternoon, to find his mother watching television by herself, because, she said, "Sophia is still very upset, and has retired to her room."

He replied, cheerfully, that he would dash upstairs, and cheer her up, and Hudson could expect the three of them for dinner. The Barton family rarely, if ever, dined out on a Monday night.

He climbed the stairs, and tapped on Sophia's door, before pushing it open and finding her face down on the far side of the bed, obviously still in tears.

"Okay," he said, briskly, "You can spring to your feet now, because it's all over. There will be no prosecution of anyone in the Fontridge case, certainly not you. That's it. So would you please dismount from that bed and walk around to congratulate me!"

Miss Morosova tried to smile, she sat up against the pillow and by any standards her face was a wreck, tear-stained, reddened, eyes slightly swollen. But she still looked beautiful.

And she did walk around, and throw her arms around Charles. They hugged each other for several minutes and then she asked him, "What exactly has happened?"

"I'm afraid I can never tell you that," he replied. "Not as long as we both live. I am not only in possession of the most marvellous girl ever to be born in the Republic of Russia, I am also in possession of a British state secret, and, if you want the truth, I will never part with either of them."

"But how do you know they won't prosecute someone for the murder?"

"That, I am afraid, is not for you to know," he said. "But they are not going to. I suppose I could say that the disgusting behaviour of a senior English Law Lord had some bearing on their irrevocable decision."

"But what about the media demanding an arrest?" she asked.

"The mightiest powers in England couldn't give a damn what the bloody media do. There's no arrest, no charges. Next case, please."

"Can I dare to be this happy," she said. "This is like a dream that's lasted for weeks and weeks, and now I am awake. I am here in this wonderful house with two people I like more than almost anyone in the world. Three if you count Hudson!"

And Charles added, "And I think it's high time we made some plans, and he advised her to wash her face, change her rumpled clothes, and bring her new happy face, to delight both him and Lady Penelope."

But first, Charles hurried upstairs to his private office and checked his email, the computer almost permanently connected to the Communications Centre of New Scotland Yard. And there it was, the statement he thought would be waiting, an announcement from the Crown Prosecuting Service, making public a decision which had been finalised that afternoon. The statement read:

"The CPS has studied all of the data, concerning the murder of Lord Justice Fontridge, a case in which there were no witnesses, either to the criminal act itself, or to any of the suspects. It was considered an abuse of the public purse to prosecute in this instance. The lack of evidence would make a conviction extremely unlikely. The Crown Prosecution Service will thus not be proceeding with charges. The decision is that Lord Justice Fontridge was indeed unlawfully stabbed to death, by person, or persons unknown."

Charles signed out, closed down the lid of his laptop, and wearing what might be described as a complacent, not to mention self-satisfied grin, made his way downstairs for a very large scotch and soda, a gin and tonic for his mother, and a vodka and tonic for his future bride.

"NOSTROVIA!" The traditional Russian toast would, in a sense, echo through Mayfair this evening, on a matter which would barely trouble the great British public. Yes, they would read the *Why oh why* ravings of the tabloid press, and probably the BBC. But it would affect no one, except Sophia Morosova, and her Chief Superintendent.

NOSTROVIA!...To your health (not to mention, your freedom).

Ends Chapter Thirty

Chapter Thirty-One
Grand Slam on Death Row

*This was a precise version, here in Buenos Aires, of the exact
same club in Moscow. There was a slightly unreliable security curtain
surrounding the owner, but the Russian attaches were
quite certain this was the business place of Boris Morosov.*

What Charles Barton did not understand was the seething cauldron of unrest which existed on a giant patch of grassland, 20-miles to the north-west of the Argentinian city of Mendoza. Senor Eduardo's body was formally identified by his nephew, Hugo, and the Surgeon-in-Residence on Monday night at Mendoza's Central Hospital, pronounced Eduardo Garcia-Romano dead on arrival.

The police made certain the documentation was correctly completed, and decided at this late hour, by now 11pm, to make their announcement tomorrow morning, *manana,* as it were.

By the time Tuesday afternoon's Metropolitan newspapers were out, and indeed in time for the national lunchtime television news, 45-million Argentine citizens were officially informed that Eduardo Garcia-Romano, one of the principal land owners and cattle barons in the country, former high-goal polo player, had indeed been murdered. Shot three times, out on the grasslands of his own estate.

His body had been discovered on Sunday evening, and was at Mendoza's Central Hospital, pending a post-mortem. This directly affected only Eduardo's big family, and a very select group of his friends and business associates, although the world of polo would mourn him in many corners of the world.

There was one corner, however, in a slightly seedy district of the capital city of Buenos Aires, where his death would be particularly concerning. Because here stood one of the city's many nightclubs, into which on a regular basis, Argentina's wealthy sidled by night, to purchase the favours of very, very young girls.

It was called, *Ode to Joy*, after Beethoven's Ninth Symphony—a trans-world echo from the city of Moscow, where once a nightclub of that very name provided an outpost of semi-legal sex with the very young. The proprietor of both clubs was one certain Mr Boris Morosov, a man who had dodged outright disgrace so many times, and yet remained a close friend of the very rich, the very dangerous, and the very sexually deviant. He was, of course, the step-father of Sophia Morosova.

And here he was, seated in a plush office, glowering at the front page of the afternoon newspaper, which pronounced the shocking death of his old friend, Eduardo Garcia-Romano. The nightclub had not yet warmed up to its nocturnal predators, but Boris Morosov was not concerned with trade, he was concerned for his own life.

No one, in the entire country, except for Boris, understood the content of the Pseudonym List that lurked on the laptop computer, owned by the deceased Lord Fontridge.

Certainly Boris did not know that Scotland Yard was in possession of that list. But he knew the pseudonyms of his six principal clients: *Birkenhead, Sweet Charity, Divine Wind, Tilden, Beauregard and Florida Garden.* These were the secret code names of the men who made their £10,000 transfers into his Moscow bank account, via the offshore organisations owned by Fontridge (that's *Birkenhead* to his closest friends).

Morosov knew that *Birkenhead* was dead. He also knew that *Sweet Charity* was dead, after that spectacular fall at the Monaco Grand Prix. He had heard through the financial grapevines of Buenos Aires business television, that *Divine Wind* had died suddenly in Hong Kong. About *Tilden,* he knew nothing, but he hoped to god that Buck Madden was still alive. And that also applied to *Beauregard.* However, the catastrophic death of his buddy, *Florida Garden,* was a stunning blow, which had raised a red flag so high it could be seen from the top of the Andes.

A dozen thoughts tumbled through the quasi-criminal mind of Boris Morosov. *Four out of six...and it may be more...that represents some kind of net closing in...I have to be potentially the seventh hit on that list—but I haven't the first idea who could possibly be on my trail.*

Boris tried to think, but the memory of his long-time client, Eduardo, was pushing everything else aside. He picked up his telephone, found the phone number for Buck Madden, and dialled the Virginia Tennis Club. To his absolute horror, the voice-recording announced a new tennis professional, not the man who had founded the Club.

The stubby fingers of Boris Morosov thumped into his telephone keypad, attempting to find a local media outfit in Charlottesville, Virginia. Finally he got through to a television station and told the editorial assistant he had critical information about Mr Buck Madden, the local tennis professional.

A new voice came on the line with a polite, "Can I help you?" Boris told him he was trying to confirm the death of Buck Madden, because he had important information to give.

"Yup, old Buck's surely dead. Some lady murdered him right on the service line of his own courts. A real local mystery, and not likely to be solved."

Boris instantly cut off the connection, simultaneously going white as the blood drained from his face.

Jesus Christ! I've gotta be next, because I'd guess that Beauregard has also gone, but it beats the hell outta me who could possibly have launched a campaign of murder like that. They must have hired several vigilantes, to cut down a half-dozen people, from all over the world, without mercy."

Boris felt physically ill. *There can be no doubt I must be on that hit-list,* he told himself. *I was the goddamned mastermind, I took the money, I provided the girls…and who the hell could have hated those men so badly they hired a killer to commit murder on their behalf?*

And try as he might, Boris Morosov could come up with only one person in all the world, with reason to harbour such a relentless hatred. He knew what had happened to Sasha, and now he faced an unthinkable reality that either the murderer, or the person who had hired the murderers, must indeed be his own step-daughter, Sophia—that cool-eyed, standoffish schoolgirl, whom he had so often caught gazing at him with icy disdain.

Could it be her? Could this girl, who had come to very little harm from my own actions…could she possibly have arranged this? I understand she could not have done it personally. The location of these murders must have spanned almost 20,000-miles. And yet…there is no one else, there just could not be any other person with that much loathing in their soul…unless, of course, Veroniya somehow escaped from that Russian nuthouse, and set off in pursuit of the men who'd simply wanted gentle sex with her daughters.

Boris Morosov found himself facing the twin demons of those who are being hunted, 1) he was scared half to death, and now was uncertain of his own judgment; 2) he was confused, uncertain of the identity of his enemy, uncertain of where that enemy might strike next.

No matter how hard he racked his brain, he always came back to Sophia, the one person, living free, and determined, who might reasonably be expected to come after him.

Sophia was by no means an average enemy. She was highly intelligent and had access to a large amount of money in a personal Trust in London, which was guided by *that absolute bastard, Rudolph Masow, a man who has always hated me.* Boris had no idea precisely what Uncle Rudy did for a living, but he was a formidable man, too cosy with the Russian oligarchs, and with Russia's most ruthless politicians, including the President.

Boris understood that if Rudolph Masow wanted him dead on behalf of his niece, Sophia, then right here in the control room of *Ode to Joy,* he could start counting the number of days he had left on this earth.

And yet…there was no proof that anyone was stabbing and shooting their way through the Pseudonym List. He had no idea that this was really happening. But the circumstantial evidence was overwhelming, and, like most lifelong businessmen, Boris did not like coincidences. There were six men on that list and five of them were dead, all of them under extremely shaky circumstances.

Boris thought this was too obvious not to be true. Five out of the six. All murdered inside the last two months. And if de Villiers was gone too, that was six out of the six—a kind of death-row Grand Slam.

And there was no escaping the obvious conclusion he, Boris, the reigning Teenage Sex King of Buenos Aires, must surely be next on the list. And so far as he could see, the only possible answer to his plight was to follow that old Russian proverb, and take out the archer, not the arrow. For as long as Sophia Morosova shall walk the streets of London, he, her step-father, must be in mortal danger. Rudolph Masow, he assessed, was impregnable inside the Russian Embassy.

There was only Sophia, and he had absolutely no idea where she lived, where she was, or what she planned. She might be in London, she might be somewhere else, she might even have gone back to Moscow to see her mother. And how the hell he was supposed to find her from a remote street in Buenos Aires? God alone knew the answer to that.

The only person he could come up with, who would without doubt know her whereabouts was, of course, her chief Trustee, Uncle Rudolph. To ask him would be much like asking God the whereabouts of the Virgin Mary. He supposed there was a slender chance that Veroniya would know her daughter's address. But Boris privately thought there was a very good chance he'd end up with a bullet in his head, if he even attempted to visit the hospital. *That bastard, Masow, would stop at nothing,* he gritted.

It took almost two hours, closing in on the hour of midnight, before Morosov had a brainwave. And that was the law firm which administered Sophia's Trust Fund. He had almost forgotten that it was he, Boris, who had set it up in the first place. He had signed the papers and actually appointed Uncle Rudolph as the senior Trustee.

Certainly there would be no telephone assistance from the law firm, in which the senior partner also held a permanent position on the Board of the Trust. They would never tell a voice on the phone, the location of the principal beneficiary of such a huge sum of money.

But they might reveal an address if he presented himself at their office in London's Leadenhall Street, in person, smartly dressed, with a request to see the lawyer who administered the Morosov family money.

Ode to Joy would run itself, under the staff appointed by Boris. At least, they would for a few days, and he elected to fly to London the following Sunday night. That flight would put him in the City around 9am, and he'd be in the lawyer's office at 9.30am. This gave him four clear days to arrange his life before departure, and to make a few phone calls to gather what assistance he could, in the matter of the vanished Sophia, whom he had not seen for almost eight years.

But those four days were not peaceful. The busy mind of Boris Morosov scanned over the possibilities, taking care not to dwell on the worst of them—a car bomb under his Mercedes; a bomb through the window of his office, a salvo of rapid bullets from an AK 47, a Kalashnikov aimed straight at him, as he came out of the nightclub around 2am.

Boris knew as well as anyone that when the heavyweights of the Russian government wish someone to be extinguished it is never subtle, and mostly decisive. The men from the *Lubyanka* always used a very large jackhammer to smash a peanut.

And what an undignified ending. Boris envisaged his own body, spread-eagled on the sidewalk right in front of *Ode to Joy,* with the haunting violins of Beethoven's Ninth providing a somewhat jarring note for his journey into the great unknown.

****

Rudolph Masow's worldwide net finally came up with a slightly vague notion of where Boris Morosov may be living. His man in the Russian Embassy in Buenos Aires revealed an almost certain connection between the *Ode To Joy* and the former Moscow sex hang-out of the same name.

The Spanish nightclub in Buenos Aires was a precise version of the exact same club in Moscow. The had made one or two enquiries, and although there was a slightly unreliable security curtain surrounding the owner, the Russian attaches were quite certain this was the business place of Boris Morosov.

Uncle Rudy telephoned his niece, and informed her that her step-father was now living in Buenos Aires. "And that means," he said, "He will definitely know that damned polo player has died. And I'd say that will be a grave warning to him, and I'm not absolutely sure what he'll do."

Sophia immediately told Charles, and confirmed that she would like, if possible, to stay in South Audley Street with him, but really should return to Paris for a couple of days, just to clear up the apartment, pay the bills and lock it up for the rest of the summer.

"I'd hate to give it up," she said, "And I cannot just leave it without checking the security, and leaving my new address with Gaston."

Charles agreed with that, and suggested she go in the early part of next week, when he personally had a couple of conferences to attend, and would be missing for much of the time.

They subsequently spent an idyllic few days in London, not only making plans for their future, but also, at last spending the nights together, while Lady Penelope turned a discreet blind eye. It was the first time Sophia had ever willingly been with a man, actually the first time she had ever willingly kissed a man.

She was 24 now, and as first dates go, this one was world-class. Charles, of course, found it difficult to avoid the ever-present truth that the girl he planned to marry may be a serial killer.

He was absolutely certain she had killed Lord Fontridge, but he had no idea whether Josh Hartley had been a victim; and he regarded it as totally impossible that Sophia could have had anything to do with the demise of Mr Takahashi. He considered she could not possibly have gone to Hong Kong and back, in that time-frame.

He knew that *Tilden* was dead, but again regarded it as impossible for her to have gone to America without his knowledge. The death of the tennis pro was outlandish, and so was the shooting of the film tycoon. At this point Charles Barton had no idea about the death of *Florida Garden.* He did not even know who or where it was.

And yet…all the other pseudonyms were gone. And only Fontridge had happened in England, where Sophia had been. One murder really was bad enough, another five seemed bizarre, out of the question, and the girl he loved even denied knowing anything about the stabbing of Freddie Fontridge.

It was a very scattered puzzle. The pieces were all over the place, and a couple of them were on the floor, under the table. Charles resolved to cast it all from his mind, let the ghost of the rapist, Fontridge, drift, everlastingly, over the misty lake of Glyndebourne House.

He had absolutely no connection to the cases, which seemed a sound reason to cast them aside, and concentrate on the beauty, wit and joy of Sophia Morosova, without visions of daggers, guns and hatred clouding his mind.

When he kissed her good-bye on Monday morning he knew it was only for a couple of days, and she'd be back by Thursday. It was unimaginable, in the minds of both of them, that they would ever be apart again.

****

Boris Morosov arrived at the offices of *Johnson, Magnus and Lowenstein,* a City law firm situated just along the street from the world's insurance hub, Lloyds of London, and just south of the Gherkin, that 600-foot high, round solar skyscraper which is supposed to run on a couple of flashlight batteries.

Johnson Magnus is traditionally more concerned with finance than with crime. Boris went to the fourth floor, tapped on the door and entered, requesting the receptionist ask one of the senior partners to see him.

The young lawyer who arrived, shook hands and asked what he could do for him. And Boris explained, in some detail, he was enquiring about the whereabouts of his step-daughter, Sophia Morosova, the principal beneficiary of a Trust he had set up for her, eight years ago.

He explained there were several Trustees involved, including a senior Russian diplomat at the Embassy, and indeed the senior partner of this law firm. Boris was invited into a small conference room, where he was asked for passport identification, and an example of his signature.

A different lawyer returned with the Trust file, and Boris recognised immediately it was Bob Lowenstein, the very man who had set the Trust up, all those years ago. The two men remembered each other and they shook hands.

The lawyer said, "I can see no reason why the person who established the Trust, and indeed placed the principal amount of money in it, should not be given the current address of the beneficiary."

Mr Morosov thanked him and Bob Lowenstein wrote on a sheet of paper, *Miss Sophia Morosova, 19, rue des Beaux Arts, Apartment 6A, Paris, 75006, France.* He wrote her telephone number underneath.

But the lawyer felt uneasy. He walked to the window and stared down at the departing Russian businessman He watched him climb into a taxi, which headed east, towards Aldgate and Whitechapel, the wrong way for Maida Vale, where he remembered Morosov lived, several years ago.

He actually watched the taxi as it made its way towards the East End, and then disappeared into Whitechapel Road. It was surprising to Bob Lowenstein that this immaculately dressed Russian should be heading towards one of the least prosperous areas of London. But he would have been even more startled if he had known the final destination.

This was a pub called *The Druids*, once a cornerstone of the capital's old gangland days, when vicious criminals gathered in such hostelries to plot and plan various robberies, swindles and murders etc. *The Druids* was in fact located just around the corner from the East End's most storied pub, the *Blind Beggar*, into which the fabled Shoreditch mobster, Ronnie Kray, walked one night in 1966, and blew rival gangster George Cornell's brains out with one shot to the forehead from a 9mm Luger—right in front of all the clients.

Ronnie went down for life on that one, to Broadmoor, Britain's most formidable high-security hospital for the criminally insane, where he died, nearly 30-years later. Not one of the drinkers would give evidence against him. *The Blind Beggar* was that sort of pub.

The Druids was not much different, and was reputed to be the world headquarters of the London gang which pulled off two of England's biggest ever gold bullion heists in the late nineties.

The days of the brutal gang bosses in East London are over now, but the folklore of the place remains. Much older men have fond, rose-coloured memories of the old days when Ronnie and Reggie Kray ruled the criminal classes. And many such men still return to their old East End haunts, which are mostly cheerful places now, also frequented by a modern, arty crowd who love the mythical past the place evokes.

It is often said, that if anyone wants a criminal act committed on their own behalf, the place to get a proper accomplice is right there in the historic gangland pubs. If the money's right, the contract villain will be at your service. Boris Morosov's mission was just beginning, and the money would be right. And one of the flat-nosed, hard men of the East End would be somewhere in the vicinity, trying to earn it.

Bob Lowenstein, of course, knew nothing of this. But a senior lawyer's instincts are usually as good as anyone else's. And he, instinctively did not like, trust or believe anything about his former Russian client. And while, in a sense, it was nothing to do with him, he was nervous about the blunt way Morosov had spoken to him, the cool manner of the demand, and why on earth did he not know the address of his own step-daughter?

It was not that Bob thought his visitor was being dishonest, or planned to steal the money. The Trust by-laws had an iron clamp around that. But he had met Sophia, and she had seemed so fragile. For reasons unknown, and instincts unidentified, he feared for her, and he did not know how to deal with it. But he talked it over with his wife before they retired that night, and he resolved to call the senior Trustee, Rudolph Masow, first thing tomorrow morning.

It was shortly before 10am when the private line in Rudolph's office rang, and his secretary answered. Immediately, she called out, "Sir, it's Bob Lowenstein from Johnson Magnus."

Anything to do with the welfare of his niece claimed the immediate attention of the cultural attaché, and he picked up immediately, and, over the next four minutes made very few responses of his own. He listened to the fears of Sophia's legal protector, and said, finally, "Bob, I'm grateful you have let me know. Your fears are also mine. Leave it with me … and thank you, thank you very much indeed."

"GET CHARLES BARTON ON THE LINE RIGHT NOW!" he shouted, and within moments he was recounting the highly alarming news of the morning. Yes, he'd traced Sophia's step-father to Buenos Aires, but Boris Morosov was in London yesterday, hunting for Sophia, asked the lawyers for her address."

"Christ," said Charles, "They didn't give it to her, did they?"

"Well, since Morosov put in the initial money eight years ago, they couldn't very well refuse him, could they? He actually appointed me chief Trustee. And now he has her Paris address, and I can't leave here this week …"

"Can we get her back to London right now?"

"I couldn't get her yesterday, but I'm going to try. And Charles … I don't trust that little rat Morosov one inch … he's low-life, dangerous, and totally dishonest. And I would not be surprised if he wanted her dead … what do you think?"

"Think!" exclaimed Charles, *"Think!* I don't even have time for that. I'm going to Paris, leaving about four-and-a-half seconds from now. I'll call you later."

The line went dead, and Rudolf Masow found himself very, very scared. He, of course, knew all about the death of Eduardo Garcia-Romano. And since Boris lived in Buenos Aires he also must know that his old London client with the polo mallet had died. And he may also know that was the sixth and final victim on Sophia's list.

As the mastermind of the Maida Vale sex ring, he would not have to be all that smart to think, wrongly, that the killer might want him next. Self-preservation, with unending violence, is a treasured component in the Russian psyche, as Napoleon and the late Fuhrer would doubtless testify.

In Uncle Rudy's opinion, Sophia was in mortal danger. She was being hunted. Boris Morosov had flown the Atlantic Ocean specifically to find her, and he had her Paris address. Rudolph thought he and Charles might be too late, and should that be so, Boris Morosov's days were numbered.

He, Rudy, would personally attend to that. As a matter of fact, too late or not, he would attend to that anyway. *How dare that unspeakable bastard Boris come skulking around the City of London in search of Sophia … if he harms one brunette hair on her head … he dies … well, he dies anyway. That's already been decided. By me … some people being too evil to live.*

Chapter Thirty-Two
Cash Down - A Contract Killing

*"Anyway, Rudy's very scared. He sent me to France, a) to
protect you if Boris turns up on the doorstep wielding a
Kalashnikov; b) to get you the hell out of Paris, because
that's the only address Boris has for you."*

Detective Chief Superintendent Barton raced down the stairs and into the back
of a waiting, unmarked BMW three-litre sedan for his fast ride to St Pancras
International Station: along the Thames Embankment, and then north at
Blackfriars Bridge, straight past Fleet Street and on to *Eurostar's* London
Terminus.

Charles hit the station running, dodging wandering passengers, as he sprinted
past the 270-foot clock tower, which dominates the enormous red-brick Gothic
Revival building on London's Euston Road. The 18th century clock showed
12.14pm as he reached the ticket office. Charles hoped the darned thing wasn't
running slow, because he needed to be on the 12.24 *Eurostar*, non-stop to Paris,
a Pegasus in high-speed travel, covering the 300-miles to the French capital in
under

two-and-a-half-hours.

The *Eurostar* would race through the green fields of Kent at 143mph, it
would charge under the Channel Tunnel still making 99mph, and then speed up
when it reached France. Charles made it by about three minutes, and sat scowling
and fretting for most of the journey, wondering why the hell the driver 'couldn't
get this French wreck moving!'

Nonetheless, even without hearing the Scotland Yard Superintendent griping
and moaning three carriages back, the driver skilfully brought the thundering
yellow and white, high-voltage monster straight into the middle of Paris right on
time. The Gare du Nord, 15.47 in the afternoon, 2hrs 23mins. Charles checked
his watch, and stopped grumbling to himself, jumped into a taxi, and said, *"Rue
des Beaux Arts, Saint Germain. Numero dix-neuf."*

Then he remembered Paris was one-hour in front of London, nearly 4pm not 3pm. *Friggin Frogs,* he growled, uncharitably. At times like this, Charles was quite certain the Battle of Waterloo 'was won on the playing fields of Eton,' where both he, and the Duke of Wellington, were educated. That Old Etonian superiority never left the Duke, and it would never leave Charles, especially in the grand railway station, of which the French were so inordinately proud.

In fact, when the Duke made his famous pronouncement he was actually watching a cricket match at the 600-year-old Thames-side school, and really meant that the entire ethos of hard competitive sport at Eton and other schools like it, always made the British mentally and physically superior. Charles Barton, a self-effacing man, nevertheless, in his heart, lined up, resolutely, with the Iron Duke.

The four-mile journey from the Right bank to the Left, took nearly 40 minutes in heavy traffic, during which time Charles reset his watch to French time, and apologised *in absentia* to the *Eurostar* driver for berating him as 'too slow' during his 170mph dash across France.

When they reached Number 19, Charles hastily handed the driver some euros, and came through the lobby like an English rocket, mistakenly wishing Gaston good-day in Italian instead of French … *Buongiorno!"* he called.

"Monsieur?" replied Gaston, staring at Charles as he bounded into the elevator. *"Je ne comprends pas!"*

"Then for Christ's sake pay attention!" snapped Charles, out of earshot and laughing, as he ascended to the rooftop hideaway of the endangered goddess he adored. "That's *amore* to you, Gaston," he added still laughing, *"Just today. Silly old prick."*

He reached #6, and tapped lightly on the door. Sophia opened it and almost went into shock at the sight of Charles. "I thought I just left you in London!" she laughed, "What could you possibly be doing here? I'm coming home to London in the morning."

"May I come in?" he asked, ingenuously.

"Any time," she said, "Any time you like. Welcome to my French residence."

Sophia shut the door, and they fell into those never-ending hugs to which new lovers are prone. Finally she asked, "Excuse me, Superintendent. But could I ask you again what precisely you are doing here?"

"Well, the main reason is you failed to answer your phone to any one of Uncle Rudy's 18 calls. So we both thought you might be dead!

"The secondary reason is my obligation to make sure you do not become dead. And that, darling Sophia, is the serious part."

"Can I know the details?"

"You can. That hideous step-father of yours just turned up in London. Rudy had traced him to Buenos Aires, where he now lives, but he's just flown the Atlantic, and has found out your address from the Trust lawyers."

"Well … perhaps he wants to give me a birthday present."

"Perhaps not. Perhaps he wants to kill you."

"Whatever for?"

"Sophia," said Charles, carefully, "A rather unfortunate series of deaths has occurred to a list of Boris Morosov's main business clients. A suspicious person like him may consider he could be next on the list, given his close dealings with the deceased. It may have occurred to him that you had something to do with those deaths, and subsequently he prefers to get rid of you, before you get rid of him."

"You mean he thinks he's in danger from me?"

"Don't know really. But if I were him, and I'd done what he'd done to his step-daughters, I would not dismiss the possibility. It's a routine question in any murder, *who hated him most?* And you'd slot in there very neatly.

"Anyway, Rudy's very scared. He almost *sent* me to Paris, a) to protect you if Boris turns up on the doorstep holding a Kalashnikov; b) to get you the hell out of Paris, because that's the only address Boris has for you."

"And where do I go?"

"Fort Barton, currently under the command of artillery Major Penelope MacLeish, Mayfair Light Dragoons."

Sophia could never help laughing at Charles, and she quickly slipped into a military mode. "And what are our tactics, if this Russian lunatic launches an assault on Fort Barton?"

"Easy. We'll Unleash MacLeish! Who will scatter the enemy into Bond Street, before accepting documents of surrender in the champagne bar at Claridge's."

Sophia laughed, nearly, but it was as if the words of the Superintendent had finally sunk in. "Do you think my own step-father would actually try to kill me, in real life, I mean."

"I do, and killings quite often are in real life. Rudy is certain that's his intention. Remember, Boris has spent much time in company with the underworld …"

"Not to mention the underwear," she added.

But Charles was no longer joking. "Sophia, I don't happen to agree with Rudy that Boris will personally make an armed attack on you—I think it more likely he will pay for someone else to do it. In the East End it's known as a *contract killing*. I believe £20,000 is the going rate, half in advance, half on completion."

"Am I worth all that?"

"Much more to me, and very much more to someone who thinks you're a serial killer."

Sophia decided this was a good time to make some tea and retreated to the kitchen. Charles called, "By the way, I'm on duty from now on. Scotland Yard protection, here to keep you safe until we go back to England."

They finished their tea, and talked more about the threat from Boris, and Sophia just could not accept that he was somehow lurking, somewhere in Paris, waiting for a chance to strike. "It seems so unreal," she said, "Like something from a movie. As if a real person might come through that door with a gun."

"Or a knife," added Charles, in a slightly backhanded way.

It was almost 6pm now and Sophia wondered what they might do for dinner. She volunteered either to cook something, or order from the excellent restaurant across the street.

"If we're going to order something from the restaurant," he suggested, "We may as well eat it there, save the washing up. We're leaving early in the morning."

And, just as he spoke, there were three firm knocks on the front door.

"You sure you'd recognise Boris after all these years?"

"Anywhere, anytime," she said, and walked directly to the peephole in the entrance door … and then, "It's not him. A lot too young."

Charles took over, had another look through the peephole and asked, "Who is this?"

"Courier service, sir. Package for Miss Mozzarella."

"Who?" said Charles.

"Can't really read the name too well, guv. Might be Molotov."

Charles opened the door and asked to see the package. The word 'guv' was pure London. And every one of his defences was up. But his copper's brain did not want this man to make a run for it, and he watched his every move carefully.

The man was not as tall as Charles but he was heavyset, with a face that was no stranger to violence. Actually the former East End policeman thought he recognised a former bank robber, Alfie someone, who'd gone down for 12 years for shooting the cashier at the Mile End branch of Barclays Bank.

Today he was wearing an open-necked white shirt with a blue blazer and dark grey trousers. He carried a slim leather briefcase, but like so many men who have spent the majority of their adult lives in jail, he had a pallor about him, a greyness to his complexion. Charles would recognise his kind a long way off. And then, from way back, he remembered the name, Alfie Cruikshank, Bethnal Green, bank robber by trade, 'dangerous little bastard,' twice went down for robbery with violence.

Just then Sophia walked into the hallway. "This her?" asked Alfie, and as he did so, Charles noticed his right hand slide towards the left inside pocket of the blazer, where there was an obvious gun. And the words of Mick Pearson flashed through his mind ... *Be first, son. Go now, Charlie boy ... right hand!*

Charles never even bothered to get centred. Never wound up. But he was up on the balls of his feet, and he slammed a terrific right hook into the soft area right below Alfie's greedy little heart.

Alfie was stunned, and his cheeks blew out like a trombone player, emptying his lungs. He dropped to his knees, struggling for air, the semi-automatic Walther PPK skidding across the floor. Charles backed up a bit, refrained from kicking him in the face, and paused for a surrender.

But Alf Cruikshank had been fighting all his life, on the hard, roguish streets of East London, and when necessary, in prison. He somehow climbed to his feet, and came straight at Charles, fists flailing ... and the tall Etonian detective actually smiled as he stood his ground and delivered a jolting left jab flush on Alfie's nose.

The punch was magnified by Alfie's incoming momentum, and blood spurted down his face. He tried to wipe it away ... but the shouts of Mick Pearson still ran through the mind of Charles Barton ... *don't let 'im off the hook, Charlie ... combinations ... the jab ... then the big right ... go for 'im, son ... he's all done!*

Before the would-be hit man could recover, Charles was on him, but still careful, coming in with a slick feint to the left, and then that steam-hammer left jab exploded again, landed with a smack on Alfie's cheek bone, breaking it in two places.

Finish him, son ... right hook ... drop him ... right now ...!

The left side of Alfie's face was now unguarded, and Charles sent in the punch Mick had told him would take him to a professional career. That fabled right hook exploded on the left side of Alfie's jaw, and his head snapped back hard, his eyes glazed as he toppled over.

Had the boxing writer from *L'Equipe* been there he would surely have written: *"The British middleweight Charles Barton stopped his opponent after 47 seconds of the first round with a lights-out right hook which scared Cruikshank's corner-men into literally throwing in the towel before their man even hit the canvas. It fluttered into the ring, and the referee signalled it was all over, never even bothered to count. The ring doctor was through the ropes in an instant."*

Charles rubbed his knuckles, and turned to see Sophia, standing rigid as Lenin's statue, the ex-German Police revolver pointed unerringly at Alfie's head. He took it from her, and put his arm around her, and could feel her trembling.

"Would you have actually shot him?" he asked.

"If he'd hurt you, yes, without question."

Charles found this in a way comforting, but also a bit ... well ... thought-provoking. "Actually, my darling," he said, "This is a bit of a mess. Alfie down there looks kind of lopsided." (as you do with a broken jaw).

What do we do now, call the French police?"

"I don't think we have much choice," he replied. "This character isn't dead, and we do have to behave properly. We can't just leave him, or toss him off the roof, can we?"

"Not really. But we don't want to get hung up all day signing documents for the *gendarmes* ... and, by the way, since I'm shortly going to marry Mayfair's answer to Mike Tyson, could you possibly tell me where you learned to fight like that."

"That wasn't fighting," he said, "That was boxing. And the two are very different. One's for thugs, one celebrates the noble art of self-defence, as laid down by the Marquis of Queensbury."

"Didn't look much like self-defence to me," she smiled.

"Not even if you consider he was brandishing a PPK 9mm, with which he intended to kill certainly you, and probably me."

"Christ!" she said, atypically. "I hadn't thought about that. Do you think Boris really did hire him?"

"Without a doubt," he replied. "The visit to the London lawyers, your Paris address. Who the hell else told him where you lived?"

"I suppose so. But for some reason I just find it hard to accept that my own step-father hired someone to murder me."

"Depends largely on the step-father," replied Charles. "Let's not forget, yours was a bit special, by any standards."

"Yes … but you still haven't told me how you learned to … er … box like that."

"Helston ABC," he said.

"Sounds like a playschool."

"Helston Amateur Boxing Club. Honorary member, proposed by the best fight trainer in the East End, Mick Pearson, Olympic medallist."

"But you don't see him much now, do you?"

"Not really, coupla times a year. But he's always in my corner when there's trouble."

"What about today?"

"Mick was there … don't ask me how."

Sophia changed the subject. "There's someone else who should have been with us today. And I think I'm going to call him right now …"

"Uncle Rudy?" he replied. "Good idea. Let me make the call."

She handed him the phone, and watched him dial the private number inside the Russian Embassy in London.

Two minutes later Rudolf Masow was on the line, and Charles outlined the events of the late afternoon. Sophia heard him mention that Rudy had been right—this was a straightforward plot to kill her.

She also heard him say that Boris had not come in person—he'd sent some cheap little hitman, who was presently unconscious on the floor, a bit bloody, and with an obviously fractured jaw.

Charles touched the button for speakerphone, and she heard Uncle Rudy shout, "Jesus! You haven't killed him, have you!"

She then heard him add, "What did you hit him with, a steel poker?"

"Right hook, actually, old boy. He went down like a sack of potatoes."

373

Rudy roared with laughter, and Sophia held out her hand for the phone. She told him they had no idea what to do. Alfie was immobile and may need oxygen. Should they call an ambulance?"

Rudy said to forget that. He just said, "Dearest Sophia, gather up your boyfriend and go out for a nice dinner. Do nothing except to tell Gaston to let a couple of visitors go upstairs. Fix him with a tip, and tell him to ignore the visitors when they make their exit. Leave everything to me, but don't let the damned hitman get away. Tie him up. We'll talk later."

Sophia found a roll of wide electrical tape in the kitchen, and Charles wound it tightly around Alfie's wrists, behind his back and ankles. He also slapped a large piece across his mouth. Which meant he couldn't speak, couldn't move, couldn't run, and was, anyway, unconscious. Safe for at least an hour.

On their way out, Sophia gave Gaston a 100-euro note and requested his discretion. And Charles, ever the romantic, took her for a stroll around the block to *Le Bistro*, the restaurant where first he had fallen in love with her.

Monsieur DeFarges remembered her well, and asked of course to be remembered to Lady Penelope. They had a perfect dinner, Dover sole and Meursault, and returned to the apartment shortly after 10.30pm

Gaston gave Charles a conspiratorial wink, and said, "Your visitors left after about 10 minutes. I think there was someone else with them."

"Good luck with that, Alfie," muttered Charles.

And with that, on this warm and peaceful Paris night, they slipped into Sophia's big bed with the windows open, and the faint bustle of the city still audible. They had never slept here together, and Charles found the entire experience magical.

They were locked in each other's arms as the great bells of the north tower of Notre Dame Cathedral chimed the midnight hour. It was so breathtakingly beautiful, as the ancient bells rang out across Paris.

They stayed, quietly listening, as the deep rolling notes echoed along the low, near deserted River Seine. They did not, however, hear another sound from a couple of miles downstream, at the dark bridge spanning the channel off the Boulogne-Billancourt.

This was an altogether less melodious noise, a sudden flat

SP-L-ASH! made by a heavy object falling into the water, and then heading 30-feet down into the muddy depths of the riverbed. And there the sounds ended, no footfalls from two hurrying Russian 'attaches,' walking softly from the lonely bridge, returning to their Embassy.

****

Charles and Sophia arrived home from Paris shortly after midday. It was a good time for arrivals. At this precise moment Boris Morosov was landing at the Ezeiza International Airport outside Buenos Aires, non-stop overnight from London.

He wore a contented smile on his face. The threats were gone. He could live his life. The avenging angel that was little Sophia from Maida Vale, was no longer alive. He'd call Mr Cruikshank in an hour, and the final words of the London gangster were clear in his mind—"Don't you worry about it, sir. It'll be quick and clean, two bullets from a silenced Walther PPK. No noise. Game over. Not a worry."

That was precisely the way Boris Morosov liked it. But all through that morning he tried unsuccessfully to call Cruikshank, and the line was permanently dead. He was preoccupied with that final link to his personal happiness, to the exclusion of all else. He postponed a meeting with his accountants, had no time for his manager, and interviewed no young, prospective prostitutes.

He spent a couple of hours in an upstairs staff apartment at the back of the building, but returned to his office to dial that cell-phone number in London over and over. He skipped lunch, and he skipped dinner, took a couple of strong vodkas which increased his worries, and made him feel even more sick.

By 10pm *Ode to Joy* was becoming busy, but it did so without the Boss. He never even stepped outside into the narrow street for a breath of fresh air. And he never saw two silent men in a black Ford SUV parked across the street. They seemed to be working in shifts, with relief coming every eight hours, next one due at 3am.

The street was very dark after midnight, and the vehicle in which Boris had arrived was parked on the same side as the club, 50 yards farther on. It took the two men just a few minutes to manhandle the magnetised IED into place on the base of the steel gas tank.

They set the contact detonator just forward of the offside rear wheel. When Boris Morosov's big Mercedes rolled forward, he would be safe for less than two seconds, as the car moved off, and the back wheel ran over the metal-strip contacts, crushing them together.

That particular IED contained enough high-explosive pentolite to detonate the two power-sections of uranium in an atom bomb, nuclear warheads being the normal spot for this deadly compound, when it's mixed with TNT.

If the IED under Boris Morosov's car functioned correctly it would probably send him into orbit. And no one had long to wait. The proprietor of *Ode to Joy* came out of the club at 2am as usual. He walked to his Mercedes, used his cell-phone for yet another call to Cruikshank, and then started the engine.

Seconds later the car moved forward, and the blast nearly took down half the street. Every window on the opposite side for 50-yards was blown out. The entire front side of the nightclub was obliterated, laying bare the inside of the building. The car burst into flames, the gasoline burned black, the tyres caught fire, and a group of three passing pedestrians was killed instantly.

The bombers were long gone, and they heard the blast from a mile away. That old Russian jackhammer just cracked another peanut. And the photograph, almost immediately faxed to Uncle Rudy, showed a blazing inferno, like a scene from a war zone. They never found Boris Morosov's body.

Back in London, even Rudy was a little surprised at the level of pure violence which had occurred in the past few days. But he shrugged it all away, as he had done so many times before, and resolved to say nothing more to Charles and Sophia.

That night he took them both out to dinner, and poured the best Russian vodka, generously. At the conclusion of the evening, he raised his glass for one last toast, and, as usual, mentioned his beloved Sasha.

"To absent friends," he said. *"Dasvidaniya!"*

Both Charles and Sophia thought he was saying yet another farewell to the little girl. But he wasn't. Rudolf Masow was sending his detested brother-in-law on his way to hell, which, in the considered opinion of the Russian assassin, was far, far too good for him.

The End

Epilogue

Charles Barton and Sophia Morosova were married at the glorious Catholic Church of the Immaculate Conception, Farm Street, Mayfair, on 23 September 2016. Their first Christmas together would be spent at the home of the Mildmays, in Winkfield Row, Berkshire.

On that cold and frosty morning, they left home early and drove out along the M4, well past the turning for Windsor, and all the way to Henley-on-Thames. And there, Sophia took her new husband on her Thames-side walk along to St Nicholas Church.

In Sophia's mind this was a pilgrimage, not a Christmas morning stroll. She had not been here since before her return from Santiago, and there were important matters she wanted her sister to know. Also she wanted her God to forgive her, and to accept her actions had been those of a Christian avenger, in the hope of achieving eternal rest, at last, for an innocent Christian martyr.

This shaded churchyard had been for almost eight years the principal place for Sophia to communicate with the Holy Mother, to beg Her indulgence, and to accept that Sasha had not meant to offend God, that the young girl had been driven to her destruction by the cruellest of men.

There was a bitterly cold east wind blowing head-on up the Regatta Course, as they made their way downstream along the towpath. Sophia, wearing high boots and a Russian fur hat, had both hands stuffed into the pockets of her heavy coat, with Charles linking his arm through hers. In her other hand Sophia clutched the beads of her rosary.

They reached the old stile and climbed over, before walking up to the deserted churchyard—two hours before the Christmas morning service. For reasons unknown, she wanted Charles here. He knew almost nothing about the suicide of Sasha, and he never would know one thing about her Crusade of Revenge. But Sophia wanted to share with him, this sacred place where her little sister rested; a place to which he had never been.

She opened the iron gate, and together they crossed the icy grass and stopped at the grave beneath the pines. Charles read the headstone, and saw the name *Sasha*, and the dates, which made her 15 years old, when she died in 2011.

Sophia, with tears running down her face, turned to Charles without wiping them away. And then she told him one of the secrets of her sister's death. "Charles," she said, "She jumped 200-feet from that roof, with the bravest prayer ever spoken, scribbled on a piece of paper they found in her school blazer pocket—the prayer of departure from the barbarously tortured Saint Agatha of Sicily ... *Lord, you have given me patience to suffer ... receive now my soul.*

Charles stared at the grave, and at the words his wife had engraved into the stone:

A Tragic Child of God
Let Eternal Light Shine Upon her

And he began to understand the depth of his wife's sorrow. He now understood this deep, all-embracing sadness which she may never cast from her mind. *Sasha, darling little Sasha* ... the words he had heard two or three times from Sophia, and several times from Uncle Rudy.

He understood the haunted despair of those imagined final terrifying moments high on the roof. The broken-hearted young girl who had done no wrong, desolate on the brink of her own death. How could Sophia ever forget? How could Rudy ever forget? How could anyone?

He turned to his wife, who stood with her head bowed, her hands clasped in prayer. But she was thinking not of this quiet graveyard with its everlasting memories, but of other times, and other places, of murder and death, daggers and guns, hatred, and above all, revenge.

Charles stepped back, and stayed silent. And he did not hear the new Mrs Barton murmur as she touched the headstone, "I did it all for you, darling. So think of me, dearest Sasha. And peace be with us both. At last. I'll come back soon."

As they walked away, Charles said, "It was always about Sasha, wasn't it?"

"Always," she replied softly. But she held her head high, and she did not dry her tears in the bitingly cold east wind.

Author's Note

Later on that Christmas Day, they gathered at the elegant home of the Mildmay family in Winkfield Row, near Windsor. Rudy, Lady Penelope, Charles and Sophia, made nine of them altogether, seated for a traditional late afternoon lunch. It was a festive combination of two very grand families. Richard loved having them all, and proposed his usual toast : *To thank you all for coming, and to wish everyone the happiest Christmas.*

Very short, very crisp and very Richard. Although this time, he added a little footnote, "Sorry about the regular tubs of Caspian Sea Beluga, chaps. They never came this year. First time old Boris has missed since 2007, since we more or less adopted Sophia."

Rudolf Masow smiled hesitantly, the secret smile of the profoundly guilty. And, under the table, he issued a light-tap from his hand-made shoes, right on the shin-bone of Charles Barton, who did not dare look up for fear of laughing, the strain of which almost caused a jet of vintage Krug to splash straight down his shirt.

Sophia looked perplexed. But only slightly.